Mary C. Darlington, Simeon Ecuyer, William M. Darlington,
Pierre-Joseph Céloron de Blainville

Fort Pitt

And Letters From the Frontier

Mary C. Darlington, Simeon Ecuyer, William M. Darlington, Pierre-Joseph Céloron de Blainville

Fort Pitt
And Letters From the Frontier

ISBN/EAN: 9783337142780

Printed in Europe, USA, Canada, Australia, Japan

Cover: Foto ©Andreas Hilbeck / pixelio.de

More available books at **www.hansebooks.com**

FORT PITT

AND

LETTERS FROM THE FRONTIER

Two Hundred Copies Printed.

PREFACE.

The increase of interest in the frontier history of Pennsylvania, caused by the establishment of the society called the "Daughters of the Revolution," has induced me to publish these historical documents.

The principal occupants of this portion of Pennsylvania, when first explored, were the Six Nations: the Mohawks, Oneidas, Onondagas, Cayugas, Senecas and the Tuscarawas.

1749, Captain Celeron, a French officer, came to the Ohio and took possession of the country in the name of his king, Louis XV, of France, and deposited leaden plates at different places on the rivers Allegheny and Ohio. This is referred to in the "Olden Time," and parts of the journal have been published by others with notes. The journal of Celeron, as now published, was copied in Paris from the original in the Public Library, procured by the kindness of Monsieur Margry. The few notes needed were written by William M. Darlington.

1754, Governor Dinwiddie claimed the Forks of the Ohio for Virginia.

Captain Trent's company was sent here, under command of Ensign Ward, and commenced the erection of a fort.

April 17th, Monsieur Contrecœur descended the Allegheny River with his forces and demanded its surrender. Resistance was impossible and the surrender was made to Contrecœur, who completed the fort, commenced by Ward,

and called it Fort Duquesne, in honor of the Governor of
Canada. The history of this settlement is given in the
"Olden Time," by Pittsburgh's historian, Neville B. Craig.

1758, General Forbes advanced towards Fort Duquesne and
it was abandoned by the French. Fort Pitt was then built
by General Stanwix and was considered a formidable fortifi-
cation. Colonel Bouquet built the redoubt, now standing, in
1764. It was during the occupation of this fort by the British that Captain Ecuyer was in command. No notes are
needed with his journal and letters—they are complete and
were copied for Mr. Darlington from the originals in the
British Museum.

The sketch of the life of General James O'Hara was compiled from documents collected by Mr. Darlington and letters
now in the possession of Mrs. McKnight and Miss Matilda
Denny. Biographies or biographical notices and journals
have been published of all the historical persons here mentioned. The letters are copies of the original letters and
sufficiently annotate these histories.

The history of the organization of Allegheny County was
written by Mr. Darlington by request of county officials. To
those interested in the early history of the West this historical collection is offered, in memory of William M. Darlington,
by his wife,

MARY CARSON DARLINGTON.

CONTENTS.

ILLUSTRATIONS.

MAPS.

CANADA—1749.

JOURNAL OF THE CAMPAIGN

Which I, Celeron, Chevalier of the Military Order of St. Louis, Captain Commanding a Detachment, sent to the Belle River by the Order of the Marquis de la Galissonnière, Commanding General of All New France and Country of Louisiana.

I LEFT de la Chine on the 15th of June with a detachment formed of a captain, eight subaltern officers, six cadets, an armorer, twenty men of the troops, one hundred and eighty Canadians and nearly thirty savages—equal number of Iroquois and Abenakes. I slept at Point Clair. On the 16th I departed at 10 o'clock A.M., and slept at Soulange with all my detachment. Several canoes were injured in the rapids. On the 17th I departed from Soulange, and ascended to the Cedars, on the side of the Lake. In this place Mr. Joncaire was shipwrecked, his canoe broken, one man drowned, and the greater portion of the effects lost.

18th, I remained at the entrance of the Lake St. Francis, to dry the few effects which were collected at the foot of the rapids.

19th, I passed Lake St. François, ascended the rapids called the Thousand Rocks, and anchored without any accident.

20th, I ascended the long fall (Sault).

21st, I passed several rapids; I did not make a list of them; they are known by every one.

22d, 23d, and 24th, I continued my route without anything

remarkable happening, excepting that several canoes were staved in by the carelessness of those who conducted them. I had them mended, and continued my way.

25th, I passed a new French establishment, founded by the Abbé Piquet, where I found nearly forty acres of cleared land; his stone fort, eight feet in height, was not yet finished. The Abbé Piquet was lodged under bark, in the manner of the savages, and was preparing wood and other material for his habitation. He had two savage guides whom he desired me to take with me; I accepted them to please him; this was all that composed his mission.

26th, I left Mr. Piquet and slept at Little Detroit.

27th, I departed early to go to Fort Frontenac,* where I arrived at 5 o'clock in the evening.

28th and 29th, I sojourned at Fort Frontenac, to mend my canoes, which had been much damaged in the rapids, and to rest my men.

30th, I departed from Fort Frontenac to go to Niagara; on the fifth day I met Mr. Nardiere, who received the Miamis. He informed me that the nations of Detroit, having known of my march, were ready at the first invitation to join me. I did not rely much on the disposition of these savages, however, as I had learned on my route that they had more people on the Belle Rivière than I had been informed of at Mr. Galissonière's. I profited at all hazard by the advice of Mr. Nardiere, and forced my march to rejoin Mr. Labrevois, who was going to command at Detroit.

I arrived at Niagara on the 6th of July, where I found him; we conferred together, and I wrote to the Chevalier de Longnaiul that which I had learned from Mr. de la Nardiere, and de-sired him, that if these nations of Detroit were in the design to come and join me, and not delay his departure, I would

* Outlet of Lake Ontario.

give the rendezvous at Strotve* on the 9th or 10th of August; that if they had changed their mind I would be obliged to him to send me couriers to inform me of their intentions, so that I may know what will happen to me. On the 7th of July, I sent Mr. de Contrecœur, captain and second in command of the detachment, with the subaltern officers and all my canoes, to make the portage. I remained at the fort, to wait for my savages who had taken on Lake Ontario another route than I had; having rejoined me I went to the portage which Mr. de Contrecœur had made. On the 14th of the same month we entered Lake Erie; a high wind from the sea made me camp some distance from the little rapid; there I formed three companies to mount guard, which were of forty men, commanded by an officer.

15th, I departed early in the morning, in the hope of making a fine journey, and went to the portage of Chatakouin,† which I could not make, there having risen a high wind—the same as on the evening. I was forced to land. The lake is extremely low. There is no shelter. If one does not foresee the wind, they run the risk of perishing in disembarking. For more than twenty acres in extent we found very large stones on which one is in danger of perishing. I fell on one, and without prompt help I would have been drowned, with all my men. I landed to mend my canoe, which had been broken in several places.

16th, I arrived at noon at the portage of Chatakouin. As soon as my canoes were loaded, I detached Mr. de Villiers and Le Borgne, with fifty men, to go clear the roads the rest of the day. I observed the situation of the place, in case one should wish in the future to make there an establishment. I did not find anything advantageous there, either for the navigation of the lake or in the situation of the place. The lake

---

* Cannot be identified.
† Barcelona or Portland.

is so shallow to the south that vessels cannot approach the portage nearer than one mile. There is no island or harbor where one could anchor and get into shelter; they must anchor and have boats to unload from—high winds are so frequent; and I think they are dangerous; furthermore, there is no village of the savages established in this place, the nearest are those of Ganaonagon and de la Paille Coupée.*

In the evening Mr. Villiers and La Borgne came to sleep in the camp; they had cleared nearly three-quarters of a league of road; they placed guards, and this order will continue all the campaign, as much for the safety of my detachment as to discipline the Canadians, of which they have need.

17th, At break of day we commenced our portage, which was conducted very vigorously. Nearly all the canoes, provisions, and munitions of war and merchandise, destined for presents to the nations of la Belle Rivière, were carried the three quarter-leagues which had been cleared the evening before. This road is very difficult, on account of the number of hillsides which are encountered, also, all my men were very tired.

18th, I continued my portage; but bad weather prevented continuing it as long as on the preceding day. I consoled myself that this delay was only caused by the rain: it was all that I wished, in order to have water in the river to pass with the load that I had in my canoe.

19th, The rain being heavy, I put myself *en route* and made this day a half league.

20th, 21st, We continued our route with extreme diligence.

22d, We have achieved the portage, which could be counted as four leagues, and we arrived on the border of Lake Chata-kium.† At this place I had my canoes repaired and rested my men.

---

* Broken straw.
† Chautauqua.

23d, At noon I departed and encamped one league from the entrance of the lake, which might be nine leagues In the evening our savages, who had been fishing in the lake, told me that they had seen people, who had hidden in the woods as soon as they perceived them.

24th, I went out of the lake early in the morning and drew into the river Chatakium. The water being found low, I had transported the greater part of the baggage by land. The portage was indicated to me by the traces of the savages. We had nearly three-quarters of a league to transport our canoes, which could not pass with the load ; we have made at least this day, by water, one half league.

25th, Before commencing our march, by the advice of the savages of my detachment, I assembled a council, composed of the officers and the natives which I had with me, to deliberate together on the measures which we should take on the occasion of the vestiges, which we had found the preceding evening, of several cabins, abandoned with such precipitation that they had left a part of their utensils, their canoes, and even their provisions, to gain the woods. This manœuvre made us judge of the fear of the savages, and that they had only retired through fear, and, consequently, they would carry the alarm to all the villages—put them to flight or make them take the part of assembling, forming a considerable corps and surrounding us with ambushes. The country was very advantageous for them, and for us very difficult of access, owing to the little water in the river. I communicated the intentions of the Marquis de la Galissonière to the officers; they saw that it was of very great importance, for the execution of the orders with which I was charged, to reassure the natives of these countries, and the unanimous opinion was that they should be desired to keep themselves tranquil in their tents, and assure them that I have only come to treat with them of good things and explain to them the opinions of their father, Onontio. I drew up in writing their opinions, which they all signed. Here is the copy:

"Council held by Mr. de Celeron with the officers of his detachment and the chiefs, July 25th, 1749.

"Having discovered yesterday, July 24th, at the base of the Lake Chatakium some signs, by which it appeared to us that the savages who were hunting in this place had been frightened by the number of canoes and people which composed our detachment, having abandoned their canoes, provisions and other utensils, useful to them, and that they had carried the alarm to the village de la Paille Coupée, and as it is important in consequence of the orders of the Marquis de la Galissonière to speak to these nations, to make known to them his intentions, and not wishing to do anything without taking the advice of the officers and of the chiefs we have with us, we have assembled them to make known to them the orders with which we are charged, in order to take the most convincible measures to dissipate the terror which our march has spread. The advice of all having been collected, the unanimous opinion has been that to reassure these nations and have the opportunity to speak to them, there should be a canoe sent to the village de la Paille Coupée in which would embark Mr. Joupere, lieutenant, with some Abenakes and three Iroquois, to carry to them three strings of wampum, and invite them to return, that their father had only come to treat with them on pleasant business.

"Executed at our camp at the entrance of the River Chanongon, July 25th."

All the officers signed.

As soon as the council finished I sent away Mr. de Jonquiere; that done, I set out on my route and made nearly a league with much toil. At many places I was obliged to put forty men on each canoe to make them pass.

26th, 27th and 28th, I continued my route not without many obstacles, and notwithstanding all the precautions which I took to manage my boats, they were often in a bad state, owing to the low water.

29th, I entered at noon into the Belle Rivière* (Ohio). I buried a lead plate, on which is engraved the possession taken, in the name of the king, of this river and of all those which fall into it. I also attached to a tree the arms of the king, engraved on a sheet of white iron, and over all I drew up a Procès Verbal, which the officers and myself signed.

Copy of the Procès Verbal, of the position of the lead plate and the arms of the king, placed at the entrance of la Belle Rivière (Ohio) with the inscription :

"The year 1749, Celeron, Chevalier of the Order Royal and Military of St. Louis, Captain Commanding a Detachment sent by the orders of Marquis de Gallissonnière, Commander General of Canada on the Belle Rivière, otherwise called the Ohio, accompanied by the principal officers of our detachments, have buried, at the foot of a red oak on the south bank of the river Ohio (Oyo) and of the Chanangon and at 40 51' 23" a lead plate with inscription :

"In the year 1749 of the reign of Louis XV, King of France, I, Celeron, Commander of the Detachment sent by the Marquis de la Gallissonnière, Commanding General of New France, to re-establish tranquillity in some villages of these cantons, we have buried this plate, at the confluence of the Ohio† and Kanaragon,‡ July 29th, as a monument of the renewal of possession which we have taken of the said river Ohio, and of all those that therein empty ; and of all the land on both sides to the source of said river, as they were enjoyed, or

* Now Allegheny.
† Allegheny.
‡ Conewago, now Warren.

should have been enjoyed by the preceding kings of France, and that they are maintained by the arms and by treaties, and especially by those of Reswick, d'Utrecht and of Aix la Chapelle; we have also affixed in the same place to a tree the arms of the king, in testimony of which we have drawn up and signed the present Procès Verbal.

"Done at the entrance of Belle Rivière, July 29th, 1749. All the officers have signed."

This operation finished, as I was not far from the village of Kanaongan, and as the savages were informed by Mr. de Joncaire of my arrival, they were anxious to find me. As soon as they had discovered my canoes they sent a deputation to invite me to visit their villages and there receive the compliments of their chief. I treated them well—the envoys. I gave a cup of brandy,* for them to drink to their father Onontio, and gave them tobacco. They returned to their villages. I went there a short time after. I passed before the village; they saluted me with several discharges of musketry; I returned them, and formed my camp at the other side of the river. Mr. de Joncaire collected the chiefs in one tent, I received their compliments and felicitations, and as this village has from twelve to thirteen cabins, I invited them to go to la Paille Coupée to hear what I had to say to them on the part of their father Onontio; the women brought me a present of Indian corn and pumpkins. I responded suitably with other little presents. Mr. Joncaire assured me that it was time he should have come to dissipate the terror which had seized on the spirits of the savages, that several had retired to the woods and that the others had made their packs to do the same. I sent M. de Joncaire to la Paille Coupée.

On the 30th I went to la Paille Coupée, where I had sent Mr. de Joncaire the previous evening. The savages of this

---

* In the French copy it is "coup de lait."

place intended to hide themselves in the woods on the report which was made to them by those we had found on the Lake Chatakium; they had told them that we were a large company and that without doubt it was to destroy them. Mr. de Joncaire had much trouble to remove this impression, although they were Iroquois of the five villages that composed these two villages, and he is an adopted child of the nation, and they have great confidence in him. As soon as I was encamped the chiefs assembled and came to my tent; here are their first words:

Speech of the Sonontonans, established at the Village de la Paille Coupée, otherwise called Kachuiodagon and Kanaonagon, to Mr. de Celeron, by two strings of Wampum, July 30, 1749:

"My Father, we wish to testify the joy which we feel at seeing you arrive in our villages in good health. It is a long time since we had the pleasure of seeing our Father in this land, and the march, of which we have heard for a month, has caused us much inquietude and fear, not only in our villages but in all those of la Belle Rivière (Ohio). It is perceived, my Father, that to reassure the children, frightened and without spirit, that you have sent our son, Joncaire, to tell us to be tranquil and wait in our villages your arrival; to hear the words of our Father, Onontio, which you bring us; the strings of wampum have entirely removed from our spirits all the fears which had possession of us. Our packs were made up for flight, and we were like drunken people, all in despair, and we have remained as thou wished us, to hear that which thou hast to say to us. We are charmed that our Father, Onontio, chose thee to make known to us his intentions. It is not only to-day that we have known thee; thou hast governed us at Niagara, and thou knowest that we have only done thy will."

Response of Mr. Celeron, in the following words, with two strings of Wampum, July 30, 1749 :

" I am charmed, my children, that the arrival of Mr. Joncaire in your village has raised your spirits and dissipated the fear that my presence in this country caused you. Without doubt it is caused by the evil intrigues of people who work always evil. That which I find surprising is that those which have the right spirit and that have always listened to the words of their Father, Onontio, should have felt this fear.

"By these two strings of wampum I open your ears, so that you will hear well that which I tell you on the part of your Father, Onontio ; and I also open your eyes to make you see clearly the advantages which your Father is going to procure for you, if, like people of sense, you will profit by it. It is his word that I bring to you here and which I am going to carry to all the villages of la Belle Rivière (Ohio.)"

Speech of the Marquis de la Gallissonnière to the first village of the Iroquois Sonontouans, established at the entrance of la Belle Rivière ; brought by Mr. de Celeron. With one belt:

"My children, since I have been at war with the English, I have learned that that nation has deceived you; and not content with breaking your heart, they have profited by my absence from this country to invade the land which does not belong to them and which is mine. This is what determined me to send to you Mr. Celeron, to inform you of my intentions, which are, that I will not suffer the English on my land; and I invite you, if you are my true children, to not receive them any more in your villages. I forbid, then, by this belt, the commerce which they have established lately in this part of the land, and announce to you that I will no longer suffer it. If you attack them you will make them retire and send them home; by that means you will be always peaceable in your village. I will give you all the aid you should expect from a good father. If you come to see me, next spring, you will have reason to be satisfied with the reception which I will give you. I will furnish you with traders in abundance, if you wish for them. I will even place here officers, if that will please you, to govern you and give you the good spirit, so that you will only work in good affairs. The English are more in the wrong in coming to this land, as the Five Nations have told them to fly from there to the mountains. Give serious attention, my children, to the words which I send you; listen well, follow it, it is the way to see always in your villages a haven beautiful and serene. I expect from you a reply worthy of my true children. You see the marks to be respected which I have attached along la Belle Rivière, which will prove to the English that this land belongs to me and that they cannot come here without exposing themselves to be chased away. I wish for this time to treat them with kindness and warn them ; if they are wise they will profit by my advice."

With two strings of Wampum :

" I am surprised, my children, to see erected in your village a cabin destined to receive English traders. If you consider yourselves my children you will not continue this outrage; further than that, you will forbid it and will never receive the English."

Response of the Iroquois of the Village of Ganaouskon and Chinadiagon, July 3, 1749. With two strings of Wampum :

" My Father, we thank you for opening our ears and our eyes to hear your speech and to see clearly that you speak to us like a good father."

With one belt:

"My Father, we are very glad to speak to-day of affairs with you. Do not be surprised at our answers. We are people without any knowledge of affairs, but speak to you from the bottom of the heart.

"My Father, you are surprised that the English have come to trade on our land; the elders have forbidden them the entrance; it is true you engaged us to descend to Montreal next year to speak of affairs with Onontio, and we acknowledge these favors; we assure you we are going to work for that during the winter, and that we will go during the spring.

"My Father, you have told us that you perceive that the English have come to invade our land, and that you are going to summon them to retire; that for this effect you will barricade the road. We thank you for your enterprise, and we promise not to suffer them here. We are not a party capable of deciding entirely of the general sentiments of the Five Nations who inhabit this river; we wait for the decision of the chiefs of our villages, as well as from the villages lower down. As for us, my Father, we assure you we will not receive the English in our villages."

With two strings of Wampum:

"My Father, you have told us that little birds have informed you that a house is building here for the English, and that if we allow it, soon they will form an establishment considerable enough to drive us away, because they will make themselves masters of our land. You have asked us not to continue this work; this we promise, and this house, which is nearly finished, will only serve to amuse the youth. We also promise not to touch the arms of the king which you have placed on this river, which prove to the English that they have no right in this part of the land."

With two strings of Wampum to the Savages of the Detachment:

"My brothers, we are pleased to see you accompany your Father in his route; you have told us that you have no other sentiments than those of Onontio. We invite you to follow the counsels, which he knows well how to give, and we are resolved to only do his will. We thank you for that which you have come to tell us; we will give attention to it."

The Council ended, I made presents to these savages, which gave them great pleasure, and in acknowledgment they assured me anew that they will never see again the English at their homes, and that they will descend next spring to see their Father Onontio.

July 31st, I sojourned at this village, having been stopped by the abundance of rain, which pleased us much. The water rose three feet during the night.

August.—The first of August I departed from la Paille Coupée. After having marched nearly four leagues, I found a village of Loups and Reynards (wolves and foxes) of six cabins. I disembarked, and only found one man, who told me that the rest had taken flight. I told these savages that these people were wrong to be afraid, that I had not come to injure them, but, furthermore, I had come to treat with them on good affairs and give courage to the children of the governor who had lost it. I added that I did not doubt but that as soon as I left they would return home; that I invited them to go to the village lower down, which was but four or five leagues distant, and that I would speak to them. I passed the same day to a little Loup village of six cabins, to whom I told, as to the others, to go to the most considerable village, where I would speak to them on the part of their Father Onontio. They arrived there a little while after me.

On the second, I spoke to these savages in the name of the General. Here are the words and their reply:

With one belt:

"My children, the Loups, the reason which has determined your Father Onontio to send me to this part of the land has been the knowledge that he has had that the English propose to form here a very considerable establishment, to invade, some day, these lands, and increase in such a manner, if they are allowed to do so, that they will make themselves masters and you will be victims, as you have been in the past. Listen with attention to the words which I bring you from him:

"The experience which you have had, my children, of the evil proceedings of the English, should be present with you; remember that you possessed at one time, at Philadelphia, magnificent lands on which you found an abundance with which to subsist your families; they approached you under pretext to give you necessaries, and, little by little, without you perceiving it, they have established forts and then towns, and when they became powerful enough they drove you away, and have forced you to establish yourselves on these lands on which to subsist your women, and will do to you as they did in Philadelphia. They could do it to-day on the Belle Rivière by the establishments which they wish to form there. It is the knowledge which I have obtained sooner than you which has determined me to send to you Mr. de Celeron, to make you open your eyes on the misfortunes which menace you and make you see that it is only their own interest which moves the English. I will send a summons for them to retire this time, not wishing them to occupy the land which belongs to me; if they have sense they will not expose themselves to being forced. The English have less right to come to this land, because the kings of France and England have agreed in all the treaties of peace, and particularly in the last, which terminated the war, that the English should never set foot on this land. You know, also, my children, that the Five Nations have absolutely forbidden them not only to make any establishment on the Belle Rivière, but to come here to trade; that they go to the other side of the mountains, on the lands of yours, which they have occupied. I do not oppose that, but on mine I will not allow them. As for you, my children, you will lose nothing there, besides that I will give you all the aid which you should expect from a good father. Delegate next spring some one of your nation, with your uncles, to come to see me, and you will see the reception which I will give you—how much I love you, and that I seek only to do you good and save you from the yoke which the English wish again to impose on you. I will give you traders, who will furnish you all necessaries and will put you into a state not to regret those which I send away from my lands; of those which you possess you will always be masters. I will even give you officers to maintain you there peaceably and tranquilly, and let no one inquiet you, seeking like a good father whatever would be of advantage to you."

Reply of the Loups, the 2d of August, by one belt :

"My Father, we pray you to have pity on us ; we are young men, who cannot reply as the old men could to what you have said to us. We have opened our eyes and taken spirit ; we see that you only work with good affairs ; we promise to have no other sentiments than those of our uncles of the Five Nations, with whom you seem content.

"Examine, my Father, the situation in which we are. If thou makest the English retire, who give us necessaries, and especially the smith who mends our guns and our hatchets, we would be without help and exposed to die of hunger—of misery in the Belle Rivière. Have pity on us, my Father ; thou canst not at present give us our necessaries ; leave us at least for this winter, or at least until we go hunting, the smith and someone who can help us ; we promise thee that in spring the English shall retire."

I said, without promising anything, that I would make the arrangement which would be for their best interest; and accord with the intentions of their father, Onontio. I confess that this representation embarrassed me very much. I made them a little present and engaged them to keep the promise which they had given me.

On the third I commenced the march; on the road I found a village of ten cabins abandoned, the savages, having had news of my arrival, had gained the woods. I continued my route to the village of the River aux Bœufs,* which is only of nine or ten cabins; as soon as they saw me they saluted; I returned it and disembarked. I had been told that there was in this place a smith and an English merchant. I wished to speak to them, but the English, like the savages, had gained the woods; there only remained five or six Iroquois, who presented themselves with arms in their hands. I scolded them for the manner of showing themselves, and made them lower their arms. They made many excuses, and said that they had only come with their guns because they had them— to salute me. I spoke to them nearly as I had spoken to the Loups and re-embarked immediately. This evening I buried a lead plate and the arms of the king by a tree, and drew up the Procès Verbal following :

Procès Verbal.

1749.—This year I, Celeron, Chevalier of the Order Royal and Military of St. Louis, Captain-Commander of the Detachment sent by order of the Marquis de la Galissonière, Commander-General of Canada, on the Belle Rivière (otherwise

---

* Venango.   Origin of name, Zynango (tobacco).

called the Ohio), accompanied by the principal officers of our detachment, having buried on the south bank of the Ohio, four leagues below the River aux Bœufs, opposite a bald mountain and near a large stone, on which are seen several figures, rather roughly engraved, a lead plate and attached in the same place to a tree the arms of the king. In faith of which we have signed the present Procès Verbal.

"Made at our Camp, August 3d, 1749. All the officers have signed."

The inscription is the same as the preceding which I have placed at the entrance of la Belle Rivière. On the 4th, in the morning, after having conferred with the officers and chief savages of my detachment, on the precautions which we should take to reassure the nations of the Belle Rivière and engage them not to fly so that we can speak to them on the part of the General, it was concluded that Mr. de Joncaire, with the chiefs, should go to the village Attickè* to announce my arrival and engage the nations of this place to wait for me without fear; for I only come to speak of good things. As soon as he had departed I put myself *en route*. We finished nearly fifteen leagues this day.

On the 5th I departed at an early hour. After having made from three to four leagues, I found a river, of which the mouth is very beautiful; and one league below I found another. They are both south of la Belle Rivière.

On the heights there are villages of Loups and Iroquois of the Five Nations. I encamped early to give time to Mr. de Joncaire to arrive at the village Attickè.

On the 6th I departed at 7 o'clock; after having made nearly five leagues I arrived at the village Attickè, where I found Mr. de Joncaire with our savages; those of this place had taken flight. This village is of twenty-two cabins. Mr.

---

* Attiquè, Kiskeminitas River.

3

de Joncaire told me that a chief with two young men, who had stopped on their discovery, seeing few accompanying him, came to him and demanded the motive of his voyage, to which he replied that I had only come to speak to the natives of la Belle Rivière and give spirit to the children of the Governor who lived there. He engaged this chief to take charge of some strings of wampum which I had given to him to take to the lower villages, and to tell them to keep themselves tranquil on their mats, that I only came to treat of affairs which will be of advantage to them.

I re-embarked and I passed the same day the ancient village of the Chaouanous, which has been abandoned since the departure of Chartier and his band, who were removed from this place by the orders of the Marquis de Beauharnais, and conducted to the river Vermillon, in the Wabash, in 1745.

I encountered in this place six Englishmen, with fifty horses and nearly one hundred and fifty packs of peltry, with which they were returning to Philadelphia. I summoned them by writing to return to their country, that the land where they had come to trade belongs to my king and not to the king of England, that if they returned again they would be pillaged, that I would this time treat them with humanity, if they would profit by the advice which I gave them; they assured me, either from fear or something else, that they would not return; they are convinced that they have no right to trade.

This I well explained to them in the summons. I wrote to the government of Philadelphia in these terms:

"Sir :—Having been sent with a detachment to this neighborhood by the orders of the Marquis de la Gallissonnière, Commanding General in New France, to collect together some savage nations who had quarreled on the occasion of the war which has just ended, I have been much surprised to find merchants of your government in this country, to which the English government never had any pretentions. I have treated them with all the gentleness possible, although I was right to regard them as interlopers and people without hope of future possession; their enterprises were contrary to the preliminaries of peace which have been signed for more than fifteen months. I hope, sir, that you will in the future forbid this commerce, which is against the treaties, and warn your merchants that they will themselves risk a great deal if they return to these countries, and that they can only blame themselves for the misfortunes which might happen to them. I know that our Commandant General will be very sorry if any violence happens, but they have strict orders not to allow strange merchants in his government.

"I am, etc."

That executed, I re-embarked and continued my route. On the 7th I passed a village of Loups, where there were only three men; they had placed a white flag on their cabins; the rest of their people had gone to Chinique, not having dared to remain at home. I invited these three men to come with me to Chinique to hear what I had to say to them. I re-embarked and visited the village, which is called the "Written Rock." The Iroquois inhabit this place, and it is an old woman* of this nation who governs it. She regards herself as sovereign; she is entirely devoted to the English.

All the savages having retired, there only remained in this place six English traders, who came before me trembling. I disembarked, and as I wished to speak to them I was much embarrassed, not having an interpreter of their language and they pretending not to understand any other. After awhile

---

* Named Queen Alliquippa.

they softened, and one of them spoke Chawenois.* I made
them the same summons as to the others, and I wrote to their
governor. They told me they were going to retire; that they
knew well they had no right to trade, but not having found
any obstacle until now, they had tried to make a living, so
much the more as the savages had attracted them; but that
they would not return again. This place† is one of the most
beautiful that until the present I have seen on the Belle
Rivière. I left this camp, and slept nearly three leagues
below. As soon as I had disembarked our savages told me
that on passing they had seen writing on a rock. As it was
late, I could not send there until the next day. I appointed
R. T. Bonnecamp and Mr. de Joncaire to go there, with the
idea that these writings could give me some light. They
were there early in the morning and reported that it was
only some names written with charcoal. As I was only
two leagues from Chinique I dispersed as much as possible
the men of my detachment to give them a greater appearance, and arranged everything so as to arrive in good order
at this village, which I knew to be one of the most considerable on the Belle Rivière.

On the 8th, as I prepared to raise my camp, I saw ap-
proaching a canoe with two men; I judged they were envoys
from the village; I waited for them. They were some who
came expressly to find out by my countenance what were
my designs. I received them with kindness, and made
them drink a cup of milk to their father Onontio. This is
always, among savage nations, the greatest mark of friendship which one can show. After talking some time, they
asked me to return to their village and to give them some
hours to prepare to receive me. Soon after their departure

* Shawnese.
† Site of Pittsburgh.

I embarked, after having viewed the arms of the men and distributed ammunition in case of need, and ordered that from the boat there should be but four guns charged with powder to respond to the salute, and eight with balls, having to take good precautions with nations frightened and riotous. As soon as I was in sight of the village I observed three French flags and one English. As soon as I was observed, salutes of musketry were sent from the village, and as the current is extremely strong at this place, and the river low, there came an Iroquois to me to indicate the passage. I was stopped instantly by the rapidity of the current. When disembarking they drew on us a discharge of balls. This salute is made by all the nations of the South ; often accidents happen from it. This fashion did not surprise me or the officers of the detachment, however, as I was suspicious and did not believe their intentions good. I told them, by Mr. de Joncaire, to cease firing in that manner or I should fire on them. I told them at the same time to lower the English flag or I should pull it down myself. This was done instantly; a woman cut the staff, and the flag has not since appeared. I disembarked, and as the shore is extremely narrow and very disadvantageous in case the savages had evil designs, being at the base of a cliff which was more than thirty feet high, I immediately lifted my canoes and the baggage on the bank so as to place myself advantageously. I established my camp near the village, which I made to appear as extensive as possible, placed a corps de garde to the right and to the left, ordered the sentries at short distances the one from the other, and all were on the watch all night. The officers who were not on guard had orders to make the rounds all night. These precautions prevented the savages from doing what they had projected. This Mr. de Joncaire discovered a short time afterward by means of some women of his acquaintance.

This village is of fifty cabins, composed of Iroquois, Shawnees and of Loups, and of a party of men of the villages
which I had passed, having come here for refuge to render it
stronger. At 5 o'clock in the evening the chiefs, accompanied by thirty or forty warriors, came to salute me—a com-
pliment on my arrival at their home.

Here is their first speech, August 8, 1749:

With two strings of Wampum :

"My Father, with these two strings of wampum we come to
testify the joy which we feel, to see you arrive in our village
in good health ; we thank the Master of Life for having preserved thee on a journey so long and so toilsome as that which
thou hast performed. It is a long time since we had the satisfaction to see some French persons in our village. We see
thee here with pleasure, my Father. Thou must have remarked, by the flags that thou hast seen in our village, that
our heart is entirely French. The young men, without
knowing the consequence, placed some which have displeased.
As soon as we saw them, thou hast seen them fall. They
were only placed for show, and to divert the young men,
without fear that the thing could displease thee. We invite
thee also, my Father, by these strings of wampum, to open
thy heart to us, and make known to us whatever can make
thee angry. We will do what thou comest to speak of, on the
part of our Father Onontio ; we are ready to hear his words,
and we pray thee to wait until the chiefs of the village, whom
we expect, shall arrive."

Response of Mr. de Celeron, with two strings of Wampum :

"I am obliged to you, my children, for the pleasure you appear to have at seeing me in your village. I have only come,
as you think, to speak to you, on the part of your Father

Onontio, of good things. This is what I will explain to you to-morrow, when you are all together.

"You are right in saying that the English flag, which I saw on your village, displeased me. This mixture of French and English flags is not seemly for the children of the govern-ment, and seems to show that their heart is divided. Let them be lowered in such a way that they cannot again be raised. The young men placed them without judg-ment. The old men have taken them away on reflection ; they have done well. By these two strings of wampum, I open, in my turn, your eyes, and your ears to hear well that which I have to say to you to-morrow, on the part of your Father Onontio."

They retired to their homes ; and, in order to hold them-selves ready for all events, they passed the night dancing, always having some of their people for watchmen.

On the 9th, before day, Mr. de Joncaire—whom I had ad-vised, as also his brother, to examine during the night the manœuvres of these savages— came to tell me that he had news that eighty warriors were about to arrive, and that the resolution was taken in the village to attack us. On this news, which I communicated to the officers, I again gave or-ders that all should be ready, in case they should come, to fight. I held all my men in good order. I placed the officers in such a manner that they would encourage them to do their duty, and waited nearly two hours for what their resolution would determine. Seeing that no one advanced, I sent to them Mr. de Joncaire, to tell them that I knew the side which they had taken ; that I waited for them with impatience, and, if they did not hasten to put into execution that which they had projected, I would go to attack them. A little while after Mr. de Joncaire's return, the savages defiled before my camp, and made the ordinary salute. There may have been fifty men, according to what several officers told me they had counted while defiling, many warriors of the village having been there before those who arrived in the night. All these manœuvres convinced me of the evil intentions of these nations; but as I knew that the intention of Mr. de la Gallissonnière was to collect these savages by gentleness, and that, furthermore, I was engaged in a country where it would be very difficult for me to retreat—it being impossible to ascend the Belle Rivière (Ohio), owing as much to its swift current as to the want of provision and the bad state of my canoes— and, furthermore, if an action should take place, all the nations would be interested in it—I took the side of dissimulation, and determined to speak firmly to these savages and impose on them by the good appearance which I made for nearly two hours after the arrival of these warriors. The men of note, with those of the village, came to my tent with calumets of peace, made me their compliments, and presented them to me to smoke. Before accepting, I reproached them for their manner of acting, in terms which were perfectly explained to them by Mr. de Joncaire. Here is the discourse which I made to them :

Speech of Mr. de Celeron to the Savages of Chenengué, with four strings of Wampum, August 9, 1749 :

"I am surprised, my children, that after having taken the trouble to send to you Mr. de Joncaire to the Paille Coupée and Attiqué to announce to you my arrival in this country, and inform you that I carry to you the words of your Father Onontio, to see you frightened, amazed and making manœuvres which are never known to the children of the Governor. I wish to say, by these strings of wampum, that I have only come to work at pleasant affairs; this has been delayed. You should have believed me, and you know enough of the French to know that they are true and that they never speak only from the lips. If I had had the designs which you have fancied, and which evil spirits have told you, I would have hidden from you—that was easy for me. I need not have arrived so quietly as I did at your village. I know how to make war, and those which we have with us should know; but I do not know how to be treacherous. By these four strings of wampum, I reopen your ears, I enlighten your minds, and I remove the bandage, which you have over your eyes, so that you can hear the words of your Father Onontio, who is full of kindness for you, although he has had reason for discontent with some among you. I wish much, presently, to smoke your calumets, to prove to you that I forget what you have done. I will speak to you to-morrow on the part of your Father Onontio. I ask you to drive away the evil spirit which seduced you and which will destroy you, without remedy, if you do not take care."

I smoked the calumets, they retired well satisfied, and all was quiet for the rest of the day and following night.

August 10th.—At 10 o'clock in the morning I assembled all the chiefs and a part of the warriors at my camp. I had prepared a place for the Council. I repeated to them the words of the general, to which they listened with much attention.

your eyes to the projects which the English make on your land. You are ignorant, without doubt, of the establishment which they propose to make, which will accomplish nothing less than your entire ruin. They hide from you their intentions, which are to establish themselves in such a manner that they will make themselves masters of this whole country and drive you away if I would let them do so. I shall, like a good father who loves his children tenderly, who though at a distance from them carries them all in his heart, avert the peril which menaces them, which is the design which the English have formed to seize your land; and to accomplish this they have commenced to spoil your minds. You know, my children, that they forgot nothing in this last war to put you at war with me. The greater part of your nation has sense enough not to listen to them. I know their good-will, and pardon, like a good father, the past, persuaded that in the future you will live quietly on your mats. Whatever war I have with the English it is for your advantage to guard the neutrality which you yourselves demanded of me when you visited Montreal, to which I willingly consented. By this means you will preserve that peace which makes the happiness of these nations. As I know that the English only inspire you with evil sentiments, and that they design, by their establishments on the Belle Rivière, which belongs to me, to seize on it, I send to them a summons to retire; and I am so much the more right in doing so, as the kings of France and England have agreed that the English should never come here, either for trade or otherwise. This is even one of the conditions of peace which we have made together. Moreover, the chiefs of the Five Nations have told them not to pass the mountains—which are their boundary. I do not wish, at this time, to use violence with the English. I tell them gently my opinions—may they pay attention to them. If, in the future, misfortune happens to them, they can only blame themselves. As for you, my children, live quietly on your mats and do not enter into the discussions which I may have with the English. I will pay attention to all which can be of advantage to you. I invite you to come to see me next year. I will give you marks of my friendship, and will put you in such a condition that you will not regret those whom I exhort you not to permit in your homes.

"I will give you all the aid of a good father who loves you and who will not let you want for anything; those who will bring it to you do not covet your land, either by purchase or usurpation; further than that I will order them to maintain you there against all, and your interests will always be mine, if you behave well. By this means you will always be tranquil, and peace will be in your villages. I have wished, my children, to tell you the sentiments of your Father before speaking to the English, whom I will seek, to tell them to retire."

The Council ended, they seemed well satisfied with what I had told them, and went to their villages to consult together on the replies, which I told them to make the next day, having a long road to travel and the season being far advanced. This village is composed of Iroquois, of Chawneese, and of Loups, which caused the Council to last more than four hours. Besides these three nations there are in the village some Iroquois, from Sault St. Louis, from the Lake of the Two Mountains; some Nepessingues, Abenakes, Ottawas and other nations. This assemblage forms a very bad village, which, tempted by the cheap market which the English offered, were drawn into a very bad disposition for us.

I had called before me the most important of the English traders, to whom I gave a summons to retire to their country with all their employees, as I had done to those whom I had

formerly met.   They replied, like the others, that they would
do so; that they knew well they had no right of trade on the
Belle Rivière.

I added that their government was bounded by the mountains, and that they should not pass beyond them.   They
agreed to that.   I wrote to the Governor of Carolina, as I had
done to the one at Philadelphia.

August 11th, The savages came to give me their response.
If they are sincere I think the General will be satisfied ; but
there is little dependence to be placed on the promises of such
people ; so much the more as I have just said that their interest engages them to look with favor on the English, who
give them merchandise at so low a price that we have reason
to believe that the king of England, or the country, bears the
loss which the traders make in the sale of their merchandise
to attract the nations.   It is true that the expenses of the
English are not nearly so great as those which our traders will
be obliged to make, on account of the difficulties of the route.
It is certain that we will never be able to reclaim the nations
except by giving them merchandise at the same price as the
English.   The difficulty is to find the means.

*Here is the Response which the Savages of Chenengué made to
the Speech of the General, August, 1749:*

" My Father, we are very glad to see you to-day and in the
manner with which you regard us.   The Commander of
Detroit and of Niagara told us to go to see Onontio ; to-day
you come yourself, you write us to descend.   We must have
lost our mind if we did not pay attention to your words.   By
this belt we assure you that all the nation which inhabits this
river will descend next spring, in order to hear the speech
of our Father Onontio.   Nothing will be able to change
the mind in which we are, even if there remained but one

person only, he would have the pleasure of seeing our Father. The shoes which we make for walking on ice will not be fit to take us to Montreal ; we pray you to provide for us some that we will find at Niagara as we pass there. My Father, have pity on us; we have no more ancient chiefs, they are only young men who speak to you. Pardon the faults which we make, for you, who are wisdom itself, make some. You come to drive the English from this continent ; to this we consent willingly, but you should also bring with you traders to furnish us with necessaries. If you have pity for us, leave us the English, so that they can give us the help which will be necessary to us until spring. You see the unhappy state in which we will be if you have not this kindness for us ; do not be surprised not to see the replies to your belts. Those whom you see here are only young men who guard the cabins until our chiefs and warriors return. We will inform them of your intentions and of the sentiments of our Father Onontio, and that we may be tranquil. We pray you to leave with us one of our children, Joncaire, to lead us to our Father and work conjointly at good affairs."

Reply of Mr. de Celeron to the demand of the Savages that they may have one of the Messrs. Joncaire:

"My children, it is not in my power to dispose of the officers which your Father has confided to me. When you descend you can ask him for one of the Messrs. de Joncaire, and I am persuaded that he will not refuse you."

Continuation of the Speech of the Savages:

"We thank you for the hope that you give us that our Father will give us one of our children ; we assure you again that we will do without reserve all that you have demanded of us. We would be charmed to see you for a longer time, and we thank our brothers who are with you for the advice they have given us, and we will give attention to it."

So soon as the Council finished I had the presents brought which I had intended for them and which were very considerable ; they were flattered by them. I encouraged them anew to keep their promises, and above all to come to see the General next year, assuring them that they would have reason to be satisfied with the reception of their Father Onontio.

My business being finished, I had my canoes placed in the water and embarked to continue my route. Nearly four leagues below there is a river from the south, on which there are several villages ; I did not disembark, having spoken to them at Chenengué.

12th, I embarked at 6 o'clock in the morning, after having made four or five leagues. I encountered two canoes, loaded with packs and guided by four Englishmen. I disembarked to speak to them ; all that I could learn from them was that they had come from St. Yotoc,* from whence they had departed twenty-five days since. I had no English interpreters, and they could not speak Iroquois ; this was the only language for which I had an interpreter. I re-embarked and marched until 3 o'clock, and having much sickness, I sent my savages to hunt, in the hope that this beautiful river— which had been described to the Governor as being abundant in game—would furnish me some to refresh my men, who cannot live longer only on mush. But I was mistaken, my savages having only killed a buck, which is a feeble resource to comfort people hungry and sick.

13th, I departed early in the morning and I encountered several pirogues, conducted by Iroquois, who were hunting on the rivers which intersect the land. At noon I sealed and

---

* Scioto.

interred a plate of lead at the entrance of the river, and attached to a tree the arms of the king, and drew up the following Procès Verbal :

Procès Verbal of the Position of a Plate of Lead at the entrance of the River Kanawha :

" Year 1749, I, Celeron, Chevalier of the Order Royal and Military of St. Louis, Captain Commanding the Detachment sent by the orders of the Marquis de la Gallissonnière, Commandant General in Canada, in the Belle Rivière, accompanied by the principal officers of our detachment, have interred at the foot of a large cone,* at the entrance of the river and on the south bank of the Kenawah, which discharges itself to the east of the river Ohio, a plate of lead, and attached in the same place to a tree the arms of the king. In faith of which we have drawn up and signed with the officers the present Procès Verbal, at our Camp, August 13th, 1749."

The 14th of August, I departed at 7 o'clock in the morning, not being able to leave sooner on account of the darkness. I passed two rivers, of which the entrances are very beautiful. The hunting has been pretty abundant to-day in bucks. The 15th, I continued my route and placed a lead plate at the entrance of the river Yenanguekouan and drew up the following Procès Verbal :

Procès Verbal of the Position of a Fourth Lead Plate, at the entrance of the River Yenanguekouan, August 15. 1749 :

On the 15th of August, 1749, I, Celeron, Chevalier of the Royal and Military Order of St. Louis, Captain Commanding the Detachment sent by the orders of the Marquis de la Gallissonière, Commanding General of Canada, on the Belle Rivière, otherwise called the Ohio River, accompanied by the

---

* Cone pine.

principal officers of our detachment, have interred, at the foot
of a maple, which forms a tripod with a red oak and a cone
pine, at the entrance of the river Yenanguekouan, on the west
shore of this river, a plate of lead, and in the same place
attached to a tree the arms of the king.   In faith of which we
have drawn up the present Procès Verbal with the officers, at
our camp, August 15th, 1749.

On the 16th, I could not depart until 9 o'clock, having
slept in the woods.   I made nearly twelve leagues.

On the 17th, I embarked at 7 o'clock; in the course of
the journey I passed two beautiful rivers, which descended,
one from the north, the other from the south of the Belle
Rivière.   I do not know their names.   I disembarked early
to hunt, being altogether reduced to a diet of bread.

The 18th, I departed at an early hour.   I camped at noon,
the rain preventing us continuing our route.   I have this day
placed a lead plate at the entrance of the river Chiniondaista
and attached the arms of the king to a tree.   This river carries
canoes for forty leagues without encountering rapids, and has
its source near Carolina.   The English of this government
come by treaty to the Belle Rivière.

*Procès Verbal of the Fifth Plate of Lead, placed at the en-
trance of the River Chiniondaista,* the 18th of August,
1749.*

The year 1749, I, Celeron, Chevalier of the Royal and
Military Order of St. Louis, Captain Commanding the Detachment sent by the order of the Marquis de la Gallissonnière,
Commandant General of Canada, on the Belle Rivière, otherwise called the Ohio River, accompanied by the principal
officers of our detachment, have buried, at the foot of a tree,
on the southern shore of the Ohio and the eastern shore of

---

* Kanawha.

Chiniondaista, a plate of lead, and have in the same place attached to a tree the arms of the king. In faith of which we have drawn up the present Procès Verbal, which we have signed with the officers at our camp, August 18th, 1749.

19th, The rain having continued with so much violence that I was forced to raise my camp to ascend the bank, the shore being inundated.

The 20th, I re-embarked. After having gone some leagues, I saw a man on the shore. I went to him, he was a savage Loup, who was returning from war on the nation du Chien. It was sixteen days since he departed alone, without food or ammunition. I gave him some to take him to Chiningue, from which he was distant. I questioned him on the number of people which there were at St. Yotoc. He replied that there might be eighty cabins, and perhaps one hundred. I continued my route until 3 o'clock and hunted.

On the 21st, The savages of my detachment came to tell me that they feared to arrive at St. Yotoc, without having given notice to the nations of that place, of my intentions; that this village was considerable, and that it might be believed that these savages having news of my march, and not being without apprehension that those who had carried the news to them of my arrival had told them, as in the villages which I have passed, many stories which induced them to make ambushes at the approach of the village. I assembled the officers to consult together on the part we should take. It was determined to send a canoe to St. Yotoc to tranquillize the nations and restore their spirits, in case any carrier of news had troubled them. It was Mr. de Joncaire, that I chose to go there with Teganakassin and Lactarquerate, both chiefs of the Sault de St. Louis and faithful servants of the king, and three Abenakis chiefs. Mr. de Niverville asked to go; I permitted him. I gave some hours for the advance of my envoys, then I re-embarked and landed as usual for the hunt.

22d, I embarked at 7 o'clock in the morning, after having delivered the munitions of war to all my people, and encouraged them to do their duty if the savages should wish to undertake anything against us. After having made about four leagues, I saw a canoe, which appeared to me to be manned with seven or eight men, and had a white flag; as soon as they saw me they landed. I went to them; it was Mr. de Joncaire with seven savages, an equal number of Shawnees* and Iroquois. As soon as I had disembarked the chiefs came and gave me their hands, the others did the same, then sat down and remained silent for some time. Their eyes appeared to me excited. I commenced the subject to Mr. de Joncaire, who told me that the nations of St. Yotoc were very much troubled, and that as soon as they had arrived they had fired on them with balls and even pierced the flag with three balls; that when they disembarked they were conducted into the cabin of the council, and when they would have told them the subject of their commission, a savage had stood up and interrupted him saying that the French deceived them and that they only came among them to ruin them and their families; then at that instant the youth had run for arms saying they must commence by killing these Frenchmen, send our families into the woods and then go and form ambuscades for the canoes. According to what Mr. de Joncaire and the savages which accompanied him told me, this would have been done to them had not an Iroquois chief turned aside the storm and quieted them and engaged himself to come before me with those who would follow him; and for surety they were guarding Mr. de Niverville and the savages. At last, after a half hour of silence, the Iroquois chief arose and said to me:

* Chaouonons.

"My Father, thou seest before thy eyes people without sense, and who have been on the point of embroiling the land forever. Regard us with pity and have no resentment for that which we have done. Our old men, now that thou hast arrived at our village, will show their repentance of the fault which they have committed. For two months we have been like drunken men, on account of the bad news which were brought to us from the village which you passed."

I replied to him :

" I do not know what you mean to tell me; when I go to St. Yotoc I will find out, and I will see what I shall do. You came to me of your own accord. Thou wouldst have done wisely to bring back the savages who were with Mr. de Joncaire. Shortly return to thy village; I will go there soon. Thou must advise thy youth not to salute in their manner, it will be dangerous for them."

I gave a cup to drink, to those who were with him, and sent them away, because Mr. de Joncaire said to me: " I know well that these savages have evil intentions and are much frightened; within twice twenty-four hours they have made a fort of stones, well doubled and fit to defend them." That made me reflect seriously. I knew the weakness of my detachment; two-thirds were of young men who have never made a sortie, and who at the aspect of ten savages attacking me would have taken flight. I had not been the master to choose others, and whatever recommendation had been made to Mr. de la Gallissonnière, on leaving Quebec, to give us chosen men, was not paid attention to. There was no other way to take than of continuing my route—wanting provisions, my canoes unserviceable, no more gum or bark. I re-embarked, ready for all events ; I had good officers and nearly fifty men on whom I could depend. At a quarter of a league from the village I was discovered ; at once the salutes commenced and the savages fired nearly a thousand times. I am sure that the powder was furnished to them gratis by the English. I disembarked opposite the village and saluted; the chiefs and the old men crossed the river and came to me with the white flag and the calumet (pipe) of peace, cut some grass for us to make seats and invited me to take seats with all the officers. They had brought with them Mr. de Niverville and the savages whom they had guarded; as we went to sit down there came up nearly eighty men, armed and equipped as warriors. I had arms taken to my detachment. These eighty men stood in line twenty paces from us and leaned on their guns. I said to the chief that I was surprised at the manner of this rashness, and if they did not retire promptly I would fire on them; they replied that they had not come with evil designs, that they came to salute anew, but that they would retire if that displeased me. This they did at once, firing their guns in the air, which were only charged with powder. The calumets were presented to me and to all the officers; after this ceremony a Shawnee (Chaouanon) chief arose and complimented me on my arrival. I told them I would speak to them the next day at my tent, where I would light the fire of the Governor. They replied to me that they had in their village a cabin for council, where they would hear, if I would go there with all my officers, all that I had to tell them on the part of their father Onontio. I refused them, and said it was for m to come to me and hear what I had to say to them, and being disappointed it would be a great imprudence to go i village. I held firm on this article, and lead them to They returned to their village. The corps de and the rounds made all night, very par-officers. It is to be observed that this village, of Shawnees (Chaouanons) and Iroquois of s had added to it more than thirty men of the Sault St. Louis, whom licentiousness had made to retire there. Abundance of hunting and a cheap market—which the English gave them—are motives very seducing for them. The son of Tenaga Kassin is there, and never has his father or myself been able to bring him away; besides the people of the Sault St. Louis, there are some from the lake, the two mountains, Loups, Miamis, and from nearly all the nations of the upper country. All these additions are worth no more than the Chaouanons and are entirely devoted to the English.

23d, I sent to give them notice by Mr. de Joncaire, to come to my camp to hear the words of their Father. They refused to come at first, saying, that it was in the council cabin that they should be spoken to. I replied that it was for the children to come to their Father, where he wished to light his fire. After some conference they came to my camp and made their excuses in these terms :

Speech of the Savages of St. Yotoc to Mr. de Celeron, with four strings of Wampum, August 23, 1749 :

" My Father, we are ashamed to appear before you after our impertinence yesterday to those you sent to us. We are in despair. We ask pardon and pray our brothers and thee to bury this bad affair ; the regret which we feel for it makes us hope that you will pardon us."

Reply of Mr. de Celeron to the Savages of St. Yotoc, on the same day :

" My children, no one could be more surprised than I was when I learned by the canoe which came before me the reception which you had given to the chiefs which I had sent to announce to you my arrival and tell you that I had come to carry to you the words of your Father Onontio ; they were that I only came to your village tranquilly. This token, so respected by all nations, has not been by you, and you have fired on it. Not content with that, you have listened, in preference to my words, to those of a wicked man who is in your village and who is a slave. I have been the more surprised knowing for a long time that the Shawnees (Chaouanons) have sense; they have appeared on this occasion more desirous to insult the envoys. What have you done, Chaouanons, with the sense which you had ten years ago, when Mr. de Longueil passed here to go to Chiachias? Thou wast in his presence and by all kinds of ways you showed to him the goodness of thy heart and thy sentiments. He even raised a troop of thy young men to follow him. He had not even given notice to you of his arrival; but you had at this time the French heart, and to-day thou lettest thyself be corrupted by the English, who dwell with you continually, and that under pretence to give you some assistance, only seek to ruin thee. Reflect on the just reproaches which I make to thee and rid thyself of these bad people who will be, if you do not take care, the ruin of the nation. Thou hast opened on my arrival the throat by four strings of wampum. I have not need of that medicine. The heart of the Governor is a pipe, good for his children; but as thou must have a stronger dose of it, by these strings of wampum, I evacuate all the bad humors. The pardon which thou demandest of the fault and the regret which thou appearest to have for it, inclines me to pardon Be wiser in the future. I bury this evil affair, as thou and I will pray thy Father Onontio not to preserve I invite thee to reject all the evil discourses be made to thee in the future and listen well to thy Father Onontio which I bring to you.

Speech of the General to the Savages of the Village of St. Yotoc, August 23, 1749. Brought by Mr. de Celeron. By one belt:

"The friendship, my children, which I have for you, although so distant, has prompted me to send Mr. de Celeron to make you open your eyes and discover the projects which the English form against you and the land which you inhabit. You are ignorant, no doubt, of the establishments which they can make here, and which aim at nothing less than your ruin; they hide from you their ideas, which are to form here, and construct forts strong enough to destroy you, if I let them do so. I am, like a good father, who tenderly loves his children, and who, although at a distance from them, thinks always on what is best for their advantage, and warns them of peril which menaces them. You know, my children, that they forgot nothing in the last war which I had with them, to engage you to declare against me; happy for you that you did not listen to them. I think kindly of you for it; of others, who let themselves be seduced, I have pardoned some of them, persuaded that they will be wiser in the future and will not listen any more to the bad people, who only seek to trouble the land. But to put us entirely beyond their seduction, I sent promptly a summons to them to retire from my land, where they never had a right to enter. The kings of France and of England agreed in the treaties of peace that the English should never come to trade, or for anything else, into la Belle Rivière. I do not wish this time to make use of force, although I would be right if I had them pillaged. I warn them gently—may they pay attention to it—if another time there happens to them any misfortune it will be their own fault.

"As for you, my children, live tranquilly on your land, and do not enter into the discussions which I may have with the

English; I will pay attention to all which can be to your advantage. I invite you to come to see us next year; I will give you marks of my friendship, and will put you in such a position that you will not regret those whom I sent from your country. I will give you all the aid which you should expect from a good father who loves you and will not let you want anything. Those who will bring it to you will not invade your lands to drive you from them; on the contrary, I will order them to maintain you there, and their interest will always be the same."

By another belt :

"For the two years I have been in this country I have been entirely occupied in learning the interests of my children and that which can be of advantage to them. I have learned with pain the affair which has happened between you and the Illinois. As you are equally my children, and as I have for you the bowels of a father, I charge Mr. de Celeron, whom I send into the villages of the Belle Rivière, to carry my words, to give you a belt from me; to engage you to be reconciled with your brothers, the Illinois. I have taken the same precautions with them, having sent a commandant of this post with orders to speak to them on my part, and to tell them to keep themselves tranquil. I hope, my children, that you will both hear with pleasure my words, and that you will determine to live in peace and union, like my true children. I will not enter upon the subject of your quarrel; I ignore even who is the aggressor; but whoever it may be, it is suitable that he should make the necessary advances for reconciliation, and that the offended forgets the injury which he has received. I will be obliged to him inasmuch as I only seek to procure for them that which is most advantageous for them."

While we were in the council, a Chaouanon entered, with a much frightened air, and told the chiefs that all the nations of Detroit were coming to fall on them, and that, while I was amusing them, they were going to see their villages destroyed. I saw that there was an alteration in this savage. I asked him the reason. I reassured them from their fright, and restored them so well that the council was not long interrupted. After having explained to them the intentions of the General, I gave them a cup to drink. They then returned to their village. As soon as they had departed, I sent Mr. de Joncaire to inform himself of the news which had just arrived. He was not long returning, and reported to me that three Ottawas had arrived at a village in the country, ten leagues from St. Yotoc, and that immediately couriers had left to carry us the news that the Ottawas would not arrive for two days. I judged they were couriers that Mr. de Sabrevois sent me, to give me advice about the disposition of the people of Detroit.

The 24th, The savages replied, after having made some objections to coming to the French camp to make their reply; but, seeing that I persisted with firmness in my system, they came, and here is their reply, very badly explained, their interpreter being very bad:

Reply of the Savages of St. Yotoc to the Speech of the General, August 24, 1749, *by six strings of Wampum :*

"My Father, we have come to tell you that we have heard the speech of our Father Onontio with great pleasure ; that all that which he has told us is true, and for our good, and that we and our brothers, the Miamis, who are here, will conform to it, having but one sole thought. For these strings of wampum we assure our Father Onontio that all those who live in our village will not work any more on evil affairs, and

will not listen again to evil discourses.   My Father, we thank
you that you wish to reconcile us with our brothers, the Illinois.   We promise you to work for that.   This speech has
given pleasure to all our village.

"My Father, by these strings of wampum, we thank you
for the manner in which you have spoken to us.   We encourage you to continue your work, and to give spirit to all your
children, so that the land may be tranquil.   As for us Chaouanons, we assure you that we will only work with good
affairs."

On the 25th I assembled all the chiefs, and made them a
present, on the part of the General, and asked them to keep
the promise which they had given me.   A little while after,
I made the traders come to me, and summoned them to retire, making them feel that they have no right of commerce
or anything else in the Belle Rivière.

I wrote to the Governor of Carolina, whom I have well
warned of the risks which their traders will run if they return here.   That was enjoined on me in my instructions, and
even to pillage the English, but I was not strong enough for
that—these traders being established in the village, and well
sustained by the savages.   I would have made an attempt,
which might not have succeeded, and would have turned
against the French.   The Ottawas sent by Mr. de Sabrevois
arrived, and brought me letters by which advice was given to
me, which was no more than that which Mr. La Naudière had
told me—of the disposition of the savages of Detroit—and,
besides that, that some efforts which Mr. de Longueil had
made to engage them to march they had constantly refused.
I gave provision to these couriers, although I was very short ;
and I wrote to Mr. de Sabrevois, and asked him to keep twenty
canoes below Detroit, with provisions for my establishment,
at the commencement of October.

The 26th, I departed, at 10 o'clock in the morning, from St. Yotoc. All the savages were under arms, and saluted when I passed before the village.

The 27th, I arrived at the Rivière Blanche at 10 o'clock in the evening. I knew that, three leagues in the country, there were six cabins of the Miamis, which induced me to sleep at this place.

The 28th, I sent Mr. de Villiers and my son to these cabins, to tell these savages to come to speak to me. They brought them, and I engaged them to come with me to the village of the Demoiselle, where I was going to carry the words of their Father Onontio. They consented, asking me to wait until the next day, to give them time to go for their equipage. There are in this village two Sonontonane cabins. The policy of these nations is to have some of them with them who are like protectors. I engaged one of the Sonontonanes, who speaks Miami well, to come with me to the home of the Demoiselle.* I needed him, not having an interpreter of this language, and I had some affairs of consequence to treat with them.

The 29th, I wrote to Mr. Raimond, Captain and Commandant at the Miamis, and asked him to send to me the one named "King's Interpreter," with as many horses as possible, to make the transport of our baggage at a portage of fifty leagues.

The 30th, The savages of the Rivière Blanche having arrived, I embarked to gain the Rivière à la Roche, and at the entrance I buried a plate of lead, and attached to a tree the arms of the king—of which I drew up a Procès Verbal.

* Fort Laramie.

Procès Verbal of the Sixth Plate of Lead, buried at the entrance of the River à la Roche,* August 31, 1749.

"The year 1749, I, Celeron, Chevalier of the Order Royal and Military of St. Louis, Captain Commanding a Detachment sent by the orders of the Marquis de la Galissonnière, Commanding General in Canada, in the Belle Rivière (otherwise the Ohio), accompanied by the principal officers of our detachment, have buried on the point formed by the right shore of the Ohio, and the left of the River la Roche, a plate of lead, and attached to a tree the arms of the king. In faith of which we have drawn up and signed with the officers the present Procès Verbal."

September.—That done, I embarked; the little water which I found in this river made me take thirteen days to ascend it.

The 12th, The Miamis of the village of the Demoiselle, having learned that I was about to arrive at their home, sent four chiefs to me with calumets of peace for me to smoke, as I had invited them to my people on land, not having water enough in the river to draw the loaded canoes through. I was informed by Mr. Courtmanche, an officer of the detachment, of the arrival of these envoys. I disembarked at the place where they were, and, when we were all seated, they commenced their ceremonies, presenting to me the calumet. I accepted it. They then carried it to Mr. de Contrecœur, second captain of the detachment, and to all the officers, and to the Canadians, who, famished for a smoke, wished that the ceremony had lasted a long time. The hour having arrived to encamp, we slept at this place. The messengers rested with us. I was obliged, notwithstanding the little provision we had, to give them supper.

13th, I arrived at the village de la Demoiselle, and I placed my camp and arranged the sentries and waited for the

---

* Miami.

arrival of the interpreter, which I had demanded from Mr. de
Raimond. During this time I sounded their minds to learn
if they were willing to return to Kiskakon. This is the
name of their ancient village. It appeared to me that they
had not a great repugnance. They had two English workmen in their village, whom I made leave ; those who had
passed the summer there trading, had retired with their
effects by land. They have roads communicating from one
village to the other.

17th, Tired—that the interpreter did not arrive, and that
my provisions were consumed waiting for him. I determined
to speak to the Demoiselle by means of an Iroquois, who
spoke Miami well. I showed them magnificent presents, on
the part of the General, to engage them to come to their village, and explained to them his intentions in these terms :

*Speech of the General to the Miamis, to the Demoiselle estab-
lished at the River à la Roche, and to Bariel, established at
the River Blanche. Carried by Mr. de Celeron, February
17, 1749, by eight strings of Wampum, for the two Villages :*

"My children, the manner in which I have dealt with
you, notwithstanding what you have done to the French—
that I have given subsistence for your women and children—
should prove to you the attachment which I have for you,
and the justice of my sentiments. I forget that which you
have done, and I bury it in the deepest part of the earth, that
I may not remember it again, persuaded that you have done
nothing but at the instigation of people whose policy is to
trouble the land and spoil the mind of those with whom they
have intercourse, and who profit by the unfortunate ascend-
ancy which you have let them gain over you, make you commit errors and engage you in evil affairs—without letting it

appear that they have any part in them—so as to injure you
with me.   It is to enlighten you that I send to you my words;
listen well to them and pay attention to them, my children.
They are the words of a father who loves you, and to whom
your interests are dear.   I extinguish by these two strings
of wampum the two fires which you have kept alight for two
years at the River à la Roche and at the River Blanche.   I
extinguish them in such a manner that not a spark shall
appear from them."

By one belt to the Demoiselle and one to Bariel:

"My children, I come to tell you by this string of wampum
that I will extinguish the fires which you have lighted on the
River à la Roche and at the River Blanche.   By these belts
I raise you up from your mats and I take you by the hand to
lead you to Kiskakon, where I will relight your fires and fill
them more solid than ever.   It is in this land, my children,
that there will be joined to you a perfect tranquillity, and
where every moment I will be in the way to give you marks
of my friendship.   It is in this country, my children, that
you will meet with the sweetness of life, it being the place
where the bones of your ancestors repose and those of Mr. de
Vincennes, who loved you so much, and who always governed
you in such a manner that affairs were always good.   If you
have forgotten the counsels which he gave you, his ashes will
recall to you the memory.   The bones of your ancestors
suffer for your remoteness; have pity for the dead who
recall you to your village; follow with your women and
your children the chief that I send to you to carry my speech
and who will relight your fire at Kiskakon in such a way that
it will never be extinguished.   I will give you all the help
that you should expect from my friendship, and know, my
children, that I will do for you that which I have never done
for any other nation."

Another Speech by four strings of Wampum and two to Bariel.

"By these strings of porcelain I place a barrier at every passage that leads to the Belle Rivière, so that you will never go there again, and that the English, who are the authors of all evil affairs, can not approach to this land which belongs to me. I make for you at the same time a good road to lead you to Kiskakon,* where I will relight your fire. I break off all commerce with the English, whom I have warned to retire from my land, and if they come there they will have cause to repent."

By two strings of Wampum to the Demoiselle and two to Mr. Bariel:

"Since you have done, my children, that which I demanded of you, which is only for your advantage, I invite you to come to see me next year, and to receive from me also sensible marks of my friendship. I give the same invitation to all your brothers of the Belle Rivière. I hope that you both have sufficient sense to respond, as you should, and, to begin to give you a proof of my friendship, I send you these presents to cover your women and your children. I join to them powder and balls, to gain a living easier on the route which you are going to take to take you to Kiskakon. Abandon the land where you are; it is pernicious to you, and profit by that which I make for you."

The council finished, every one retired. They carried the presents to their village, where they assembled to make their replies. On the 18th, at 9 o'clock in the morning, they came to make their reply.

---

* Now Fort Wayne.

*Reply of the Demoiselle, Chief of the Miamis, established at
the River à la Roche, and of Bariel, established at the River
Blanche, February 18, 1749, by two Calumets of Peace :*

"It is the old custom among us, when good affairs are
spoken of, to present some calumets. We pray you to listen
to us; we are going to reply to what you have said to us.
This calumet is a testimony of the pleasure which I have to
smoke together, and we hope to smoke the same calumet
with our Father next year."

By one belt :

" My Father, we heard with pleasure yesterday your speech.
We see well that you have only come for good affairs. We
have only a good response to make to you. You have made
us remember the bones of our ancestors, who groan, and we
see in this place that which recalls us continually. You made
for us a fine road to return to our ancient nest. We thank
you for it, my Father, and we promise you to go there in the
early spring. We thank you for the good words which you
have given us. We see well that you do not forget us. Be
sure that we will always work at good affairs with the
Chaouanons. We recall the good advice which Mr. de Vincennes gave us. My Father, you have business with people
without sense, and who cannot reply to you perhaps as you
hoped; but they speak truth. It is not with the lips they
speak to you; it is from the bottom of the heart. You have
told us to make serious reflections upon what you have said
to us. We have done so, and we will continue to do so all
winter.

" We hope to have the pleasure to give you a good speech
in the spring. If the hunting is good we will repair our
faults. We assure you, my Father, that we will listen no
more to the evil discourses or the evil news. We have at
present some sense."

Reply to the Demoiselle and to Bariel in the same Council by Mr. de Celeron :

"I have listened to my children, and I have well weighed your speech; either because you have not well understood, or you pretend so, you do not reply to that which I said to you. I proposed to you, on the part of your Father Onontio, that you should come with me to Kiskakon, to there relight your fire and remake your nest. You put it off until next spring. I would have been charmed to be able to say to your Father Onontio that I had led you there. That would have given him pleasure, on account of the interest which he takes in what concerns you. You tell me you will go there at the end of winter. Be true to your promise. Assure him of that, for he is stronger than you, and if you fail, fear the resentment of a father, who has but too much reason to be irritated against you, and who has offered you the means of regaining his favor."

Reply to these Words by the Demoiselle and Bariel :

"My Father, we will be faithful in executing the promise which we have given thee. We will go at the close of winter to our ancient cabin, and if the Master favors our hunting we hope to repair our passed faults. Be convinced that we do not speak from our lips, but from the bottom of our hearts. We cannot, at present, return to where you have come to lead us. The season is too far advanced."

The council finished. I stopped some old men, to attempt to discover whether what they had told me was sincere; I spoke with these savages, who assured me that both villages would return in spring to Kiskakon, and that which delayed them was that they had no cabins built where I could conduct them, and that when hunting in the winter they would approach their village, and that they would return there certainly. Roi, for whom I had asked Mr. de Raimon, arrived on the 19th. I remained, to try, by the means of Roi, to persuade the Demoiselle, with some other chiefs, to return with me to relight their fires, and make their nests at Kiskakon. I did not succeed. They continued always to say and assure me that they would return next spring. On the 20th, all being ready for our departure, we raised our camp, after having burned our canoe, with which we could not make the transport. We began our march by land, everyone carrying his provisions and his baggage, excepting the officers, for whom I had procured horses, and some men to lead them. I had formed all my people in four brigades, of which each one had an officer at the right and the left. I conducted the right and Mr. de Contrecœur the left. We only spent five and a-half days in making this route, which is estimated at fifty leagues.

The 25th, I arrived at Mr. de Raymond's, who commands at Kiskakon. I only rested here long enough to purchase some provisions, and some pirogues, to take me to Detroit.

The 26th, I caused to come to me the Pied Froid, chief of the Miamis, established at Kiskakon, and some others of consequence, to whom I repeated, in the presence of Mr. Raymond and the officers of our detachment, that which I had said at the village of Demoiselle and the reply which I had to it. After they had listened with a great deal of attention, they arose and said to me : " I wish I was mistaken, but I am attached enough to the French to say that the Demoiselle will lie. My only sorrow is to be the only one who loves you and to see all the nations of the south incensed against the French."

The 27th, I left Mr. de Raymond's, not having found enough pirogues for all my people. One party went by land,

under the guidance of some officers, and some savages to
guide them through the woods. I spent eight days in going
to the lower part of Detroit. When I arrived, the 6th of
February, I found some canoes and provisions for my detachment. I would have left the same day, if my savages would
have followed me, but they amused themselves drinking, in
the lower part of the river Miamis. I waited for them on
the 7th and they arrived at the close of the 8th. I left on
the 9th of February the lower part of Detroit, and slept at
the Pointe Pellé. During the traverse of Lake Erie nothing
happened to us that merits attention.

I arrived at Niagara on the 19th, where I was delayed three
days by bad weather. The 22d I left Niagara by the south of
Lake Ontario, to go to Fort Frontenac. I spent fourteen
days in passing this lake, in which I have had several canoes
broken by the violence of the winds, and I arrived on the 6th
at 9 o'clock at said fort.

November, I departed from Fort Frontenac. I passed to
the establishment of Mr. Piquette. I had received orders from
the Marquis de la Gallissonnière to see the addition which he
had made to it during my voyage. I did not see any change
since I had passed at the beginning of July. His fort had
been burned since his departure for Montreal, by the savages,
who were thought to have been sent by the English of Cho-
ueginus. A large field of grain was also burned, and a kind
of redoubt, which was in the angle of a bastion, has been saved,
although the fire had been put to it several times. There
were only three men on guard at this fort, of which one had
an arm carried off by a gun, which burst in his hands when
firing on those who made the fire.

I asked if anyone knew the nation who had done this deed.
I was told that it was two Goyoquines, who had passed the
summer with Mr. Piquette, and who had been hired by the

English to take away his negro.   I departed, and slept at the
foot of the Rapids.

10th, At 9 o'clock I arrived at Montreal, where I remained two days.   I descended to Quebec to give an account
to the Marquis de la Jonquiere of my voyage.   I have been
very happy—notwithstanding the fatigue of the campaign,
and the bad fare, and the quantity of sickness—to lose
but one man, who was drowned in the shipwreck of Mr.
de la Jonquiere.   In the estimation of Father Bonnecamp,
Jesuit and great mathematician, who has given great attention
to the route, the journey was 1,200 leagues; by mine and that
of the officers of the detachment it is longer.   All that I can
say is, that the nations of these places are very ill-disposed
against the French and entirely devoted to the English.   I
do not know by what means they can be reclaimed.   If
violence is employed they would be warned and take to flight;
they have a grand refuge in the flat plains, from which they
are not far.   If we send to trade with them, our traders can
never give our merchandise at the price the English do,
because of the great expense they would be at.   Furthermore,
I think it would be dangerous to make easier conditions
with the nations who inhabit the Belle Rivière than in the
roads to Detroit, Miamis and others.   It would be to people
our old posts and perpetuate the nations on the Belle Rivière
and who are within the reach of the English Government.
They have nevertheless sent their armies, but they had fewer
English and they had not credit as they have to-day ; and if
the French traders would tell the truth, they would admit
that their profits proceed but from the trade which they make
with the English by the exchange of peltry, cats, otters and
skins, all at a low price, in England, and with us very high.
Thus have we seen come from this place only peltries and
no beaver,—they are given in exchange to the English.

A substantial establishment could be useful to the Colonies, but there are many inconveniences to sustain from the difficulties of the road on which to transport provisions and effects necessary. I doubt if one would succeed except by making a strong defence. I feel obliged, by the knowledge which I have of all these places, to put these reflections at the end of my Journal, of which such use may be made as is thought proper.   Signed,

CELERON.

Copy of the Summons made to the English of la Belle Rivière.

I, Celeron, Captain, Chevalier of the Royal and Military order of St. Louis, Commanding a Detachment sent by the Marquis de la Gallissonnière, Commanding General of New France, have summoned you English traders, who trade in an Indian village situated on the Belle Rivière, to retire to their country with their effects and baggage, under pain of being treated as interlopers ; in case of refusal, to which summons the said English have said that they were going to retire to their country with their effects.

Executed in our camp of la Belle Rivière.

[Copied.]   Signed,

DE LA JONQUIÈRE.

Notes on Celeron's Expedition, by William M. Darlington.

Kannaigai River and Village, doubtless the same as Conewango or rapids—a carrying place for canoes.

Venango—Rivière aux Bœufs—otherwise Zynango (tobacco).

Hart's Rock is two miles below Pittsburgh.

Attiquè, Kiskiminitas River, about twenty-five miles above

Pittsburgh, emptying into the Allegheny.   Village of Loups.
Alliquippa, opposite Brunot's Island.   North shore.

Leaden Plates Deposited.

First, on the 29th of July, 1749, at the junction of Conewango Creek and Allegheny River, now Warren.

Second, on the 3d of August, at the Three Rivers (Pittsburgh). -

Third, on the 16th of August, at the mouth of the Muskingum (Marietta).

Fourth, on the 18th of August, at the mouth of the Kaskaskia (Point Pleasant).

Celeron descended to the mouth of the Wabash.

CAMPAIGN OF 1758.

LETTERS OF GENERALS GRANT. FORBES AND BOUQUET.

COPY OF MAJOR GRANT'S LETTER TO BRITISH GENERAL FORBES, UPON THE AFFAIR OF SEPTEMBER 14, 1758.

(Endorsed by Col. Bouquet.)

September 14. 1758.

Sir:—If it had been in my power to write sooner, you will do me the justice to believe that I should have troubled you long before this time with an account of the detachment which marched the 9th of September from the Camp of Loyal Hanna.

We were lucky enough not to be discovered in our march, though several scouting parties passed very near us. We got to an advantageous post the 12th, about three in the afternoon, which, according to the information of all our guides, was ten or twelve miles from the French fort. I thought it was a proper place to encamp in, as I did not think it advisable to go nearer, for fear of being discovered ; but I afterward found that our guides were much mistaken about the distance, for, as near as I can judge, the camp is about sixteen miles from the top of the Hill, where we were to take post. The 13th, at break of day, I sent Major Lewis, with 200 men, and our Indians, with orders to post men in ambuscade, about five

miles from the fort, which was all the precaution I could take
to prevent our being discovered in the camp. I flattered
myself that, if a reconnoitering party was sent out, it might
possibly fall into the ambuscade, and, in that case, in all
probability they must have been killed or taken ; and, if they
had sent, in the event our plans succeeding, a second party
from the fort, would have found the whole party ready to
receive them. I ordered Mr. Chew to march with a party of
fifteen or twenty men to reconnoitre the ground and to try,
without exposing himself or the men, to draw a party of the
enemy into the ambuscade.

He only went with three Indians, who soon left him, and,
by that means, in place of returning to Major Lewis' about
ten o'clock as I expected, he was obliged to conceal himself
till night came on, and he joined me upon the march about
eleven o'clock at night. But I would not be understood to
reflect upon him ; he is a good, brisk young lad. About three
in the afternoon I marched forward to the rest of the detachment, and I found Major Lewis advantageously posted about
four miles from our camp. The post, I was assured, was not
seven miles from the fort, though I found it was above twelve.
After giving orders to the troops, and particular instructions
to the captains, I proceeded about six in the evening toward
the fort, expecting to get to the top of the Hill about eleven
at night ; but, as the distance was so much greater than I
imagined, it was after two in the morning before we got
there. The instructions, when I left Loyal Hanna, were that
a particular party should be sent to attack each Indian fire,
but, as these fires either had not been made, or were burnt
out before we got to the ground, it was impossible to make
any disposition of that kind. Major Lewis was informed of
every particular of our project before we marched from Loyal
Hanna, and was told there that he was to command the

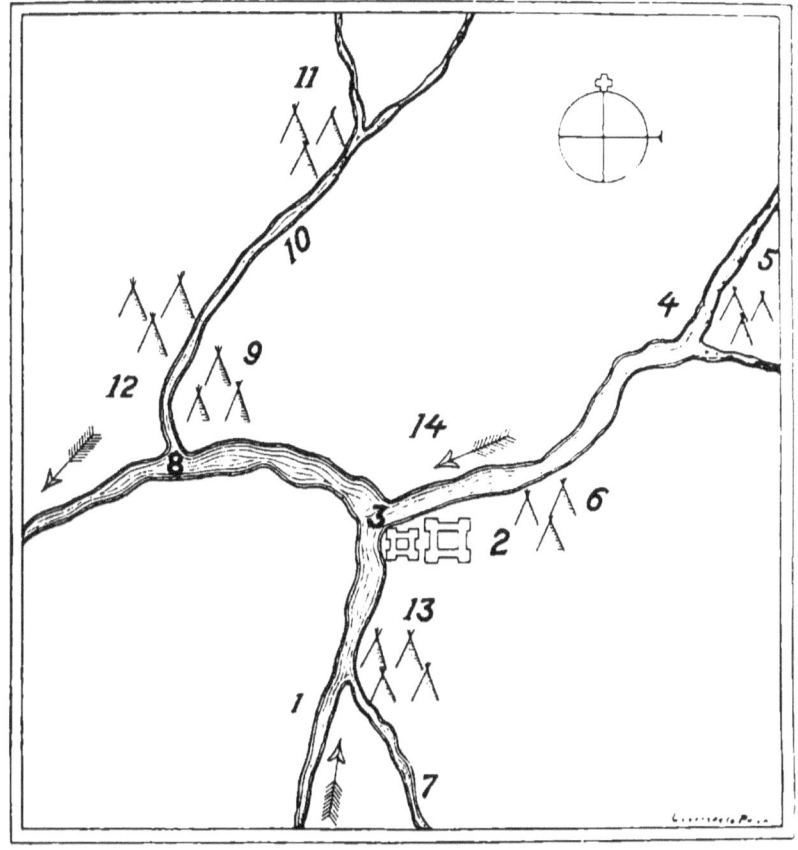

FORT PITTSBURGH AND ITS ENVIRONS.
January, 1759.

REFERENCES TO THE ABOVE SKETCH OF FORT DU QUESNE, NOW PITTSBURGH, WITH THE ADJACENT COUNTRY.

1. Monongehela River.
2. Fort Du Quesne. or Pittsburgh.
3. The Small Fort.
4. Allegheny River.
5. Allegheny Indian Town.
6. Shanapins.
7. Youghiogheny River.
8. Ohio, or Allegheny River.

9. Logs Town.
10. Beaver Creek.
11. Kuskuskies, the Chief Town of the Six Nations.
12. Shingoes Town.
13. Alliquippa.
14. Sennakaas.

The arrows show the course of the rivers.

troops that were to be sent upon the attack. As I was to
continue upon the height to make a disposition for covering
his retreat (which we did not desire to be made in good order)
and for forming the rear guard in our march from the fort,
you will easily believe that he and I had frequent conversations upon the march about our plan of operations. I sent
for him the moment the troops arrived upon the hill opposite
the fort, and told him that as we had been misinformed by
the guides in regard to the distance, and had got there much
later than we expected, it was impossible to make the projected disposition of a party of men for the attack on each
fire ; but that it was impossible to continue another day without being discovered, and that as the night was far advanced,
there was no time to be lost. I therefore ordered him to
march directly, with 100 Americans,* 200 Highlanders and 100
Virginians, and to attack anything that was found about the
fort. I gave orders that no attention should be paid to the
sentries, who probably would challenge, and, in case they were
fired upon they were not to return it upon any account—but
to march on as fast as possible—and were not to fire a shot till
they were close to the enemy ; and that after they discharged
their pieces they were to use their bayonets without loading a
second time. I told the Major that I would order all our drums
and pipes to beat the retreat when it was time for the troops
to relieve, that I was indifferent what order they came back in,
that it was the same thing to me if there was not three of them
together, provided they did the business they were sent upon.
The Major had not half a mile to march into the open plain
where the fort stands, the 400 men under his command had a
white shirt over his clothes to prevent mistakes and that they
might even at a distance distinguish one another. I saw the
Americans and Highlanders march off and gave directions that
the Virginians should fall in in the rear. Sending a greater

* Royal Americans, 60th Regiment.

number of men might possibly, I thought, occasion confusion, and I was of opinion that 400 men were quite sufficient to carry the service into execution. I was absolutely certain we were not discovered when the troops marched from the hill. I thought our loss must be inconsiderable, and never doubted but that everything would succeed beyond our most sanguine expectations.

After posting the remaining part of the troops in the best manner I could, I placed myself and the drums and pipes at the head of the Highlanders who were in the centre and exactly opposite the fort. During the operation the time passed. The day advanced fast upon us, I was turning uneasy at not hearing the attack begin, when to my great astonishment Major Lewis came up and told me "that it was impossible to do any thing, that the night was dark, that the road was bad, worse than anything I had ever seen, that there were logs of wood across it, that there were fences to pass, that the troops had fallen into confusion and that it was a mercy they had not fired upon one another, that they had made so much noise he was sure they must be discovered and that it was impossible for the men to find their way back through those woods." These were really the words he made use of ; this behaviour in an officer was new to me ; his conduct in overturning a long projected scheme and in disobeying such positive orders was so unaccountable that I could not speak to him with common patience, so that I just made answer to his last words, that the men according to the orders that had been given would have found their way back to the drums when the retreat beat. So I left him and went as fast as I could to Lieutenant Mc-Kenzie and Mr. Fisher to see what the matter was and to give directions for the attack if the thing was practicable. I found the troops in the greatest confusion I ever saw men in, which in truth was not surprising, for the Major had

brought them back from the plain when he returned himself
and everybody then took a road of their own. I found it
was impossible to think of forming them for an attack, and
the morning was too far advanced to send for the other
troops from the other places where they were posted ; thus I
was reduced, after all my hopes of success, to this melancholy
situation. That something at least might be attempted, I sent
Lieutenants Robinson and McDonald with fifty men, to make
an attack at a place where two or three fires had been seen
the night before. I desired them to kill a dozen of Indians
if possible, and I would be satisfied. They went directly to
the place they were ordered, and finding none of the Indians
they set fire to the house, but it was day-light before they
could return. I mention this last circumstance that it might
appear clearly to you, it was not in my power to send a
greater number. The surprise was complete, the governor
knew nothing of us or our march, and in all probability the
enterprise must have succeeded against the camp as well as
against the Indians if the attempt had been made. So
favorable an opportunity, I dare say, never was lost.

The difficulties which Major Lewis had represented to me
to be insurmountable, appeared to me, as they certainly were,
absolutely imaginary. I marched above twelve miles that
night, with an advanced guard and flanking parties before it
without the least confusion. The Major had not a mile to
march to the fort, and above two-thirds of that was in an open
plain, and I can safely declare that there is no part of the
road in getting into the plain worse than what I had passed
without any great difficulty in coming up the hill. I made
no secret to the people who were then about me that I was
so much dissatisfied with the Major's conduct that I was
determined to carry him back to camp in arrest, that he
might answer to you for his behaviour. Several officers

heard me say so. Mr. Bentinck, if he escaped, has no doubt informed you that such was my intention. However, I did not think it advisable to take any step of that kind till we were out of reach of the enemy. I therefore sent Major Lewis the 14th, at break of day, with the Americans and Virginians to reinforce Captain Bullet, whom I had left with about fifty men as a guard upon our horses and provisions within two miles of the fort, directly upon the road by which we were to return to our camp. I was afraid the enemy might possibly send a detachment that way to take possession of some passes to harass us in our march or perhaps to endeavor to cut us off in case we were forced to make a retreat, and I directed the Major to place these troops in ambuscade that he might have all the advantage possible of any party that could be sent out. About 7 in the morning, after the fog was gone and the day cleared up, it was found impossible to take a plan of the fort from the height where the troops were posted, and as Colonel Bouquet and I had settled that a plan should be taken "a la barke de la Garrise" in case an attempt did not succeed in the night.

I sent Mr. Rhor with Captain McDonald and a hundred men to take the place, with directions not to expose himself or the troops. About the same time, being informed that some of the enemy Indians had discovered Captain McKinzie, who was posted upon the left, almost facing the Monongehela, in order to put on a good countenance and to convince our men they had no reason to be afraid, I gave directions to our drums to beat the Reveille. The troops were in an advantageous post, and I must own I thought we had nothing to fear. In about half an hour after, the enemy came from the fort in different parties without much order, and getting behind trees, they advanced briskly and attacked our left, where there were 250 men. Captain McDonald and Lieutenant Campbell were soon killed, Lieutenant McDonald was wounded at the same time, and our people being overpowered gave way where those officers had been killed. I did all in my power to keep things in order, but to no purpose; the 100 Pennsylvanians who were posted upon the right at the greatest distance from the enemy, went off without orders, without firing a shot; in short, in less than half an hour all was in confusion, and as soon as that happened we were fired upon from every quarter.

I endeavored to rally the troops upon every rising ground, and I did all in my power in that melancholy situation to make the best retreat I could. I sent an officer to Major Lewis to make the best disposition he could with the Americans and Virginians till I could come up, and I was in hopes to be able to make a stand there and at least to make a tolerable retreat. Unfortunately, upon hearing the firing the Major thought the best thing that could be done was to march to our assistance, unluckily they did not take the same road by which I marched the night before and by which they had passed that morning, and as I retired the same way I had advanced, I never saw them when I found Captain Bullet and his fifty men alone. I could not help saying to him that I was undone. However, though there was little or rather no hopes left, I was resolved to do the best I could, and whenever I could get any body to stay with me made a stand, sometimes with 100 and sometimes with 50, just as the men thought proper, for orders were to no purpose. Fear had then got the better of every other passion, and I hope I shall never see again such a pannick among troops—till then I had no conception of it.

At last, inclining to the left with about fifty men, where I was told a number of the Americans and Highlanders had gone, my party diminished insensibly, every soldier taking the road he liked best, and I found myself with not above a dozen of men and an officer of the Pennsylvanians who had been left with Captain Bullet. Surrounded on all sides by the Indians, and when I expected every instant to be cut to pieces, without a possibility of escaping, a body of the French with a number of their officers came up and offered me quarters, which I accepted of. I was then within a short league of the fort; it was then about 11 o'clock, and, as far as I can judge, about that time the French troops were called back and the pursuit ended. What our loss is, you best know, but it must be considerable. Captains McDonald and Munroe, Lieutenants Alex. McKenzie, Collin Campbell and Wm. McKenzie, Lieutenants Rider and Ensign Jenkins and Wollar are prisoners. Ensign J. McDonald is prisoner with the Indians; from what I hear they have got two other officers, whose names or corps I know not. Mr. Rhor and the officer who conducted the Indians were killed. Major Lewis and Captain McKenzie are prisoners. I am not certain that Lieutenant McKenzie was killed, but I have seen his commission, which makes it very probable. I spoke to Lieutenant McDonald, Senior, after he was wounded, and I think he could hardly make his escape. I wish I may be mistaken. This is the best account I can give you of our unlucky affair. I endeavoured to execute the orders which I had received to the best of my power; as I have been unfortunate, the world may possibly find fault in my conduct. I flatter myself that you will not. I may have committed mistakes without knowing them, but if I was sensible of them I most certainly should tell you in what I thought I had done wrong. I am willing to flatter myself that my being a prisoner will be no detriment to my promotion in case vacancies should happen in the army, and it is to be hoped that the proper steps will be taken to get me exchanged as soon as possible.

I have the honor to be, Sir,

Your most obedient and most humble servant.

P. S.—As Major Lewis is prisoner, I thought it was right to read to him that part of this letter which particularly concerns him. He says when he came back to speak to me, that he gave no orders for the troops to retire from the plain. That Captain Saunder, who was the next officer to him, can best account for that step ; for they did retire, and I took it for granted that it was by the Major's orders, till he assured me of the contrary. Mr. Jenkins, of the Americans, is a pretty young lad, and has spirit. He is the oldest ensign, and is much afraid that being a prisoner will be a detriment to his promotion. He begs that I may mention him to you, and I could not think of refusing him.

[British Museum.—Bouquet Papers.]

LETTER TO COLONEL BOUQUET.

(No Endorsement or Address.)

Raestown, September 23, 1758.

Sir:—Your letter of the 17th, from Loyal Hanning, I read with no less surprise than real concern, as indeed I could not well believe that such an attempt would have been carried into execution without my previous knowledge and concurrence, as you well know my opinion, and dread of the consequences of running any risque of the troops meeting with the smallest check. As well as my fears of alienating and altering the disposition of the Indians, at this critical time, who (tho' fickle and wavering), yet were seemingly well disposed to embrace our alliance and protection. But I need not recapitulate to you my many good reasons against any attempt of this kind being made at this time ; nor repeat to you how happy your assurances made me, of all my orders and directions having been (and would be) complyed with.

For which I rested secure, and plumed myself in our good fortune, in having the head of our army advanced, as it were, to the beard of the enemy, and secured in a good post well guarded and cautioned against surprise. Our roads almost completed; our provisions all upon wheels, and all this without any loss on our side, and our small army all ready to join and act in a collected body whenever we pleased to attack the enemy, or that any favourable opportunity presented itself to us.

Thus the breaking in upon—not to say disappointments of —our hitherto so fair and flattering hopes of success touches most sensibly. How far we shall find the bad effects of it, I shall not pretend to say. At present I shall suspend judging, altho' I have languished for the officer you promised to send me down—whom I have expected hourly—and a letter from you of your present situation, with the state of the posts, and the strength at them, that the escorts may be proportioned. I acquainted you of the state of our provisions, and the hopes I have of being immediately supplied with 1,000 barrels of pork and at least 1,200 barrels of flour, all of which, by this time, is actually upon its march, and will arrive here daily. So, I shall forward it as fast as I can, altho' large convoys and escorts are very inconvenient. The description of the roads is so various and disagreeable that I do not know what to think or say. Lieutenant Evans came down here the other day, and described the Laurell Hill as, at present, impracticable, but said he could mend it with the assistance of 500 men, fascines and fagots, in one day's time.

Col. Stephens writes Col. Washington that he is told by everybody that the road from Loyal Hannon to the Ohio and the French fort is now impracticable. For what reason, or why, he writes thus I do not know ; but I see Col. Washington and my friend, Col. Byrd, would rather be glad this was true than otherways, seeing the other road (their favourite scheme) was not followed out. I told them plainly that, whatever they thought, yet I did aver that, in our prosecuting the present road, we had proceeded from the best intelligence that could be got for the good and convenience of the army, without any views to oblige any one province or another ; and added that those two gentlemen were the only people that I had met with who had shewed their weakness in their attachment to the province they belong to, by declaring so publickly in favour of one road without their knowing anything of the other, having never heard from any Pennsylvania person one word about the road ; and that, as for myself, I could safely say—and believed I might answer for you—that the good of the service was the only view we had at heart, not valuing the provincial interest, jealousys, or suspicions, one single two-pence ; and that, therefore, I could not believe Col. Stephen's descriptions untill I had heard from you, which I hope you will very soon be able to disprove.

I fancy what I said more on this subject will cure them from coming upon this topic again. However, I beg you will cause look into the Laurell Hill, and let it be set to rights as fast as possible ; and let all the different posts, and the different convoys and escorts, as they pass along, repair the bad steps, and keep the roads already made in constant order.

I have sent Mr. Basset back the length of Fort Loudoun, in order to divide the troops from thence to Juniata, in small partys, all along that road, who are to set it all to rights, and keep it so ; and as the partys are all encamped within five or six miles one of another, they serve as escorts to the provisions and forage that is coming up, at the same time. I am extreamly sorry for your loss of De Rhorr ; nor can I well conceive what I had to do there. Mr. Gordon, who, it seems, had the direction of the works here, left this without leaving

6

the plan or sketch of this place or environs, or leaving any directions, as far as I can yet learn, either with the people employed to carry the general plan into execution, or how that they were further to proceed ; and, notwithstanding the multiplicity of working-tools, I am at a loss to find a sufficient number for helping the roads and clearing the stumps or other impediments about the camp ; nor can I well imagine what is become of all the rest.

There are two wounded Highland officers just now arriv'd, who give so lame an account of how matters proceeded, or any kind of description of the ground, that one can draw nothing from them—only that my friend Grant had most certainly lost the *tra mon tânc*, and, by his thirst of fame, brought on his own perdition, and run a great risque of ours, which was far wide of the promises he made me at Carlisle, when soliciting to command a party, which I would not agree to ; and, very contrary to his criticisms upon Gen. Abercromby's late affair, has unhappily fallen into the individual same error, by his inconsiderate and rash proceeding.

I understand by these officers that you have withdrawn the troops from your advanced post, which I attribute to its being too small for what you intended it, or that it did not answer the strength that you at first described it to me. I shall be glad to hear all your people are in spirits, and keep so, and that Loyall Hannon will be soon past any insult without cannon. I shall be soon afraid to crowd you with provisions, nor would I wish to crowd the troops any faster up, untill our magazines are thoroughly formed, if you have enough of troops for your own defence and compleating the roads ; and I see the absolute necessity there is for my stay here some days, in order to carry on the transport of provisions and forage, which, without my constant attention, would fail directly. The road forward to the Ohio must be reconnoitered again in order to be sure of our further progress, for it would grieve me sadly that Mr. Washington or Mr. Byrd should have any reason to find fault with that, which without their knowledge they have so publickly exclaimed against. When you have settled things to your mind, I beg you will write me, and as soon as you conveniently can, come down, were it only for a day, and if Colonel Armstrong could be spared, should be glad he came along, in order to settle our further proceedings, and to seize the first favourable opportunity of marching directly forwards. The artillery that is left here I would march in two divisions to prevent a long train of waggons, and the tearing up the roads. The Congress at Eastown had the most favourable appearance, as there was 500 Indians already come in, but what they will now do, God knows. Pray make up a hovell or hutt for me at L. Hannon or any other of the posts with a fire place if possible. Sir John St. Clair says that if I say he was in the wrong to Colonel Stevens, he will readily acknowledge it. I do not choose meddling, but I think Colonel Stevens might act, and trust to Sir John's acknowledgment.

I am, dear sir,

Your most obedient servant,

Jo. Forbes.

[British Museum.—Bouquet Papers.]

LETTER BY COLONEL BOUQUET.*

(Endorsed.)

Loyal Hanna, Sept. 17, 1758.

Camp at Loyal Hanna, Sept. 17, 1758.

Sir:—In the situation in which you are, sick, etc., it is with double regret, that I must inform you of the misfortune

---

* To General Amherst.

which has happened to Major Grant, who after a long engagement has been defeated on the 14th current.

I do not make any apology for the part which I took in this affair. I leave the detail of facts to condemn or justify me.

The day on which I arrived at the camp, which was the 7th, it was reported to me that we were surrounded by parties of Indians, several soldiers having been scalped, or made prisoners.

Being obliged to have our cattle and our horses in the woods, our people could not guard or search for them, without being continually liable to fall into the hands of the enemy.

Lieutenant Col. Dagworthy and our Indians not having yet arrived, I ordered two companies each of a hundred men to occupy the path ways and try to cut off the enemies in their ambush and release our prisoners. These detachments being ready to march, Major Grant drew me aside and said that he was surprised that I took this method, after so many proofs that these little parties never did anything, and served to lose our men and discourage our people; but if I would give him five hundred men, he would go to the fort, reconnoitre the roads and the forces of the enemy, which according to all our reports does not exceed six hundred French and Indians, that this was confirmed by a party which had entered the town, and that whatever detachments they could make, they could not send out more than they have, and that by erecting an ambuscade he could take prisoners.

I made some objection to letting him go, but he insisted, and influenced by his reasons and the situation in which we found ourselves I consented and countermanded the two parties who were under arms. Having sent for Col. Burd and Major Lewis (Lieut. Col. Stephen being under arrest I told his Major to inform him of the affair), I informed these

gentlemen of the proposition made by Major Grant to procure for us sure intelligence which would give us some advantage over the Indians, who insulted us every day with impu-
nity, and that this would be the way to cure our men of the
fear which they had of them. Those who had escaped from
their attacks had thrown down their arms that they might fly
faster.

I begged them to give me their opinion upon a project
of which I had several times spoken to Major Grant at Raystown, which was to attack during the night the Indians who
camped around the Fort in huts, and that the disposition could
be made thus: Lieutenant-Colonel Dagworthy (who should
arrive this evening or to-morrow with the Indians) should
march with 900 men to the post, which was known to be 10
miles distant, there construct an entrenchment and remain
with 200 men. The Major should march with 300 Highlanders, 100 R. A., 150 Virginians, 100 Marylanders and 100
Pennsyia, and all the Indians to the neighborhood of the
fort, regulating their march so as to be five miles from
the fort in the evening, with the precautions necessary to
prevent a surprise; and from there he would send the Indians
and such of the officers as knew the environs of the place to
reconnoitre, and if he found by the appearance of the enemy
that he had not been discovered, he would advance on the
hill, half a mile from the fort, when he would reconnoitre
himself the fires of the Indians and make his arrangements
accordingly. In case he saw them around their fires, he
should send parties of his detachment with white shirts over
their clothes to attack them soon after midnight, the bayonets
on the guns and only fire in extremity, it not being difficult
to surprise them, as they do not keep sentinels. This *coup*,
made or missed, he should beat a retreat to the height,
where they should stop with the rest of the troops and the

Indians, and as soon as his people, directed by the sound, should have joined him, he should immediately retire six miles from the fort before day, and there form an ambuscade of all his men and the Indians, in case the enemy should follow, leaving a small company round the post to observe their movements and inform him of them. If he should conquer them at the ambuscade he could then return safely to the fort to take a plan of it and reconnoitre the environs. But if by his spies or himself he finds that he was discovered, he should only think of retiring. This is the plan that was proposed, and to execute it preparations were made the next day.

On the 9th he departed, and I joined him on the 10th at the post, where Lieutenant-Colonel Dagworthy should have stopped. I remained here all night, and saw him depart on the 11th with his detachment in good order. This post being nearly ready for defence, I returned to the camp. Instead of this plan, which did not compel him to fight, or which gave him in that case every advantage of disposition, and choice of ground with all his troops together, here is what he appears to have done: Having arrived at the height only one fire was seen, but Ensign Chew, who had reconnoitered, said that all the Indians lay in the block houses, which were easy to force. He sent there Major Lewis with 400 men; some confusion being among the troops he feared he had been discovered and returned to join Major Grant, who sent there at once two companies of Highlanders. They visited the block houses, and found no one. They put out the fire and returned. The Major, according to his orders, should have retired, but unfortunately he thought that the garrison was too weak to dare risk a sortie, and in consequence he remained on the height untill morning. He then beat the *reveille* in different places, and ordered Major Lewis to place himself in ambuscade with the baggage and 100 R. A., 150 Virginians, 200 Highlanders, 100 'Maryl' and 100 Penns. were placed on the heights, and he sent Captain McDonald with 100 Highlanders, drums beating, straight to the fort. Some one had seen a party leave the garrison as though they would cut off the retreat. Hardly had McDonald gone half the distance, when he heard the whoop of the Indians, followed immediately by a sortie of nearly 300 French and Indians, who fell upon them. He killed so many of these people at his first fire that they turned aside and surrounded him. He pierced through them, where he was killed. The companies of Monro and McKenzie, who descended to their assistance, were put in disorder and the Captain killed. As the enemy continually received reinforcements, all the troops were soon engaged, and the fire sustained a long time after our men yielded. Major Lewis, who was distant about two miles, heard the firing, urged by his officers and the soldiers, quit his post to go to their assistance. He arrived just at the moment our men retired in disorder towards his post. He had gained a height which had put his men out of breath, and, stopping, they found themselves under fire of the enemy. The action was, nevertheless, still very lively and for a long time disputed. At last our men yielded, and there remained only a scene of confusion, notwithstanding all the efforts of Major Grant to rally them. They would have been cut to pieces probably had not Captain Bullet of the Virginians, with 100 men, sustained the combat with all their power, until, having lost two-thirds of his men, he was driven to the shore of the river, where he found the poor Major. He urged him to retire, but he said he would not quit the field of battle as long as there was a man who would fight. My heart is broke (said he) I shall never outlive this day. They were soon surrounded, and the Frenchmen, calling him by his name, offered quarter. He would not accept it. They would not fire on him, wishing to take him prisoner. Captain Bullet continued firing. At last they also fired and drove his party into the Ohio, where a great number were drowned. Bullet escaped, but I have no news of the Major.

At the first news of his misfortune I sent Lieutenant-Colonel Stephen with 300 men to join Lieutenant-Colonel Dagworthy to cover their retreat. The Indians did not pursue them far. Our post misses some officers and it lacks yet 270 men. Many have crossed the river, and it is thought many will escape. Our Catawbas did not fire and the Tuscararas and Nottaways did very well.

It appears from the testimony of the Indians and of our men that the French have lost many men, mostly Indians. The French did not try to kill but to make prisoners, and it seems for the first time they shewed humanity, which makes me hope that the Major and several others of the officers whom we miss are saved.

I have written to Colonel Washington to march to Rays Town, leaving 100 men at Cumberland, until the arrival of the militia of Maryland. This reinforcement is necessary to secure to our convoys communication. Contrary to my expectations the troops do not appear depressed by this check, and if all was ready elsewhere, they would be more ready than ever to go to the front. Reports of an action in the woods are so confused that I cannot render you an exact account of what happened there, but I will send to you an officer as soon as I know what is best to do. Many of the arms are broken, some lost. We must have others to replace them. We are assured that the Delawares and the Shawnees were against us, and among the men taken and scalped around the camp is a German who came, it is said, from Ohio, and who, I suppose, was sent by the Governor of Pennsylvania. The enemy had received a considerable reinforcement the evening of the action. The account of their number varies from 3000 to 1200. There was discovered on the island a camp with more than 100 tents. For the state of the roads and the fort I refer you to the report which the officer will deliver to you. The post is much more considerable than we had thought and many new works have been added. We have not seen an Indian for eight days, we think that after this success it will be difficult for the French to keep them. I will send a letter to the Governor to make known the fate of those who are missing.

The Provincials appear to have done well and their good men are better in this war than the regular troops.

I will not add any reflections on this affair, they are too unpleasant. If the French wish to attack us in their turn, we will be in two days ready to receive them, being all reunited at this post.

I have the honor, to be, Sir,

Your very obedt. servant,

HENRY BOUQUET.

[British Museum.—Bouquet Papers.]

LETTER OF COL. BURD UPON THE ATTACKS.

(On his Majesty's Service.)

CAMP AT LOYAL HANNON, October 12, 1758.
To Col. Bouquet at Stoney Creek on the Laurell Hill:

Dear Sir:—I had the pleasure to receive your favours of this date this evening at 7 P.M. I shall be glad to see you. I send you, through Lieut.-Coll. Lloyd (who marches to you with 200 men), the 100 falling axes, etc., you desire.

This day, at 11 A.M., the enemy fired twelve guns to the
southwest of us, upon which I sent out two partys to surround them ; but instantly the firing increased, upon which I
sent out a larger party of 500 men.   They were forced to the
camp, and immediately a regular attack ensued, which lasted
a long time; I think about two hours.   But we had the
pleasure to do that honour to his majesty's arms, to keep his
camp at Loyal Hannon.   I can't inform you of our loss, nor
that of the enemy.   Must refer you for the particulars to
Lieut.-Col. Lloyd.   One of their soldiers, which we have
mortally wounded, says they were 1200 strong and 200
Indians, but I can ascertain nothing of this further.   I have
drove them off the field ; but I don't doubt of a second attack.
If they do I am ready.

Being most sincerely,

My dear sir,

Your most sincere friend and

Obe't humble serv't,

JAMES BURD.

[Since writing we have been fired upon.]

COL. BOUQUET.

[British Museum.—Bouquet Papers.]

[The address torn away all but the word "Rays Town."]

RAYS DUDGEON, October 13, 1758, 10 P.M.

Sir:—After having written to you this morning, I went to
reconnoitre Laurell Hill, with a party of eighty men, some
firing of guns around us made me suspect that it was the signal of an enemy's party.   I sent to find out, and one of our
party having perceived the Indians, fired on them.   We continued our march and have found a very good road for ascend-

ing the mountain, although very stony in two places. The old road is absolutely impracticable.

I have had this afternoon a second letter from Colonel Burd. The enemies have been all night around the entrenchements, and have made several false attacks. The cannon and the cohortes* have held them in awe, and until the Colonel had sent to reconnoitre the environs, he was not sure that they had retired. At this moment is heard from the mountains several cannon shots which makes me judge that the enemies have not yet abandoned the party, and at all events I am going to attempt to re-enter this post before day. The 200 men which Colonel Burd sent to me, have eaten nothing for two days. I received this moment provisions from Stoney Creek and will depart in two hours.

I have not got any report of our loss, two officers from Maryland have been killed, and one wounded. Duncannon of Virginia mortally wounded, also one officer of the first Battalion of Pennsylvania, and nearly fifty men.

The loss of the enemy must be considerable to judge by the reports of our men and the fire which they have clearly wasted. Without this cursed rain we would have arrived in time with the artillery and 200 men, and I believe it would have made a difference.

As soon as it is possible, I will send you word how we are. Be at rest about the post. I have left it in a state to defend itself against all attacks without cannon, and I learn that they have finished all that remains to be done.

I am with entire devotion, Sir,

Your very humble and very obedient servant,

HENRY BOUQUET.

---

* Troop of 500 fort soldiers.

BOUQUET PAPERS.

S. Ecuyer, Commandant at Fort Pitt, 1763.

JOURNAL, LETTERS AND ORDERLY BOOK AND A LETTER FROM GENERAL BOUQUET.

Fort Pitt, May 14, 1763.

A number of Six Nation Indians that lived about 90 (miles distant on the) Ohio below this, came up and settled at Pine Creek and began to (plant corn).

17th, Their chiefs collected a number of horses their young men had stolen and delivered them up. From this to the 26th they continued planting their corn.

27th, Two men that went up the Ohio about 7 miles, to where the Munsies were settled, returned and informed me that all the Indians the night before had removed from their towns and carried everything with them, leaving their corn-fields open : this made us suspect that some mischief about here was immediately intended. A number of Delawares with a large quantity of skins came in and dealt them ; the uncommon dispatch and indifference of what they took for them, and their chief seeming to press Mr. McKee to go down the country and not to stay above four days, still gave us more suspicion of the Indian designs and caused the inhabitants to arm themselves.

28th, Two Shawnese came in from hunting.

29th, At break of day this morning three men came in from

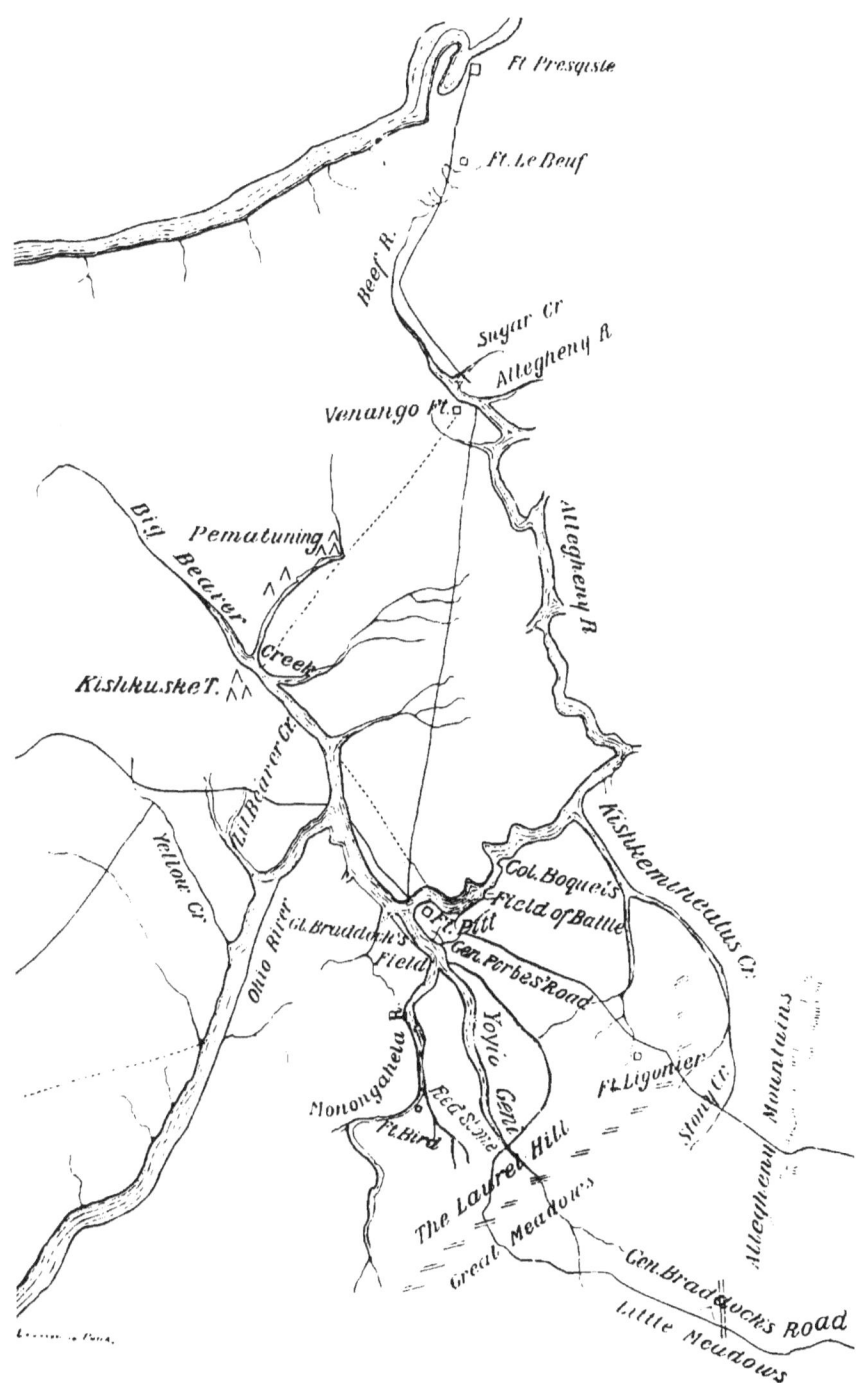

Ft. Presquisle

Ft. Le Beuf

Beef R.

Sugar Cr

Alleghenŷ R

Venango Ft.

Alleghenŷ R

Pematuning

Big Beaver

Creek

Kishkuske T.

Little Beaver Cr.

Yellow Cr.

Kishkeminneutus Cr.

Ohio River

Col. Boquet's Field of Battle

Ft. Pitt

Gl. Braddock's Field

Gen. Forbes' Road

Alleghenŷ Mountains

Ft. Ligonier

Stony Cr.

Monongahela R.

Redstone

Loyal Cr.

Ft. Bird

The Laurel Hill

Great Meadows

Gen. Braddock's Road

Little Meadows

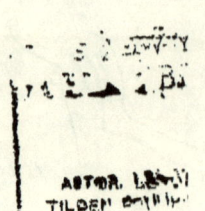

Colonel Clapham's, who was settled at the Sewickly old town, about 25 miles from here, on the Youghyogane river, with an account that Colonel Clapham, with one of his men, two women and a child were murdered by Wolfe and some other Delaware Indians, about 2 o'clock the day before. The 27th Wolfe, with some others robbed one Mr. Coleman on the road between this and Ligonier, of upwards of 50£. The women that were killed at Colonel Clapham's were treated in such a brutal manner that decency forbids the mentioning. This evening we had two soldiers killed and scalped at the saw-mill.

May 30th, All the inhabitants moved in to the fort. About 4 o'clock one Coulson came in who had been a prisoner (at the lower) Shawnese town, and gave the following account. We came to the town with some traders, where an Indian arrived from the Lakes (with a) belt to acquaint the Delawares that Detroit was taken, the post at Sundusky burnt, and all the garrison put to death, except the officer whom they made prisoner. Upon this news, the Beaver and Shingess (the two Chiefs of the Delawares, commonly called King B and King S) came and acquainted Mr. Calhoon (the trader there) with it, and desired him to move away from there as quick as possible, with all his property, and that they sent three Indians to conduct him and the rest of the white people safe to this post, and yesterday as they were crossing Beaver Creek, being fourteen in number, they were fired on and he believes all were killed except himself.

31st, Two of Mr. Calhoon's men came in and confirmed the above account. A second express was despatched this night to the general.

June 1st, Two men who were sent off express last night to Venango returned, being fired on at Shanipin's Town and one of them wounded in the leg. About 12 o'clock two men came from Redstone and the same night were sent back with orders for the Sergeant to repair to this post and bring the country people with him with 600 lbs. powder that was there belonging to some traders. About 6 o'clock in the afternoon Mr. Calhoon came in and brought the following account which he took in writing from the Indians at Tuskarawas.

Tuskarawas, May 27, 1763, 11 o'clock at night, King Beaver with Shingess, Windohala, Wingenum and Daniel and William Anderson came and delivered me the following intelligence (by a string of Wampum).

Brother: Out of regard to you and the friendship that formerly subsisted between (our) grandfathers and the English, which has been lately renewed by us, we come to inform you of the news we had heard, which you may depend upon as true.

Brother: All the English that were at Detroit were killed ten days ago, not one left alive.

At Sandusky all the white people there were killed 5 days ago, nineteen in number, except the officer who is a prisoner and one boy who made his escape, whom we have not heard of. At the mouth of the Twigtwee River (about 80 miles from Sandusky by water) Hugh Crawford with one boy was taken prisoner and six men killed. At the Salt Licks five days ago 5 white men were killed, we received the account this day ; we have seen a number of tracks on the road between this and Sandusky not far off, which we are sure is a party coming to cut you and your people off, but as we have sent a man to watch their motions, request you may think of nothing you have here, but make the best of your way to some place of safety, as we would not desire to see you killed in our town ; be careful to avoid the road and every part where Indians resort.

Brother: What goods and other effects you have here you

need not be uneasy about them, we assure you that we will take care to keep them safe for six months, perhaps by that time we may see you or send you word what you may expect from us further. We know there is one white man at Gichanga, don't be concerned for him, we will take care to send him safe home.

Brother: We desire you to tell George Croghan and all your great men (that they) must not ask us any thing about this news, or what has happened, as we are not all concerned in it : the nations that have taken up the hatchet against you are the Ottawas and Chipawas and when you first went to speak with these people you did not consult us upon it, therefore we desire you may not expect that we are to account for any mischief they do, what you would know further about this news you must learn by the same road you just went, but if you will speak with us you must send one or two men only, and we will hear them.

Brother: We thought your king had made peace with us and all the Western Nations of Indians, for our part we joined it heartily and desired to hold it always good, and you may depend upon it we will take care not to be readily cheated or drawn into a war again, but as we are settled between you and these nations who have taken up the hatchet against you we desire you will send no warriors this way till we are removed from this, which we will do as soon as we conveniently can ; when we will permit you to pass without taking notice, till then we desire they may go by the first road you went.

Gave a String.

The following is what Mr. Calhoon learned on his journey from one of these three Indians who were sent (to conduct him) safe there, viz. Daniel before mentioned as one of their chiefs. That Detroit was not really taken but had been attacked by the Indians four days before the messenger who brought the account left it, which Mr. Calhoon imagines must have been from about the 13th to the 17th of May and that the Indians had not then met with much success, but strongly persisted in carrying on the attack and said they were determined not (to) give over till they took it, and that the English had sent out three Belts of Wampum and the French two, desiring them to desist, which they refused. Mr. Calhoon says that when he and his people left Tuskerawas fourteen in number the Indians refused to let them bring their arms, telling them that the three Indians who were going along with them were sufficient to conduct them safe, and that the next day passing Beaver Creek they were fired upon by a party of Indians, when their guides immediately disappeared without interfering for them, and he is convinced that they were led by their guides knowingly to this party in order to be cut off, from which himself with three of his people only have escaped.

Mr. Calhoon further says that having lost his way and falling in upon the road leading to Venango, about seventy miles above this post he saw a number of Indian tracks, which had gone that way—two men were sent to the General with the intelligence received.

This morning an order was issued by the (commander of the fort), to pull down and burn all the out-houses.

June 2d, Three men, who were sent a second time express to Venango, returned after going about twenty miles, having fallen in with a party of (Indians). While our people were engaged to-day in burning the houses on the hill, the Indians set fire to Thompson's house, about half a mile from the fort.

3d and 4th, All the garrison were employed in repairing and strengthening the fort.

5th, 2 o'clock at night one Benjamin Sutton came in, who

says he left Redstone (or Fort Burd) two days ago and found
that place evacuated, and saw a number of shoe tracks going
towards Fort Cumberland which he supposes was the garrison, that there was with him there a white man named Hicks
and an Indian named Keeois, who would have burnt the fort
had he not persuaded them from it, that Hicks told him that
an Indian war had broken out and that he would kill the white
people wherever he found them, and went with intention to
murder Madcalf's people, nine miles from here, who had
removed some time before ; he says they intended to have
taken him prisoner, but the wind blowing hard and it growing
very dark when he came nigh the fort he made for it and called
to the sentinel.   Hicks and the Indian went by in their bark
canoes.

6th, Nothing extraordinary.

June 7th, This morning Mr. Wilkins, with his wife and one
child arrived here in a day and a half from Venango.

The following intelligence which arrived the day before
they left, was brought by express from Presqu' Isle :

That Lieutenant Cuyler, an officer of the Queen's Rangers,
had arrived there, who informed us that he had been as far as
the mouth of Detroit River with an escort of about one hundred men, ten batteaux and 139 barrels of provisions, where he
was attacked the 28th May, at 11 o'clock at night, that he had
2 sergeants, 52 privates, a woman and a child killed, himself
with three privates wounded, two since dead of their wounds,
that he saved only two batteaux with five barrels of pork, that
he then retreated to the Fort Sandusky, which place he found
destroyed, and from thence he made the best of his way to
Presqu' Isle where arrived; he also says that Lieutenant
Schlosser's post was destroyed and the garrison cut off.   A
number of canoes were brought and left in the night on the
other side of the Monongehela River, opposite to the fort.

7

9th, By a great smoke which rose up the river, we suppose the enemy has burnt Mr. Croghan's house, the smoke rising where we imagine his house stood. Nine o'clock, two more expresses were sent to Venango.

10th, This morning the two expresses returned, having lost themselves in the night. About 10 o'clock in the morning as some of the militia were putting up some fences about 1000 yards from the fort the enemy fired on them, they returned the fire and retreated safe to the fort.

June 11th, At break of day some Indians were discovered among the ruins of the upper town.

About 10 o'clock at night they set fire to a house, on which a shell was thrown among them, some time after Indians were seen in the lower town and some hallooing heard at a small distance from the fort.

12th, An Indian was discovered from the garden; about 11 o'clock a party, out cutting spelts, saw two Indians and fired on them, on which a number more appeared and fired on our people, who returned it; on some round shot being fired from the cannons in the fort the Indians ran off.

13th and 14th, Nothing worth notice.

15th, A party was sent out to cut spelts and were fired on. Sergeant Miller of the militia, contrary to orders, with three others advanced to Grant's Hill, and just as they had gained the summit, Miller was shot dead, a party advancing drove the enemy off and prevented their scalping him. Between 11 and 12 o'clock at night, as an express from Bedford was challenged by one of the sentinels from the rampart the enemy fired a number of shots at him and the sentinels in the fort.

16th, Four Shawnees appeared on the opposite side of the Ohio, and desired that Mr. McKee would go over and speak to them, which he did and they made him the following speech :

"*Brother*, We received the message you sent us on the death of Colonel Clapham, and our chiefs desired us to inform you that they will take care of the traders in our towns. Mr. Baird and Gibson were taken by the Delaware Indian called Sir William Johnson and his people at the Muskingum town and carried to our town. Our chiefs say they will take care of them until the war is over. We came to enquire news, we have heard none since the time the message with the belt and bloody hatchet came from the Lake Indians to the Delaware and Tuskarawas, acquainting them that they had struck the English and desired that they would join them. The captains and warriors of the Delawares pay no regard to their chiefs, who advised them not to accept the hatchets, but are determined to prosecute the war against you. It was the Six Nations that left this and the Delawares that killed your people at Beaver Creek with Mr. Calhoon."

An express was sent off in the night to Bedford.

June 17th, The same Indians came and called again and desired Mr. McKee would come over, he refused; they then recommended him to set off for the inhabitants in the night, or to come over to them and they would take care of him at their towns till the war was over; they acquainted him that all the Nations had taken up the hatchet against us and that they intended to attack this post with a great body in a few days, that Venango and all the other posts were already cut off, that they were afraid to refuse taking up the hatchet against us as so many nations had done it to force us to come to them. About 12 o'clock at night two expresses came in from Ligonier with letters from the General.*

18th, The enemy set fire to another house up the Ohio. One o'clock in the morning the two expresses that came last set off for Ligonier again with letters.

---

* Amherst.

June 19th, Two Indians crept along the bank of the Monongehela towards the sentinel who was posted on the bank
of the river and fired at him.   Soon after a number of Indians
were seen at the head of the fields, taking off some horses,
as the garrison was turning out a soldier's gun went off by
accident and mortally wounded him, of which he died the
next day.

20th, Nothing extraordinary.

21st, About 11 o'clock at night the Indians on the opposite
side of the Monongehela repeated all's well after our sentinels.

22d, Between 9 and 10 o'clock in the morning a smoke was
seen rising on the back of Grant's Hill, where the Indians had
made a fire, and about 2 o'clock several of them appeared in
the Spelt's* field, driving off the horses and cattle.   About 5
o'clock one James Thompson, who it was supposed was gone
after a horse, was killed and scalped in sight of the fort; on
this a great number of Indians appeared on each river and on
Grant's Hill, shooting down the cattle and horses.   A shell
was thrown amongst a number of them from a howitzer, which
burst just as it fell among them.   About an hour after they
fired on the fort from Grant's Hill and the other side of the
Ohio, a shot from the opposite side of the Ohio wounded a
man in Monongehela Bastion.   About 7 o'clock three Indians
were seen about 150 yards from the fort on the Monongehela
bank.   Mr. McKee and two others fired on them and killed
one of them.

23d, About 12 o'clock at night, two Delawares called for
Mr. McKee and told him they wanted to speak to him in the
morning.

24th, The Turtle's Heart, a principal warrior of the Delawares, and Mamaltee (a chief) came within a small distance of
the fort, Mr. McKee went out to them and they made a speech,

* Spelts, German wheat.

letting us know that all our posts, and Ligonier was destroyed, that great numbers of Indians were advancing, but that out of regard to us they had prevailed on six nations of Indians not to attack us but give us time to go down the country, and they desired we should set off immediately.

The commanding officer thanked them, let them know that we had everything we wanted, that we could defend it against all the Indians in the woods, that we had three large armies marching to chastise those Indians that had struck us, told them to take care of their women and children, but not to tell any other Nations, they said they would go and speak to their chiefs and come and tell us what they said, they returned and said they would hold fast the chain of friendship. Out of our regard to them we gave them two blankets and an hand-kerchief out of the Small Pox Hospital. I hope it will have the desired effect. They then told us that Ligonier had been attacked, but that the enemy was beaten off.

The 25th, A Shawnee Indian came across the river and spoke to Mr. McKee and told him that two days ago, sixty miles off, he left a large body of Indians on their march for this place, to attack it, and the Delawares that were here, were going to join them.

About 5 o'clock in the afternoon, two soldiers belonging to the garrison of Le Bœuf came in and informed us that Ensign Price would be here the next morning.

The 26th, Six o'clock in the morning Ensign Price, with five men came in from Le Bœuf and gave the following account of his miraculous escape from that place, and while they were bringing him across the river seven Indians showed themselves on Grant's Hill.

Early in the morning of the 18th instant five Indians came to his post and asked for some tobacco and provisions, which he gave them. Soon after they went off, about thirty men

came down the road leading to Presqu' Isle, laid their arms
a short distance off, and came and asked liberty to come in
and said they were going to war against the Cherokees, would
stay with him that night and that they proposed to pass by
Fort Pitt in order to speak with Mr. Croghan ; Mr. Price
suspecting their design had all his people under arms and
would not suffer them to go in, upon this the Indians took up
their arms and got to the back of an out store, where they
picked out the stones it was underpinned with and got into it,
then they began to roll out the barrels of provisions and shoot,
fired arrows into the top of the block house which was put
out several times, this continued till some time in the night,
when Mr. Price, finding it impossible to defend the place any
longer or prevent its being consumed, took advantage of the
night, got all his people out at a window and made off without
being observed, but unfortunately left six of his men and a
woman who he supposes fell into the hands of the enemy,
some time after he left the block house, the Indians began to
fire upon it, when he came to Venango he found it in ashes,
kept the road all the way here and saw the bones of several
people who had been killed while going to Venango : they
were Six Nation Indians who attacked him.

Mr. Price gives an account likewise which some persons in
the sloop from Detroit had brought to Presqu' Isle. About the
beginning of May a large body of Indians (1,500 in number)
came to Detroit under pretence of holding a treaty with
Major Gladwin, but Monsieur Baubee finding out their design
apprised Major Gladwin of it, who immediately ordered his
garrison under arms and would not permit them to come in,
upon this the Indians sent two of their principal warriors in,
to desire he would come out and treat with them, which he
did not think proper to do, but detained the two warriors and
sent out Capt. Campbell and Lieutenant McDougal to know

what they wanted, whom the Indians made prisoners and
then rushed up and endeavoured to force the gate, but the
garrison being under arms and prepared for them, fired upon
them, killed forty on the spot and wounded many more ; the
Indians carried on the attack for two weeks before the sloop
left it ; it was three weeks before she arrived at Presque Isle,
owing to contrary winds.   The garrison at, De Troit had no
provisions but a little corn which Baubee furnished them,
the French inhabitants there are not concerned in this war
but live on their farms as usual, the sloop was attacked all
the way down the De Troit River and the Indians sent Capt.
Campbell on board of her to desire Capt. Newman to deliver
her up, who sent for an answer that he was determined to
fight them, he is gone to Niagara and proposes to return to
Detroit with provisions.   6 o'clock in the afternoon a soldier
who made his escape from Presqu' Isle and says that on the
19th inst. that post was attacked by 250 Indians which continued for two days and that the Indians had made holes in the
bank and fired through, that the officer Mr. Christy capitulated, that the Indians were to give them 6 days' provisions
and escort them safe to this post.   It was the Ottawas, Chipawas, Wayondotts, and Senecas that took the post, and after
they had delivered the Indians their arms, while the Indians
were engaged in carrying out the provisions and other stores,
he being at some distance hearing a woman scream he
imagined they were beginning to tomahawk the garrison he
made his escape, that another soldier likewise attempted to
make his escape but fears he did not get off, that the Indians
had fired the roof of the Block House a great many times
before they capitulated and that they as often put it out, he
further says that the schooner was in sight and kept there
sounding with their boats to try if they could get in to their
assistance, but that there was not water enough, that the

Indians told them they had destroyed 800 barrels of provisions at the store house where the schooner was to load and that he believes the schooner had no provisions on board. Nine o'clock at night two expresses were sent off to the General by way of Fort Cumberland on the other side of the Monongehela with these accounts.

27th, Six o'clock in the afternoon four men and one woman, of the garrison of Le Bœuf came in, who, it was feared, had fallen into the hands of the enemy; they say they left the other two men of that garrison about thirty miles off, not being able to come along. The other soldier from Presqu' Isle, who, it was thought, was captured, came in with these people and confirms the account already received respecting that garrison. These soldiers say, soon after they left the fort they heard two guns and the death halloo. Mr. Price says that the schooner brought an account of Sir Robert Davers, Captain McKay and Captain Robinson being killed by the Indians before the attack begun at D'Troit, while they were sounding the depth of the water in the lake near the mouth of D'Troit River.

28th, Several Indians have been seen to-day on Grant's hill and about the fields. About 9 o'clock at night the sentinels discovered some canoes in the river and presently after saw some people in the ditch. The garrison turned out to their alarm posts, remained under arms till 12 o'clock, then went to their barracks, all but the guard. A great smoke was seen up the river this morning, supposed to be a house on fire.

29th, This morning numbers of Mockeson tracks were seen in the ditch where the enemy were last night.

30th, Nothing extraordinary. A few Indians seen who called to a man that went to drive some cattle in.

July 1st, Six or seven Indians showed themselves this morning at the upper end of the garden.

2d, About 7 o'clock this morning some Indians appeared on Grant's Hill; at 12 o'clock they came into the cornfield, drove off a number of cows and shot at several; this night several Indians were seen near the Glacis.

3d, At 10 o'clock this morning as a party of men went to the gardens for greens, etc., they were fired upon by some Indians who had hidden within thirty yards of the fort; our people hurried forward and fired upon them, and it was thought that Adam Terrence either killed or wounded one badly, as the others were seen helping or carrying him away. Our people pursued them till they were ordered back; they found his tomahawk, pipe and a handkerchief which he dropped. At 10 o'clock two guns were heard on the opposite side of the Allegheny, and immediately four Indians appeared naked and their bodies painted with different colors, singing as they came along according to their custom when appearing as friends; they had two small sets of British colors. Mr. McKee went down and asked who they were and what their business was; they answered him they were Ottawas and came from D'Troit ten days ago, where they said everything was settled between them and us in that place, and that they had brought letters from the commanding officer there, therefore desired to be brought over. Notwithstanding the fair appearance they came under, McKee directed them to go up the river and cross at a place where the Indians were frequently seen crossing, and while they were away a canoe was sent and left for them on the other side. When they came over Mr. McKee went and met them a small distance from the fort. One of them (commonly called Chatterbox) displayed two large belts of wampum tied on a stick. They made the following speech to Mr. McKee: "*Brother:* (Showing the belts, one of which he called the Friendship Belt, the other for clearing the path between them and us) "This is what we called the writing we had for you and we are sent by our chiefs (who will be here to-morrow) to acquaint you that they are coming to renew their friendship by their belts and to assure you that they are coming with a good intent and hope to be received as friends. This is all we have to say; we propose to go and meet our chiefs this afternoon and will return to-morrow." Then asked for some thread and tobacco. During this time on Grant's Hill a number of Indians appeared, very uneasy, and came running down toward us; five more appeared over the Ohio or Alleghany. Upon this the Ottawas went to their canoes, where they met those Indians that came from Grant's Hill; they talked some time together; During this our people fired several shots at those that came from the hill, which they returned. At 6 in the afternoon three of the Ottawas, with their colours, came to the same place and Mr. McKee went to them; they informed him that their chiefs had come to the opposite side of the river and desired them to deliver the following speech:

"*Brother the Commanding Officer:*—By this string of wampum we open your ears, wipe the tears from your eyes and remove everything that is bad from your heart, that you may hear and receive them in friendship to-morrow." Gave a string painted with blue clay. Mr. McKee gave them some bread and tobacco and they returned across the river.

As soon as it was dark our sentinels began to fire at some Indians in the ditch, the whole garrison turned out and remained under arms until 1 o'clock, then went to their barracks and lay on their arms till daylight.

July 4th, This morning the canoe we had lent the Indians yesterday, was seen aground in the middle of the river on a bar.

About 11 o'clock the Ottawas appeared on the opposite side of the river, ten in number, and requested to be brought over, upon which Mr. McKee desired them to take the canoe which lay on the bar and cross in her, but they made many excuses saying they intended no harm. Upon their fair promises the commanding officer sent two soldiers in a canoe for them, and at their landing on the other side several halloos were heard on Grant's hill and the Ottawas began to sing, five of them came down to the canoe, three of which seized the soldier at the head, the two others made toward the man in the stern who threw himself into the water, they followed and stabbed him with their knives in two places; the other soldier they had got up to the bank, but on some shots being fired from small arms and a cannon with grape shot they all retreated into the woods and left their kettle with one set of their colours on the bank; both soldiers got back without further damage though one of the wounds is thought dangerous.

Three o'clock, the Indians returned and took their colours and kettle, then fired several shots at the fort. A cannon with grape shot was fired at them, the Indians on Grant's hill likewise fired several shots, this continued till dark; several bullets came into the fort, but did no damage.

July 5th, Eleven o'clock in the morning the Indians fired from both sides of each river and Grant's hill; several crossed in a canoe up the Monongehela. Five o'clock in the afternoon they crossed back again.

July 6th, Five o'clock this morning an Indian appeared on the point of Grant's hill and fired his piece at the fort, in the night the sentinels discovered a large fire up the Ohio.

7th, Early in the morning one Indian was seen over the Monongehela and one by Hulings'. By their being so quiet we imagine they are gone down to meet our troops, attack Ligonier or fall on the country people.

8th, Nothing extraordinary.

9th and 10th, None of the enemy appeared. The people grown careless and straggle about the fields in as much security as if no enemy ever had appeared about us. I doubt we shall pay dear for it.

11th, All quiet. 12th, ditto. 13th, ditto, the first night I have stripped since the beginning of the alarm.

14th, One of the militia fired on and wounded in three places by some Indians within two hundred yards of the fort as they were taking care of some cattle, we sent out a party and brought him in, but fear he will die, being shot through the arm, body and thigh and the bones broken.

15th, 16th and 17th, Nothing more than a number of Indians appearing and the man wounded on the 14th dying.

18th, A party was sent out to cut the Spelts. An Indian killed near Grants' Hill and scalped by Mr. Calhoon one of Mr. Fleming's party who went out before day to scour the hill while our people were at work, getting in part of the spelts, a large body of the enemy appeared over the Monongehela, at the mouth of the Saw-mill Creek, they called from this side over each river, on which the covering and working parties came in. Soon after a large body of the enemy appeared about the upper end of the field where our people had been at work. Three of the Indians from the Monongehela came over, they are Delawares, they say they are for peace and will go to war against the Ottawas and Chipawas. Another Indian, one James Willson, came down from Grant's Hill without arms and walked close to the fort, being known and without arms prevented his being killed, he likewise says that the Beaver and chiefs of the Delawares are coming here, as well as three Indians who came from the other side of the river, they can tell nothing of Mr. Lowry and our people. They say that Mr. Gibson, Baird, Cammel and one Robinson, a hired man, was at Beaver Creek waiting for their canoe coming up the river;

that the canoe was just by when the enemy began to fire on
them, that Gibson and the rest jumped to their arms to go to
their assistance, but they persuaded them not to, that they
would be all killed, but they persisted. That they seized
Gibson, Cammel and Robinson, but Mr. Baird who got to his
arms fought bravely till he was killed. There is a letter from
Gibson from Wills Town desiring we will pay some goods for
getting him off, which I have proposed to do.

10th, The commanding officer returned them thanks for
their offer of joining us against the Ottawas and Chipawas
and for the intelligence they gave us of a great number of
the enemy being about us; but told them until General Bouquet
arrived he could hold no treaty with them.

July 20th, The Indians, men, women and children, continued passing over the Allegheny in canoes and on horseback, near the fort, supposed to be going to fetch Indian corn,
and I believe endeavouring to make us believe their numbers
much greater than what they are.

21st, 9 o'clock in the morning, three Shawnese waded across
the Ohio to the Point, just by the fort, and asked for some
provisions for their chiefs, who were just come. The commanding officer told them he had none, and that he would not
speak any more with them till their chiefs came themselves.
Three o'clock in the afternoon a Shawnese chief came to the
Point and acquainted Mr. McKee that they were in council,
not to think the time long, that when they had done they
would come; that they had got an account from Detroit sixteen day since, that the officer commanding there had settled
matters with the Indians on promising that if they had had
any injury done them they should be redressed; that the
Indians had all gone home. They said that, hearing we had
given the Delawares a set of colours, induced them to come
and make everything easy. They were forbidden to pass

backwards and forwards near the fort with arms, and up and down the river.

22d, Gray Eyes, Wingenum, Turtle's Heart and Mamaulter came over the river, told us their chiefs were in council, and that they waited for Custaluga, whom they expected that day. The Indians passed backwards and forwards, men, women and children, up the river in canoes. It appeared that they were carrying things down to the saw-mill in their canoes, and several horses passed with loads, in sight of the fort, which I took to be Indian corn from the deserted plantations and leather from Anthony Thompson's tan-yard, though many suspect it is plunder from the frontier inhabitants. They were told not to go backwards and forwards in their canoes or they would be fired on.

July 23d, We heard nothing from the Indians to-day ; two of them appeared over the Ohio but said nothing.

24th, Four Indians discovered at the upper end of the garden ; several tracks found about the River Ohio bank, where they had been last night. At dusk three Indians came on the opposite side of the Ohio and told us that Custaloga was come. They were throwing the water out of the canoes, that lay on the shore where they were, with the intention, as I suppose, of coming over when it is dark. While we were talking with them we heard three death halloos. Mr. McKee asked them who it was. They said they knew nothing of it (perhaps they were Ottawas), but said they would let us know in the morning.

25th, Four Indians passing up the Monongehela, close by the opposite shore, contrary to orders, a six-pounder with grape was fired on them. They all made their escape (the shot fell all around them), leaving their canoe. Four of the militia set off in a canoe to a bar in the middle of the river, and then one swam and brought off their canoe. They left four rifles, with eight pair of new Indian shoes, all their powder-horns and pouches full of powder and ball, and two pairs of leggings for each, with five blankets—a sure sign they were going to war.   We are partly sure these Indians want to lull us into security, that they may get the advantage of us—but they will be disappointed.   We saw where they had been under the bank during the night, spying.   In the evening two Indians came to the opposite shore of the Ohio and asked why we fired on their people.   They were answered, they were in canoes passing by the fort with arms.   They said they supposed it was on account of the death hallooes we heard the night before, and said it was some of the Ottawas or Wyandottes, who had been down the country.   They said their hearts were good, but perhaps we were angry.   They desired to know if we would hear their chiefs if they came. They were answered yes, but no one else.

26th, The Indians came over—Shingess, Wingenum, Gray Eyes (sometimes called Sir William Johnson), with several other warriors, the Beaver not with them.   They made a speech, desiring us to quit this place, and let us know that we, by taking possession of their country, were the cause of the war ; and let us know that the Ottawas and Chippewas were coming to attack us.   While in council heard a death halloo at the saw-mill.

27th, Fifty-seven Indians all on horseback were seen from the fort, going down the road and some on foot.   Soon after some were seen returning, some appeared in Hulings field cutting some wheat with their knives and a scythe, we imagine they are hungry.

A gun was fired according to agreement to call them over to get their answer, soon after they appeared on the other side ; as soon as they came over, Captain Ecuyer's answer to this speech was delivered them, letting them know that we took this place from the French, that this was our home and we would defend it to the last, that we were able to defend it against all the Indians in the woods, that we had ammunition and provisions for three years (I wish we had for three months), that we paid no regard to the Ottawas and Chippawas, that we knew that if they were not already attacked, that they would be in a short time in their own country which would find enough for them to do.

That they had pretended to be our friends, at the same time they murdered our traders in their towns and took their goods, that they stole our horses and cows from here, and killed some of our people, and every three or four days we hear the death halloo, which we know must be some of their people who have been down the country and murdered some of the country people. That if they intended to be friends with us to go home to their towns and sit down quietly till they heard from us or else to send some of their people down to Bedford to the General who had only power to treat with them of Peace, they say they will come to-morrow and let us know when they will go home.

The Yellow Bird, a Shawnee chief, asked for the four rifle guns we had taken from the four Indians the 25th, they were answered, if it appeared that their nation had done us no harm, and that they continued to behave well, when we were convinced of it that then they should either have their guns or pay for them. He was very much enraged, and the whole changed countenance on the speech that was made them. White Eyes and Wingenum seemed to be very much irritated and would not shake hands with our people at parting.

28th, In the morning the Indians were seen crossing the river by Shanopins' Town on horseback or swimming. Half an hour after, about 2 o'clock, they fired on our people in the garden, who I had desired not to stay as I was positive they were coming down, but they paid no regard to it, they got in with only one man wounded in the knee. Soon after they began firing on the fort and continued it the whole day and night. Captain Ecuyer was wounded in the leg with an arrow, a Corporal and one of the men, mortally.

29th, Continued firing on the fort, the whole day, from the Ohio bank, they kept up a very smart fire, this day and yesterday a number of shells were thrown to disperse them, but they only shifted places, this day and yesterday about 1,500 small arms fired on them from the fort. Wounded this day : Marcus Huling's leg broken, Sergeant Hermon shot through the lungs, a grenadier shot through the leg, fired three round shots from a six pounder, as they were passing the river in canoes; obliged them once to throw themselves into the river, one of them said to be cut in two by one of the shot. These two days killed several of them from the fort, one of them wounded and drowned in the river, attempting to swim over and five more seen carried out of the canoe on the farther side of the Ohio, supposed to be wounded. The roofs of the Governor's House and the Barracks much hurt by the enemy's fire. In the night they shot several arrows at the fort, some with fire, mostly fell short.

30th, The enemy at night gathered under the bank and we imagined they intended to make an attack, they fired at the fort random shots all day and night, the whole under arms all night. But few shot fired from us.

31st, The enemy continued firing random shot. Two shells thrown at some reaping in Huling's field. In the evening they called to the fort and told us they had letters from Colonel Bouquet and George Croghan and desired me to go for the letters and they would give them to me. Continued firing at the fort all night, threw some hand grenades into the ditch, where we imagined some of the enemy were.

8

August 1st, The enemy continued firing random shots from under the bank of the Ohio till about 3 o'clock, when they withdrew, and soon we saw large numbers crossing from this to the opposite side of the Ohio with their baggage, about 6 o'clock they put up a paper fixed on a stick from under the bank.

August 2d, All quiet till about 11 o'clock when two Indians and a white man came down on the opposite side of the Ohio and called over that they were expresses from Colonel Bouquet and G. Croghan at Bedford; they were desired to come over, the white man made answer that he was a prisoner and would not come, the Indian came over in a small bark canoe and produced his letters; he was a Cuyuga Indian named John Hudson, he says that the Indians took him and detained him three days, broke open the letters and made a white prisoner read them; one letter they kept and suffered him to bring the other two to the fort. The white, on the other side was an express, taken between this and Fort Cumberland, they had all his letters but would not let the Indian bring them over after they had read the letters and heard the message he delivered them from Mr. Croghan, some set off home, and some few to war against the settlements, and some Wayandotts to reconnoitre our army. The Wayandotts, in a council had declared that they would carry on the war against us while there was a man of them living, and told the Delawares and Shawnees that they might do as they pleased. In the evening they set off with letters down the country.

3d, On viewing the bank of the river where the enemy fired from, we saw blood in many places, the Indian who was killed was the son of John Butler, of Philadelphia, the huntsman, by an Indian woman. For the last six nights the whole have been under arms, the garrison having two reliefs.

4th, Everything quiet. Some Indians lying yet on the oppo-

site side of the Ohio.   This afternoon heard three death halloos on the opposite side of the river.

5th, Three expresses came in from Colonel Bouquet, whom
they left with the troops at Ligonier.   These expresses report they heard at Small's plantation at Turtle Creek, about
18 miles from here, a great deal of cheering, shooting and
bells, and some Indians.   We imagine they are gathering
there to attack the Colonel, and 9 o'clock 2 expresses were
dispatched to meet the Colonel.

6th, 7th and 8th, Nothing extraordinary, but the troops not
arriving according to expectation, makes us fear they have
been attacked on their march.

9th, Everything quiet, no word of the troops.

10th, At break of day, in the morning, Miller, who was sent
by express, the 5th, with two others, came in from Colonel
Bouquet, whom he left at the Nine Mile Run.   He brings an account that the Indians engaged our troops for two days, that
our people beat them off.   About 10 o'clock a detachment from
the garrison, under the command of Captain Philips, marched
to meet the troops and returned about 2 o'clock, having joined
the Colonel at Bullet's Hill.   The following is the best account
I have been able to learn of the action, which happened the
5th, about a mile beyond Bushy Run :

Our advanced guard discovered the Indians where they were
lying in ambush and fired on them about 3 o'clock in the afternoon ; this brought on a general engagement which continued
through the next day and night.   Our people behaved with the
greatest bravery and also the Indians who often advanced
within a few steps of our people.

The action continued doubtful till the enemy by a stratagem
was drawn into an ambuscade, where they were entirely
routed, leaving a great many of their people dead on the spot.

Our loss in this affair is about 50 killed and 60 wounded.
It is thought by our people the enemy left as many.

11th of August, raised our bateaux that we had sunk.

12th, Twenty-two bateaux were manned and rowed up both rivers for some distance; during this we could see the enemy on a hill on the opposite side the river looking at us; this was done to make the enemy believe we were going to attack their towns in order to clear our communication, as our horses, with most of the women and children, were going down with the escort.

13th, Major Campbell with the escort marched for Ligonier.

14th, 15th, 16th, 17th, 18th, 19th, 20th, and 21st, no enemy appeared. We have been employed in reaping and getting in all the grain, plowing for turnips and getting coal.

22d, Major Campbell arrived with the convoy with provisions.

23d and 24th, Nothing extraordinary. Mr. McKee with a number of the militia went up to Mr. Croghan's plantation. Found his with all the houses between here and there burnt.

25th, An Indian called Andrews arrived here express from De Troit. Since he left De Troit he says he heard from the Indians that Major Rogers who went out from De Troit, to attack an Indian village, was attacked by the Indians and brought back, being shot himself through the thigh and saved by his men. By all the accounts from De Troit it appears that Indians have been spirited up by the French to massacre all our troops in the Indian country.

26th, 27th, Major Campbell left this with all the wagons and pack-horses and carried down all the women and children.

28th, An Indian was seen over the river.

29th, Andrews (the Indian) was sent express to Presqu' Isle to see if our troops were rebuilding that post.

30th, 31st, Andrews returned; he went within a little of Venango and met four Wyandotts who came from Presqu' Isle; they told him there was no white people there, but that 150 Ottawas were lying there waiting for a party of our people,

expected from Niagara; that several small parties of Lake
Indians came this way; that one of 15 in number crossed to
this side of Ohio, at Mr. Croghan's place, the 30th.

Sept. 5th, Indian Andrew went to hunt over the Ohio; returned in the evening, met four Shawnese; they informed him
that the Delawares had all left their towns; that they were
sent to see if any more troops were on the road here; they
had been 18 miles down the road, were returning home again;
that they had tried to take a scalp from a party of ours cutting fascines, but were afraid.

6th, Andrew went over the Ohio to hunt; he returned to
the opposite shore with Killbuck and his son, who wanted
some person to go over and speak to them.   Colonel Bouquet
let them know that unless they came by order of their chiefs
he would have nothing to say to them; they went off.

7th, In the morning Andrew came over.   He saw two of his
own nation; they confirm the account of an engagement
between the troops under Major Rogers and the Indians near
De Troit, of his being shot through the thigh and losing 150
men with several officers, and his retreat to the fort, being
pursued by the Indians.   These Indians informed him that
there were three parties of Delawares gone down in search
of our expresses.   They informed him that the schooner was
returned from Niagara with provisions just before they came
away, and that 800 Indians in 80 canoes were gone to cut off
the communication between Niagara and the landing where
the vessels load for De Troit.   Some Indians seen to-day by
the Bullock Guard.

At dusk Andrew was sent to Ligonier to meet our express
expected.

8th, This morning some Indians seen over the Ohio.

10th, Our Bullock Guard saw 5 Indians.   In the evening
Andrew returned, having met our express 9 miles on this side

Ligonier, brought the letters, the express returned ; he saw 5 Indians a little way from the fort.

13th, Andrew saw whereabout 30 Indians had encamped the night before at Chartier's Creek.

15th, About 11 o'clock a few Indians fired on the Bullock Guard, without doing any damage ; on the Guards firing some shot at them they ran off.

16th, The officer of the Bullock's Guard sent to acquaint the Colonel that his sentinels had discovered ten Indians; he was ordered to attack them if they appeared again ; they saw nothing of them till the evening ; when the guard was marching in, one showed himself.

October 17th, I went with a detachment of 60 men over the Monongehela to get coal. Some Indians who were on the top of the hill ran off on our taking possession of it and left some corn behind them just pulled.

19th, A Highlander was shot up the Monongehela ; he was a sentinel from the Bullock Guard ; there were but two or three Indians. They scalped him.

[Bouquet Papers.]

LETTER OF CAPTAIN ECUYER.

(Endorsed.)

(Received 5th of February. Addressed.)

FORT PITT, January 8, 1763.

Sir:--I send according to your orders the return to Colonel Amherst the same that a Court of Inquiry considered in regard to the Conductor of Artillery accused of having taken powder from the magazine of the king. His officer does not wish to trust anything to him until we have a reply from his Excellency about it. The conductor is not liked, it appears. I pity him and do not think him guilty. I received the letter you did me the honor to write to me from Lancaster. I long for others and for news, for the months at Fort Pitt are eternal. Four prisoners of the Shawnese have arrived here –two boys and two girls ; we expect every day more with the chiefs. The families who brought these appeared well content with the presents of the province, which for the four amounted to 30£. Parties of warriors of the Six Nations pass here frequently, going to war against the Indians, who are in the interest of the Spanish. Mr. Croghan asks constantly for powder, lead and knives for them ; that embarrasses me. Sometimes I refuse, at other times I give a little, and at other times I do not know on which foot to dance ; I fear to do too much. Mr. Croghan says we cannot refuse these trifles, which, nevertheless, would be 45 lbs. of powder, 90 lbs. of lead, knives, vermillion, &c. I informed him that I would not give them anything without having received your orders, which I will obey promptly. As to the fort and garrison, all goes on the same way. Our gentlemen send you their compliments, and I have the honor to call myself very respectfully, Sir, your very humble and

Very obedient servant,

S. Ecuyer.

[To Colonel Bouquet.]

P. S.—I forgot to tell you, Sir, that we have a club every Monday and a ball on Saturday evening, composed of the most beautiful ladies of the garrison. We regale them with punch, and if it is not strong enough the whiskey is at their service. You may believe that we are not altogether the dupes.

Captain Philips sends you his compliments. I hope he will soon have a company. They tell me there are two vacancies in the 3d Battalion. I wish for it for him.

[British Museum.—Bouquet Papers.]

FORT PITT, Jan. 26, 1763.

Sir:—All is here very quiet; it is not the same at Bedford. Captain Ourry wrote to me that his corporal and five men are in prison for having robbed the magazine. I have just sent him a detachment to relieve his rascals and a party to escort them here, where they will receive the punishment so justly merited. They have even stolen the stores; it was thought to have been the settlers. I hope that will be discovered. An example will be very necessary; four or five hung would have a good effect.

Sergeant Clark tells me these returns should be sent to the General, but as I am not certain, I send them to you until a new order.

I have the honor to be, very respectfully, Sir, your
Very humble and obedient servant,

S. ECUYER.

[COLONEL BOUQUET.]

[British Museum.—Bouquet Papers.]

FORT PITT, Feb. 8, 1763.

Sir:—The second express arrived here the fourth of the month; the package for Detroit left the 6th in the morning by an Indian, who chose to go alone to go faster. Mr. Croghan vouches for his fidelity and diligence. I sent one by the same envoy to Venango, with orders to the officer to send the orders of his Excellency to Le Bœuf and Presqu' Isle. I have also written to the officer who commands at Sandusky. I desired Major Gladwin to give a receipt to bearer, who will be paid here on his return (he left here on horseback). As the regiment of Virginia is disbanded, I have been obliged to

send a Corporal and four men to Fort Cumberland to guard
the magazines of the king. Those at Redstone desert every
day. I wait your orders to know if it is your intention to
maintain a garrison from the battalion at these two posts. I
have been obliged to relieve all the detachments at Bedford.
They are accused by Captain Ourry of having stolen the flour
of the king. If that is clearly proven I will have them punished with the greatest severity, they belong to my company.
We have also trapped a robber of flour here, he received 500
lashes, but has not told on his accomplices. We have also
three deserters under guard, they are Wheeler, Higges and
Marks, the last of whom has already been tried by a general
court-martial. Childers has been condemned to receive 1000
lashes. Mr. Hutchins will not depart until a new order is
received. The last express having arrived too soon for him.
I have offered the flour for sale, it is worth nothing at all, the
cattle refuse to eat it. As regards the Matross* of Detroit, he
left here two days before the express arrived.

The Indians have brought us eight prisoners, of whom four
are women and four young boys; they will leave here with the
first horses that return. There, my dear Colonel, is all that
I know that is at all interesting to send you. I do not neglect anything that I undertake. Permit, Sir, that I thank
you for the news that you have had the kindness to communicate to me; may I pray you to continue? It seems to me that
we will have a grand reform, and that I only hold by a thread.
That is why I pray you if you learn anything on this subject,
do not flatter me for my experience, but render me a real
service, for then I will conduct myself accordingly. You will
find here annexed the declaration of a Shawnee Indian, who
is very intelligent, and who has travelled a great deal among
the French of the Mississippi. I forgot to tell you that Mr.

* Artillery soldier.

Donnalan joined us the 2d of the month; if he does not think of revenge he talks a great deal of it.

I have the honor to be, very respectfully, Sir,

Your very humble and very obedient servant,

S. Ecuyer.

P. S.—Dare I pray you to send the enclosed for Mr. Grandidier at Quebec?

[British Museum.—Bouquet Papers.]

Fort Pitt, Feb. 21, 1763.

Sir:—I take advantage of Mr. Davenport leaving for Philadelphia, to inform you that I have received an Indian from Detroit with letters from Major Gladwin for his Excellency; this express arrived here ten days after the departure of ours and as his excellency could still send orders for this post, I have thought it best to keep it here until the arrival of another courier, that will save the cost of an express.

Captain Campbell.

Mr. Croghan has received two expresses from the Delawares, which inform him that they will bring all their prisoners in the spring. All is well here, no appearance of deluge. I wait for news from you with great impatience. All our gentlemen assure you of their very humble respect, and I particularly, having the honor to be very sincerely,

Sir, your very humble and very obedient servant,

S. Ecuyer.

[British Museum.—Bouquet Papers.]

LETTER TO COLONEL BOUQUET.

(Endorsed.)

Fort Pitt, March 11, 1763.

Sir:—I send you the returns of the past month with an

account of the inundation of this post. The sixth of March
the two rivers being somewhat swollen but with little ice, the
6th, 7th and 8th great rain. The 7th in the morning, the
berme or turf of the flank of the bastion of the south and a
part of the stone edging had fallen into the fosse. The river
continuing to swell, I had the provisions removed from the
ground floor and the various ammunitions, worked all day
closing the drains, preparing everything against inundation
as I best could. At 10 o'clock in the evening the two rivers
united and the water around the fort increased one foot an
hour. On the 8th, at 2 o'clock P.M., the flats and boats have
been drawn to the bridge. At 4 o'clock in the morning six
inches of water in the fort and the Allegheny full of ice. Two
hours after midday I detached two officers and thirty men to
the upper town with fifteen days' provision for all the garrison.
At midnight I brought all the boats and flats into the fort,
prepared to save all and abandon the place the following
day, but happily on the 9th, at 8 o'clock in the morning, the
water was at its greatest height and at midday it fell two
inches (the highest means twenty-two inches higher than last
year).

All the provisions and ammunition are saved and in good
condition. I have followed your plan as best I could. Here
is an account of our losses.

The shop of the blacksmith entirely gone, the little wood
gathered for the construction of the boats has followed several
houses of the lower town. I believe our garden is lost by the
fault of the sergeant, who did not inform me of the danger,
this subject was entirely out of my head. All the fences of
the garden carried off by the ice. The poor deer has had its
leg broken. We are occupied in repairing the little devastations in the interior of the fort. The greater part of the turf
on the sides not covered has fallen into the fosse. I cannot

sufficiently recommend to you Burrent, or enough praise his conduct, and to say all in one word he is invaluable. I send you this letter by an express from post to post, with orders to be expeditious, and on this subject I will write to Captain Ourry. Tomson the tanner, and Shepherd the carpenter, are drowned, the first at Turtle Creek and the other at Two Mile Run. I should tell you that I have given a short account of the affair to Colonel Amherst when sending returns to him. I await for news from you with great impatience.

I have the honor to be, very respectfully Sir,

Your very humble and very obedient servant,

S. ECUYER.

[TO COL. BOUQUET.]

P. S.—I have made two remarks on the manner in which this fort has been sodded. I do not know if you will find them judicious. The first is that it was neglected in placing the turf to plant in each four or five sticks of wood, dry and thin and about two feet long, this wood would support it until the turf would take root; the second, they should mow the grass at least once a year; this long grass holds more water, and in consequence, its weight draws out the turf. I leave this to be decided by those who know more about it than I do, for I am nothing less than Engineer.

[British Museum.—Bouquet Papers.]

LETTER TO COLONEL BOUQUET.

(Endorsed.)

[CAPTAIN ECUYER.]

FORT PITT, March 19, 1763.

Sir:—The Express which I had sent to Detroit has arrived, and immediately I sent one from here with the package of

Major Gladwin, for his excellency. I learn from Captain
Campbell that one of our soldiers has been killed at Michilimakinack by accident. They send me by the same the account
of the accident of Lieutenant Jamet, who has been obliged
to abandon his post during the month of December. The
house where his detachment lodged having caught fire, which,
being joined to his, both were in flames before it was perceived, so that he had much difficulty in saving himself from
the flames that burned his shirt and his body; he has not
marched with his party, which not having provisions has returned to Michilimakinack.

I have been much mortified by this miserable return. It
causes me an excessive vexation every time that I think of it;
although it was not my fault, the Adjutant telling me that
the discharged people will not be returned. He is so positive
and so obstinate that he believes yet and even at this time
that the return is just.

I have ordered the coopers to work at the barrels. I hope
to have managed to your satisfaction, for I do not think it
would be possible to embark the provisions without casks,
either to go up or down the river. Mr. Schlotter is following
your orders in the returns for the month.

I have without delay packed up the teeth and horns, but
you did not tell me to whom to address them. I have had
our trees replanted and enclosed the garden, simply to prevent
the cows from finishing the destruction, as it appears that we
will not enjoy them; those that come after us will do as they
fancy. Our people complain a great deal since this last order.
They do not understand why they should work without pay,
and what they do they do with an ill grace. I have had a
great deal of trouble since the inundation to please everybody.
I do not think I have succeeded. Everyone wants lodging
above; the lower town has suffered most. I wish that not

one house had escaped, so as to force them to build elsewhere; the merchants have not lost anything. I assisted them with all my power, although few or none deserved it. I warned them the day before and offered them the wagons of the king, but the miserable fellows always waited until the last extremity. Mr. Hutchins has departed, hoping to return at the time appointed.

With regard to my intentions, Sir, it is not my intention to sell at present; but as I do not doubt that I will be placed on half-pay, I hope it will be as soon as possible. It appears it would be cruel and inhuman to send an officer so far and shut him up there. I declare that if that happens to me I will be entirely ruined, without the power to sell out; my voyage from Quebec here cost me 50 guineas. I hope the first packet will bring good news for reform; it is very hard, after having served well, to suffer for a troop of rebels, whatever may be said of them by the way. You will find joined to this all the vouchers which it has been possible for us to collect. There is a list among them which will explain all and two which are not here. We are occupied to-day in the chapel and have at midday divine service; afternoon for the Germans. The Rev. Mr. Post gives us a service in his manner. We had St. Patrick's fetes in every manner, so that Croghan could not write by this express.

I have the honor to be, very respectfully, Sir,

Your very humble and very obedient servant,

S. ECUYER.

[To COLONEL BOUQUET.]

P. S.—A merchant coming from Sandusky has presented an account to me of £11 : 12 : 6 pence curr. which poor Pauly will perhaps be obliged to pay; this was for the little presents which he was obliged to give to the Indians—tobacco, paint, &c.

LETTER OF CAPTAIN ECUYER.

(Endorsed.)

(Received the 16th of April, answered the 17th.)

FORT PITT, March 30, 1763.

Sir:—We are very busy with our boats ; Burrent has taken all possible pains. I hope he will be well paid ; he deserves it, and he would be foolish to take this trouble for 18 cents a day. I continue to recommend him to you ; I wish that my situation and my circumstances would enable me to be useful to him ; I would do so with all my heart.

Sir, I pray you to fix a price with Mr. Swain ; by the way, it is not just that he should take so much trouble for nothing.

I have written to Captain Basset on the communication, and sent him a list of articles which are wanting here. I prayed him to send horses from Bedford and Ligonier ; we must, however, at least have four, as well as collars or draw-gears, for all those we have are rotten. The poor mare always limps.

I have made known publicly that all those who are in debt to the king for flour must pay on the 15th of April, or in default of which I will sell their effects ; it is no use to speak mildly to this race.

We expect the Shawnese with our captives, from day to day. I begin to get tired of Fort Pitt, and this winter has seemed very long to me. Return quickly, that will give us back life. We expect you with impatience, particularly he who has the honor to call himself, very respectfully,

Sir, your very humble and very obedient servant,

S. ECUYER.

[British Museum.—Bouquet Papers.]

FORT PITT, April 9, 1763.

Sir:—It appears by the return of Mr. McKee that the Shawnese are no longer so well disposed as they were last autumn. The Delawares have sent a message for them not to give up their captives, that they were resolved not to give up any until they saw what turn things would take at this place. Notwithstanding all that, the Shawnese will be here in a few days with five prisoners, escorted by 100 beggars. We have determined to receive them very coldly; our boats advance very slowly (we need nails, iron and four or five horses more), nevertheless every one is employed. I forgot in my last to tell you, Sir, that your snuff-box has been found, but with a square piece cut out. After the flood the servant of Mr. Poffs and mine were walking along the river near the kitchen of Mr. Bassett; they found the pieces in the sand in such a way that I can not doubt a moment but that this theft was done by that rascally negro of Capt. Basset; he has buried the pieces in the sand, near the kitchen, and forgot them after the flood. There, Sir, is my opinion. I hope you will not shrug your shoulders at it.

This instant I have finished an affair which was on the point of making trouble, here in a few words is the case.

Lieut. Donnellan and Surgeon Boyd gave each other blows with their fists and sticks for three days, but upon other preparations to fight again, I was forced to put them under arrest to prevent other disorders. The officers tried to reconcile them, on which they wrote to me that they would not quarrel again. I will take care that the letter is signed by both.

I made them come before all the officers of the garrison and give their word of honor that they would not again quarrel, and set them free. Lieut. Francis was present during the whole affair.   If you will question him, you will know all the minutiæ; he heard more than I did.

I have the honor to be very respectfully, Sir,

Your very humble and obedient servant,

S. ECUYER.

[COL. BOUQUET.]

LETTER TO COLONEL BOUQUET.

(Endorsed.)

[CAPTAIN ECUYER.]

FORT PITT, April 23, 1763.

Sir:—I have sent your mare (nearly cured) to your farm by a confidential soldier, who should not mount her, she only carries oats to Bedford.   I have written to Captain Ourry to provide enough to convey him to the farm.   I gave him money for the journey.   Before the arrival of your letter I had sent four horses to Ligonier, they have returned with a wagon loaded with iron, harness and tools.   I have sent an order to Mr. Blane to send to me all the king's horses, having great need of them here, for the boats and for the gardens.   But he replied that he has not any, and that the horses which he has belong to himself, and that he had arranged with you on this subject when you came down.   I believe that living so long at this post has made him believe at last that the place belongs to him.

I do not know, sir, if I have told you that we have found one of our bellows, and the second is some place at the bottom of the river, found by a trader from whom I wait to have an explanation, before I send to find it.   I have three forges and six blacksmiths working at a great rate, eight hand saws and the mill, which is repaired and works.   I think

9

that when you return here I will have all my wood sawed, all
the stakes are made, 300. It must be confessed that Captain
Bassett is a lazy man. I am told he has horses on the road;
he has not deigned to write the least word, it seems to me he
should have let me know what he sends if only to tranquillize me.

I spare neither care nor trouble to push on the work, it is
my duty as much for the good of the service (which you
have much at heart) as to prove to you, sir, my entire
devotion, desiring nothing more than the power to be useful
in something.

As with regard to Burent, Captain Basset can not sufficiently pay him for his diligence; he is absolutely a slave
and does more than all the rest together. I do not know
whether I do wrong, for without your orders I employ four
coopers. We need casks. As well as for up as down the river
we must have them. I have published that all who are in
debt for flour or beef to the king must replace them the 15th
of April; but hardly any one has come. I will then be
obliged to take stronger measures, considering that all who
are here (excepting the garrison) are the dregs of nature. I
have had a thousand difficulties before I succeeded in collecting a part of the tools belonging to the king. I know that
the old Clapham has his house full of them, but I leave that
case to Captain Basset. The old man should furnish us by
contract, sixteen beeves, he has only delivered thirteen, saying he lost the other three, that is why I put it at nearly the
total.

You will find, sir, joined to this the declaration of Mr.
McKee, on his journey to the Shawnees, as well as the
council which we have held here; I can not absolutely refuse
to give them powder, lead, vermillion, swivel guns, knives and
tobacco. I think we are cheaply rid of them. They told us

that the Illinois and other Indians lower than them will
oppose our passage, at the instigation of the French ; their
story seems very probable. Several soldiers demand their
discharge, as many here as in the detached posts. Where is
your camp bed ? I am told that the one in your chamber
belongs to Captain Barnsley, and his valet asks for it every
day.

The Indians depart at last to-morrow, very much dissatisfied, although I have done for them more than I should
perhaps ; but one cannot free one's self from Mr. Croghan.
He gave up to them because they would have eaten all our
provisions ; think, that during one month Mr. Croghan has
drawn 17,000 pounds, as much flour as beef ; that makes one
tremble. I use the skins which the Indians have given, to
dress the five prisoners and the rest of the product they will
take home. I take this trouble myself, because where there
is nothing no one will take care of it—nothing without
money and everything for money.

Have the goodness, sir, to have sent to us for the officers
good flour, the fine which we have will be finished in a short
time.

[British Museum.—Bouquet Papers.]

LETTER OF CAPTAIN ECUYER.

(Endorsed.)

(Received the 19th. On the back : " M. Repeat that no soldiers but such
as act as .   . are to be paid, and those at 15s. Tell it to Baillie."\)[*]

FORT PITT, May 4, 1763.

Sir:—I hope that my letter of the 24th April with the
returns has reached you. I have just received a package from

* Nearly illegible.

Detroit which I send immediately, with a speech of the Miamis to Mr. Holmes. Mr. Croghan is at Bedford, and proposes to go to Carlisle. It will be well that he should not delay, for those rascally Delawares are coming; they are all assembled in one of their towns for a grand council, to know whether they will deliver our men or not. Major Gladwin writes to me that I am surrounded with scamps. He complains a great deal of the Delawares and of the Shawnees; these are the rascals that try to put the others in action. Our boats go well; I have seven of them in the water. I have been obliged to send to Bedford for pitch or tar.

I have the honor to be, very respectfully,

Your very humble and very obedient servant,

S. ECUYER.

[COLONEL BOUQUET.]

[British Museum.—Bouquet Papers.]

LETTER FROM CAPTAIN ECUYER.

(Endorsed.)

FORT PITT, May 29, 1763.

Sir:—A large party of Mingoes arrived here at the beginning of the month and have delivered to us ten miserable horses. They demanded presents from me, but I have refused all their demands excepting eight bushels of Indian corn, which they have planted opposite Croghan's house, where they have formed a town. Before yesterday evening Mr. McKee reported to me that the Mingoes and Delawares were in motion, and that they had sold in haste £300 worth of skins, with which they have bought as much powder and lead as they could. Yesterday I sent him to their villages to get information, but he found them all abandoned. He followed their traces, and he is certain that they have descended the river; that makes me think that they wish to intercept our boats and prevent our passage. They have stolen three horses and a cask of rum at Bushy Run ; they at the same time stole £50 from one called Coleman (on the road to Bedford) with the gun at his breast. They say the famous Wolf and Butler were the chiefs, and it is clear that they wish to break with us. I pity the poor people on the communication. I am at work to put the fort in the best possible condition with the few people we have. Mr. Hutchins arrived here yesterday with six recruits. We have twenty boats in the water ; I would like to know the number you wish, and what the carpenters must do. As I was finishing my letter three men arrived from Clapham's with the bad news that yesterday at 3 o'clock P.M., the Indians had killed Clapham, and all that were in the house were robbed and massacred. These three men were at work and escaped through the woods. I sent them immediately with arms to warn our men at Bushy Run. The Indians told Byerly to quit the place or they would all be killed in four days. I tremble for our small posts. As for this one, I will answer for it.

If any person should come here, they must take an escort, for the affair is serious.

I have the honor to be, very respectfully, sir,

Your very humble and very obedient servant,

S. ECUYER.

[COLONEL BOUQUET.]

If you do not receive letters often from me it will be a proof that communication is cut off.

LETTER FROM CAPTAIN ECUYER.

(Endorsed.)

[Received June 5th. Colonel Bouquet.]

FORT PITT, May 3, 1763, 9 o'clock P.M.

Sir:—Yesterday evening the Indians massacred the two men we had at the saw-mill, they scalped them and have left a head breaker or Tomahawk, which signifies I believe a declaration of war, they at the same time stole four horses of the king, which were working there. One Daniel Collier, horsedriver, who has just arrived, has made the declaration as follows, that being at Tuscarawa with forty-four ladened horses, King Beaver had warned Thomas Colhoun to depart immediately with all the whites that he could take and that he would give them three Indians to escort them, but being at Beaver Creek they were attacked, and only he himself has arrived here, with much difficulty. He believed all the party were killed, having heard seven or eight death cries. He said that the Indians that carried the belt to the Delawares have said that Sandusky was cut off and the officer made prisoner and that when the Indian express had departed from Detroit the party was attacked by them.

I fear the affair is general. I tremble for our posts. I fear according to the reports that I am surrounded by Indians. I neglect nothing to receive them well, and I expect to be attacked to-morrow morning. God wills it, I am passably ready. Every one works, and I do not sleep; but I fear that my express will be stopped.

I have formed two companies of militia, which amount to 80 or 90 men. I have had the oxen and cows brought near for service. In one word I have neglected nothing and have spared neither care nor trouble.

I hope to be capable to do more for the service of the king, whom I have the honor to serve. Whatever happens I will do all that is in my power. Excuse haste as they say.

I have the honor to be very sincerely, Sir,

Your very humble and very obedient servant,

S. ECUYER.

P. S.—You will have the goodness to translate my letters for the General as you like. Joined to this is a discourse which we sent to the Indians after their first murders; no reply, it is too soon.

[British Museum.—Bouquet Papers.]

LETTER FROM CAPTAIN ECUYER.

(Received the 10th, and the Duplicates sent to the General.)

(FIRST LETTER.)

FORT PITT, June 2, 1763, 9 o'clock P.M.

Sir:—Here is the third express I have sent to Philadelphia, the first the 30th of May, the second on the 31st.

This will inform you of the arrival of Mr. Calhoun at this post with a harangue from the Delawares. I am going to continue my last letter. On the 31st I sent two inhabitants to Venango, but they could not pass; at one mile and a half they were attacked and obliged to return; one of the two slightly wounded on the leg. Two young men arrived yesterday from Fort Burd and returned with orders to the Sergeant to engage all the inhabitants to join me here with 100 lbs. of powder and 1,000 lbs. of lead, which a merchant sent there a few days since; they should come either by water or by the woods. I hope to reap some advantage from the Indian's peltry. He told me that he will come with a party as soon as he has sent his wife and his cattle to Fort Cumberland. The two men from Bushy Run have retreated to Ligonier. Last night three inhabitants also departed for Venango. I do not know whether they can pass. To return to that which concerns this place.

My garrison consists in all of 250 men, as many regulars as militia, all very determined to conquer or die; our men are high-spirited and I am glad to see their good will and with what celerity they work. I have little flour, the inhabitants receive half rations of bread and a little more meat, to the poorer women and children a little Indian corn and some meat. I manage as well as I can. I have collected all the animals of the inhabitants and placed them under our eye. We kill to spare our provisions, for the last resource and in order that the savages shall not profit by our animals. They are around us at the distance of a mile; they have not yet dared to appear, perhaps they are too feeble; it is not my business to go to find them. I have distributed tomahawks to the inhabitants; I have also gathered up all their beaver traps which are arranged along the rampart that is not finished. The merchant Trent is an excellent man, he has been of great help to me. He is always ready to assist me, he has a great deal of intelligence and is very worthy of recommendation. I will say no more in his praise. Burent is always the same, indefatigable. I pray you to leave nothing undone to induce his Excellency to procure a commission for him; I do not know any man that merits it more.

Here is an abridgement of our work; I have demolished the lower town and brought the wood into the fort. I have burnt the high town; every person is in the fort, where I have constructed two ovens and a forge. I have surrounded our bastion with barrels full of earth, made good even places and embrasures for our cannon. I have a good entrenchment on the mined bastion and on the two curtains at the right and left. All around the rampart my people are covered by strong planks joined with stakes and an opening between two for firing the guns, without being exposed in any manner. If there were any open places I would place across them bales of skins of deer which belong to the merchants. I have in the same way made galleries at the gorge (breast) of the bastion which corresponds with that of the barracks.

I have placed all the powder of the merchants in the king's magazine. I have also prepared every thing in case of fire. My bastions are furnished with casks full of water, as well as the interior of the fort. The women are appointed for this service. One must take service from all in this life.

The rascals burned the houses in the neighborhood. They have shot balls at the saw-mill. If I had foreseen it I could have saved all. Burent, my right arm, does not let me forget anything. A king would be happy to have 100,000 such subjects.

I have made Trent Major-Commandant of the militia, but as that does not agree with my fancy, I have incorporated the militia in our companies, having given the best to the grenadiers. Being mixed with our men we can draw from them better parties. Three companies serve twenty-four hours. At two hours after midnight all the garrison is at its post or place of alarm, so that I believe we are guarded from all surprises. I have been obliged to make some outlay, but I hope his Excellency will find them just, reasonable and necessary. My pocket is empty, nothing remains there but ten shillings. I would like very much to have a little more rum to give from time to time a drop to my brave men, they know my will and say nothing. I will be well recompensed if you approve of the measures which I have taken. I have done all for the best. If I have erred it is from ignorance. I would wish to be a good engineer to be able to do better, in short I have neglected no care, no trouble, be persuaded of that.

I am very respectfully, Sir,

Your very humble and very obedient servant,

S. ECUYER.

P. S.—The three men who left here yesterday for Venango have been obliged to retrace the road nearly twenty miles this way, where they discovered two parties of Indians coming from this side. I tremble lest the posts should be cut off.

[British Museum.—Bouquet Papers.]

LETTER FROM CAPTAIN ECUYER.

(Endorsed.   Received the 23d.)

FORT PITT, June 16, 1763.

Sir:—I do not know whether this will reach you the same as my three preceding ones. According to all reports, it appears to me that the Indians march to the neighborhood of our colonies. I believe that there are but few around us; however, there are enough to interrupt our communication.

A man has arrived here who has assured me that Fort Burd is abandoned; I suppose they have retreated to Fort Cumberland. The Indians have burned Croghan's house and that of Thomson ; they wish to decoy me and make me send out detachments, but they do not give me the chance. I am determined to guard my post, spare my men and not expose them uselessly. I believe that is what you expect of me. We are so confined in the fort that I fear sickness, for notwithstanding all my care I cannot keep the place as clean as I wish, thus the smallpox is among us on this account. I have had constructed a hospital under the bridge above the reach of rising waters. The three expresses (of which I made mention in my last) for Venango were obliged to return the next day. In the meantime, on the morning of the 7th, a boat arrived with a soldier and a trader and a letter from Mr. Christie. He informed me that Lieutenant Cuylor of the Queen's Rangers going from Niagara to Detroit was

attacked at the entrance of that river on the 28th of May, at
11 o'clock in the evening   His detachment was of 97 men,
some R. A. some rangers.   He had 139 barrels of provisions.
He was himself wounded, two sergeants killed ; Cope was one
of them and 16 of our regiment.   Ferlinger and 44 rangers,
a woman and some others wounded.   He only saved two
boats with which they retreated to Sandusky, but he found
no one there and all was burned.   From there he went to
Presqu' Isle with the rest of the people.   He there left six
men, and departed for Niagara.

My fort is formidable at present, 16 pieces mounted on
good platforms.   I have a sufficiently good retrenchment
joined to a fraise, which is not set out over all, so it is not
altogether as regular as it should be.   But without engineers
and being much hurried this should pass, and I think is good
enough against this rabble, so that I begin to breathe.   We
have worked during eleven days in an incredible manner, our
men are much fatigued, but I do not complain.   In the future
they will have rest.   I have divided my little garrison into
two divisions, each one with three officers, five sergeants,
one drum, and from 68 to 70 men.   We are all doubly armed,
so that I have 500 shots to give them as they are in the moat
(*fossé*).   These are the measures which I have taken, during
our work.   I had 100 men on the rampart all night, and at
2 o'clock in the morning the rest of the garrison were under
arms until 5 o'clock, when they went to work.   I have collected all the beaver traps which could be found with our
merchants and they were placed in the evening outside the
palisades.   I would be pleased to send you one with the leg
of a savage, but they have not given me this satisfaction.   I
have had made a quantity of crow-feet traps for the fossé,
they are pointed enough for their moccasins.

No one has offered to help me but Mr. Trent, to whom I am

much obliged, as well as to Mr. Hutchins, who has taken no rest.
He oversaw the works and did his duty, at the same time, that
is praiseworthy and he merits recompense. I wish Detroit
could be sustained, but provisions and ammunition are scarce
there. I hope to see you soon at the head of some regiments;
for if they are sent as formerly, in small parties, one after
the other, they would be cut off. This slovenly kind of war
costs us an infinite number of men, that is the reason they
should be driven back by one stroke and exterminated. I
sent two men to Venango, but I have no news of them or from
any other place.

On the 15th a party went out to cut grass. A militiaman
was killed on the top of the mountain, where he had nothing
to do. If he had followed my orders this would not have happened to him. The same night the savages crossed the garden, fired on the fort and on our oxen and cows which are in
the park meadow where the deer were. Your letters also
arrived on the night of the 15th and 16th by a good express
from Bedford, who killed an Indian on the road. Mr. Blane
was attacked on the second of June without results. We
have often little alarms, but we laugh at them. I am assured
that they are in very small numbers about us. I have only
seen ten at a time, who showed themselves at the house of
Hulings, perhaps to make us go out. I do not fear them. I
wish they would desire to give me an assault, were they 5,000,
for the more there were the more we would kill. No one more
alert could be seen than our people. At the least sign everyone is at his post of alarm. I never knew the number of boats
you wished for until now the carpenters told me. Mr. Basset
had ordered thirty from them. I have 19 in the water and three
nearly finished, but I have been obliged to discontinue from
the moment the savages appeared so near to us. I can not
send them actually until an escort is offered. I employ them

in the fort and they have been a great help in my work. Captain Ourry sends me word that a party of nearly thirty men from his garrison will be here soon. As soon as I see them I will have a party ready to sustain them. If I knew the day and if I could give them a position I would be certain to catch ten or twelve.

I have the honor to be very respectfully, Sir,

Your very humble and very obedient servant,

S. ECUYER.

[COLONEL BOUQUET.]

P. S.—Grandidier remarked to me that Meyer is detested in the 2d Battalion; I do not doubt it. The rascally Shawnees have come from the other side of the Ohio; they asked to speak to Mr. McKee. You will see, Sir, what they have said. They had a Frenchman with them, and fierce looks; they have not wished to come to this side; they have made demands as usual, but there was nothing for them but balls at their service. They said they had many Indians around us, but I believe nothing of it.   S. E.

[British Museum.—Bouquet Papers.]

LETTER OF CAPTAIN ECUYER.

(Endorsed.)

(Private.   Received the 29th at Carlisle.)

FORT PITT, June 18, 1763.

Sir:—I received your letter May 3d, and one of June 9th yesterday at midnight. The carpenters being discharged, I will certify the accounts of our artisan soldiers and nothing more. Captain Basset wrote to Mr. Baillie to put him on the book for one shilling a day. I will never certify to such an article; he has done nothing, only Burent. Mr. Basset is angry at me; as it appears in his letter, he has very bad manners. I have done his duty here, and I am actually still doing it. Mr. Hudson deserves to be paid more than others; moreover, Burent has used more shoes, &c., which these 2£ 6s. cannot pay for. I do not know why any one would put money into the hands of people who do not do what they should do. I will say no more about it until I have the honor to see you.

I am respectfully, Sir,

Your very humble and very obedient servant,

S. ECUYER.

[COLONEL BOUQUET.]

P. S.—Burent has just given me the warrant which he received from Mr. Basset; he does not want pay for what he has done. I have done what I could to appease him, but uselessly. Really I can not blame him; he is not paid for the tenth of his services. He has been a slave, and one who has done nothing has all the profit. I will never certify to an unjust thing if it is within my knowledge, for that would be wronging the king. Moreover, here is a paragraph of an order from the General-in-Chief, which I have received from you : "Where any work is carried on by artisans or laborers, the accounts of the several workmen must be kept by the commanding officer and the person who directs the work, from which accounts only the men will receive their wages." Thus, you will see, Sir, if it is just that Mr. Baillie, who keeps no account, can adjust them, and I pass and sign.   S. E.

I have sent to Venango 25 barrels of flour and beef; I would have sent it at any rate without the alarm. Lieutenant Gordon must have sent a great deal to Le Bœuf. In his last letter he remarks to me that he has only provision for six

weeks. He has been very imprudent in sending two expresses by land, which have not arrived here, and one by boat
without necessity; this is how they strip a post unreasonably.
I have the honor to be, very respectfully and without reserve,
 Sir, your very humble and very obedient servant,

          S. ECUYER.
[COLONEL BOUQUET.]

 P. S.—Mr. Croghan departs on the 25th for Bedford and
Carlisle. The Dulcinia has given the itch to poor Baillie and
others.

[British Museum.—Bouquet Papers.]

LETTER FROM CAPTAIN ECUYER.

(Endorsed.)

(Received the 29th at Carlisle.)

       FORT PITT, June 18, 1763.

 Sir:—In my last, dated the 16th, I sent you a short discourse between four Shawnees and Mr. McKee. The next
morning they recalled him and addressed to him the discourse
here added. Mr. McKee gives great credit to it. As to me,
I do not believe such vagabonds. I have seen but few Indians
around us until this time. However it may be, they will come
when they wish. The post is in a good state, and I cannot
imagine that they will dare attempt an assault. I wish they
would do it; they would remember it for more than four days.
I have no news from any post but from Bedford and Ligonier. All is well.

 I have the honor to be, very respectfully, Sir,

  Your very humble and very obedient servant,

          S. ECUYER.

[British Museum.—Bouquet Papers.]

LETTER FROM CAPTAIN ECUYER.

(Endorsed.)

(Received at Carlisle, July 3d.)

FORT PITT, June 26, 1763, at 11 o'clock P.M.

Sir:—Since my last, dated the 18th, nothing extraordinary has happened, excepting some slight alarms from time to time, until the afternoon of the 22d, when the savages showed themselves and descended into the plain, driving into the woods a part of our horses, and killing some cattle, after which they attacked the fort from all sides excepting from the other side of the Monongehela, but at a great distance. I had, however, a militia killed and another wounded. I dispersed them a little later with a howitzer and two cannon shots, which assuredly were not without effect. We fired but three guns against these Indians, of whom one was killed. They came to take a horse opposite here, where Fleming's house was. On the night of the 23d and 24th they prowled around the fort to reconnoitre, and after midnight the Delawares asked to speak to Mr. McKee. You will find annexed our different conversations. The returns of the month : the three deaths are three of my men killed. I have besides that a regular wounded, two militia killed and two wounded. The garrison consists of 330 men all counted, 104 women, 106 children. Total 540 mouths, of which nearly 420 receive the provisions of the king. Mr. Price arrived this morning with seven men of his garrison, and as he has the honor to write to you, I will say no more about him, having had little time to talk to him since his arrival.

I have the honor to be, very respectfully, Sir,

Your very humble and very obedient servant,

S. ECUYER.

The 26th, five hours after noon.

Declaration of Benjamin Gray, soldier of the company of Cochran. He had left Presqu' Isle the 22d: Monday, the 19th, in the morning, 250 Indians attacked the place; they fought all the day and the next day. The day after Mr. Christie capitulated they should have given him an escort to here with provision for six days, but after having pillaged, they massacred our people. He and two others fled to the woods. He assures us that the Indians were of four nations —Ottawas, Chipawas, Wyandotts and Senaccas. He had himself seen the schooner going to Detroit, but he does not know if it was loaded with provisions. He passed by Le Bœuf and Venango, which were destroyed.

S. ECUYER.

[British Museum.—Bouquet Papers.]

LETTER FROM CAPTAIN ECUYER.

(Endorsed.)

(Received the 6th of November, 1763.)

FORT PITT, August 2, 1763.

Sir:—I have at this moment received John Hudson with one of your letters only. I hastened him off instantly. He was three days among our enemies. He will tell you more of it than I can. I have not received letters in reply to mine of the date June 26th. I have had ten days of council with the Indians; you will see their demands and my reply which Mr. McKee sent to Mr. Croghan.

On the 28th, of the afternoon, they came to attack us very briskly, and very soon all the bank of the lower town was surrounded. The garden of Mr. Rosgruge, behind our brick barrier, just to where the house of Captain Basset was, there was a mob. They were well covered and ourselves the same.

They did us no harm,—no one killed. Seven wounded— myself lightly. Their attack lasted 5 days and 5 nights. We are certain of having killed and wounded 20 of their men, without counting those which we have not seen. I did not permit any one to fire until they saw the object, and as soon as they showed their noses they were picked off like flies, for I had good marksmen. They recrossed the Ohio on the arrival of your express, and after having read your letters. I will tell you more about it when I have the honor to see you. I have at present four legs of beef and no flour. Bring a great deal of it or the jaws will rest immovable. Nothing to wash our throats. No Indian herb for the morning, and none of that kind of cabbage to mix with it; however, an old soldier can dispense with all that as well as with other things, and in the meanwhile I have the honor to be very perfectly, Sir,

Your very humble and very obedient servant,

S. ECUYER.

[TO COLONEL BOUQUET.]

[British Museum.—Additional Manuscript, 21,649.]

LETTER TO S. ECUYER.

(The Bouquet Papers, Volume VII., page 153.)

(Endorsed.)

(Captain Ecuyer, November 8, 1763. Received the 13th. Addressed, on His Majesty's Service, to Henry Bouquet, Esq., Colonel of the First Batt. R. A. R., etc., at Fort Pitt.)

BEDFORD, November 8, 1763.

Sir:—We arrived here the 4th of the month and departed the 9th. I do not know when we will arrive at Ligonier, for the roads are terrible for the chariots. Our escort is very weak. We have only six militia, and our detachment diminishes every day. We have two invalids and eight deserters, viz. : Armstrong, Childers, Cope, Arneld, Negely, Townhawer, Grenadiers Darks and Fill. I suppose several will depart this night. I have done all that it was in my power to retain them, but all useless. They are rascals and mutineers of the first order, above all the Grenadiers. I suppose that Cotton and the scamp de Mains will go also ; that will only be a benefit, for these two wags are capable of corrupting a whole regiment. I never had a detachment so disagreeable in my life, occasioned by their bad conduct.

I have written to Messrs. Belneves and Dow to have them put in prison if they show themselves in the province. I made a distribution of clothes to-day. The eight scamps left with their old people. The soldiers which are here and at Ligonier in garrison complain bitterly that they are not provided for, and I have no money to give them. We prepare to suffer rain, snow and cold without counting fatigue before we will have the pleasure of seeing you.

Waiting for that desired time, I have the honor to be very respectfully, sir,

Your very humble and very obedient servant,

S. ECUYER.

[COLONEL BOUQUET.]

[British Museum.—Bouquet Papers.]

LETTER FROM CAPTAIN ECUYER.

(On the back : Nov. 14th, 1763, 11 o'clock forenoon, met an express from Captain Stewart at Bedford, the contents of which obliges me to proceed with the utmost expedition to Bedford.)

CHAS. FORBES.

(A mile nearer Ligonier than the crossings of the road. Endorsed Captain Ecuyer, Nov. 13th, 1763. Answered the 16th, addressed, on His Majesty's Service, To Henry Bouquet, Esq., Commanding his Majesty's Forces to the Westwards, etc., at Fort Pitt.)

BEDFORD, Nov. 13, 1763.

Sir:—I hope you have received the express which Captain Stewart sent you with a letter dated from camp four miles from Bedford, November 11th.

We marched on that day to the foot of the Allegheny and when our carrier guard joined us they reported to us, that four different parties of Indians had been discovered; they killed for us one driver and one horse, and in the neighborhood of Bedford two of the inhabitants were cruelly massacred and a third carried off.

Captain Ourry came this morning to the camp to see us, but we had left, and he came near being among the victims, for the driver was killed very near to him. Their intention was to take him prisoner, but not being able to do that, they mortally wounded him. Our rear guard ran up and they took to the woods.

After all this intelligence Captain Stewart sent an officer with a party to reconnoitre the top of the mountain and escort two expresses to carry letters to you, but being near to the breastworks, they discovered and saw six savages coming to reconnoitre our camp ; they were followed as they believe by several others. Warned by the noise of the stones and other things they retreated and arrived at the camp at midnight; we were all under arms. After all these discoveries Captain Stewart called together all the officers and demanded their opinion which was unanimous, to return to Bedford, to save the convoy and wait for a sufficient escort, for eighty men in all was not a sufficient escort for twenty-three wagons, 300 horses, 160 cattle. I think they wished to attack us before we should arrive at Ligonier, perhaps hoping to be more fortunate than between Ligonier and Fort Pitt. It is desolation on our frontiers. It is said here for certain, that the province of Pennsylvania is going to raise three battalions and some rangers.

The Cherokees have refused the presents and have declared that so long as there is one man living they will not treat with us. It is said also, that the Senaccas have been so badly received when they have demanded to renew the chain of friendship, that they have all taken the hatchet and it was they who made the attacks (coup) at the portage of Niagara. What will the five other nations do? We have several men in my detachment incapable of marching. I have also the great scamps, Maines and Coyle, prisoners for desertion. Here are the names of those who have deserted since my letter of the 8th, Hurst, Miller, Colton, Green, Hook, Ward, Smith, Grend. Burgess, Higgs and Anderson, Grenadiers, total eighteen and two prisoners, besides those who departed before we marched here. I have served more than twenty-two years, but I have never seen the like, a troop of mutineers, of bandits, of cut-throats, above all the Grenadiers. I have been obliged after all imaginable patience to have flogged two on the field and without court-martial. One wished to kill the Sergeant and the other wanted to kill me. I was on the point of blowing out his brains, but the fear of killing or wounding some one of those who were around us prevented me. What a disagreeable thing. In the name of God let me retire to my country seat. It is in your power, Sir, to let me go, and I will be eternally grateful. Do not refuse me this favor I pray you, otherwise I will not get better and I do not know if I will be in a state to mount with the convoy.

Waiting for news of you, I pray you to believe me, very respectfully, Sir,

    Your very humble and very obedient servant,

                                               S. ECUYER.

[COLONEL BOUQUET.]

[British Museum.—Bouquet Papers.]

LETTER FROM CAPTAIN ECUYER.

(Endorsed.)

(Received the 29th. Addressed—On His Majesty's Service, to Henry
Bouquet, Esq., Colonel Commanding His Majesty's
Forces to the Westward, etc., at Fort Pitt.)

BEDFORD, November 20, 1763.

Sir:—I have received your two letters by Captain Forbes,
dated the 13th and 16th of the month. We have not had any
desertions since my last letter. I am distressed to be obliged
to remain here, my health does not permit me to undertake
the journey to Fort Pitt. Doctor Boyd will tell you the same,
that I am not capable of bearing the fatigue. I have a great
cold in my head and fever every night, sick stomach and head-
ache, accompanied by an abscess in the place where I was
wounded at Quebec, which causes me inexpressible suffering.
However, I hope that this complication of ills will have no
evil result and as you cannot give me a furlough, I will join
the battalion as soon as possible; in the meanwhile I will
remain here ready to receive your orders.

I have desired Mr. Hutchins to arrange all my accounts
and pay the balance to my men and that he will have the
goodness to send me some linen, for I am naked as the hand,
having only brought with me four woven shirts. I congratulate you on the journey of Sir Jeffry, he is much regretted by
all the army.

General Gage will command, it is said, until the arrival of
General Moncton. There you see the changes more prompt
than could have been expected from them. I acknowledge
that the American army is agreeably surprised. The great
Babylon has fallen, and all the undermined world rests on its
foundation. What cries of universal joy, and what bumpers of
Madeira will be drunk on his prompt departure. God knows
whether he will deign to reply to our last letters; he is sufficiently pleased to leave you in the lurch. I know that you
will draw good from it, notwithstanding his jealousy. I pray
very humbly, Sir, to you to take the trouble to speak to Captain Barnsley with regard to my subsistence. I would be
charmed if things could be arranged pleasantly. He charges
me ten shillings . . . more than it cost. There is the way
some people make money in the world. It seems to me that
after having spent foolishly my money during 18 months he
might as well give me the change. He has lost nothing by me;
but when one is a Jew he is a Jew, and remains so, besides
that there is due me two sch. sterling a day, too much pay
for the music, from the 25th of April, 1762, until October 24,
1763. Never was detachment more disagreeable than this
one, above all for poor Captain Stewart as commandant. He
has been very badly served and obeyed by some of the officers,
so that after all the patience imaginable he sees himself in the
hard necessity to send to you Lieutenants Guy and Watson,
prisoners for faults and crimes for which in all other services
the last would have had his head broken. I am not surprised
if the soldiers mutiny when the officers conduct themselves
in that way. I will say no more about it; you will see in the
papers more than you wish to. Mr. Guy has surely neglected
his duty; he left his guard the day of the mutiny, took lodgings in town without permission, while I, though sick, camped
with the soldiers. One evening, when he was on duty, he did

not make his round. I spoke of it to him the next day, on
which he replied that if he knew the reporter he would kick
him on the back. I replied that it was me, and that it was my
duty, and it seemed to me that every one should do his. He
retired, some days after he was put under arrest. I wrote to
him and advised him as a friend, but he did not deign to reply.
I abandon him to his unhappy fate and pity him. He is an
idiot who lets himself be led, and who follows a bad guide. He
is uncourteous to be obstinate when he is entirely in the wrong.
It is true that when one breakfasts with a toddy one is liable
to commit great faults during the day and to repent in the
evening. However it may be, he comes out badly from it.

I continue to recommend myself to the honor of your
remembrance and to call myself very respectfully, Sir,

Your very humble and very obedient servant,

S. ECUYER.

[COLONEL BOUQUET.]

P. S.—I must not neglect to recommend to you Mr. Hutchins as a worthy officer. He has given himself all imaginable
trouble and has been of great use to Captain Stewart and the
detachment. His diligence and good will merits more than I
can tell you.

[The Bouquet Papers.]

LETTER TO MAJOR GLADWIN.

FORT PITT, August 28, 1763.

Dear Sir:—I had last night the very great pleasure to receive your letter of the 28th of July by your express Andrew,
who says he was detained by sickness at Sandusky. Your
letters for the General are forwarded.

A Mohawk having reported to Sir Wm. Johnson that De Troit was taken, I could not help being uneasy, tho' long acquainted with Indian lies. It was a great satisfaction to me to know from yourself that you have been able to defend that post, with so few men, against that multitude. What was known below of your firm and prudent conduct from the beginning of the Insurrection had obtained the General's approbation, and does you the greatest honor.

The loss of all our detached posts is no more than could be expected from their defenceless state ; but Captain Campbell's death affects me sensibly.

I pity the unfortunate who remain yet in the power of the barbarians, as every step we take to rescue them may and will probably hasten their death. Your express says that after he left the De Troit two Wiandots told him that the detachment of 300 men from Niagara had joined you with provisions. This will give you some ease till more effectual reinforcements can be sent.

You know that you are to have the command of all the troops destined for De Troit and to retake possession of the country now fallen into the hands of the enemy. To that effect the General collects all the troops that can be spared at Niagara, and Presque Isle.* The remains of the 42d and 77th were ordered to join you this way, when we had intelligence that Venango had been surprised, Lieutenant Gordon and all his unfortunate garrison massacred. Le Boeuf† abandoned and Presque Isle surrendered, to my unspeakable astonishment, as I knew the strength of that block house, which would have been relieved from Niagara.

Fort Pitt was attacked and invested by all the Delawares and parts of the Shawnese, Wiandots and Mingoes, to the

* Erie.
† On French Creek.

number of 400, by their account, but much more considerable, as we found afterward, besides their women and children, which they had brought here to carry the plunder to their towns, not doubting to take the place. Fort Burd, on the Monongehela, Bushy Run and Stoney Creek were abandoned · for want of men.

Ligonier,* a post of great consequence to us, was defended with a handful of men by Lieut. Blane, and Capt. Ecuyer baffled all their efforts here, though the fort was open on three sides ; the floods having undermined the sodwork, the rampart had tumbled in the ditch. He pallissadoed and fraised the whole, raised a parapet all around, and in a short time with a small garrison he has made it impregnable for savages. Besides their attack on the forts, they kept parties on the communication and interrupted all expresses, while others falling upon the frontier settlements spread terror and desolation through the whole country.†

Things being in that situation I received orders to march with the above troops, the only force the General could collect at that time for the relief of this fort, which was in great want of provisions, the little flour they had being damaged.

In that pressing danger the provinces refused to give us the least assistance. Having formed a convoy, I marched from Carlisle the 18th of July with about 460 rank and file, being the remains of the 42d and 77th regiments, many of them convalescents. I left thirty men at Bedford, and as many at Ligonier, where I arrived on the 2d instant. Having no intelligence of the enemy, I determined to leave the waggons at that post and to proceed with 400 horses, loaded with flour, to be less incumbered in case of an action.

---

* Red Stone, old fort. one mile above the mouth of Red Stone Creek; east side of Loyalhanna Creek.

† Battle of Bushy Run.

I left Ligonier on the 4th, and on the 5th instant, at 1 o'clock
P.M., after marching seventeen miles, we were suddenly attacked by all the savages collected about Fort Pitt. I shall
not enter into the detail of that obstinate action, which lasted
till night, and beginning early the 6th continued till 1 o'clock,
when at last we routed them. They were pursued about two
miles and so well dispersed that we have not seen one since :
as we were excessively distressed by the total want of water,
we marched immediately to the nearest spring without
inquiring into the loss of the enemy, who must have suffered
greatly by their repeated and bold attacks in which they were
constantly repulsed. Our loss is very considerable. Of the
42d: Captain-Lieutenant Graham, Lieutenant McIntosh, Rangers Lieutenant Randall killed. 42d : Captain John Graham,
Lieutenant Dun Campbell wounded. 77th : Lieutenant
Donald Campbell. Volunteer People : killed, 50 ; wounded,
60 ; in all, 110.

After delivering our convoy here, part of the troops were
embarked and sent down the river to cut off the Shawnees ;
the rest went back to Ligonier, and brought our wagons on
the 22d. The great fatigues of long marches, and of being
always under arms has occasioned great sickness, which, with
the loss in the action, puts it out of my power to send you
the remains of the two regiments ordered to join you by
Presque Isle, till I receive a reinforcement. This gives me
great uneasiness, as I know that they are much wanted.

But you may be assured that we shall do everything in the
power of man to assist you. I am to remain here myself,
ready to go down the river with a strong body, which is to be
ordered for that service.

As I have no means to procure intelligence from Presque
Isle, I am obliged to send your express that way, and at his
return I will dispatch him by Sandusky, with what news I

may then have received and a duplicate of this. It is very agreeable to me to hear that our officers with you have been so happy as to obtain your approbation of their services, and I am much obliged to you for the honor you have done them.

I enclose the latest papers we have. Two of our battalions are reduced. I know nothing certain of the numbers of corps remaining.

I am, dear Sir,

Your most obedient and humble servant,

H. BOUQUET, *Col.*

ORDERLY BOOK.

Fort Pitt, Saturday, May 28, 1763. G. O. parole, Devonshire. The battalion to be under arms to-morrow morning at 6 o'clock, the men's arms and accoutrements to be clean and in good order for to-day, to-morrow Lieutenant Carre.

For Guard 1 sergeant, 2 corporals, 22 privates.

Fort Pitt, May 29, 1763. Sunday, G. O. parole, George. The officer of the day in case of an alarm to take the command of the main guard and wait under arms for further orders.

R. O. for the day to-morrow, Lieutenant Guy.

Fort Pitt, Monday, May 30, 1763. G. O. parole, Vesel. The bridge to be drawn up at retreat beating till further orders. The artillery to give a sentinel to the flag bastion. The officer of the day to visit all the sentinels in the forts once every night, at any hour he pleases after 11 o'clock and order paroles from the main guard twice in the night.

R. O. for the day to-morrow, Lieutenant Baillie.

G, after orders. The officer of the day to take the command of a picket of 1 , 1ᶜ, 1ᵈ, 20ᵖ at retreat beating, who are to lodge on the grenadier bastion all night, to keep four sentinels which the adjutant will place. All the men off duty to lay on their arms without stripping off their clothes, and no man whatever to be permitted to sleep out of the fort. The whole garrison to be under arms every morning one hour before day till further orders. And the sergeants and corporals are requested to see their men turn out without the least noise and acquaint their officers who are immediately to join them.

Fort Pitt, Tuesday, May 31, 1763, G. O. parole, Plymouth ; countersign, Canterbury. The militia to march into the fort this evening at the retreat beating, with their arms, ammunition and accoutrements, after which the rolls of the companies are to be called ; no man whatever to be permitted to leave the fort without permission from the commanding officer. In case of an attack the women to provide and serve the men upon duty with water and to take care not to make the least noise in going backwards and forwards in the fort or they will be turned out of it. Quartermaster Clark to provide all the tents that can be had for the militia to pitch on or near the bastions.

The R. A. to give for picket to-night   1': 2. 12th } 2. 3. 24
The militia to give   1': 1. 12th }

R. O. for the day to-morrow, Lieutenant Donalon.

Fort Pitt, Wednesday, June 1, 1763. G. O. parole, Dublin ; countersign, Cooke.

The whole garrison to be under arms this evening at 6 o'clock ; the musicians, drummers and servants to fall in with their company with arms and accoutrements. The Drum Major to act as orderly drummer till further orders.

A return of the effective strength of each company, including the militia, to be given in at the same time to the commanding officer.

The militia to draw provisions on Saturday next with the companies they are incorporated into. Commanding officers

of companies are to see that their militia are immediately
provided with powder, flints and such balls as are fit and
suitable for their fire-locks and rifles.

R. O. for the day to-morrow, Lieutenant Carre.

Fort Pitt, Thursday, June 2, 1763. G. O. parole, London;
countersign, Chatham. Quatermaster Clark to get the
provision return of each company, including the militia,
to-morrow morning at 8 o'clock, and inform the commissary
what fresh provisions there will be occasion to kill. Picket
as usual.

R. O. for the day to-morrow, Lieutenant Grey.

Commanding officers of companies to examine their militia
this evening at roll calling, if they are all provided with a suf-
ficiency of ammunition and balls fitted to their pieces, and to
see those provided that are deficient.

Fort Pitt, Friday, June 3, 1763. G. O. parole, DeTroit.
The picket and guard to join under the command of the
officers of the day, and to be relieved every evening at
retreat beating; in the day, the whole to lodge in the guard
room, and in the night upon the grenadier bastion, as usual.
The adjutant will give every evening to the officer of the day
the signal, that the patrols of the outposts will give to the
sentinels when challenged by them, which he will communicate to his sentinels. All the men to receive a dram this
evening for their good behavior and another to-morrow to
drink his Majesty's health, it being his birthday. The commanding officer desires his thanks to be given to the garrison
in general for the assiduity in carrying on this work with
such good spirit and dispatch, and for the future orders that
but one half of the garrison off duty be ordered for work in
the forenoon and to be relieved by the other half in the afternoon.

For the parade to-night 3 sergs., 3 corps., and 60 p's for the
day. To-morrow Ensign Hutchins.

Fort Pitt, Saturday, June 4, 1763, G. O. parole, the King; countersign, George, which is to be given by all rounds and patrols within and without the garrison to the sentinels when challenged by them, upon which they are to be allowed to pass. As it is necessary (for more ease to the men) to divide the garrison into two reliefs, and a Captain being wanting, the commanding officer is pleased to appoint Lieutenant Carre to do duty as Captain Lieutenant for the time being, and he is to be obeyed as such. Captain Phillips' division for duty to-night to consist of Lieutenant Grey, Donallon, McKee and Milligan. 6^s, 1^s, 2^l, 96^p to be relieved to-morrow morning by Captain Lieutenant Carre, Lieutenants Baillie, Hutchins, Fleming and Graber 5^s 9^l 96^{ps}. The Quarter Master to visit the barracks every other day, to see that they are kept clean and void of all nuisance that might infect the Garrison, which he will report to the commanding officer. He is also to deliver this evening to a Sergeant of each company two quarts of loose powder, which they are to distribute to those men that have cartridges, and see that they strengthen each cartridge by adding one-third of an inch in length to it. The commanding officer recommends it to the men (that in case of an attack) they will keep themselves cool and not rashly throw away their ammunition, by firing without being sure of seeing the enemy before them and by such caution and conduct they may assure themselves of success, and he begs that all the officers will have a particular attention to see this order obeyed. The commanding officer of artillery to order one-half of his detachment to their posts at picket mounting in the evening, to remain there all night. Work to-morrow as usual, and when the drum beats for the morning working party to leave off the afternoon party to fall on for work. Each man to have one pint of beer issued to him to-morrow at noon by the Sergeant-major. All orders concerning the men to be read to them by an officer of a company at roll calling in the evening.

Fort Pitt, Sunday, June 5, 1763. G. O. parole, Westminster, countersign York. No horses to be suffered to go loose about the fort. The Quartermaster to see this order obeyed. He is also to take a list of the number of the women and the children in each barrack room, which is to be given in to the commanding officer at 2 o'clock, in order to have a proper number put together and prevent the men from being crowded and disturbed. As the dogs about the garrison make daily great disturbance, and in case of an attack might make great confusion in the garrison by their noise, that no orders could be heard or executed. It is therefore the commanding officer's positive order that all the dogs without exception that are not tied up after 4 o'clock this afternoon shall be killed and that a party be ordered immediately to put this order in execution. It is likewise the commanding officer's orders that the wolf and bear be immediately killed or put out of the fort.

Fort Pitt, Monday, June 6, 1763. G. O. parole, Philadelphia; countersign, Bath. All the men's arms to be discharged or drawn this day between the hours of 11 and 1 o'clock, on the Monongahela curtain, an officer of each company to be present and to see that every man, after having unloaded his piece, wipes her clean and loads her again. Captain Carre to order those men on duty to do the same, permitting only one-half of his guard to unload at one time. The cattle to be watered once every day, and fed with spelts twice, viz., at 10 o'clock in the morning and 4 in the afternoon, at which time the women to turn out to cut the spelts, and in case any of them refuse so to do, they are to be confined in the guard-room. A covering party of 1^s, 1^c 20^{ns} to be sent with them from the guard. The captain and the guard to continue a corporal and 8 privates to kill or drown the dogs.

Fort Pitt, Tuesday, June 7, 1763. G. O. parole, Jersey; countersign, Grant. In case of an alarm, the guard to take the post they occupy at night, and all the men off duty to take their usual post of alarm, viz., the grenadiers upon the Grenadier bastion, the general company upon the Ohio bastion, Captain Ecuyer's upon the Monongehela bastion, Captain Gordon upon the Flag bastion, Captain Cochran upon the Music bastion. The Lieutenant-colonels, the reserve, under Major Trent's orders. This disposition to take place till further orders ; and no women at that time to be suffered upon the ramparts or to appear out of their rooms, except such as are bringing water to men. Regular sentinels always to be posted at the bridge gate and sally-ports, who in case of an alarm are to permit nobody to go out of the fort without leave from the Captain of the guard.

Fort Pitt, Wednesday, June 8, 1763. G. O. parole, Harwick ; countersign, Pearth. Return of the strength of each company to be given in to the Sergeant-major at 2 o'clock. A covering party of an officer, 1, 1, 30[ns] to parade at half an hour past 2 o'clock, and to march to the spelt field, turning out all the women that are able to use and cut with a sickle, also 5 or 6 men to mow the spelts. It is then to be brought into the charge and care of the cattle guard, who are to dry it in the sun and stack it, and the Sergeant of that guard to be answerable that a proper quantity be equally given to the cattle daily, once in the forenoon and once in the afternoon.

Fort Pitt, Thursday, June 9, 1763. G. O. parole, Cumberland ; countersign, Cork. As the commanding officer thinks it necessary for the benefit of the garrison to have three reliefs, a return to be given in to-morrow morning of

11

each company, including for duty the servants (who are to
mount guard with their masters), 4 drummers and all the
artificers except the following, viz., 8 shipwrights, 2 bakers,
1 gunsmith, 2 wagoners, 1 gardener—the names of which
the Sergeant-major will acquaint a sergeant of each company.

Fort Pitt, Friday, June 10, 1763. G. O., Buckingham ; countersign, How. The provision store to be surveyed immediately ; for that duty, Captain Phillips, Lieutenant Donalon,
Ensign Hutchins. Captain Phillips will report to the commanding officer the quantity they may find a necessity for
condemning. Ensign Hutchins and Mr. McKee are appointed to duty with the artillery till further orders. For
guard to-night, Captain Phillips, Lieutenant Donalon and
Davenport 5^s, 1^d, 69^{ms}. The sergeant of each company that
is off duty to give in to the adjutant every morning a return
of the effective strength of the company for duty that day,
mentioning those excused and unfit for duty on the back.

Fort Pitt, Saturday, June 11, 1763. G. O. parole, Boston ;
countersign, Wales. For guard to-night, Captain Carre,
Lieutenants Fleming, Milligan and Christy 5^s, 1 , 71^{pls}. All
the chimneys to be swept this afternoon, but none of them to
be cleaned by setting them on fire. The Quartermaster to
see this order complied with, and also give orders to all the
women against washing in the barrack rooms and governor's
house.

Fort Pitt, Sunday, June 12, 1763. G. O. parole, Salsbury ;
countersign, Watch. For guard to-night, Captain Phillips,
Lieutenants Baillie and Greber 5 , 1^d and 71 R. & F.

The women to wash at the batteau-shed in the lower town
twice a week, viz., Mondays and Thursdays, at which time
they will have a covering party from the guard of a corporal
and six privates.

Fort Pitt, Monday, June 13, 1763. G. O. parole, England ;

countersign, John. For guard to-night, Captain Carre, Lieutenants Donalon and Davenport 5°, 1ᵈ and 70 R. & F.

Fort Pitt, Tuesday, June 14, 1763. G. O. parole, Annapolis ; countersign, Job. For guard to-night, Captain Phillips, Lieutenants Fleming, Milligan and Christy 5°,1ᵈ and 70 R. & F.

Fort Pitt, Wednesday, June 15, 1763. G. O. parole, Charlotte ; countersign, M.

The commanding officer is very much surprised and displeased at the exorbitant price (he is informed) some persons have charged the poor and unfortunate people in the garrison for Indian corn, and it is his orders that none of it be sold above the rate of 6s per bushel, and that whoever has sold it higher since their coming into the fort to return to the buyer the overplus. Sergeants of company to see all their men provided with two firelocks and all the militia with tomahawks when under arms this evening. The militia always to parade with their tomahawks. One relief to march at 2 o'clock this day with single firelocks, to destroy the fences and chimneys of the upper town; for this duty Lieutenants Donalon and Davenport, 4 . 40 R. and F., with arms, 30 rank and file, with falling axes, pickaxes and spades. All the women to carry water, to fill the empty casks upon the ramparts, at 4 o'clock this afternoon, the casks to be equally distributed and properly placed upon the bastions and curtains. For guard to-night, Captain Carre, Lieutenants Baillie and Graber, 5°, 1ᵈ, 69 R. and F. No work this afternoon.

Fort Pitt, June 16, 1763. G. O. parole, Amherst.

Headquarters, New York, May 4, 1763.

Orders.—His Excellency, the Commander-in-Chief, makes known to the army that the definitive treaty of peace between His Majesty and the most Christian and Catholic kings is signed, to which order observance will be had. Signed, Jeoffry Amherst.

General orders.—Whenever a covering party is ordered out, whoever may command the party is not upon any account to allow any man to pass his sentinels without a written order from the commanding officer of the garrison, and none of the men to run upon any occasion before their officer, but keep themselves cool and wait for orders and directions; then they may always assure themselves of success ; but by running without directions they will fall in disorder and be out of breath when they come up to engage the enemy, which would be of the greatest disadvantage to them and bad consequence. An officer of each company to see the men's arms drawn immediately, and the spare balls to be delivered by the sergeant to the Quartermaster ; none of the arms to be fired off except the rifles. The commanding officer is pleased to appoint John Robertson, of the grenadier company, Sergeant of militia, in his own company, in the room of Sergeant Miller, dead, and he is to be obeyed as such. For guard to-night, Captain Phillips, Lieutenants Donalon and Davenport, 5 , 1 and 70 R. and F.

Fort Pitt, June 17, 1763. G. O. parole, America. As a party is expected daily from Bedford, the commanding officer makes known to the garrison that that party will have white garters tied round their heads, to distinguish them from the enemy, tho' their dress will be something like the Indian manner. And as expresses may be expected daily or nightly, sentinels are to challenge 1, 2 or 3 persons that may appear in the night two or three times before they fire. For guard to-night, Captain-Lieutenant Carre, Lieutenants Fleming, Christy and Milligan, 5 sergeants, 1 drummer and 70 rank and file.

Fort Pitt, the 18th, 1763. G. O. parole, Bedford. The sentinels not to allow any person to cut grass upon any part of the rampart or parapet without leave in writing from

the commanding officer, nor to suffer anybody but the workmen to go near the fascines, as machines are fixed, these not
showing where they are placed, might be wounded or hurt.
For guard to-night, Captain Phillips, Lieutenants Baillie and
Graber, 1 sergeant, 1 drummer and 70 rank and file.

Fort Pitt, June 19, 1763.   G. O. parole, Granby.   The garrison to be under arms to-morrow morning at 2 o'clock, each
company at their alarm posts.

For guard to-night, Captain Lieutenant Carre, Lieutenants Donelon and Davenport, 5 sergeants, 1 drummer and
68 rank and file.

Fort Pitt, June 20, 1763.   G. O. parole, Darby.   As those
people who have Indian corn for sale think 6s a bushel too
little, refusing to sell it at so reasonable a price, by which the
poor and necessitous in the garrison are much distressed,
the commanding officer thinks proper to allow them to sell
it at one dollar per bushel, and that whoever shall presume to
ask a higher price or refuse to sell it at that rate shall be
punished for disobedience of this order.   The garrison to be
under arms at 2 o'clock to-morrow morning.

For guard to-night, Captain-Lieutenant Phillips, Lieutenants Grey, Milligan and Christy, 5 sergeants, 1 drummer and
69 privates.

Fort Pitt, June 21, 1763.   G. O. parole, Sunderland.   As
the people who have cattle are desirous of repairing the
fences near where Colonel Burd's house stood, they are to
be under arms at 2 o'clock this afternoon, and to march there
together ; they are desired to be very cautious and hurry their
work ; two pieces of cannon will cover their retreat.

For guard to-night, Captain-Lieutenant Carre, Lieutenants
Baillie, Fleming and Greber, 5 sergeants, 1 drummer, 69 rank
and file.

Fort Pitt, June 22, 1763.   G. O. parole, Aberdeen   As the

small quantity of wood within the fort may be wanted for
the works, and is not sufficient to serve for the common
uses of the garrison, the commanding officer desires the
several officers' messes to be very saving of it, and orders
the private men and women to gather their fire-wood in the
lower town, that the wood within the fort may be used at the
last extremity. The dogs being still noisy at night, and hinder-
ing people of their rest, whoever keeps dogs are desired to
have them tied up at night. Patroles will go round the fort
for the future to kill them, and for every dog they kill they
will get a half crown reward. For guard to-night, Captain-
Lieutenant Phillips, Lieutenants Donellon and Davenport, 5
sergeants, 1 drummer, and 67 rank and file.

Fort Pitt, June 23, 1763. G. O. parole, Dublin. The
monthly returns to be given to-morrow at orderly time. For
guard to-night, Captain-Lieutenant Carre, Lieutenants Grey,
Milligan and Christy, 5 sergeants, 1 drummer, 69 rank and file.

Fort Pitt, June 24, 1763. G. O. parole, Westminster.
For guard to-night, Captain-Lieutenant Phillips, Lieutenants
Baillie, Fleming and Greber, 5 sergeants, 1 drummer, and 69
rank and file.

Fort Pitt, June 25, 1763. G. O. parole, Chatham. The
townspeople who have cattle, to go together at 3 o'clock this
afternoon, to make a fence across the spelt field,* beginning so
far down as the spelts are cut, in which part the cattle may
feed. For guard to-night, Captain-Lieutenant Carre, Lieutenants Donellon and Davenport, 5 sergeants, 1 drummer and
68 rank and file.

Fort Pitt, June 26, 1763. G. O. parole, Edinburgh. For
guard to-night, Captain-Lieutenant Phillips, Lieutenants Guy,
Milligan and Christy, 5 sergeants, 1 drummer, 71 rank and
file.

* German wheat.

Fort Pitt, June 27, 1763.   G. O. parole, Scarborough.   A
court-martial to sit immediately, Captain-Lieutenant Carre
President, Lieutenant Baillie (members) Lieutenant Guy.
The men that came in from Le Bœuf and Presque Isle
yesterday to be armed and accoutred and provided with the
necessaries they want immediately.   For guard to-night, Captain-Lieutenant Carre, Lieutenants Baillie, Fleming and
Greber, 5 sergeants, 1 drummer, 69 rank and file.   The Captain of the guard to send the keys of all the gates of the
garrison to the commanding officer, to whom they are always
to be applied for (when wanted) by a sergeant and six men.

Fort Pitt, June 28, 1763.   G. O. parole, Woolwich.   No
fires to be kept in the barracks after tattoo beats.   The rooms
will be visited and any person found with fires in their rooms
after that time will be punished for disobedience of orders.
For guard to-night, Captain-Lieutenant Phillips, Lieutenants
Donellon and Davenport, 5 sergeants, 1 drummer and 67
rank and file.

Sergeant Robinson of Captain Gordon's company being
appointed to remain orderly over the commanding officers.
The commanding officer is pleased to appoint William Campbell (additional to the artillery) to do duty as sergeant in
Captain Gordon's company and the artillery to take another
man (in) his room.

Fort Pitt, June 29, 1763.   G. O. parole, Chelsea.   For
guard to-night, Captain-Lieutenant Carre, Lieutenants Guy,
Milligan and Christy, 5 sergeants, 1 drummer and 69 rank
and file.

Fort Pitt, June 30, 1763.   G. O. parole, Norwich.   For
guard to-night, Captain-Lieutenant Phillips, Lieutenants Baillie, Fleming and Greber, 5 sergeants, 1 drummer, and 68
rank and file.

Fort Pitt, July 1, 1763.   G. O. parole, Edinburgh.   For

guard to-night, Captain-Lieutenant Carre, Lieutenants Don-ellon, Price and Davenport, 5 sergeants, 1 drummer and 70 rank and file.

Fort Pitt, July 2, 1763. G. O. parole, Yarmouth. If any woman, drawing provisions, refuse to carry water when ordered they shall be struck off the provision return and turned out of the garrison as soon as the communication is clear. There-fore, all the women to turn out this afternoon at 4 o'clock to fill all the casks round the ramparts, and the commanding officer hopes they will do it without grumbling, it being for the good of the service. Whoever keeps horses or cows in the fort is ordered to clean the place where they stand every day, or the cattle will be turned out into the field, this being to prevent sickness in the garrison. For guard to-night, Cap-tain-Lieutenant Phillips, Lieutenants Milligan and Christy, 5 sergeants, 1 drummer, 68 rank and file.

Fort Pitt, July 3, 1763. G. O. parole, Dover. For guard to-night, Captain-Lieutenant Carre, Lieutenants Fleming and Greber, 5 sergeants, 1 drummer, 71 rank and file. The men to lie upon their arms every night till further orders, without taking off their clothes.

Fort Pitt, July 4, 1763. G. O. parole, Chester. No body allowed to smoke upon sentry or upon guard. Command-ing officer of post to be answerable for it. The back win-dow shutters of all barrack rooms to be shut as soon as it is dusk. For guard to-night, Captain-Lieutenant Phillips, Lieutenants Donellon, Price and Davenport, 5 sergeants, 1 drummer, 74 rank and file.

Fort Pitt, July 5, 1763. G. O. parole, Frankfort. For guard to-night, Captain-Lieutenant Carre, Lieutenants Guy, Milligan and Christie, 5 sergeants, 1 drummer, 73 rank and file.

Fort Pitt, July 6, 1763. Parole, Greenwich. For guard

to-night, Captain-Lieutenant Phillips, Lieutenants Baillie, Fleming and Greber, 5 serjeants, 1 drummer and 70 rank and file. After orders : As the traders have lost many of their deerskins out of the bundles that are piled up in the fort, whoever shall be found with any of them in their custody shall be most severely punished, as well as pay for the skins ; and whoever will discover such persons will be rewarded for it.

Fort Pitt, July 7, 1763. G. O. parole, Glasgow. As troops are daily expected from our colonies, the relief that is last off guard to hold themselves always in readiness to turn out on the first notice to support them. They are to parade in their waistcoats, and with one firelock only. A proper disposition will be made before they march out. For guard to-night, Captain-Lieutenant Carre, Lieutenants Donellon, Ensign Price, Lieutenant Davenport, 5 sergeants, 1 drummer and 71 rank and file.

Fort Pitt, July 8, 1763. Parole, Falmouth. For guard to-night, Captain-Lieutenant Phillips, Lieutenants Guy, Milligan and Christie, 5 sergeants, 1 drummer and 73 rank and file. A working party of a sergeant and 12 privates, and a covering party of 12 privates to parade, all with their arms, to-morrow morning at 7 o'clock to work in the King's garden.

Fort Pitt, July 9, 1763. G. O. parole, New Castle. A working party for the King's garden to parade to-morrow morning at 7 o'clock, as usual. A court-martial to sit at 3 o'clock this afternoon, Captain-Lieutenant Carre, President ; Ensign Hutchins (members), Ensign Price.

For guard to-night, Captain-Lieutenant Carre, Lieutenants Baillie, Fleming and Greber, 5 sergeants, 1 drummer and 71 rank and file.

Fort Pitt, July 10, 1763. G. O. parole, Brunswick. A

working and covering party for the King's garden to parade
to-morrow morning at 7 o'clock, to consist of 12 men of the
regulars for work, and a sergeant and 12 ditto to cover them,
the whole to parade with arms.   All the men off duty to parade
at the same hour to collect wood.   The artillery to collect for
themselves.   They are to work from 7 o'clock to 11, and from
1 to 5 in the afternoon.   For guard to-night, Captain-Lieutenant Phillips, Lieutenants Donellon, Price and Davenport,
5 sergeants, 1 drummer and 73 rank and file.   The clapboards
and shingles to be burned by the baker only, none of them
to be used in the barrack rooms, nor any of the long timber
to be cut by any body for fire-wood, as it may be wanted for
the works about the garrison.

Fort Pitt, July 11, 1763.   G. O. parole, Carlisle.   All the
old iron and nails that is found in the ashes of the wood
used for fire to be brought to the serjeant-major's room.
For guard to-night, Captain-Lieutenant Carre, Lieutenant
Guy, Christie and Milligan, 5 sergeants, 1 drummer and 72
rank and file.

Fort Pitt, July 12, 1763.   G. O. parole, Brussels.   For
guard to-night, Captain-Lieutenant Phillips, Lieutenants
Baillie, Fleming and Greber, 5 sergeants, 1 drummer, 70 rank
and file.

Fort Pitt, July 13, 1763.   G. O. parole, Sumersett.   For
guard to-night—Captain-Lieutenant Carre, Lieutenants Donellon, Price and Davenport, 5 sergeants, 1 drummer, 71 rank
and file.

Fort Pitt, July 14, 1763.   G. O. parole, America.   Captain Ecuyer gives his thanks to the militia for their diligence
hitherto at work, and for the future he exempts them from
all kinds of fatigue, except such as the service may absolutely
require, and assures them that he will acquaint the General-
in-Chief of their services and good behavior, and shall always

acknowledge they have done their duty with spirit, like true
British men.   At the same time desires the inhabitants who
have cows to sell them to Mr. Murray, the commissary, for
the benefit of the garrison, as he is determined not to allow a
man to go out any more with them, having lost already three
men by them, whose lives were too valuable at this post to
be lost on such occasions.   In case of an alarm everybody
to be at their alarm posts, as per order of June the 7th, and
not to run to such parts as where they may hear firing, but
remain at their own posts, and whoever will be found from it
will be punished for disobedience of orders.   The commanding officer recommends to the officers commanding at the
several posts not to suffer the men so easily to throw away
their ammunition without paying a proper attention to the
orders they receive from their officers as to their firing, and
desires they will confine such of them as do not pay a due
observance to their orders on that head.   For guard to-night,
Captain-Lieutenant Phillips, Lieutenants Guy, Milligan and
Christie, 5 sergeants, 1 drummer and 73 rank and file.

Fort Pitt, July 15, 1763.   G. O. Burlington.   For guard to-
night, Captain-Lieutenant Carre, Lieutenants Baillie, Fleming and Greber, 5 sergeants, 1 drummer and 73 rank and file.

Fort Pitt, July 16, 1763.   The garrison to be under arms
to-morrow at 11 o'clock, the company to form before their
barracks, and march to their alarm posts.   The guard to remain at their posts and as soon as the whole are upon the
ramparts the officers are to make their disposition and wait
for further orders.   Garrison weekly returns to be given to-
morrow at 9 o'clock.   All the sickles in the garrison to be put
in good order to-day.   Mr. McCallister and Sergeant Campbell
are desired to have them repaired.   A court-martial to sit at
11 o'clock, Captain-Lieutenant Phillips, President; Lieutenant Donelon (members), Ensign Price.   For guard to-

night Captain-Lieutenant Phillips, Lieutenants Donelon, Price and Davenport, 5 sergeants, 1 drummer, 73 rank and file. After orders Mr. Clarke; the Quartermaster to see the flour belonging to the king most exactly weighed and also the bacon, pork, salt beef, hung beef, rice and salt. The commis-sary to give a true and just return the 22d inst. to the com-manding officer of all the several articles under his care. The troops being served up to that day inclusive, at the same time he is to give in also a return of the provisions belonging to the townspeople.

Fort Pitt, July 17, 1763. G. O. parole Deal. The spelts to be cut to-morrow morning; a covering party of regulars to be under arms to-morrow morning at 5 o'clock, to consist of one captain, 4 subalterns 5 sergeants, 1 drummer, and 80 rank and file, to be distributed as follows; 1 subaltern, 1 sergeant and 20 rank and file men, near the coopers' shop, along the ridge of Hulins field. 1 subaltern, 1 sergeant and 20 rank and file along the Allegheny River, and the captain with 2 subalterns 3 sergeants and 40 rank and file in the centre; besides there will be a party of 1 subaltern and 30 volunteers which will take post upon Grant's Hill. The whole to be under the command of the captain.

For the above duty Captain-Lieutenant Phillips, Lieuten-ant Guy, Baillie, Price, Davenport, 5 sergeants, 1 drummer and 80 regulars.

To take post upon Grant's Hill, Lieutenant Fleming and 30 volunteers. Major Trent will be pleased to find 30 men among the militia to cut and tie the corn. The whole will be covered with cannon and howitzers. The commanding officer of the artillery will give proper directions for that purpose. The whole will take a little bread and cold meat with them, sufficient for a day.

For guard to-night, Captain-Lieutenant Carre, Lieutenants

Milligan, Christy and Greber, 5 sergeants, 1 drummer, 76 rank and file.

Fort Pitt, July 18, 1763. G. O. parole, Brussels. For guard to-night, Captain-Lieutenant Phillips, Lieutenants Baillie and Fleming, 5 sergeants, 1 drummer, 73 rank and file.

Fort Pitt, July 19, 1763. G. O. parole, Bergenupzoom. The people who had cattle taken by the commanding officer's orders, are desired to settle with Mr. Murray, who will pay them at the rate of 4½d per pound.

For guard to-night, Captain-Lieutenant Carre, Lieutenants Donelon, Price and Davenport, 5 sergeants, 1 drummer, 74 rank and file.

Fort Pitt, July 20, 1763. G. O. parole, Peterborrow. The commanding officer is very much surprised to find most of the guards at 3 o'clock in the morning fast asleep in-stead of being under arms from 2 o'clock till broad day, that being a general rule, as well in time of peace as in time of war, to guard against a surprise ; and as a large number of Indians appear about us, the garrison to form two relieves till further orders.

For guard to-night, Captain-Lieutenant Phillips, Lieuten-ants Potts, Baillie, Price, Milligan and Christie, 7 sergeants, 1 drummer, 112 rank and file. They are to take post as follows, viz.:

	CAPT.	LIEUT.	SERG.	D.	R. F.
Grenadier Bastion	1	1	3	1	36
Ohio Bastion		1	1		24
Monongehela Bastion		1	1		20
Music Bastion		1	1		20
Flag Bastion		1	1		12
Total	1	5	7	1	112

Half of the men of each bastion to be on sentry at night, sentinels in the day as usual. The artillery to keep two gunners on each bastion all day. Mr. Price not to mount to-night, he being on guard.

Fort Pitt, July 21, 1763. G. O. parole, Tinmouth. For guard to-night, Captain-Lieutenant Carre, Lieutenants Guy, Donalon, Davenport, Fleming and Greber, 7 sergeants, 1 drummer, and 110 rank and file.

Fort Pitt, July 22, 1763. G. O. parole, Lincoln. For guard to-night, Captain-Lieutenant Phillips, Lieutenants Potts, Baillie, Price, Milligan and Christy, 7 sergeants, 1 drummer, and 112 rank and file.

Fort Pitt, July 23, 1763. G. O. parole, Hanslow. For guard to-night, Captain-Lieutenant Carre, Lieutenants Guy, Donalon, Fleming, Davenport and Greber, 7 sergeants, 1 drummer, 111 rank and file.

Fort Pitt, July, 1763. G. O. parole, Middlesex. A court-martial to sit immediately. Captain-Lieutenant Phillips, President ; Lieutenant Baillie (members), Ensign Hutchins. For guard to-night, Captain-Lieutenant Phillips, Lieutenants Potts, Baillie, Price, Milligan and Christie, seven sergeants, 1 drummer and 112 rank and file. The monthly and garrison returns to be given this evening.

Fort Pitt, July 25, 1763. G. O. parole, Colebrook. For guard to-night, Captain-Lieutenant Carre, Lieutenants Guy, Donalon, Davenport, Fleming and Greber, 7 sergeants, 1 drummer, 112 rank and file.

Fort Pitt, July 26, 1763. G. O. parole, Maidenhead. For guard to-night, Captain-Lieutenant Phillips, Lieutenants Potts, Baillie, Price, Milligan and Christie, 7 sergeants, 1 drummer, 112 rank and file.

Fort Pitt, July 27, 1763. G. O. parole, Hambleton. A working party of one sergeant and eight privates to parade every morning at 5 o'clock to thresh the "spelt,"* when the weather will permit, till it is all done. For guard to-night, Captain-Lieutenant Carre, Lieutenants Guy, Donalon, Davenport, Fleming and Greber, 7 sergeants, 1 drummer, 112 rank and file.

Fort Pitt, July 28, 1763. G. O. parole, Oakham. As several firelocks have gone off at half-cock, an officer of each company to examine all the arms carefully this evening at roll-calling, and have such of them repaired immediately, to prevent further accidents. For guard to-night, Captain-Lieutenant Phillips, Lieutenants Potts, Baillie, Price, Christie and Milligan, 7 sergeants, 1 drummer, 112 rank and file.

Fort Pitt, July 29, 1763. G. O. parole, George. N. B.— Being attacked.

Fort Pitt, July 30, 1763. G. O. parole, Buckingham. A redoubt to be built in Croghan's Point of 18 feet in square, with high and strong pickets and embrasures to it ; for that purpose a party of a sergeant and twelve men to parade to help the carpenters, who are to be kept off duty till further orders.

Fort Pitt, July 31, 1763. G. O. parole, Aberdeen. The relief of guard to march to their several bastions at sunset. The officers to take their posts of alarm as yesternight ; the whole to remain upon the ramparts all night ; the men to be divided into four reliefs for sentries, and if nothing extraordinary happens in the morning, the relief upon guard at present to march to their post at 6 o'clock. The officers commanding at bastions are desired not to allow on any account the men to raise fixed shades against the parapet in the night time, as it would not only very much prevent the men from doing their duty in case of attack, but also stop the passage from sending orders back and forwards when re-

* German wheat.

quired. In the daytime the men may be allowed loose shades, made with their blankets only, which are to be taken off at night. The ship-carpenters to compose part of the reserve, and also the musicians till further orders.

Fort Pitt, August 1, 1763. Parole, Stonehave. As the wood begins to be very scarce, and wanted to carry on the works, the commanding officer desires the garrison once more to be very saving of it, especially the women, who destroy such a quantity in washing and ironing. They are, therefore, for the future, to wash the linen only, without ironing it at all, till we can get more wood. The whole garrison to be acquainted with this order. The relief of guard to march to their bastions at sunset as usual.

Fort Pitt, August 2, 1763. G. O. parole, Bouquet. The commanding officer has the pleasure to inform the garrison than an army arrived at Bedford the 25th of July under the command of Colonel Bouquet and may be expected very shortly at this post, to our relief; also that another army is on their march by the Lakes into the heart of the enemy's country. If any Indians should appear before the fort with green boughs in the muzzles of their guns, they are not to be fired upon, but looked upon as friends, and to be reported to the commanding officer immediately on their appearance. The garrison to take post to-night as usual.

Fort Pitt, August 3, 1763. G. O. parole, Glasgow. The garrison to be divided into two relieves. For guard to-night, Lieutenants Potts, Baillie, Price, Fleming and Milligan, 7 sergeants, 1 drummer, 116 rank and file, the eldest subaltern to command; the whole to take post at the grenadier bastion and to report all extraordinaries to that commanding officer. One-half of the men at each bastion to be sentry at a time.

Fort Pitt, August 4, 1763. G. O. parole, Dublin. A court-martial to set at 11 o'clock; Captain-Lieutenant Phillips, President ; Lieutenant Donelon (members), Ensign Hutchins. For guard to-night, Lieutenants Guy, Donelon, Davenport, Christie and Greber, 6 sergeants, 1 drummer, 106 rank and file.

Fort Pitt, August 5, 1763. G. O. parole, Porchester. For guard to-night, Lieutenants Potts, Baillie, Price, Fleming and Milligan, 6 sergeants, 1 drummer, 106 rank and file.

Fort Pitt, August 6, 1763. G. O. parole, Norwich. For guard to-night, Lieutenants Guy, Donelon, Davenport, Greber and Christie, 6 sergeants, 1 drummer, 106 rank and file.

Fort Pitt, August 7, 1763. G. O. parole, Deptford. For guard to-night, Lieutenants Potts, Baillie, Price, Fleming and Milligan, 6 sergeants, 1 drummer, 106 rank and file.

Fort Pitt, August 8, 1763. G. O. parole, Southampton. For guard to-night, Lieutenants Guy, Donnelon, Davenport, Greber and Christie, 6 sergeants, 1 drummer, 106 rank and file.

Fort Pitt, August 9, 1763. G. O. parole, Petersfield. For guard to-night, Lieutenants Potts, Baillie, Price, Flemming and Milligan, 6 sergeants, 1 drummer, 106 rank and file.

Fort Pitt, August 10, 1763. G. O. parole, King George. For guard to-night, Lieutenants Baillie and Milligan. Garrison orders : The sergeants and corporals on guard to stand fast till to-morrow morning, the guards of the several bastions to join immediately the guard at the grenadier bastion, leaving their sentries posted as usual, and from that bastion the sentries will be relieved till further orders.

Fort Pitt, August 11, 1763. G. O. parole. Countersign. Garrison orders : The guard to be relieved at 10 o'clock. For guard, Ensign Price, 2 sergeants, 1 drummer and 36 rank and file.

Colonel Bouquet orders his thanks to be given to the officers, soldiers and inhabitants who have so bravely de-

fended the post against the repeated attacks of barbarians
and malicious enemies. Captain Ecuyer by his firm and
prudent conduct has obtained the General's entire approbation
and it is with the greatest satisfaction that the Colonel informs him of it. The Colonel takes a particular pleasure in
expressing to Major Trent how agreeable his services and
those performed by the brave militia under his command are
to him, and returns him his sincere thanks for the ready assistance he has constantly given to the commanding officer,
desiring he will inform his officers and men of the grateful sense
the Colonel has of their behavior. Nothing can be more
agreeable to the Colonel than to have to represent to the General the merit of the officers and men who have contributed to
the preservation of this important post, which particularly
curbs the insolence and pride of the faithless savages and con-
tinues an immovable barrier against the impotence of their rage
and perfidy. All the double arms employed in defence of this
post to be drawn and delivered with the ammunition to the
officer of the artillery who will have them put in order. All
the women and children and useless people to hold themselves
in readiness to-morrow night to go to the settlement. A
party to be ready to reap to-morrow morning, who will be
covered by a company of light infantry. The effects of a deceased officer of the 42d Regiment to be sold at vendue to-
morrow morning in camp at 10 o'clock.

For guard to-morrow, Lieutenant Donelon, 1 sergeant, 2
corporals, 1 drummer, 36 privates.

Fort Pitt, August 12, 1763. G. O. parole, Middlesex;
countersign, Allegheny. Two days provisions to be issued
to the detachment immediately, viz.: to the 13th, inclusive.
The regular troops off duty to parade at the front of the
camp at 5 o'clock this afternoon. All the militia to line the
bastions at the same hour. The 60th Regiment to furnish

a captain, 2 subalterns, 2 sergeants, and 60 rank and file, to encamp to-morrow in the line and march with the escort to Ligonier. The same number of the troops of the line under the command of Captain Stewart, of the 42d, are to join the garrison of this fort ; the men most unfit to march are to form this detachment. The rations are reduced till further orders to seven pounds of bread and seven pounds of beef per week.

N. B.—Four pounds of pork is equal to seven pounds of beef. The detachment of the Royal Artillery, and the officers and men of the garrison who have done duty with them, have distinguished themselves in the attack of this fort, and Colonel Bouquet desires that his thanks be particularly given to that corps for their important services on that occasion.

Royal order by Colonel Bouquet : The detachment of Royal Americans that is to march to be completed to thirty rounds per man and three flints each. They are to march without their coats, or any baggage except their blankets. For that duty Captain-Lieutenant Phillips, Lieutenant Baillie and Ensign Price, 2 sergeants, 1 drummer, and 60 rank and file.

Fort Pitt, August 13, 1763.   G. O. parole, Bristol ; countersign St. Andrew. The troops under the command of Major Campbell, consisting of the remains of the 42d and 77th Regiments and a detachment of the Royal Artillery Regiment, are to march this evening for Ligonier, with Captain Barret's Rangers, and take under their escort the women, children and useless people of this garrison, and all the pack-horses, with 200 empty bags. Major of brigade will furnish a list. Commissary Herren and his assistant to march and return with this detachment. Mr. Clinton, mate of the hospital, and Mr. Murdoch, mate of the 42d Regiment, are to return with this detachment and take with them a medicine chest. Mr. Lister to take charge of the sick and wounded of

the 42d Regiment left here, and Dr. McLean of the 77th, and
of all the wounded rangers, pack-horse men or other people
not belonging to the regiment.   The troops above-mentioned,
the women and children, pack-horse, bullock and sheep-
drivers discharged, are to draw bread or flour to the 16th
instant, and pork to the 20th, inclusive.

N. B.—The children to have half a ration only.   Commissary Herren will take sheep to march with that detachment.
A return to be given to the Major of brigade of the horses
wanted for the officers, which Mr. Preter is to furnish.   He is
likewise to lend horses to the women, but not to load any of
them with above 160 pounds weight of baggage.   Axes to be
taken to clear the roads.

After orders : All letters are to be sent this day to Captain
Bassett, who goes express.   It is the commanding officer's
order, no person of any condition whatsoever sends any letters
by anybody else, as they will be destroyed if found, and the
carrier punished for disobedience of orders.

Fort Pitt, August 14, 1763.   G. O parole, Windsor.   For
guard to-morrow two subalterns, three sergeants, four corporals, seventy privates.   For picket to-night, one captain,
one subaltern, three sergeants, four corporals, seventy privates.   Officers for guard, Lieutenant Allen Grant, Lieutenant Greber.   The officers of the picket once every
night to go the rounds.   The picket to parade at retreat
beating, for that duty this night Captain Stewart and Lieutenant Davenport.   Any person knowing of any women and
children being hid in the fort who are ordered away, are to
discover them immediately to the Major of brigade, and whoever dares to screen any of them must be treated with the
utmost severity.   Royal order for guard to-morrow : two sergeants, two corporals, twenty-four privates.   For picket to-
night, one sergeant, one corporal, twenty-four privates.

Fort Pitt, August 15, 1763.   G. O. parole, Harwick.   For guard

Fort Pitt, August 16, 1763.   G. O. parole, Cork.   For guard, 2 subalterns, 3 sergeants, 4 corporals, 61 privates.   For picket, 1 subaltern, 1 sergeant, 1 corporal, 30 privates.   The brigade Major and Major of militia will take an inventory of all the provisions in the fort, including cattle and grain, and all inhabitants who have cattle, dried meat, corn, or any other kind of provisions are to inform the Major of brigade of it, who will order it to be received into the King's store and give certificates for the payment to the owners.   A gill of salt per man to be issued to the troops.   Royal order: for picket tonight, 1 subaltern, 1 sergeant, 1 corporal, 11 privates.   For picket, Ensign Hutchins.   For guard to-morrow: 1 subaltern, 1 sergeant, 3 corporals, 22 privates.   For guard, Lieutenant Donelon.

Fort Pitt, August 17, 1763.   G. O. parole, Darby.   For guard 2 sergeants, 3 subalterns, 4 corporals, 60 privates; for picket, 1 subaltern, 1 sergeant, 4 corporals, 30 privates.   A return of the sick and wounded to be given to the brigade Major by the surgeons, distinguishing those who are to be on full and those on half allowance of provision.   The bridge to be drawn and the gates to be shut at retreat beating.   R. O.   For guard, Ensign Hutchins, 2 sergeants, 2 corporals, 22 privates; for picket, 11 privates.   The men's accounts to be balanced and the men settled with to the 22d July inclusive, being 26 weeks from the time they were last settled with.

New York, April 9, 1763.   Orders.—The Secretary at War having transmitted in a letter to the Commander-in-Chief copies of a letter from the Speaker of the Honorable House of Commons with resolution of that House, the Commander-in-Chief takes the earliest opportunity of communicating the same to the officers under his command, with a copy of the

Secretary at War's letter.   The Commander-in-Chief with the warmest gratitude must express to the officers and soldiers he has the honor to command the pleasure and satisfaction he has in communicating to them this honorable testimony of their services ; and he cannot omit on this occasion to signify to them that their constant steady good conduct, and unwearied exertion of their abilities in carrying on the extensive and successful war in this country, not only entitles them to the most sincere acknowledgments, but has imprinted in him such strong marks of affection and esteem for them, that their happiness and glory must always be inseparable from his.

Signed, WILLIAM AMHERST,
Dy. Adjt. Gen.

[Copy.]

Sir:—The Speaker of the Honorable House of Commons having transmitted in a letter to my office a resolution of that House to give their thanks to the officers of the navy and army, for the meritorious and eminent services they have done to their King and Country during the course of the present war, I send you herewith copies of the said letter and resolution which you will communicate to the officers of the army in North America.   The good conduct, courage and zeal of the officers and soldiers of his majesty's army, so uniformly exerted for the glory and honor of this nation, oblige me at the same time to express the great satisfaction I feel in communicating this public mark of honor conferred upon them, which I beg you will be pleased to signify to the officers and soldiers under your command.

I have the honor to be, Sir, &c.
WILLIAM ELLIS.

[MAJOR-GENERAL SIR GEOFFRY AMHERST, &c., &c., &c.]

Copy of a letter from the Right Honorable Sir John Lust, Bart., Speaker of the Honorable House of Commons, to His Majesty's Secretary at War.   Dated the 9th of December, 1762.

Sir:—In obedience to an order of the House (of) Commons, 1 have the honor of transmitting to you a resolution to which they have this day unanimously agreed.   It is a singular satisfaction to me to receive the commands of the House on this occasion and to convey through you, sir, to the officers of the army, so honorable a testimony of the meritorious and eminent services performed by them for His Majesty and this Nation.

Jovis, 9th Die Decembris, 1762.

Resolved, Nemine Contradecentie—That the thanks of this House be given to the officers of the navy and army for the meritorious and eminent services which they have done to their king and country during the course of the present war, and that Mr. Speaker do signify the same by letter to the commissioners for executing the office of Lord High Admiral of Great Britain, and to His Majesty's Secretary at War. [A true copy.]   H. BOUQUET, *Col.*

Fort Pitt, August 18, 1763.   G. O. parole, Norfolk.   For guard, 2 subalterns, 3 sergeants, 4 corporals, 60 privates. Picket, 1 captain, 1 subaltern, sergeant, 1 corporal, 30 privates. Mr. Jossa. Davenport is appointed captain and Mr. Calhune, lieutenant of the militia, who are to do duty and be obeyed as such.   R. O.   For guard, 0 subaltern, 2 sergeants, 2 corporals, 22 privates.   Picket, 1 sergeant, 1 corporal, 11 privates.

Fort Pitt, August 19, 1763.   G. O., parole, Athlone. For guard, 2 subalterns, 3 sergeants, 4 corporals, 60 privates. Picket, 1 captain, 2 subalterns, 2 sergeants, 2 corporals, 48 privates. Provision returns to be given to the brigade Major signed by the commanding officer of each corps in which are to be included all the people drawing provisions, and underneath to be deducted the rations for the sick and wounded, etc., to be drawn by the hospital. The picket consisting of 1 captain, 2 subalterns, 2 sergeants, 1 drummer and 50 rank and file to parade to-morrow morning at the first signal of the drum to go over the Monongehela with a working party of men to bring coals and lime. The floating battery to be equipped with patteraroes and two artillery men to go in her. The necessary flats and batteaus, bags and tools to be kept ready. The men ordered on this service to take provisions with them, as they are not to return till the evening. One gun will be fired from the fort as a signal for their retreat. The captain of the picket is to receive his instructions from the colonel. R. O. For guard 2 sergeants, 2 corporals, 22 privates. Picket, 1 sergeant, 1 corporal, 18 privates. Some soldiers of the first battalion having very indiscreetly applied this day to the Colonel for their discharge, he orders it to be said to those who may have a right to it, that they must be sensible of the impossibility of discharging them at this critical juncture, when the inhabitants themselves must be detained for the defence of this important post. But they may be assured that they will not be kept a moment longer than the service will absolutely require. And as two of the battalions are to be reduced this will be easily completed without detaining the soldiers who have served out their time. If, after this, any man should be so base as to mention again his discharge during this time of danger, he must expect to be treated with the just indignation and contempt he would incur by a behavior so unbecoming the character of a Briton and a Soldier, and so contrary to the duty we all owe our King and Country.

Fort Pitt, August 20, 1763. G. O. parole, Rochford. For guard, o captain, 2 subalterns, 3 sergeants, 4 corporals, 1 drummer, 60 privates. Picket, 1 captain, 1 subaltern, 1 sergeant, 1 corporal, o drummer, 30 privates. R. O. For guard, Lieutenant Guy, 1 sergeant, 2 corporals, 1 drummer, 22 privates; picket, 1 captain, 1 sergeant, o drummer, 11 privates.

Fort Pitt, August 21, 1763. G. O. parole, Coventry. For guard, o captain, 2 subalterns, 3 sergeants, 4 corporals, 1 drummer, 60 privates ; picket, 1 captain, 1 subaltern, 1 sergeant, 1 corporal, 1 drummer, 30 privates. Weekly returns to be given to the Major of Brigade every Sunday, of the garrison, by the corps, including all the persons who draw provisions ; another of all kinds of provisions in the fort, including grain and cattle ; another of the batteaus and flats, etc. All officers, servants and, in general, every person able to bear arms, to mount the guards and picket in their turn. R. O.: For guard, Lieutenant Donelon, 2 sergeants, 2 corporals, 1 drummer, 22 privates ; picket, 1 sergeant, 1 corporal, o drummer, 11 privates.

Fort Pitt, August 22, 1763. G. O. parole, Suffolk. A company of grenadiers and a company of light infantry to parade to-morrow morning at 6 o'clock, to take possession of Grant's Hill and of the hill on the Monongahela to cover the wood-cutters. Eighty men of the Royal Americans and Militia, with axes and their arms, under the command of two subalterns, to cut wood for the winter. Those who have no axes, to load. The two wagon-masters to have their wagons fitted to haul the logs on the glacis. The ship-carpenters to go out with the wood-cutters, with their axes. The camp to furnish the grass guard. These troops to return in the evening when a gun is fired from the fort. Provisions for the two companies of the line to be carried to them. For guard,

1 subaltern, 1 sergeant, 2 corporals and 36 privates. R. O. For guard to-morrow, 1 sergeant, 2 corporals, 21 privates; for fatigue, Lieutenant Guy, 4 sergeants, 4 corporals and 46 privates.

Fort Pitt, August 23, 1763. G. O. parole, Charlestown. A company of grenadiers and a company of light infantry to cover the working party to-morrow, to parade at 6 o'clock. The same number of Royal Americans and Militia to parade to-morrow morning at 6 o'clock, as was to-day, for the working party. A man of the mess to be left to receive and cook the provisions. No soldier to go into the gardens on any account, nor any of the rails to be burnt. R. O. For guard to-morrow, Ensign Hutchins, 0 sergeant, 1 corporal, 21 privates; fatigue, Lieutenant Baillie, 4 sergeants, 4 corporals, 46 privates. The monthly returns to be given in to-morrow.

Fort Pitt, August 24, 1763. G. O. parole, Birmingham. R. O. A court-martial to sit at 4 o'clock this afternoon to examine the accounts and vouchers which Lieutenant Phillips will lay before them concerning the effects of the late Captain Mather, deceased, and to certify the same at the bottom of the general account, to be transmitted to his heirs.

For the above duty Captain Ecuyer, President; Lieutenant Bailey (members), Ensign Price.

When the men's accounts are balanced, the men to be completed with necessaries and the balance paid them to July 22d, inclusive, which when done the commanding officers of companies to report the same to the commanding officer. G. O. For guard: 1 sergeant, 1 subaltern, 2 corporals, 1 drummer, 36 privates the working party of this day. The wagons to make four trips in the forenoon and two in the afternoon. Only one light infantry company to cover them with 12 men from the force. Captain Grant's Light Infantry company to be ready for duty to-morrow morning at 9 o'clock.   All the women ordered down, to be ready to go the 26th in the morning with their children.   The commanding officer orders all the dogs to be sent down with the escort, as those seen here afterwards will be killed.   The officers, if they choose it, may keep one each. R. O. For guard: 1 sergeant, 2 corporals, 21 privates. For fatigue, Lieutenant Guy, 4 sergeants, 4 corporals, 46 privates.

Fort Pitt, August 25, 1763. G. O. parole, Nottingham. For guard, 1 sergeant, 1 subaltern, 2 corporals, 1 drummer, 36 privates, the wood cutting party as this day.   The wagons to make four trips and then leave off.   One light infantry company to cover with 12 men from the grass guard. R. O. For guard, 0 sergeant, 1 subaltern, 1 corporal, 21 privates; for fatigue, Ensign Price: 0 sergeant, 4 subalterns, 4 corporals, 46 privates.

Fort Pitt, August 26, 1763. G. O., Blenheim: A detachment of Royal Americans of 2 subalterns, 2 sergeants, 1 drummer and 50 rank and file to encamp this afternoon in the line and march with the troops to-morrow; they will be replaced by 1 captain, 2 subalterns, 3 sergeants and 50 rank and file of the 42d and 77th Regiments.   A detachment of 2 lieutenants, 1 sergeant and 25 men of the militia to march to Bedford and return with the first convoy.   All the wounded, sick or invalids of any of the corps here, which the surgeon will judge able to go down, to be inside with the wagons. The surgeons or mates of the regiments to march with their different corps.   All the sick and wounded here to be left under the care of mates of the hospital.   The remains of the 42d and 77th Regiments with the detachment of the 60th and of the militia to march to-morrow morning under the command of Major Campbell, taking under their escort all the wagons and pack-horses. Mr. Clark, Quartermaster of the

60th, will give this afternoon to the women and children, ordered down, the number of the wagons allotted to them and do the same for the sick and wounded not able to walk. The baggage of the troops to go in the wagons and no pack horses to be loaded in going down. The troops and other persons going down to be served with bread to the 29th inst., and meat to the 2d of September, inclusive, in which will be included some live cattle for the officers, the sick and wounded. The salt meat to be served this afternoon and the bread to-morrow morning. A return to be given in immediately for what ammunition is wanting to be completed—36 rounds per man. R. O. For the above detailment: Lieutenant Carre and Donelon, 2 sergeants, 2 corporals, 1 drummer and 48 privates. The men who are going on detachment to-morrow morning that are not yet settled with, to have their accounts balanced immediately and the balance paid them, also eight weeks subsistence to be given to Lieutenant Carre for (each) man going on detachment.

Fort Pitt, August 27, 1763. G. O. parole, Lisbon. R. O. For guard, Lieutenant Baillie, 1 sergeant, 1 corporal, 1 drummer, 20 privates. For picket, 12 privates.

Fort Pitt, August 28, 1763. Parole, Brunswick. For guard, 0 captain, 2 subalterns, 3 sergeants, 4 corporals, 1 drummer, 15 privates. For picket, 1 captain, 1 subaltern, 1 sergeant, 1 corporal, 0 drummer, 24 privates. No soldier to go out of the fort without leave from the commanding officer of his company or detachment, who will not grant it without a sufficient reason. The sentries are not to suffer anyone to pass the gates or sally-ports without a verbal order from an officer, as it is probable the savages will soon be skulking again about the fort. The officer of the grass guard will keep his guard and sentries very alert, that on the first appearance of an enemy the cattle may be brought near unto the fort.

That officer is not to suffer any person to straggle for plums, as they will be in evident danger of being scalped. The gates of the fort are not to be opened without an order from the commanding officer, the sally-port toward the Monongahela will be opened every day in the following manner: The captain, with a sergeant, a corporal and 8 men of his picket will every morning at 7 o'clock, if the weather is clear (if not, after the fog is gone), open that sally-port and shut it again, then open the barrier toward the point of the two rivers, send out a corporal and four privates to reconnoitre the banks all round and going through come back along the Monongahela to the other barrier, which, upon their report, will then be opened for the cattle to go out; the first barrier to the west is to be locked again as soon as the corporal and 4 men are out. All horses and cows to be kept out of the fort with the King's cattle and sent along with the grass guard, to prevent their going into the corn-fields.

R. O. For guard to-night, Ensign Price, 1 sergeant, 1 corporal, 1 drummer, 14 privates. For picket to-night, Captain-Lieutenant Phillips, Ensign Hutchins, 1 sergeant, 1 corporal, 1 drummer, 11 privates. For guard to-morrow, Ensign Hutchins, 1 sergeant, 2 corporals, 0 drummer, 24 privates. For picket to-morrow, 0 sergeant, 1 corporal, 0 drummer, 11 privates.

Fort Pitt, August 29, 1763. G. O. parole, Portland. For guard to-morrow, 0 captain, 2 subalterns, 3 sergeants, 4 corporals, 1 drummer, 50 privates. For picket, to-night, 1 captain, 1 subaltern, 1 sergeant, 1 corporal, 1 drummer, 24 privates. R. O. For the garrison guard to-morrow evening, 0 captain, 0 subaltern, 1 sergeant, 1 corporal, 0 drummer, 15 privates. For the bullock guard to-morrow morning, 0 captain, 0 subaltern, 0 sergeant, 2 corporals, 0 drummer, 9 privates. For picket to-morrow night, Captain Ecuyer, Lieutenant Baillie,

0 captain, 0 subaltern, 0 sergeant, 0 corporal, 0 drummer, 11 privates.

Fort Pitt, August 30, 1763. G. O. parole, Lisbon. For guard to-morrow, 0 captain, 2 subalterns, 3 sergeants, 4 corporals, 1 drummer, 50 privates. For picket, 1 captain, 1 subaltern, 1 sergeant, 1 corporal, 1 drummer, 24 privates. The commanding officer desires that nobody goes near any person that has smallpox, except the doctor and the people attending them, who are themselves to be very careful not to go near any person that has not had them. R. O. For bullock guard to-morrow morning, Lieutenant Baillie, 1 sergeant, 1 corporal, 8 privates. For the garrison guard to-morrow evening, 1 sergeant, 2 corporals, 15 privates. For picket to-morrow evening, 1 sergeant, 0 corporal, 10 privates.

Fort Pitt, August 31, 1763. G. O. parole, Pensacola. For guard to-morrow, 0 captain, 2 subalterns, 3 sergeants, 3 corporals, 1 drummer, 50 privates. For picket to-morrow, 1 captain, 1 subaltern, 1 sergeant, 1 corporal, 1 drummer, and 24 privates. In case of any alarm the troops are immediately to repair to the following posts, viz.: Bastions, Ohio, the 42d Regiment.

Grenadier: The grenadier company, Captain Cochran's company, Captain Ecuyer's company, of the 60th Regiment.

Music: Colonel Provost's company, Colonel Bouquet's company, Captain Gordon's company, of the 60th Regiment. Flag, the 77th Regiment. Monongahela the militia. The reserve to be in the area of the fort, which is to consist of the storekeeper, contractor, artificers, butcher, baker, bullock and sheep drivers. The King's and contractor's clerks, etc., under the command of Captain Trent. A list to be given in by corps of the names of such persons who have not had the smallpox. The garrison to be under arms to-morrow at 7 o'clock. The guard to join, leaving the sentries at their posts. N. B.—The

redoubt guard and the corporal and six, with the cattle to
standfast. R. O. For the bullock guard to-morrow morning, Ensign Price, 1 sergeant, 1 corporal and 8 privates.
Guard to-morrow evening, 1 corporal, 15 privates. Evening,
Ensign Hutchins, 1 sergeant, 1 corporal, 10 privates. After
orders : A court of inquiry to be held to-morrow morning at
10 o'clock. Captain Stewart, President ; Captain Hay and
Captain Ecuyer, members. The President to wait on the
commanding officer for his instructions.

Fort Pitt, September 1, 1763. G. O. parole, Colchester.
For guard to-morrow, o captain, 2 subalterns, 3 sergeants, 4
corporals, 1 drummer, 50 privates. Picket to-morrow, 1 captain, 1 subaltern, 1 sergeant, 1 corporal, 1 drummer, 24 privates. The men to turn out to work at the beating of the
long roll, and to leave off on the beating of the three ruffs.
R. O. For guard to-morrow morning, Ensign Hutchins, 1
sergeant, 2 corporals, 9 privates. For guard to-morrow evening, 1 sergeant, 1 corporal, 15 privates. For picket to-morrow evening, Captain-Lieutenant Phillips, 1 corporal, 11 privates.

Fort Pitt, September 2, 1763. G. O. Parole, Kingston.
For guard to-morrow, o captain, 3 subalterns, 2 sergeants, 4
corporals, 1 drummer, 50 privates. For picket to-morrow, 1
captain, 1 subaltern, 1 sergeant, 1 corporal, 1 drummer, 24
privates. R. O's For bullock guard to-morrow morning, 1
sergeant, 1 corporal, 9 privates. For guard to-morrow evening, Lieutenant Baillie, 1 sergeant, 2 corporals, 15 privates.
For picket to-morrow evening, 1 corporal, 11 privates.

Fort Pitt, September 3, 1763. G. O. parole, Louisburgh.
For guard, 2 subalterns, 3 sergeants, 4 corporals, 1 drummer, 50 privates. For picket, 1 captain, 1 subaltern, 1 sergeant, 1 corporal, 1 drummer, 24 privates. A court of inquiry to be held immediately to inquire into the effects left

by the late Captain Clapham, and to settle his affairs as far
as it can be done here. Captain Barnsley, President; Captain Trent and Captain Davenport, members. The garrison
to be under arms to-morrow morning at 9 o'clock. R. O.
For the bullock guard to-morrow morning, 1 sergeant, 1 corporal, 9 privates. For guard to-morrow evening, Ensign Price,
1 corporal, 15 privates. For picket to-morrow evening, Captain Ecuyer, Ensign Hutchins, 1 sergeant, 1 corporal, 11 privates.

Fort Pitt, September 4, 1763. G. O. parole, Kingston.
For guard to-morrow, 2 subalterns, 3 sergeants, 4 corporals, 1 drummer, 50 privates. For picket to-morrow, 1
captain, 1 subaltern, 1 sergeant, 1 corporal, 1 drummer, 24
privates. R. O. For bullock guard to-morrow morning, 1
sergeant, 2 corporals, 9 privates. For guard to-morrow evening, Ensign Hutchins, 1 sergeant, 2 corporals, 15 privates.
For picket to-morrow evening, 11 privates. All the men off
duty to parade to-morrow morning at 7 o'clock, with their
arms, in order to cut fascines. No washing to be allowed at
either of the pumps or wells. The sentry in the area of the
fort to observe that this order is strictly obeyed.

Fort Pitt, September 5, 1763. G. O. parole, Tunbridge.
For guard to-morrow, 2 subalterns, 3 sergeants, 4 corporals, 1
drummer, 50 privates. For picket to-morrow, 1 captain, 1 subaltern, 1 sergeant, 1 corporal, 1 drummer, 24 privates. The
captain of the picket to visit the hospital every morning, the
subalterns every afternoon, who are to take notice if the rooms
are kept clean and the sick and wounded are properly attended.
The adjutants to visit the barrack rooms once every day to
see that they are kept clean and in good order, the two adjutants to take this duty week about. One captain, 1 subaltern, 2 sergeants, 2 corporals and 50 men to parade to-
morrow morning, with their arms, in order to cut fascines.

R. O. For the bullock guard to morrow, 2 sergeants, 1 corporal, 9 privates. For guard to-morrow evening, 1 corporal, 15 privates. For picket to-morrow evening, Ensign Price, 1 sergeant, 1 corporal, 11 privates.

Fort Pitt, September 6, 1763. G. O. Parole, Worchester. For guard to-morrow, 2 subalterns, 3 sergeants, 4 corporals, 1 drummer, 50 privates. For picket to-morrow, 1 captain, 1 subaltern, 1 sergeant, 1 corporal, 1 drummer, 24 privates. Any person that can give information concerning the effects, accounts of debtor, credits or any other thing relating to the late Mr. Wm. Clapham, are desired to communicate them to the court of inquiry to-morrow morning at 10 o'clock, at Captain Barnsley's room. For bullock guard to-morrow morning, Lieutenant Baillie, 1 sergeant, 1 corporal, 9 privates. For guard to-morrow evening, 1 corporal, 15 privates. For picket to-morrow evening, 11 privates.

Fort Pitt, September 7, 1763. G. O. Parole, New Castle. For guard to-morrow, 0 captain, 2 subalterns, 3 sergeants, 4 corporals, 1 drummer, 50 privates ; for picket to-morrow, 1 captain, 1 subaltern, 1 sergeant, 1 corporal, 1 drummer, 24 privates. All the men off duty to parade to-morrow morning in order to repair the ramparts and clean the fort, etc. R. O. For the bullock guard to-morrow morning, Ensign Price, 1 sergeant, 2 corporals, 9 privates ; for guard to-morrow evening, 1 sergeant, 1 corporal, 15 privates ; for picket to-morrow evening, Ensign Hutchins, 1 sergeant, 1 corporal, 11 privates.

Fort Pitt, September 8, 1763. G. O. Parole, Carlisle. For guard to-morrow, 0 captain, 2 subalterns, 3 sergeants, 4 corporals, 1 drummer, 50 privates ; for picket to-morrow, 1 captain, 1 subaltern, 1 sergeant, 1 corporal, 1 drummer, 24 privates. R. O. For the bullock guard to-morrow morning, Ensign Hutchins, 0 sergeant, 1 corporal, 9 privates ; for guard to-morrow evening, 1 sergeant, 2 corporals, 15 privates; for picket to-morrow evening, Captain Ecuyer, o sergeant, 1 corporal, 11 privates.

Fort Pitt, September 9, 1763. G. O. Parole, Gravesend. For guard to-morrow, o captain, 2 subalterns, 3 sergeants, 4 corporals, 1 drummer, 50 privates; for picket to-morrow, 1 captain, 1 subaltern, 1 sergeant, 1 corporal, 1 drummer, 24 privates. R. O. For the bullock guard to-morrow morning, 1 sergeant, 1 corporal, 9 privates; for guard to-morrow evening, Lieutenant Baillie, 1 corporal, 15 privates; for picket to-morrow evening, 1 corporal, 11 privates.

Fort Pitt, September 10, 1763. G. O. Parole, Killdare. For guard to-morrow, o captain, 2 subalterns, 3 sergeants, 4 corporals, 1 drummer, 50 privates; for picket to-morrow, 1 captain, 1 subaltern, 1 sergeant, 1 corporal, 1 drummer, 24 privates. The garrison to be under arms to-morrow at 9 o'clock. A pint of Indian corn to be served out to each man. R. O. For the bullock guard to-morrow morning, 1 sergeant, 2 corporals, 9 privates; for guard to-morrow evening, Ensign Price, 1 sergeant, 1 corporal, 15 privates; for picket to-morrow evening, Ensign Hutchins, 1 sergeant, o corporal, 11 privates.

Fort Pitt, September 11, 1763. Parole, Orkney. For guard to-morrow, o captain, 2 subalterns, 3 sergeants, 4 corporals, 1 drummer, 50 privates; for picket to-morrow, 1 captain, 1 subaltern, 1 sergeant, 1 corporal, 1 drummer, 24 privates. For Court of Inquiry to be held to-morrow morning at 10 o'clock. Captain Stewart, President; Captain Hay (members), Captain-Lieutenant Phillips.

To inquire into the reasons of the loss of Presque Isle and Le Bœuf. Ensign Price and all evidences to attend the court.

His Excellency, Sir Geoffry Amherst, has been pleased to

appoint Lieutenant Belnearis, of the Royal Highlanders, Captain-Lieutenant and Mr. Robt. Peples, gentleman, to be ensign in the said regiment, who are to be obeyed as such.

New York, July 19, 1763.—Orders.—His Excellency, the Commander-in-Chief, having received from His Majesty's Secretary of State, a copy of the Proclamation of Peace, thinks proper to make the same known, that it may be duly observed.

WHEREAS, a definitive treaty of peace and friendship between us, the most Christian King, and the King of Spain, to which the King of Portugal hath acceded, hath been concluded at Paris on the 10th day of February last, and the ratification thereof have been exchanged on the 10th day of this inst. (March). In conformity thereunto we have thought fit hereby to command that the same be published throughout all our Dominions, and we do declare to all our loving subjects our will and pleasure, that the said treaty of peace and friendship be observed inviolable as well by sea as land, and in all places whatsoever. Strictly charging and commanding all our loving subjects to take notice hereof and conform themselves thereunto accordingly.

The King's pleasure is that the clothing for all regiments in America shall be delivered out every year on the 22d day of September, being the day of His Majesty's coronation.

(Signed)   WM. AMHERST,
Adjutant-General.

R. O.   For the bullock guard to-morrow morning, 1 sergeant, 1 corporal, 9 privates ; for guard to-morrow evening, Ensign Hutchins, o sergeant, 2 corporals, 15 privates ; for picket to-morrow evening, Captain-Lieutenant Phillips, 1 sergeant, 11 privates.

Fort Pitt, September 12, 1763.   G. O. parole, Jamaica.

For guard to-morrow, o captain, 2 subalterns, 3 sergeants, 4 corporals, 1 drummer, 50 privates; for picket to-morrow, 1 captain, 1 subaltern, 1 sergeant, 1 corporal, 1 drummer, 24 privates. None of the wood now in the fort to be used for fire—that is, to be cut upon the glacis. No other sick to be returned and exempted of doing duty, but such as the surgeons shall return as unfit. The reports of the guards, etc., are to be given every morning to the colonel at 10 o'clock. When anything new occurs he is to be immediately informed. R. O. For the bullock guard to-morrow morning, 1 sergeant, 1 corporal, 9 privates; for guard to-morrow evening, 1 sergeant, 1 corporal, 15 privates; for picket to-morrow evening, Lieutenant Baillie, o sergeant, 1 corporal, 11 privates.

Fort Pitt, September 13, 1763. G. O. parole, Tobago. For guard to-morrow, o captain, 2 subalterns, 3 sergeants, 4 corporals, 1 drummer, 50 privates; for picket to-morrow, 1 captain, 1 subaltern, 1 sergeant, 1 corporal, 1 drummer, 24 privates. R. O. For the bullock guard to-morrow morning, Lieutenant Baillie, o sergeant, 2 corporals, 9 privates; for guard to-morrow evening, 1 sergeant, 1 corporal, 15 privates; for picket to-morrow evening, Captain Ecuyer, o sergeant, 1 corporal, 11 privates.

Fort Pitt, September 14, 1763. G. O. parole, Halifax. For guard to-morrow, o captain, 2 subalterns, 3 sergeants, 4 corporals, 1 drummer, 50 privates; for picket to-morrow, 1 captain, 1 subaltern, 1 sergeant, 1 corporal, 1 drummer, 24 privates. R. O. For the bullock guard to-morrow morning, Ensign Price, 1 sergeant, 1 corporal, 9 privates; for guard to-morrow evening, o sergeant, 2 corporals, 15 privates; for picket, Ensign Hutchins, 1 sergeant, 1 corporal, 11 privates.

Fort Pitt, September 15, 1763. G. O. parole, Crown Point For guard to-morrow, o captain, 2 subalterns, 3 sergeants,

4 corporals, 1 drummer, 50 privates ; for picket to-morrow, o captain, o subaltern, 1 sergeant, 1 corporal, 1 drummer, 24 privates.   At any time that a cannon is fired from the fort all parties out are to come in.   The grass guard and other parties going out of the fort are either to march in file or in a rank entire, and the soldiers must keep from three to five paces distance between one another.   The King's Commissary to be present when beeves or sheep are killed, and, if the meat does not appear to him fit to be issued, he is to report it to the Major of brigade to have it inspected and regularly condemned.   R. O.   For the bullock guard to-morrow morning, Ensign Hutchins, 1 sergeant, 1 corporal, 12 privates ; for guard to-morrow evening, o sergeant, 1 corporal, 12 privates ; for picket to-morrow evening, o sergeant, 1 corporal, 11 privates.

Fort Pitt, September 16, 1763.   G. O. parole, Leeds. For guard to-morrow, o captain, 2 subalterns, 3 sergeants, 4 corporals, 1 drummer, 50 privates ; for picket to-morrow, 1 captain, 1 subaltern, 1 sergeant, 1 corporal, 1 drummer, 24 privates.   R. O.   For the bullock guard to-morrow morning, 2 sergeants, 2 corporals, 12 privates ; for guard to-morrow evening, Lieutenant Baillie, o sergeant, 1 corporal, 12 privates ; for picket, Captain-Lieutenant Phillips, 1 sergeant, o corporal, 11 privates.

Fort Pitt, September 17, 1763.   G. O. parole, Guernsey. For guard to-morrow, o captain, 2 subalterns, 3 sergeants, 4 corporals, 50 privates ; for picket to-morrow, 1 captain, 1 subaltern, 1 sergeant, 1 corporal, 24 privates.   The captains or officers who pay companies are from this day, inclusive, to keep into their hands four shillings, New York currency, per week from the pay of every sergeant, corporal, drummer and soldier, and will account for the same to their men when they receive orders for that purpose ; and they are in the meantime to pay them only the remaining part of their subsistence, in money or in such necessaries as they may want; this order to be observed by the detachment of Royal Artillery and all the regular troops in this department. The garrison to be under arms to-morrow morning at 10 o'clock. The Artificers and men attending them are not to parade. R. O. For guard to-morrow, o captain, 1 subaltern, o sergeant, 1 corporal, o drummer, 11 privates; for picket to-morrow, 1 captain, o subaltern, 1 sergeant, o corporal, o drummer, 6 privates; for bullock guard, Lieutenant Calhoun, o subaltern, o sergeant, o corporal, o drummer, 6 privates; Captain Trent for picket.

Fort Pitt, Sunday, September 18, 1763. Parole, Quebec. G. O. For guard to-morrow, o captain, 2 subalterns, 3 sergeants, 4 corporals, 50 privates; for picket to-morrow, 1 captain, 1 subaltern, 1 sergeant, 1 corporal, 24 privates. All the men off duty to go out to cut the tops and leaves of corn as soon as the fog hath cleared up. The picket to cover them. R. O. For guard to-morrow, o captain, o subaltern, 1 sergeant, 1 corporal, 11 privates; for picket to-morrow, Lieutenant Fleming, o captain, 1 subaltern, o sergeant, 1 corporal, 6 privates; for bullock guard to-morrow, o captain, o subaltern, 1 sergeant, 1 corporal, 6 privates.

Fort Pitt, Monday, September 19, 1763. Parole, Bermudas. For guard to-morrow, o captain, 2 subalterns, 3 sergeants, 4 corporals, 50 privates; for picket to-morrow, 1 captain, 1 subaltern, 1 sergeant, 1 corporal, 24 privates. R. O. For guard to-morrow, o captain, 1 subaltern, 1 sergeant, o corporal, 11 privates; for picket to-morrow, Captain Davenport, o subaltern, 1 sergeant, o corporal, 6 privates; for bullock guard to-morrow morning, Lieutenant Fleming, 1 sergeant, o corporal, 6 privates.

Fort Pitt, Tuesday, September 20, 1763. G. O. parole,

Williamsburgh. For guard to-morrow, o captain, 2 subalterns, 3 sergeants, 4 corporals, 50 privates ; for picket to-morrow, 1 captain, 1 subaltern, 1 sergeant, 1 corporal, 24 privates. The men off duty to parade to-morrow morning for work to finish the drains and to level the barrack yard. R. O. For guard to-morrow, o captain, 1 subaltern, 1 sergeant, 1 corporal, 11 privates ; for picket to-morrow, o captain, o subaltern, o sergeant, o corporal, 6 privates ; for the bullock guard to-morrow, Lieutenant Calhoun, o captain, o subaltern, 1 sergeant, 1 corporal, 6 privates.

Fort Pitt, September 21, 1763. G. O. parole, Goree. For guard to-morrow, o captain, 2 subalterns, 3 sergeants, 4 corporals, 50 privates ; for picket to-morrow, 1 captain, 1 subaltern, 1 sergeant, 1 corporal, 24 privates. R. O. For guard to-morrow, o captain, o subaltern, o sergeant, 1 corporal, 11 privates ; for picket to-morrow, Captain Trent, o subaltern, o sergeant, o corporal, 6 privates ; for bullock guard, o captain, o subaltern, o sergeant, 1 corporal, 6 privates.

Fort Pitt, September 22, 1763. G. O. parole, Oswego. For guard to-morrow, o captain, 2 subalterns, 3 sergeants, 4 corporals, 50 privates ; for picket to-morrow, 1 captain, 1 subaltern, 1 sergeant, 1 corporal, 24 privates. R. O. For guard to-morrow, o captain, 1 subaltern, o sergeant, 1 corporal, 11 privates ; for picket to-morrow, Lieutenant Calhoun, 1 subaltern, o sergeant, 1 corporal, 6 privates ; for bullock guard to-morrow, o captain, o subaltern, 1 sergeant, o corporal, 6 privates.

Fort Pitt, Friday, September 23, 1763. G. O. parole, Charlestown. For guard to-morrow, o captain, 2 subalterns, 3 sergeants, 4 corporals, 50 privates ; for picket to-morrow, 1 captain, 1 subaltern, 1 sergeant, 1 corporal, 24 privates. R. O. For guard to-morrow, o captain, o subaltern, o sergeant, 1 corporal, 11 privates ; for picket to-morrow, o captain, o sub-

altern, 1 sergeant, 0 corporal, 6 privates; for bullock guard
to-morrow, 0 captain, 0 subaltern, 0 sergeant, 1 corporal, 6
privates.

Fort Pitt, Saturday, September 24, 1763. G. O. parole,
Piedmont. For guard to-morrow, 0 captain, 2 subalterns, 3
sergeants, 4 corporals, 50 privates; for picket to-morrow, 1
captain, 1 subaltern, 1 sergeant, 1 corporal, 24 privates. No
parade to-morrow morning. One pint of Indian corn to be
given to each man to-morrow. The monthly return to be
given to-morrow at orderly time. R. O. For guard to-
morrow, 0 captain, 1 subaltern, 1 sergeant, 1 corporal, 11
privates; for picket to-morrow, 0 captain, 0 subaltern, 0 sergeant, 0 corporal, 6 privates; for bullock guard, Lieutenant
Calhoun, 0 subaltern, 1 sergeant, 1 corporal, 6 privates.

Fort Pitt, Sunday, September 25, 1763. G. O. parole,
Louisburgh. For guard to-morrow, 0 captain, 2 subalterns, 3
sergeants, 4 corporals, 50 privates; for picket to-morrow, 1
captain, 1 subaltern, 1 sergeant, 1 corporal, 24 privates. For
work to-morrow morning at half after seven, 1 officer, 1 sergeant, 1 corporal, 30 men of the garrison, who are to work
four hours and to be relieved in the afternoon by the same
number, who are to work from half-past one to half-past five.
The subaltern of the picket takes the command of the working
party. The grass guard are to take their dinners with them,
and no man to be allowed to carry them provision. R. O.
For guard to-morrow, 0 captain, 0 subaltern, 1 sergeant, 0
corporal, 11 privates; for picket to-morrow, 1 captain, 1 subaltern, 0 sergeant, 0 corporal, 6 privates. Captain Trent and
Lieutenant Fleming for picket.

Fort Pitt, September 26, 1763. G. O. parole, Montreal.
For guard to-morrow, 2 subalterns, 3 sergeants, 4 corporals,
50 privates; for picket to-morrow, 1 captain, 1 subaltern,
1 sergeant, 1 corporal, 24 privates. R. O. For guard to-

morrow, 1 subaltern, 1 sergeant, 1 corporal, 11 privates; for picket to-morrow, Lieutenant Fleming, 1 subaltern, 1 sergeant, 1 corporal, 6 privates.

Fort Pitt, September 27, 1763.   G. O. parole, Norwich. For guard to-morrow, 2 subalterns, 3 sergeants, 4 corporals, 50 privates.   For picket, 1 captain, 1 subaltern, 1 sergeant, 1 corporal, 24 privates.   For work, 30 privates.

A court of enquiry, of Captain Stewart, Captain Hay and Captain-Lieutenant Phillips, is to sit to-morrow morning at 10 o'clock, to examine into the cause of the deficiency of 16,308 lbs. of flour, discovered in the King's store at this post in July last; the commissary to attend, and such persons who can give any information to the court.

R. O. For guard to-morrow, 1 subaltern, 1 sergeant, 1 corporal, 11 privates.   For picket, 1 captain, 6 privates.   Bullock guard, 1 corporal, 6 privates.   Working party, 7 privates.   For guard to-morrow, Lieutenant Calhoun and Captain Davenport.

Fort Pitt, Wednesday, September 28, 1763.   G. O. parole, Poole.   For guard to-morrow, 2 subalterns, 3 sergeants, 4 corporals, 50 privates.   For picket, 1 captain, 1 subaltern, 1 sergeant, 1 corporal, 24 privates.   R. O. For guard, 11 privates. Bullock guard, 6 privates.   For picket, 1 sergeant, 6 privates. Working party, 7 privates.

Fort Pitt, Thursday, September 29, 1763.   G. O. parole, Minden.   For guard to-morrow, 2 subalterns, 3 sergeants, 4 corporals, 50 privates.   For picket, 1 captain, 1 subaltern, 1 sergeant, 1 corporal, 24 privates.   The commanding officer orders that the sergeants, drummers, corporals and soldiers receive their subsistence as it was usual before his orders of the 17th inst., and the four shillings New York currency stopped from their pay in consequence of the said order be made good to them.   An express will be dispatched to-morrow for Detroit, the 1st of October another for Philadelphia.

The letters to be sent to the Major of Brigade. R. O. For guard to-morrow, 1 subaltern, 1 sergeant, 1 corporal, 11 privates. Bullock guard, 6 privates. For picket, 1 captain, 6 privates. Working party, 7 privates. Lieutenant Fleming for guard, Lieutenant Calhoun for picket.

Fort Pitt, Friday, September 30, 1763. Parole, Torbay. For guard to-morrow, 1 captain, 1 subaltern, 2 sergeants, 3 corporals, 44 privates; for picket to-morrow, 1 captain, 1 subaltern, 1 sergeant, 1 corporal, 21 privates. R. O. For guard to-morrow: 0 captain, 1 subaltern, 1 sergeant, 1 corporal, 11 privates; bullock guard, 0 captain, 0 subaltern, 0 sergeant, 0 corporal, 6 privates; for picket to-morrow, 1 captain, 1 subaltern, 1 sergeant, 6 privates; working party, 0 captain, 0 subaltern, 0 sergeant, 0 corporal, 7 privates.

Fort Pitt, October 1, 1763. Parole, New Castle. G. O. For guard to-morrow, 0 captain, 1 subaltern, 2 sergeants, 3 corporals, 44 privates; for picket, 1 captain, 1 subaltern, 1 sergeant, 21 privates. The men to be served with a pint of corn each to-morrow. R. O. For guard to-morrow, 0 captain, 1 subaltern, 0 sergeant, 1 corporal, 11 privates; for picket to-morrow, 1 captain, 0 subaltern, 0 sergeant, 0 corporal, 6 privates; for bullock guard to-morrow, 0 captain, 0 subaltern, 0 sergeant, 0 corporal, 5 privates. Lieutenant Calhune for guard, Captain Davenport for picket.

Fort Pitt, Sunday, October 2, 1763. G. O. parole, Eaton. For guard to-morrow, 0 captain, 1 subaltern, 2 sergeants, 3 corporals, 44 privates; for picket to-morrow, 1 captain, 1 subaltern, 1 sergeant, 1 corporal, 21 privates. R. O. For guard, 0 captain, 0 subaltern, 1 sergeant, 0 corporal, 11 privates; bullock guard, 1 sergeant, 0 corporal, 5 privates; for picket, 1 subaltern, 0 corporal, 6 privates; working party, 0 sergeant, 0 corporal, 7 privates.

Fort Pitt, Monday, October 3, 1763. G. O. parole, Cardigan. For guard to-morrow, 0 captain, 1 subaltern, 2 sergeants, 3 corporals, 44 privates; for picket to-morrow, 1 captain, 1 subaltern, 1 sergeant, 1 corporal, 21 privates. R. O. For guard to-morrow, 0 captain, 0 subaltern, 1 sergeant, 1 corporal, 11 privates; bullock guard, 0 captain, 0 subaltern, 0 sergeant, 1 corporal, 5 privates; for picket to-morrow, 0 captain, 1 subaltern, 0 sergeant, 0 corporal, 6 privates; working party, 0 captain, 0 subaltern, 0 sergeant, 0 corporal, 7 privates. Lieutenant McKee with a sergeant, a corporal and 30 men, to go to Mr. Croghan's plantation to-morrow morning at 8 o'clock, who are to take a batteau with them in order to bring down staves for casks, etc. Any person having claims against the Crown to deliver their accounts forthwith to the Major of brigade, with the vouchers, that they may be settled and transmitted to the General. The grass guard to report to the officer of the main guard, who is (to) include it in his report to the commanding officers. R. O. For guard, 0 captain, 0 subaltern, 1 sergeant, 2 corporals, 10 privates; body guard, 1 sergeant, 1 corporal, 4 privates; for picket, 0 captain, 1 subaltern, 1 sergeant, 0 corporal, 5 privates; working party, 0 sergeant, 0 corporal, 6 privates. Lieutenant Calhune for picket to-morrow.

Fort Pitt, Tuesday, October 4, 1763. Parole, Embden. G. O. For guard to-morrow, 1 subaltern, 1 sergeant, 1 corporal, 40 privates; for picket to-morrow, 1 captain, 1 subaltern, 1 sergeant, 1 corporal, 21 privates. R. O. For guard, 1 sergeant, 1 corporal, 11 privates; for picket, 1 captain, 1 corporal, 5 privates; bullock guard 4, working party, 7 privates. Captain Trent for picket to-morrow.

Fort Pitt, Wednesday, October 5, 1763. Parole, St. Domingo. G. O. For guard to-morrow, 1 subaltern, 2 sergeants, 3 corporals, 40 privates; for picket to-morrow, 1 captain, 1 subaltern, 1 sergeant, 1 corporal, 20 privates.

R. O. For guard to-morrow, 1 subaltern, 1 corporal, 11 privates; for picket to-morrow, 1 captain, 1 sergeant, 5 privates; bullock guard, 4 privates; working party, 7 privates. Captain Davenport for picket to-morrow and Lieutenant Calhune for guard.

Fort Pitt, Thursday, October 6, 1763. Parole, China. G. O. For guard to-morrow, 1 subaltern, 2 sergeants, 3 corporals, 40 privates; for picket to-morrow, 1 captain, 1 subaltern, 1 sergeant, 1 corporal, 20 privates. The chimneys of the garrison to be swept very clean as soon as possible. The rooms of the garrison to be completed to twenty men per room. R. O. For guard to-morrow, 1 sergeant, 1 corporal, 11 privates; bullock guard, 1 sergeant, 4 privates; for picket to-morrow, 5 privates; working party, 7 privates.

Fort Pitt, Friday, October 7, 1763. Parole, Epsom. G. O. For guard to-morrow, 1 subaltern, 2 sergeants, 3 corporals, 40 privates; for picket to-morrow, 1 captain, 1 subaltern, 1 sergeant, 1 corporal, 20 privates. One of the bales of skins lying on the rampart hath been cut open, and several stolen. Whosoever shall be found guilty of that crime will be punished with the greatest rigor. The corporal of the redoubt guard is not to suffer, at his peril, any man of his post, or any other (person), except the Grenadier Frazier, to take any turnips. R. O. For guard to-morrow, 1 sergeant, 1 corporal, 11 privates; for picket to-morrow, 1 sergeant, 5 privates; bullock guard to-morrow, 1 corporal, 4 privates; working party to-morrow, 7 privates.

Fort Pitt, Saturday, October 8, 1763. Parole, Rumney. G. O. For guard to-morrow, 1 subaltern, 2 sergeants, 3 corporals, 40 privates; for picket to-morrow, 1 captain, 1 subaltern, 1 sergeant, 1 corporal, 20 privates. R. O. For guard to-morrow, 1 sergeant, 1 corporal, 11 privates; for picket to-morrow, 1 captain, 1 sergeant, 1 corporal, 5 privates; bullock guard,

4 privates ; working party, 7 privates ; Captain Trent for picket to-morrow.

Fort Pitt, Sunday, October 9, 1763.   Parole, Saltash.   G. O. For guard to-morrow, 1 subaltern, 2 sergeants, 3 corporals, 40 privates.   For picket to-morrow, 1 captain, 1 subaltern, 1 sergeant, 1 corporal, 20 privates.

The people that live in the huts are not to allow any fire to be made in them and they are to be cleaned all round and the dirt wheeled away into the large ditch on the outside of the fort.   No ashes or dirt to be thrown into the area of the fort, but to be carried to fill up the holes on the Grenadier bastion. R. O. For guard to-morrow, 1 subaltern, 1 corporal, 10 privates. Bullock guard, 4 privates.   For picket to-morrow, 1 captain, 5 privates.   Working party, 6 privates.   Captain Davenport for picket and Lieutenant Calhoun for guard.

Fort Pitt, Monday, October 10, 1763.   Parole, Rochester. G. Os. For guard to-morrow, 1 subaltern, 3 sergeants, 4 corporals, 40 privates.   For picket, 1 captain, 1 subaltern, 1 sergeant, 1 corporal, 20 privates.   R. O. For guard to-morrow, 1 sergeant, 10 privates.   Bullock guard, 1 sergeant, 4 privates. For picket, 1 subaltern, 1 corporal, 5 privates.   Working party, 6 privates.

Fort Pitt, Tuesday, October 11, 1763.   Parole, Funday.   G. O. For guard to-morrow, 1 subaltern, 2 sergeants, 3 corporals, 40 privates.   For picket, 1 captain, 1 subaltern, 1 sergeant, 1 corporal, 20 privates.

Fort Pitt, Wednesday, October 12, 1763.   Parole, Cornwell. G. O.   For guard to-morrow, 0 captain, 1 subaltern, 2 sergeants, 3 corporals, 40 privates; for picket to-morrow, 1 captain, 1 subaltern, 1 sergeant, 1 corporal, 20 privates. R. O. For guard, 0 captain, 1 subaltern, 1 sergeant, 1 corporal, 10 privates ; bullock guard, 0 captain, 0 subaltern, 1 sergeant, 0 corporal, 4 privates ; for picket to-morrow, 1 captain, 0 subaltern, 0 sergeant, 5 privates ; working party, 0 captain,

o subaltern, o sergeant, o corporal, 6 privates.   Captain Trent
for picket, Lieutenant Fleming for guard.

Fort Pitt, Thursday, October 13, 1763.   Parole, Torbay.
G. O.   For guard to-morrow, o captain, 1 subaltern, 2 sergeants, 3 corporals, 40 privates; for picket to-morrow, 1
captain, 1 subaltern, 1 sergeant, 1 corporal, 20 privates; for
work to-morrow, o captain, o subaltern, o sergeant, o corporal,
26 privates.   R. O.   For guard to-morrow, o captain, o subaltern, 1 sergeant, o corporal, 10 privates; bullock guard, o
sergeant, o corporal, 4 privates; for picket to-morrow, 1 captain, 1 sergeant, 5 privates; working party, o sergeant, o corporal, 6 privates.   Captain Davenport for picket.

Fort Pitt, Friday, October 14, 1763.   Parole, Andover.   G.
O.   For guard to-morrow, o captain, 1 subaltern, 2 sergeants,
3 corporals, 40 privates; for picket to-morrow, 1 captain, 1
subaltern, 1 sergeant, 1 corporal, 20 privates.   R. O. For guard
to-morrow: o captain, 1 subaltern, 1 sergeant, 2 corporals, 10
privates; bullock guard, o sergeant, o corporal, 4 privates;
for picket to-morrow, o captain, 1 subaltern, o sergeant, o
corporal, 5 privates; working party, o sergeant, o corporal,
6 privates.   Lieutenant Calhune for guard, and Lieutenant
Fleming for picket.

Fort Pitt, Saturday, October 15, 1763.   Parole ———.   G.
O.   For guard to-morrow, 1 subaltern, 2 sergeants, 3 corporals, 40 privates; for picket, 1 subaltern, 1 sergeant, 1 corporal, 20 privates.   The guards to be relieved every morning
at long roll beating.   The garrison to be under arms to-morrow forenoon, if the weather permit, in order to fire three
rounds per man at a mark.   Each corps to provide themselves a target.   R. O.   For guard to-morrow, 1 sergeant, 1
corporal, 10 privates; for bullock guard, 4 privates; for
picket, 5 privates.

Fort Pitt, Sunday October 16, 1763.   Parole, Bridge-
water.   G. O. For guard to-morrow, 1 subaltern, 2 sergeants,

3 corporals, 40 privates; for picket, 1 captain, 1 subaltern, 1 sergeant, 1 corporal, 20 privates; for work, 1 captain, 1 subaltern, 2 sergeants, 60 privates, R. F.

The batteaus and flats necessary to bring coals and the bags with strings to be ready to-day; the floating battery likewise. A party of 1 captain, 1 lieutenant, 3 sergeants and 60 rank and file to go to-morrow at 9 o'clock, over the Monongahela for coals. For that party Captain Trent and the subaltern of the picket. The detachment of Royal Artillery are to furnish their proportion to lay in fuel for the winter. Nobody is to go out of the fort while the above party and the grass guard are out. Captain Hay will give orders to the gunsmith of the Royal Artillery to repair the arms of the garrison and to begin to-morrow. R. O. For guard, 10 privates; for picket, 1 captain, 1 subaltern, 1 sergeant, 5 privates.

Fort Pitt, October 17, 1763. Parole, ———. The detachment under the command of Captain Stewart to march as soon as possible after the following manner: Major Field and his rangers to march where the service most requires. Captain Stewart and two subalterns to march in the front with the first division of regulars; Major Trent, with the garrison of militia, to march in the rear of the first division. The pack and baggage horses next to them; Captain Ecuyer and two subalterns with the second division of regulars to march in the rear. Ensign Hutchins is to do adjutant's duty, and all orders received from him are to be obeyed. A return of the number of wounded men to be given in immediately to the adjutant by Doctor Boyd, that a sufficient number of horses may be applied for to Captain Ourry, to carry them on. The detachment to march to-morrow at daybreak.

The men to be completed with ammunition and provisions this afternoon. The horses for the sick to be received to-morrow morning, immediately before the detachment marches. Mr. Prather will deliver a driver with every six horses.

SKETCH OF THE LIFE OF GENERAL O'HARA.[*]

THE O'Haras are an ancient Milesian family, settled in County Mayo, in the West of Ireland. The first mention of the family was in 1348. Bishop Murcherd MacMael Moi. 1396, a Bishop of the same diocese. 1409, Bishop Bryan O'Hara. 1485, Archbishop O'Hara. General Sir Charles O'Hara in 1706 was created a baron and took his title from the castle and demesne of Tyrawley, in County Mayo. His son, General Sir James O'Hara, whose first title was conferred during the life of his father for military services during Queen Anne's reign, was also from the demesne of Kilmaine in that part of Ireland. This district is still wild and savage, the roads are few and almost impassable for ordinary carriages. The O'Haras spread from thence to other parts of Ireland, viz., Tyrone, Donegal, Antrim, etc. James O'Hara had always hanging in the hall of his house the coat-of-arms of the barony of Tyrawley, in recognition of his descent from the ancestors of the barons of the O'Hara family of County Mayo—vert on a pale radiant or, a lion rampant sable. James O'Hara, afterward General O'Hara, emigrated to America about 1772, landed in Philadelphia, and after a short residence there wandered to Western Virginia, where he was engaged as Indian trader by a Philadelphia firm. From December, 1773, to March, 1774, he was in the service of Devereux Smith and

---

[*] Compiled from books and documents collected by William M. Darlington, and letters now in the possession of Mrs. McKnight and Miss Matilda W. Denny.   M. C. DARLINGTON.

MRS. MARY O'HARA.

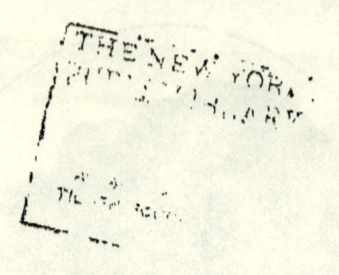

Ephraim Douglas, of Pittsburgh, as Indian trader at Kus-
kusky, an Indian town, near the junction of the Mahoning and
Shenango rivers, in what is now Lawrence County, Pennsylvania.

The accounts of the trades with the Indians are kept in
bucks', does' and fawns' skins.   Here is a sample of some of
the entries :

"Captain Pipe's account, Pea-meet-chease, lives over the
creek : Captain Pipe promises to pay this account if the other
would not.   Deer skins received of his wife, 10s; 1 buck skin,
paid Joseph 1s.   Deer skins got of Mamalteas, 6s 1d.   Remainder of raccoon and foxes got at his camp.   Account
with the white woman who lives in the smith's shop, Dr Captain Pipe's brother-in-law.   Dr The little Muncy man who
bo^t the gun at the Muncy town, 1 pint powder."

After March, 1774, James O'Hara was government agent
among the Indians until the commencement of the Revolution.
Having been three years ensign in the British army, in the
Coldstream Guards, he was thought capable of commanding a
company.   He raised and equipped a company of volunteers.
The equipment of soldiers at that time was their usual dress,
hunting shirt, buckskin breeches and the rifle which always
hung on the wall ready for use.   The equipment supplied them
would be little more than ammunition ; but in this case boats
were supplied, which carried besides the company of volunteers
such articles as were of use in trading with the Indians.   The
fort at Canhawa, now Kanawha, to which they were sent, was
erected by the State of Virginia, and was protected and pro-
visioned by the efforts of Captain O'Hara's company until
1779.   It had escaped the perspicacity of the Virginia states-
men that the sources of the Indian devastations were Detroit,
Vincennes and Kaskaskia, then in possession of the British.
Major George Rogers Clark represented that if these posts

14

were reduced, a counter-influence would be established over the Indians.

In December, 1777, Major Clark submitted to the executive of Virginia a plan for the reduction of these posts. January 2, 1778, he received orders from Patrick Henry, to raise seven companies of soldiers, to consist of fifty men, officered in the usual manner and armed properly, and with this force to attack the British posts at Kaskaskia. He set out as soon as possible on the enterprise. On arriving at the Kanawha River, he was joined by Captain O'Hara's company, then on its way to the Ozark. General Clark was successful and took possession of the town of Kaskaskia, which was situated on the river of that name, seven miles from its junction with the Mississippi. Also Vincennes on the Wabash River. This fort was called by the English Fort Sackville. The name Vincennes was derived from François Morgan de Vincennes, who was commandant at the post in 1735. The march to Vincennes was long, the season inclement, the road passed through an untrodden wilderness. He could only muster one hundred and thirty men; but inspiring this handful with his own heroic spirit, he resolved to strike the enemy in the citadel of his strength. For days his route lay through the drowned lands of Illinois. One plain, called Horse-shoe Plain, about four miles long, was covered with water breast-high. The men, holding their rifles above their heads, plunged in among the floating ice and reached the high land beyond safely. In a few days after the surrender an amazing number of savages flocked into the towns to treat for peace, and soon the enlisted companies returned to their former stations. The inhabitants were mostly French. Speaking French with fluency and understanding some of the Indian dialects, Captain O'Hara must have been of great service to General Clark. Letters from General Clark show the strong friendship be-

tween them for many years after.   In 1779, Captain O'Hara's
company, having had the greater part of the soldiers killed by
the Indians while hunting about Canhawa and other parts of
the country, was reduced to twenty-nine, which was too small
a garrison to answer any purpose, or protect the inhabitants
living in the vicinity of that post.   The fort was evacuated
and the garrison, cattle and horses removed to Pittsburgh.
The few men surviving were annexed to the Ninth Virginia
Regiment, by General Brodhead, December 13, 1779.   Captain
O'Hara was sent to headquarters with letters from General
Brodhead to General Washington, and to James Wilkinson,
asking for a supply of clothing for the soldiers.   Captain
O'Hara was then made commissary for the General Hospital,
and stationed at Carlisle.   The following letter was written
by Captain O'Hara to Devereux Smith, Esq.:

PITTSBURGH, April 8, 1777.

Dear Sir:—I arrived here yesterday from the Indian country
and must say that I have great reason to suspect that numbers of the savages are determined to annoy our frontier as
much as they dare.   On the 2d day of this month, as I was
preparing to start with my horses from the Moravian town,
there were three runners arrived from Tuscarawas, about thirteen short miles off, with intelligence that there were a party
of eighteen, consisting of fifteen Mingoes, two Shawnees and
one Wiandot at that place, on their way to war, and that they
intended to come for the ministers and other white people
who live with the Moravians, upon which all the white people
of the upper town fled that night to the principal Delaware
town; however I stayed till next morning and got two of the
Moravian Indians to go meet the warriors and find out, if possible, what they intended to do.   We got for answer that they
looked on themselves as free men, that they had no king nor

chief, therefore would do as they pleased, and that in the first place they would visit the neighborhood of Fort Pitt; they then set off from Tuscarawas, and as I knew that I certainly must have fallen in with them, if following my course. I thought best to send my horses by the Delawares and came home, myself and man, by way of the Mingoes' town on the Ohio. I was informed by good authority, that a party of sixty-four, who had gone some time ago to the Kentucky, have returned to Pluggin's town, they have brought only one prisoner, and have lost a Shawnee man; they have again held a council of war, and seventy have turned out to visit the Big River. The Muncies have in general turned off from the Delawares, and are much inclined to listen to the Mingoes. The Shawnees are divided, about one half of them have joined the Mingoes, the Wiandots seem more inclined for peace.

I have nothing further material to communicate at present but that I have lost one of your buckles. Please make my best compliments to Mrs. Smith, and Miss Polly, and the rest of your family.

I am, sir, your humble servant,

JAMES O'HARA.

The following account was written by John Heckwelder, the Moravian : On seeing the death of General O'Hara announced in the public papers, the following occurrence, respecting him, was brought to my recollection :

Some time after the commencement of the revolutionary war, when the northern Indians were beginning to make inroads on the people living on the east side of the Ohio River, this gentleman, having come out the upper Moravian town on the Muskingum, on business, and there taken lodgings with a respectable and decent family of Indians in the village, I had one evening scarcely laid down to sleep, when I was suddenly roused from my bed by an Indian runner (or messenger), who in the night had been sent to me nine miles, with the following verbal message:

"My friend: See that our friend O'Hara, now at your town, be immediately taken off to the settlement of the white people, avoiding all paths leading to that river. Fail not in taking my advice, for there is no time to lose, and hear my son further on the subject."

The fact was, that eleven warriors from Sandusky were far advanced on their way to take or murder O'Hara, who at break of day would be at this place for the purpose. I immediately sent for this gentleman and told him that I would furnish him with a conductor, on whom he might depend, and having sent for Anthony (otherwise called Luke Holland), informed him of the circumstances, and requested his services. He (the Indian) first wished to know, whether my friend placed confidence in him and trusted to his fidelity, which question being answered by O'Hara himself, and to his full satisfaction, he replied: "Well, our lives cannot be separated! We must stand or fall together! But take courage, for no enemy shall discover us!" The Indian then took Mr. O'Hara through the woods, and arriving within a short distance of the Ohio River, pointed out to him a hiding place, until he, by strolling up and down the river, should discover white people on the opposite shore; when finally observing a house, where two white men were cleaning out a canoe for use, he hurried back to bring on his friend, who, when near the spot, advised his Indian conductor to hide himself, knowing those people to be bad men, he feared they might kill him for his services. The Indian finally seeing his friend safe across the river, returned and made report thereof.

The young Indian, who had been the bearer of the message from his father to me, had immediately returned on seeing

O'Hara off, in order to play a further deception on the war party, for the purpose of preventing them even from going to our town, fearing, that if there, and not finding their object, they might probably hunt up his track, and finding this, pur· sue him.   He indeed effected his purpose so completely, that while they were looking for him in one direction, his conduc- tor was taking him off in another.   The father of the young lad, who was the principal cause that O'Hara's life had been saved, had long been admired by all who knew him for his philanthropy, on account of which the traders had given him the name of " The Gentleman."   Otherwise this Indian was not in connection with the Christian Indian Society, though a friend to them.   He lived with his family retired and in a decent manner.   While I feel a delight in offering to the relatives and friends of the deceased this true and faithful picture of Indian fidelity, I regret that on necessarily having had to recur to the names " Anthony " and " Luke Holland," I am drawn from scenes of pleasure to crimes of the blackest hue.   The very Indian just named, who at that time joyfully reported to me his having conducted his friend out of danger to a place of safety, some years after approached me with the doleful news that every one of his children (all minors) to· gether with his hoary-headed parents, had been murdered by the white people at Gnadenhutten on the Muskingum.

JOHN HECKWELDER.

1780, Captain O'Hara was appointed Commissary of the General Hospital and was stationed at Carlisle, Pennsylvania.

1781, he received the appointment of Assistant Quarter- master.

The winter of 1779 and '80 set in with unusual severity. Supplies for the troops could not be supplied in sufficient quantities, all the channels of transportation were closed. But the most serious cause of distress was the derangement

of the currency, which left Congress almost without power to
assist the commissary department. The distress consequent
thereto caused the revolt of the Pennsylvania line in 1781.
After that trouble was ended, General Greene was put in
command in the Southern army and Wayne was ordered to
join it.

Captain O'Hara, Assistant Quartermaster, used every means
to provide for the campaign. Warehouses were rented in
Carlisle and Philadelphia for the storing of provisions and
means of transportation procured. Of the history of his
efforts for this purpose there remains now in the possession
of his descendants but one small memorandum book; in that
can be traced his journey with the army, and a record of provisions procured by himself and his assistant, Mr. Elliot.
Names of places are given which correspond with the most
noted places of the Southern campaign. Charleston and almost all of South Carolina had been conquered by Lord Cornwallis. The British army was preparing for an invasion of
North Carolina. An engagement between Tarleton and
Morgan took place at the Cowpens, January 17, 1781. The
British were defeated. Tarleton marched through North
Carolina to the banks of the Dan, where there was another
engagement. From there the British army pursued Morgan
and crossed the Yadkin. General Greene made his escape
from North Carolina. Cornwallis returned to Hillsborough;
General Greene receiving intelligence of this again crossed
the Dan and returned to North Carolina. From want of pro-
visions the British retired. Greene advanced, crossed the
Haw, and posted himself between Troublesome creek and
Reedy Fork.

On the 15th of March began the battle of Guilford Court
House. It was one of the severest of the war. Although
the Americans were repulsed and the British remained masters of the field, they were too much shattered to follow up

the victory. General Greene retreated to Reedy Fork creek. After this General Greene re-entered South Carolina and attacked Lord Rawdon at Camden; he was defeated, and retreating crossed the Wateree and took a strong position for offensive and defensive operations. At Eutaw Springs was the next battle. Both sides claimed the victory. It was the last battle of any note which took place in South Carolina.

These and other places are mentioned in this memorandum book, showing that active personal attention was given to his duties in his department. He continued with the army until July, 1783, when having seen the last of the Pennsylvania troops embarked on board the transport, he travelled himself to Philadelphia with General Wayne. After settling the affairs of his office he returned to Pittsburgh, accompanied by his newly-wedded wife in a wagon, the only means of transport. She was Mary, the daughter of a Scottish gentleman, William Carson; although the house that received her was only built of logs, she took with her all the luxuries that could be transported. The carpets astonished the western country people. They expressed their astonishment that Mrs. O'Hara should spread coverlets on the floor, and hesitated to walk on them. The house stood near the Allegheny River, above Fort Pitt, in what was called the officers' orchard.

By the Act of Congress, passed April 13, 1782, "All officers in the late General Hospitals, who were inhabitants of or belonged to this State at the time of entering into service, and who became supernumerary by the arrangement of October, 1780, or resigned before 10th April, 1780, and were not otherwise provided for by law, are entitled to the depreciation of their pay. I am, therefore, of opinion, that Mr. O'Hara is within the meaning of the Act, and that the account is properly passed."

WM. BRADFORD, JUN.

Philadelphia, Sept. 10, 1786.

When peace was concluded with Great Britain, a portion of their Indian auxiliaries refused to bury the hatchet, but continued their depredations upon the settlements bordering on the Ohio. From 1783 to 1790, it was estimated that fifteen hundred men, women and children had been slain or taken captive by the Indians.

Captain O'Hara took the contract for furnishing provisions for the Western army, then under the command of General Harmar.

PHILADELPHIA, August 28, 1784.

CAPTAIN JAMES O'HARA.

Sir:—Your having assisted the Continental Commissioners in procuring the Indian goods so much to their satisfaction, has induced the Indian Commissioners on the part of this State to request your assistance in obtaining and safe-packing the goods to be provided by them. Enclosed you have a list of such as are wanted, and must beg you will lose no time in furnishing the several articles therein specified, in order that they may be sent, if possible, with the goods of the continent. The list should have been furnished sooner had we been sooner authorized. The Treaty at Fort Stanwix will be held the 20th of September next, so that it will require your utmost exertions, as many of the articles must be made here. A second treaty will be held at Cuyahoga, on the bank of Lake Erie on the 20th of November next, so that the articles in the list No. 1 will be equally divided, the one-half only immediately for the first treaty, by which means you will have sufficient time to make up such articles as shall be required for the second. As the State means to convince the natives that she can and will furnish the best assortment of goods, we must beg you will be careful to answer her good intentions in these particulars. Sundry little articles, agreeable to list No. 2, will be wanted for the accommodation of the Commissioners, who beg you will give yourself the additional trouble of furnishing the same, and having them carefully put up, marked, and sent on with the goods. When they are ready to be shipped you will be pleased to call upon Captain Joseph Stiles, the keeper of the magazine, who will deliver you ten quarter casks of powder for the first treaty, ten other quarter casks will be ready for the second, and likewise delivered you.

We are, sir, your humble servants,

SAMUEL ATLEE,

FRANCIS JOHNSTON.

P. S.—Captain Stiles will also furnish you with three horseman's and one soldier's tent.

Another letter of the same purport was written to Captain James O'Hara, by Francis Johnston, Commissioner, and Colonel Josiah Harmar.

FORT McINTOSH,* February 15, 1785.

Sir:—On the 21st of December I proceeded from Fort Pitt with five men for this post in a large boat, heavy laden with flour, rum, soap, candles, plank, etc., for the use of the troops under your command, and that night was driven on a fish dam by the ice, where we stuck fast until the night of the 22d, when, after our broadside was beat in, and no prospect of relief, two of the men nearly frozen to death, we were obliged to cast over-board twelve thousand weight of flour, five hundred weight of bread and biscuit, with a considerable quantity of other vegetables were lost, yet we did not get to shore till the 23d, and then in that distressed condition which the melancholy situation of Corporal Shaw (now present) evinces.

* Beaver.

As these losses of provision may probably be considered under the fifth article of my contract with the Secretary in the War Office, and you being acquainted with the circumstances, I shall esteem it a particular favor if you will please to furnish me with the necessary certificate thereof, and oblige,

Sir, your most humble servant,

JAMES O'HARA.

I do hereby certify that the above statement of facts relative to the loss of the contractor's boat and cargo is just and true, agreeable to the best information that can be collected. Given under my hand at Fort McIntosh, Feb. 16, 1785.

JOSIAH HARMAR,

Lt.-Col. Com. 1st Am. Reg.

The contract made by Captain O'Hara included provisioning and clothing the armies then in the field, and supplying the forts, Oswego, Niagara, Presqu'isle, Fort le Boeuf, Greenville, Washington, Fort Wayne, Fort McIntosh, Defiance, Detroit, Michillimacknac, Franklin, Miamis, Massac, Chickasaw Bluffs, Knox, Rapids of Ohio, Hamilton, Kaskaskias, Natchez, etc. To understand the difficulty of this undertaking, it must be remembered that this war was against the Indians, the most ruthless of enemies, assisted by the lately-conquered British army and American Tories, and that during this time occurred the disastrous defeats of Generals Harmar and St. Clair. General O'Hara was not only contractor for furnishing all necessaries for these armies, but he was also appointed to act as Quartermaster and Treasurer for payments to the soldiers *pro tem.* His accounts were kept with the utmost exactness, as will be proven by the following certificate:

TREASURY DEPARTMENT,

REGISTER'S OFFICE, March 6, 1792.

These are to certify that James O'Hara, Esq., late Contractor for supplying the army with Provisions, and who occasionally acted as Quartermaster of the troops and agent for the supply of Indian goods, is not charged with any moneys on the treasury books. That he has from time to time settled his accounts in a regular manner at the Treasury, and has given general satisfaction to the Treasury officers with whom he settled said account.

(Signed)   JOSEPH NOURSE,

Register.

WAR DEPARTMENT, May 21, 1792.

Sir:—I have the honor to transmit you, enclosed, your commission as Quartermaster-General of the Army of the United States.

The Secretary of War requests that you will please to purchase a bat-horse* for Brigadier-General Putnam, who is about setting out for Fort Washington† on special business. The horse will be left at Pittsburgh, under care of Major Craig, subject to your order; a saddle and bridle will also be wanted.

I am with great respect, your humble servant,

JO. STAGG, JR.,

Chief Clerk of the War Department.

To JAMES O'HARA, ESQ., QUARTERMASTER-GENERAL.

The defeat of General Harmar, in 1790, carried dismay throughout all our western settlements, and inspired the Indians with courage. A new army was raised and placed

---

* Pack-horse.
† Cincinnati.

under the command of Major-General St. Clair. On the 4th of November, 1791, he suffered a total defeat near the Miami villages by the Indians and their confederates, the English. The whole country was thrown into consternation. Petitions were sent from posts on the frontier to the officers of the government for protection. One was sent from Pittsburgh, December, 1791, representing the defenceless situation of the town, should it be attacked by the Indians. This petition was signed and addressed to Governor Mifflin by James O'Hara, John Irwin, John Wilkins, Jr., A. Tannehill, John McMasters, William Turnbull.

December 26, 1791, orders were sent through Governor Mifflin by H. Knox, Secretary of War, to Major Craig, to construct immediately a block-house at Fort Pitt, and to surround it with palisades, so as to contain about 100 men. Two companies, with the necessary officers, were ordered to the fort, and the lieutenants of Westmoreland, Allegheny and Washington were authorized to employ scouts or patrols at the expense of the general government. The scouts were to be the best of hunters and woodsmen. In 1792 General Wayne received the appointment of Commander-in-Chief, and the western army was reorganized. It was called the Legion of the United States. Anxious to conciliate the Indians, he called a council twenty-two miles below Pittsburgh, which he called Legionville. The Indians insisted that they should be the undisturbed possessors of all the land north and west of the Ohio River. In 1793, when the United States Commissioners proposed another council, General Wayne playfully expressed a wish to be present with 2,500 of his commissioners in company, with not a single Quaker among them.

On the 10th of October, 1794, General Wayne wrote from the Miami villages, that owing to the unfortunate death of

Mr. Robert Elliot, the acting contractor, who was killed by the savages, the affairs of that department were deranged and famine threatened, and General O'Hara must at once proceed to Fort Washington, visiting all the forts on the way, taking an invoice of the stores belonging to the contractors at each place, and of the means of transport, forwarding to the Miami village as great a supply of flour, salt and cattle as every means of transport in his own department as well as that of the contractors will permit. For which purpose the General-in-chief ordered a detachment of dragoons and riflemen, under the command of Captain Gibson, as far as Greenville to escort the convoy. General O'Hara also received orders that if there should be any deficiency in the contractors' stores, he should supply the deficiency.

July 26, 1794, headquarters* Greenville, General O'Hara wrote to Major Craig that a Potawatomie, who was in the action of the 30th of June, at Grand Glaize, was captured and being examined says, that by every account of the Delawares from Roche de Bout, the British have from fifteen to twenty pieces of cannon at that place; that the British called upon all the Indian Nations to bring on all their warriors, and that they would bring more British soldiers than they could bring warriors. This was one moon before the action at Fort Recovery. The Indians having prepared for war, told the British to raise their strong arm and come on; their answer was to proceed and go on before and they would wait with their strong arms to strike the Americans; that the Great Man of Canada ordered them to go and take the fort, overset General Wayne's army, and roll them into the Ohio. He could not tell the number of Indians killed before Fort Recovery; the Indians carried off all their dead, except a few that lay too

---

* Southwest branch of the Miami.

near the fort.   Some of the wounded were carried off on horseback, and some by water.   General O'Hara adds, "that the
present prospects of supporting the Quartermaster's Department with general approbation are very flattering.   The
Legion and auxiliaries are in good spirits and well supplied,
and you may be perfectly assured that we shall be in possession of Grand Glaize and Roche de Bout before the 15th of
next month."

"July 27th.—The General beats to-morrow instead of the
Reveille.   The whole army is ready to move in the most complete order at sunrise, and you may expect to be informed of
an end being put to the business of war in this quarter and
of Simcoes'* retrograde or defeat by my next letter.

"JAMES O'HARA, Q. M. G."

After the successful termination of General Wayne's campaign General O'Hara wished to resign his office as Quartermaster-General, but the resignation was not accepted until
May, 1796, when he was succeeded by Lieutenant-Colonel
John Wilkins.   He continued in the service of the government as contractor for supplying the Western army until
1802.   It was during the time of Wayne's campaign that there
occurred the revolt against government officials, called the
"Whiskey Insurrection."   The rioters had burned the country
house of General Neville, and had assembled before General
Abraham Kirkpatrick's house for the same purpose.   H. H.
Brackenridge addressed the mob and appealed to them in a
manner which they could not resist.   He showed them that
it would be impossible to burn the house of Kirkpatrick without at the same time burning that of General O'Hara, which
was close by, both built of wood; that they knew General

---

* Governor of Canada.

O'Hara was from home with General Wayne, fighting the Indians; to destroy his property under such circumstances would be an act for which they would never forgive themselves. If the house must be destroyed, let it be pulled down, not burned. The crowd dispersed.

In the spring of 1796 General O'Hara built a saw-mill in Allegheny and made arrangements with Major Isaac Craig for the erection of glassworks. Mr. Eichbaum was engaged to erect the works. It was a very difficult and expensive undertaking. They made their own pots. Some of the clay was brought from Germany; all had to be brought from Philadelphia in wagons. Thirty thousand dollars were expended before the first bottle was made. After that the furnaces were reconstructed and the manufactory became very profitable. After the partnership with Major Craig was dissolved he carried on the business alone. In 1805 he built the ship "General Butler." On March 4th it lay in the stream at Pittsburgh, ready to weigh anchor the moment the water answered. She was to go down the river with a cargo of glass for intermediate ports, take a cargo of cotton at Natchez for Liverpool, and to return to Philadelphia or New Orleans with goods for either of these markets. She was commanded by Captain Samuel Lake. The General's eldest son, William Carson O'Hara, was supercargo. General John Wilkins was owner of one-fourth of the ship and cargo.

Strict orders were given by General O'Hara and General Wilkins to Captain Lake that he would not suffer on board any stores, wares or articles of any kind that could possibly be conceived to be contraband of war, nor attempt to touch at any prohibition port. The ship was insured in Philadelphia for $10,000 by Joseph Carson; it was valued at $14,000. The cargo was to be insured in Liverpool. On account of the war Captain Lake was authorized to sell it in Liverpool. "We do not wish to sell at any considerable loss, but being engaged in building another and desirous to encourage shipbuilding at place, we are willing to sell this without profit." It was not sold. May 3, 1807, the "General Butler" again sailed from New Orleans for Greenock with a cargo of cotton. October 3, 1807, the ship was captured by a Spanish schooner within sixty miles of Havanna and taken into Vera Cruz.

Several other vessels were built by O'Hara and Wilkins for the river trade. One other, the "Betsey," traded between Baltimore and the West Indies. It was consigned to John Holmes, a merchant in Baltimore. He never rendered any account or answered letters addressed to him by General O'Hara. It was not known what became of the vessels during the owner's life.

1789, General O'Hara was elected Presidential elector and cast his vote for General Washington. He assisted General Wilkins and others in building the First Presbyterian Church, Pittsburgh, and gave the handsome chandelier which ornamented and illuminated the building, until it was torn down and replaced by the present edifice. 1802–4, he was a candidate for election to Congress and was defeated by Lucas, a Democrat. During the time of his contract for supplying the northwest army with provisions he ascertained that salt from the Onondaga works in New York could be furnished in Pittsburgh cheaper than from Baltimore. He packed his flour and provisions in barrels suitable for salt. These barrels were reserved in his contract. Vessels were built on the lakes and river for its transportation and the salt sold for $4 a bushel.

1804, General O'Hara was appointed a director of the branch of the Bank of Pennsylvania, established that year in Pittsburgh. 1811, he entered into partnership with John Henry Hopkins—afterwards Bishop of Vermont—in an iron

15

works at Ligonier. It was a failure. Among other noble qualities, Mr. Hopkins possessed the rare one of acknowledging and being grateful for a pecuniary obligation.

General O'Hara at various times made extensive purchases of property in Allegheny County and elsewhere. The first tract of land he purchased was in 1773, nineteenth day of November, being a plantation and tract of land containing four hundred acres, situated on Coalpit Run. His mercantile knowledge was acquired in 1770 and 1771 in a counting-house in Liverpool. The exactness of his accounts with government is proved by the following certificate:

BOARD OF TREASURY, July 19, 1786.

I certify that there is due to Mr. James O'Hara, from the Commissioners of the Board of Treasury, for sundry warrants by him endorsed and delivered this day to the Treasurer of the United States, the sum of Three Thousand Dollars: for the amount of which I am accountable agreeably to a receipt given to me by Mr. James O'Hara of this date.

WILLIAM DUER,
Secretary of the Board of Treasury.

Other certificates of the same kind have been preserved by his family. His compeers were men whose talents have never been excelled in this community, viz.: James Ross, Hugh Henry Brackenridge, W. Forward, Judge Baldwin, etc.

Letters from many officers of the army prove their esteem and confidence in him. To some he was allied by marriage. General Febiger was his brother-in-law. His son James married the daughter of Pressley Neville, who was also the granddaughter of General Daniel Morgan, of whom it was said, "Served everywhere, surrendered nowhere, served to the end of the war." His daughter, Elizabeth Febiger

O'Hara, married the son of Major Denny, and soon after his death his daughter Mary married the son of Major Croghan. General George Rogers Clark was a brother-in-law of Major Croghan. During his residence in Pittsburgh he was noted for his hospitality. To his house all were welcome, from the countryman who came in for rest or refreshment, to his guests of honor, Louis Philippe, General Moreau, and his friends, the French officers. At that time the higher classes in Ireland sent their sons to France for their education. It is probable that it was thus he acquired his perfect knowledge of French.

James O'Hara died December 21, 1819, in the 67th year of his age. Mary O'Hara died April 8, 1834, aged 73. William Carson, James and Charles died s. p. d., before their father. The only descendants of his name are James O'Hara and his son Richard W. O'Hara, descendants of Richard Butler O'Hara.

NOTES BY GENERAL O'HARA.

	Miles
From the mouth of Tennessee to Fort Masac	12
From Fort Masac to the mouth of Ohio	36
From the mouth of the Ohio to Fort Jefferson	6
From the mouth of the Ohio to Iron Bank	14
From the mouth of the Ohio to Chalk Bank	17
From the mouth of the Ohio to Chickasaw River	25
From the mouth of the Ohio to New Mexico	50
From Fort Jefferson to Masac, by land	18
From Fort Jefferson to the mouth of Tennessee	24

Raystown, Bedford.

Fort Burd, Redstone Old Fort.

Fort Franklin, Venango County, near mouth of French Creek.

Fort Harmar, right bank of Muskingum, opposite Marietta, built 1785 by Major Doughty.

Le Boeuf, on the south or west fork of French Creek.

Fort Ligonier, east side of Loyalhanna Creek, Westmoreland County, erected 1757 or 1758.

Fort McIntosh, built by General Lachlan McIntosh 1778. Beaver.

DuQuesne. Pittsburgh. Fort Pitt.

Presqu' Isle, erected 1756, on Lake Erie, about 30 miles above Buffalo Fort.

Fort Reed, erected 1773, near Hannas Town.

Fort Washington, Cincinnati.

THE

LEVYTYPE CO. PHILA

GUYASUTA'S GRAVE.
(KIASHUTA)

O'HARA TOWNSHIP,
ALLEGHENY COUNTY, PENNA.

LETTERS FROM OFFICERS OF THE CONTI-
NENTAL ARMY. FROM 1776 TO 1799.

FORT PITT, 6 July 1776.

AT a meeting held this Day at this place, present : Kiashuta, a Mingoe chief, just returned from the treaty at Niagira ; Captain Pipe, a Delaware chief ; The Shade, a Shawnese chief, with several others, Shawnese and Delawares ; likewise Major Trent, Major Ward, Captain Nevill, his officers and a number of the Inhabitants, after being seated, Kiashuta made the following Speech :

" *Brothers :* Three Months ago I left this Place to attend a Treaty at Niagira, to be held between the Commanding Officer of that Place and the six nation, Shawnese, Delawares, etc.; But I was stopped near a month at Connywagoe. As the Commanding officer had sent word to the Indians not to assemble until He should hear from Detroit. while I was at Connywagoe, 800 Indians of the six nations hearing my Intentions of going to the Treaty, came to meet me and go with me. just as we arrived at a small Village beyond Connywagoe, they received a message from the Commanding Officer, acquainting them that the Treaty was over, but they, notwithstanding, persisted in going. "I received a message at the same Time inviting me to come, and assuring me that the Council Fire was not yet entirely extinguished. upon my arrival with the rest of the Indians, I informed the Commanding Officer that I had come a great Distance to hear what He had to say, and desired that he would inform me ; but he told me that he was not yet prepared to speak with me, which ended our Conference."

Kiashuta then produced (his Belt, and is ordered by the Six nations to send it through the Indian Country) a Belt of Wampum, which was to be sent from the six nations to the Shawnese, Delawares, Wyandotts and Western Indians, acquainting them that they were determined to take no Part in the present War between Great Britain and America, and desiring them to do the same. He then addressed himself to the Virginians and Pennsylvanians in the following manner :

"*Brothers:* We will not suffer either the English or Americans to march an army thro' our Country. Should Either attempt it, We shall forewarn them three times from Proceeding, but should they then persist, they must abide by the Consequence. I am appointed by the Six Nations to the Care of this Country, that is, to the Care of the Indians on the West side of the river Ohio, and I desire you will not think of an Expedition against Detroit, for I repeat it to you again, we will not suffer an army to march through our Country." *A String.*

Kiashuta again rose and spoke as follows :

"*Brothers:* Should any Mischief chance to be committed by any of our People, you must not blame the Nations nor think it was done by the approbation of the Chiefs ; for the six Nations have strictly forbid any of their young men or Tributaries to molest any People on these Waters, but if they are determined to go to War, let them go to Canada and fight there." *A String.*

Kiashuta then addressed Himself to Captain Pipe (a Delaware chief), desiring him to inform his nation of what he had heard, and to request them to be strong and join with the other nations in keeping Peace in his country. *A String.*

He also recommended it to the Shade, a Shawnese Chief, to do the same.

He then desired that the foregoing speeches might be distributed through the Country, to quiet the minds of the people, and convince them that the six nations and their adherents did not desire to live at Variance with them ; To which Captain Nevill returned the following answer :

"*Brother Kiashuta:* I am much oblig'd to you for your good speech on the present occasion. you may depend We shall not attempt to march an army through your Country without first acquainting you with it, unless we hear of a British Army coming this Course. In such Case, we must make all possible speed to meet, and endeavor to stop them."

To which Kiashuta replied that there was not the least Danger of that, as they should make it their Business to prevent Either an English or American army from passing through their Country.

Captain CARSON.

First Lieutenant FINDLY.

Second Lieutenant ALEXANDER SIMERAL.

Indian Conference at Fort Pitt, July 6, 1776.

FORT PITT, 4th June, 1777.

Sir:—I am favored with your letter of this date Informing me that you can't relieve the post at Kittanning except I can Supply you with Arms and Ammunition. Arms I have not until the Wagons arrive, consequently the 50 men who Escort the Wagons may march from here as early as any other Body of men I could arm. Ammunition I suppose to be already at that Post, you complain of the expence attending calling the Militia out. You must keep an account of what necessarily arises on that service and draw for it agreeable to the Act of Assembly.

I am, Sir, with Esteem,

Your obedient Humble Servant,

EDWARD HAND.

FORT PITT, 6th July, 1777.

Sir:—I received your letter by Captn. Martin, and am glad that by your late instructions you have it in your Power to punish the refractory Members you mention. Captn. Martin's small Party & two others, 15 Privates in the whole, are all I have yet heard of, pray, inform me if any more have joined him; it is very awkward & irregular to see men droping in by twos and threes without Officers and the least Order.

Captn. Martin is Stationed at the Kiskimmenitas. You will see by the Militia Act the proportion of Officers to a Certain number of men, which can't be exceeded.

I am, Sir,

Your Obedient, Humble Servant,

EDW. HAND.

[COL. A. LOCHRY.]

FORT PITT, 29th July, 1777.

Dr Sir:—Your favor of yesterday I received & have furnished thirty Guns and accoutrements to Captns. McKee & Leech agreeable to your desire. I expect you will Please to direct them to be careful of them, that I may receive them fit for service. Captn. McKee received ten yesterday and one some time ago. Captain Leech rec'd nineteen to-day. I intend requesting the Principal Militia Officers of Westmoreland County to meet me at Hannas Town as soon as the Hurry of Harvest is over; I wish to confer with them on public business. I will give you further notice & fix a day. If you will take the Trouble to examine the Articles of War you will see that the men who deserted from Captain Martin's detachment are Guilty of Breach of the 4th & 14th Articles of the 13th Section of the Articles of War, and, as they were then in Actual Service, you will find by the 1st Article of the 17th Section that they are as liable to be punished as regular

Soldiers. I enclose a copy of the Articles of War lest you may not have one by you

and am, Dr Sir, Sincerely yours,

EDW. HAND.

[COL. A. LOCHRY.]

FORT PITT, 6th August, 1777.

Sir:—I last evening received your favor of the 2d Instant, and am convinced that what you have done is occasioned by your Zeal for the Common Cause; but you may remember that a Magazine was ordered to your Quarter by myself, &, as I did not know the most proper place, I consulted the General I met at Ligonier the 18th Ultimo. By their Common Voice, Col. Mountis was fixed on, & Col. Morgan has only acted by my express Command. I have the Pleasure to acquaint you that, as far as can be ascertained, the Suspicions of that Gentn's Infidelity are quite groundless; would to God those formed of every other Person were so! I find Col. Lochry is gone to Phila.; I therefore request you will please immediately to forward the wagons laden with Salt to Col. Mountis, and Redstone agreeable to prior order; those wagons carrying other stores I beg you will send here. It will be necessary to send an Escort with the Wagons, which must continue at Col. Mountis' as a Guard for the Magazine, & be relieved by you, agreeable to my directions, to Colonel Lochry, which I find you are acquainted with. I beg to know in what Forwardness the Militia from your County, destined for the Expedition, are in,

and am, Sir, Very respectfully Yrs.,

EDW. HAND.

[JAMES PARRY, Lieut. of Westmoreland.]

FORT PITT, August 8, 1777.

General Hand wishes to meet the Militia officers, & other principal Inhabitants of the Counties of Bedford and Westmoreland, at Ligonier, on Monday, the 18th instant, to consult on the best Measures to be taken on the present alarming Occasion.

By order of the Genl.,

J. EWING, *M. B.*

[To COLONEL ARCHIBALD LOCHRY, Westmoreland County.]

FORT PITT, August 22, 1777.

Sir:—As the Commissary has been directed to Erect a Magazine of Provisions at Colonel Mounces', near Stewart's crossing, and one at Redstone old Fort, he will send from Ligonier, by the way of the Nine Mile Run, a Number of Wagons, Laden with Stores, to the above-mentioned places. I therefore Request that you will please to furnish a Party of Militia to Escort the Wagons & serve as Guides, & to remove any obstructions the Wagons may meet on the road, the same party, or another, consisting of a carefull Subaltern officer, a sergeant & ten Privates, must remain at Colonel Mounces' as a Guard to the Magazine; they are to be kept up until further Orders, and may be delivered as often as you think necessary.

I am, Sir, Your obedient, Humble Servant,

EDW. HAND.

[COL. A. LOCHRY.]

FORT PITT, 13 October, 1777.

Sir:—I hope in a few days to move the Provisions & other stores destined for the Indian Expedition from here to Wheeling, & I will, at the same time, march all the troops here assembled to that place. I beg you may be as expeditious as possible in furnishing your proportion and ordering them to march immediately for this garrison. Send an Officer and fifteen or twenty of your Militia to meet and Escort David Tate's Brigade of Horses laden with flour, they will also take under their protection any other Continental Pack-Horses they meet.

I am Sir, Your Obed, H'ble Servant,

EDW. HAND.

FORT PITT, 18 October, 1777.

Dear Sir:—The protection of your County has, since I have had the Honor to Command, been an object equally attended to with that of any other Frontier County. I have repeatedly requested from you a number of men for that purpose, but (from what cause I can't determine) I never yet could obtain them agreeable to my wish. If you will now send me your proportion, I think that will be sufficient, added to the numbers already arrived and daily expected from different Quarters, to protect the Frontiers. Congress ordered a Post in your County (The Kittanning); I could not support that and have ordered another to be Erected at the expence of the Continent. This I think Sufficient, & will Support, if you lend me your aid; at the same time, beg leave to assure you that I don't mean to interfere with your Command of Westmoreland County, or your Plan in Erecting as many Forts and magazines as you please at the expence of the State of Pennsylvania, and puting the whole County in its Pay. Presuming you have proper authority for so doing, and every State will, no doubt, have a particular regard to the Situation of Different Counties, the People you mention are surely Defending their own Property, and, if the Spirit of Discord would permit them, have it in their Power, by Uniting to march in Bodies, to collect the Grain of every man in the Frontier parts of the County. I again request you may not delay the proportion from your County for the Expedition; the Season advances apace. I shall to-morrow proceed to Wheeling with what Troops I have, yours will receive every necessary I can Afford them when they arrive here, & when they join me shall be put on the same footing with the Militia of any other County. In the meantime, Subscribe myself,

Dr Sir, very Sincerely yrs,

EDW. HAND.

[COLONEL A. LOCHRY.]

FORT PITT, 5 Nov., 1777.

Dear Sir:—I was duly fav'd with yours of the 2d by Colonel Barr, who, instead of 53, has no more than 31 Rank and file.

To my very great mortification I find I can't collect a sufficient number of men to enter the Indian country this season, therefore, as the Frontier of Westmoreland County lies much exposed to the Ravages of the Savages, I beg that you may immediately draw out 150 men, with officers in proportion, to cover that part of the Country and Assist the Inhabitants in securing their Crops and other property, the whole to be under the direction of a Field Officer, who must report to me from time to time what number of men and officers are on duty & where they are. Col. Barr's party are now armed & will remain here subject to your Orders. I wish to render this Body of men as useful as possible to the public, shall for that reason leave the destination of them to yourself. Except 30 to be kept with Captain Moorhead, you are to continue the 150 men & no more on continental pay untill Further orders or untill the necessity for it ceases. You must apply to Col. Geo. Morgan or his agent here for Instructions how to Victual them, a sufficient number of cattle are already purchased for that purpose.

I am, Sir, your Obedt, Humle Servant,

EDW. HAND.

[COLONEL A. LOCHRY.]

[Collection of W. M. D.]

Sir:—I wrote to the honorable the Continental Congress on the 15th Ultimo, which I hope they have received. I would at that time have wrote to you, but was not certain of your being in Congress ; but as Mr. John Anderson informs me he left you in Congress, I take the liberty of communicating to you some matters that have occurred to me since my letter to Congress upon hearing the speeches of the Delawares, and request the favour of you to lay them before Congress, and that Part with respect to the Delawares I have communicated to Col. Morgan. I believe we shall have an Indian war and a general one. If the Delawares were ever so well inclined they will be awed into it by the other nations. I would be for supporting them if possible in order to lessen the strength of our enemy. They should be invited into our Country. Their wives, Children and Old people would be then secure, and we then should reap great Advantage from the service of their young Men and Warriors. And if any other Tribe or Nation would follow their Example they should be encouraged. If we have a general Indian war, it is my humble Opinion four expeditions will be necessary : One to the Southward, one to the Northward, one down the Ohio to establish a Strength on the Ohio, so as to cut off any communication with the Western and Southern Nations, and one other expedition to De Troit or to some part of the Country to the Westward, to cut off the communication between the Northern and Western Nations. Each of those expeditions should be carried into execution under the command of an experienced officer. And it is my humble opinion not less than 3,000 men should be employed in each of those expeditions, and they should be well equipped ; that those who went down the Ohio and those to Detroit should have some field pieces, and those troops should not return but establish posts and reduce the Indians and convince them of an error that they have been led into by the governments formerly, that they may at any time make war with us and have peace granted them on their own terms. I would recommend that large numbers of hostages should be taken from every tribe or nation that we may reduce, and take none but their chiefs or ruling men as hostages, that the tribe or nation should support those hostages, and that they should not be exchanged till we had good proof of their tribe or nation becoming agreeable people. That all the lands of the unoffending tribes or nations should be preserved to them, and a generous trade well regulated. And that all the lands of the offending Tribes or Nations should be forfeited, and that they should be restricted to hunt or live on such parts of it as should be directed by the commanding Officer or Governor who might be appointed to rule them. We undoubtedly should have a greater number of the Indians in our interest. If we had a sufficient quantity of goods for that purpose, our enemy have great advantage of us for they out treaty us, and the highest bidder will have the greatest Number of the Indians. This I know from my acquaintance with them for upwards of twenty years.

To the Delawares we made promises of protection, and they now put our friendship to the test, and if we do not fulfil our promises they will undoubtedly be obliged to look for protection elsewhere, and we must suffer in their opinion and also in the opinion of all the other nations. If I should receive Intelligence, or if anything should occur to me that may serve the general cause, I shall write to you.

I am, sir, with great respect,

Your most obedient humble servant,

EDW. HAND.

[COLONEL JAMES WILSON, Esq.,

A Member of the Honorable Continental Congress.]

FORT PITT, March 22, 1778.

Sir:—I am instructed by the hon'ble, the Commissioners appointed by Congress, to fix on a plan for the defence of these frontiers, to desire that you may continue 150 Privates of the Militia of your County, properly officered, on constant duty on its frontiers. Thirty of them to be added to Captain Moorhead's company, stationed at Fort Hand, and the remaining 120 placed at such stations as you find best calculated for the defence of the County. Instead of Militia call'd out in the ordinary way, the Commissioners are desirous of engaging a like number of volunteers for a longer time than the Militia generally serves. I perfectly agree with them in sentiment and wish you to fall on that Plan, provided no delay arises for its execution.

I am, sir, your obed't h'ble serv't,

EDW. HAND.

[COLONEL ARCHIBALD LOCHRY.]

FORT PITT, June 14, 1778.

Sir:—I am at a Loss to conceive the Meaning of the Intelligence I this day received from the Delaware Indians, yet as the Term old Hunting ground may, and probably does imply the Place that gentleman has been at war the last season, it it is not unlikely; but it may be your County, therefore wish you to take every Precaution to prevent a surprise by keeping

out Scouts and having a force ready to oppose the Invaders.
I will not be remiss in doing my Part. I shall give you Information of anything that comes to my Knowledge and concerns you, and expect a like Information from you, as I mean
to give you timely assistance if necessary.

I am, dear sir, y'rs sincerely,

EDW. HAND.
[COLONEL A. LOCHRY.]

Extract from intelligence receiv'd from the Delaware Indians 14th June, 1778.

The Inclosed Billet I received yesterday from the lake will,
perhaps, be of some use for you.

THE BILLET.

There is a small army of French—150 or 200 men—that is
for the frontier, commanded by one Mr. Jenot. I imagine
that he is for his old hunting ground or for Redstone.

FORT PITT, July 9, 1778.

Sir:—I have just received yours of the 7th and 8th Current,.
and am much distressed to find the unhappy situation of your
county, and the more so as I am at a loss how to relieve you.
Colonel Campbell has ordered a body of the militia of Yoho-
gania County to assemble here. I intended them for you, but
they are not yet come ; if I can't do otherwise will endeavor
to send you a few Regulars to scour your Frontier, which will,
I hope, enable you to collect your Harvest, as you may reason-
ably expect their Hay can't be long, and I hope the Militia
will exert themselves and collect in bodies to save the grain
under the Protection of this Guard ; prepare to receive them
at Hannas Town ; they will be Victualed from here to that
place ; you shall have farther notice of their approach.

Yours, etc.,

[COLONEL A. LOCHRY.]   EDW. HAND.

Fort Pitt, July 10, 1778.

Sir:—Captain James Sullivan, with a Detachment of regular Troops under his Command, will march this Evening, or to-morrow Morning, to your assistance. He will halt at Hannas Town until he sees you; he has written Instructions, which I beg you may peruse and assist him in executing. I hope his Party will produce the desired salutary Effects.

I am, sir, very cordially yours,

[COLONEL A. LOCHRY.]   EDW. HAND.

Fort Pitt, July 27, 1778.

Sir:—I have good reason to suspect that many parties of Indians are now out; you will, therefore, plan to be on your guard.

Plan to furnish twenty-five or thirty men to protect the houses, collecting forage in your county.

I am, sir, your hble svt.,

EDW. HAND.

[COLONEL A. LOCHRY.]

Fort McIntosh, Beaver Creek, Oct. 30, 1778.

Sir:—I had the Honor of writing to you on the 27th September, and hope your People are about the Block Houses I recommended for the protection of your County during my absence. The repeated murders committed by the Indians upon your Inhabitants must show the necessity of them.

The Magistrates of your County have asked my consent for 150 Volunteers to go and rout or remove a few Indian Towns upon Allegheny River, who, probably, are the most troublesome to you, which I very much approve of. It will be greatly to your honor and advantage; they shall have provisions and ammunition, either from this place or Fort Pitt, with every reasonable Encouragement I can give them, as nothing can be better

times, if they are expeditious and secrete. I propose going in
two or three days to Cochocking, or the Delaware Towns, and
leave Colonel Broadhead to wait for our stores, and the attention of most of their Warriors will be upon our motions, which
will probably make them an easy prey. It is what I had in
View myself, if I was not otherwise employed. I shall be glad
to hear of your proceedings and success in it.

I have the pleasure to inform you that my plan of securing
as I go begins to have its proper effect upon several tribes of
the Savages already, who have earnestly applied to me for
peace, but have given them no Encouragement yet, and perhaps will not if I am properly supported, until they give me
substantial proofs of their Sincerity. I intend building a Fort
at Cochocking before I proceed any further, to secure these
Indians in our Interest, from which I may probably make ex-
cursions to some of the Hostile Towns; but, unfortunately, the
time of the Militia I have with me will expire the first day of
January next, which will disappoint all my Schemes, unless I
have a fresh Supply of men before that time, which I cannot
expect from these Counties, who have already Exerted themselves so much; therefore, as I have Spared yours this time,
for the security and protection of your own Frontiers, I hope
and expect you will use your utmost Endeavours to procure
only two hundred men, properly Officered, armed and accout-
ered, whom I request you will send off the first of December
at farthest, that they may be up with me in time, and that I
may not be obliged to relinquish any Ground I gain; and must
also intreat the time of service of your Militia, if possible, may
be six Months from the Day they arrive at my headquarters,
if required so long, as short engagements will be of no use in
my design, and for their encouragement I expect they will
have the honor of finishing the campaign, and all the toil and
labor will be over before they come. In hopes that you will use

your utmost Exertion on the occasion to serve your country
and yourselves.

I am respectfully, sir,

Your most obt. servt,

LACH'N McINTOSH.

[COLONEL LOCHRY.]

I request you will forward the inclosed letter to Colonel
Piper immediately by express.

HEADQUARTERS, FORT PITT, May 10, 1780.

Dear Sir:—I find that it will not be in my power to provide
for the number of men I have ordered to be called into service so soon as I expected. Besides, I have heard officially
that a number of Artillery, Cannon and Stores are now on the
March to this place, and by report, that two Regiments are on
their march to reinforce my command. I must recommend
it to you, and all the leading Officers of your county, to excite
industry in planting and sowing the Summer crops, and to
have your troops here by the second day of next Month.

The stroke at Brush Creek was quite unexpected and has
given me great uneasiness, because I had reason to hope that
the Country eastward of this place would have enjoyed some
quiet. But I see the villains are determined to perplex us
as much as they possibly can. The Militia should be drafted
for two months, although the expedition will probably end in
one, and let them be as well armed and accoutred as circumstances will admit. I request you to encourage them to
bring with them two weeks' allowance of Provisions, lest
there should be a deficiency. I trust you and all the good
people of your County are convinced of the necessity there is
for prosecuting some offensive operations against the Savages,
and I hope that, being favored by a well-timed movement

from the new settlements down the river, we shall be able to strike a general panic into the hostile Tribes. I do not intend to put too much to hazard, as a Defeat would prove fatal to the Settlements, and therefore expect the full Complement of men will be furnished, which alone, with the blessing of Divine Providence, can ensure success. Indeed, I expect that upon this Expedition many will turn and voluntarily to procure to themselves the blessings of Peace. I have the Honor to be, with great regard and Esteem,

Dear, Sir, your most obedient servant,

DANIEL BRODHEAD,

Colonel Commanding No. D.

[COLONEL ARCHIBALD LOCHRY, Lieutenant of Westmoreland County.]

HEADQUARTERS, FORT PITT, July 9, 1780.

Dear Sir:—I am honored with your favor of this date. I am well satisfied with the proposed indulgence to the Inhabitants of Turtle Creek Waters until they have reaped their harvests of Wheat and Rye ; but it will be very inconvenient to provide for the men at such a distance ; besides, our magazines are very low, and I conceive the inhabitants who wish their protection particularly ought to feed them at their own expense—this, I believe has been the usual custom.

I hear nothing of the sixty men you were ordered to draft, which were to receive their supplies from the State, and I am desirous to know what has been done in regard to that order, for I am so circumstanced with regard to resources that my duty will require the strictest economy to subsist the troops in Continental service. If I can possibly obtain supplies, I shall yet make an excursion into the Indian country in time to destroy the corn, etc. But I conceive that the best method will be to march on horse if they can be furnished.

I am, with much respect and esteem,

Your most obedient servant,

DANIEL BRODHEAD.

[COLONEL ARCHIBALD LOCHRY.]

FORT PITT, October 8, 1782.

Sir:—I am honored with your Excellency's two letters of the 4th and 18th of September; the last by Mr. Carnaghan with the money did not arrive here till the 5th instant. This delay and the detachment of General Wayne's regiment not coming at the time proposed will unavoidably prevent my moving so soon as was intended. I have sent an officer Express to meet and hasten General Wayne's men, and though I am not certain what day they can arrive, take for granted, if at all, they will be here before the 20th, and as the business would be impracticable later, have fixed on that day to march from Fort McIntosh—a post thirty miles advanced of this place. Sixty Rangers are counted to me as part of the men for the expedition; these I am not yet informed where they are to come from. Three hundred Militia ordered by Congress from below the mountain are also counted; those are not only so far short of the number, but so few of them are fit, or in any manner Clothed or Equipped for such service, that most of them would be a dead weight or incumbrance; add to this their term of service is nearly expired. I must therefore depend solely on the few Regulars and what volunteers can be raised on this side the Mountain. If about 600 actually assemble, I am determined to make the attempt, particularly as I have some reason to hope General Clark, will co-operate with us if this last delay does not prevent it, as I had concerted measures with him that he should attack the Shawnese at the same time I did Sandusky. One of the Expresses to him was wounded on his way down the river and narrowly escaped falling into the enemy's hands. I have sent another to him since that time, and a third since I received your last dispatches in order to halt him a few days till I could get ready. The Estimate will be found in general too low, and several things omitted which cannot be dispensed with. The calculation for a horse to carry 200 is too high; however you may depend I will spare no pains to have the business done on the lowest terms. I have appointed Mr. John Irwin, of Pittsburgh, the principal agent. If you should think proper to send any money in my absence, you will be so good as to address it to him, subject to my orders. It would not be possible to procure the supplies in so short a time on any other plan than to purchase provision from the Volunteers, which they had collected for their own use on the original plan of carrying the Expedition. I mean, therefore, to order the whole to the place of general Rendezvous, there have the whole appraised and pay for it in bulk; though some unavoidable waste will take place, yet I hope, on the whole, it will come within the price the Rations are estimated at. The greatest difficulty with me is the uncertainty of the Quantity, which cannot be ascertained till the whole is collected, but there is no alternative.

I have the honor to be with great resp'ct, sir, your Excellency's most obedient servant,

[His Excellency,   WM. IRVINE,
Wm. Moor, Esq.]

FORT PITT, April 12, 1782.

My Dearest Love:—I received your two letters by Captain Craig and Mr. Hughes. I am therefore in arrears in the letter way, but the fault is not in me, being extremely anxious to inform you of my arrival here, but have not had a single opportunity. I had very cold weather, though dry, and made a speedy march. Got up the Monday after I left you. One of my horses took lame, and I was oblig'd to leave him about half-way. Things were in a strange state when I arrived. A number of the Country people had just returned from the Moravian towns, about 100 miles distant, where, 'tis said, they did not spare either age or sex. What was more extraordinary they did it in cool blood, having deliberated three days, during which time they were industrious in collecting all hands into their Churches (they had embraced Christianity) where they fell on, while they were singing Hymns, and killed the whole. Many children were killed in their wretched Mother's arms. Whether this was right or wrong I do not pretend to determine. Things were still in greater confusion nearer home, for on the morning before my arrival here a party of Militia attacked some friendly Indians, who were not only under our protection, but several actually had commissions in our service, at the very nose of the garrison on a small island in the River, of whom they killed several, and also made prisoners of a guard of Continental troops, and sent Colonel Gibson a message that they would also scalp him. A thousand lies are propagated all over the country against him, poor fellow, I am informed. The whole is occasioned by his unhappy connection with a certain tribe, which leads people to imagine for this reason that he has an attachment to Indians in general. However false this reasoning may be, yet no reasoning will or can convince people to the contrary.

People who have had Fathers, Mothers, Brothers or Children butchered, tortured, scalped by the savages—reasoning very differently on the subject of killing the Moravians to what people who live in the interior part of the country in safety do—their feelings are very different. Whatever your private

opinion of these matters may be, I conjure you by all the ties
of affection, and as you value my reputation, that you keep
your mind to yourself and that you will not express any sentiment for or against these deeds, as it may be alleged the
sentiments you express may come from me or be mine also.

No man knows whether I approve or disapprove of killing
the Moravians. I called a meeting of most of the principal
Militia Officers. They were convened here last Friday after
long conferences which lasted nearly two days. They parted
seemingly pleased with the plans I proposed to adopt for the
protection of the country, and promised they would support
me. I have also been fortunate enough to suppress the
mutinous disposition of the Troops without Blood-shedding.
From all this you make yourself easy respecting my personal
safety. Some people are killed and some taken by the Indians
in almost every quarter. I lost five of my men a few days
since, who were wood-cutting and carelessly laid down their
arms to load the wagon, when a party rushed on them. This
was at a Fort we have thirty miles down the river. Whether
my mind may change or not I cannot say, but from the state
of things at present I would not consent for the Universe to
your coming up. If your sister, Niell, lives in the country
this summer and you could accomplish taking the children
with you, I should have no objection to your spending some
weeks with her.

Yrs affectionately,

WM. IRVINE.

FORT PITT, December 29, 1782.

My Dearest Love:—This day I expected my Express, but
there is as yet no account of him, but I hourly look for him.
The Bearer, Mr. Jno. Bull, is an elder of the Moravian Indians'
congregation, who, together with the Ministers, Converts, etc.,

had built a pretty town and made good improvements and lived for some years past quite in the style of Christian, White people, but were last fall taken prisoners by a party of Indians commanded by that infamous rascal, Matthew Elliot, and carried away to the number of 100 families from their fine farms into the Wilderness, where they are starving. Mr. Bull is going down to Bethlehem to represent the sufferings of his people to the society of Moravians. I wish I could appoint a day to be with you, but that is impossible.

I am, my dearest love, yours most affectionately,

WM. IRVINE.

[MRS. IRVINE.]

PHILADELPHIA, August 26, 1784.

Sir:—We understand it is your Intention to contract for those Things which will be necessary for the table and support of the Commissioners during the Negotiations. We are apprehensive of much inconvenience in being supplied by a Contractor, and therefore it is our wish that the articles which we have noted as necessary, should be purchased by Mr. O'Hara, in whom we can Confide. You can best judge, sir, whether this will make any material difference in the Expense to the Public. If it will not, we hope the Mode we desire will be agreeable to you, and that Mr. O'Hara will be enabled to provide the Things necessary without a moment's Delay, as the time fixed for the Treaty at Stanwix presses hard upon us.

We have the honor to be, with great respect, sir,

Your most obed and humble Servts,

ARTHUR LEE,

RICHARD BUTLER.

[The Honorable the Superintendent of Finance.]

PHILADELPHIA, September 10, 1784.

Sir:—The Indian Goods destined for the Westward, and which you are now purchasing, you will please to have carefully packed up, marked and numbered and placed in some safe and convenient store, to remain there till the arrival of my Colleagues, which I expect will be to-morrow or next day at farthest. It is my wish that you should take charge of them to Fort Pitt and Cyahoga, and I make not the least doubt but Colonel Atlee and Mr. McClay will agree with me in your appointment to this business. I order that they may be forwarded with all dispatch; You had better begin to engage the necessary Teams immediately. With regard to additional Stores to accommodate the Commissioners, it will be absolutely necessary that they should be laid in. This, however, may be delay'd until the arrival of my brother Commissioners, when you shall be furnished with a list.

I am, Sir, your very humble servant,

F. JOHNSTON, *Commissioner.*

Approved by SAM. ATLEE.

[CAPTAIN JAMES O'HARA.]

PHILADELPHIA, August 28, 1784.

Sir:—You having assisted the Continental Commissioners in procuring the Indian goods so much to their satisfaction, has induced the Indian Commissioners on the part of this State, to request your assistance in obtaining and safe-packing the goods to be provided by them. Enclosed you have a list of such as are wanted, and must beg you will lose no time in furnishing the usual articles therein specified, in order that they may be sent, if possible, with the Goods of the Continent. The list should have been furnished sooner had we been sooner authorized. The Treaty at Fort Stanwix will be held the 20th of September next, so that it will require your utmost exertions, as many of the articles must be made here. A general treaty will be held at Cuyahoga, on the bank of Lake Erie, on the 20th of November next, so that the articles in the enclosed List No. 1, will be equally divided, the one-half only immediately for the first Treaty, by which means you will have sufficient time to make up such articles as shall be required for the second. As the State means to convince the natives that she can and will furnish the best assortment of Goods, we must beg you will be careful to answer her good Intentions in these particulars. Sundry little articles, agreeable to List No. 2, will be wanted for the accommodation of the Commissioners, who beg you will give yourself the additional trouble of furnishing the same and having them carefully put up, marked and sent on with the Goods. When they are ready to be shipped, you will be pleased call upon Captain Joseph Stiles, the keeper of the magazine, who will deliver you 10 quarter Casks of powder for the first Treaty; 10 other quarter Casks will be ready for the second, and likewise delivered you.

We are, Sir, your h'ble servants,

SAMUEL ATLEE,

FRANCIS JOHNSTON.

P. S.—Captain Stiles will also furnish you with three horseman's and one soldier's tent.

[CAPTAIN JAMES O'HARA.]

FORT PITT, December 3, 1785.

Sir:—I am sorry to inform your Excellency that this country has got a severe stroke by the loss of Colonel Lochry and about one hundred ('tis said) of the best men of Westmoreland County, including Captain Stockely and his company of Rangers. They were going down the Ohio on General Clark's Expedition; many accounts agree that they were all killed or taken at the mouth of the Miami River— I believe, chiefly killed. This misfortune, added to the failure of General Clarke's Expedition, has filled the people with great dismay; many talk of retiring to the East side of the

Mountains early in the Spring. Indeed, there is great reason to apprehend that the Savages and, perhaps, the British from Detroit will push us hard in the Spring, and I believe there never were Posts nor a County in a worse state of defence. Notwithstanding, I am well informed there has been sundry meetings of people at different places for the purpose of concerting plans to emigrate into the Indian country, there to establish a Government for themselves. What the result of these meetings were I cannot say, and, as I do not intend to interfere in Civil matters, have not taken any notice of the affair. From what observations I have been able to make, I am of opinion there is many obvious reasons why no time should be lost in running the line between Virginia and Pennsylvania. Civil government will never be fairly established till then, nor even the Militia drawn out with regularity for their own defence. I have no reason, as yet, to complain of the people, for the refractory, ungovernable, low manners generally ascribed to them. I assure you, sir, my pity for their situation is rather excited, than wrath or indignation kindled. I have good grounds to believe that the settlements at Cantuke and the Falls will break up, in which case, I fear, a number of adventurers, who talk of going down to New Orleans with flour, will be killed or taken. Council may depend that during my stay here, that no exertions in my power shall be wanting in everything that may tend to the welfare of the State, or protection of the Inhabitants, as far as consistent with my duty as an officer of the United States. I have the honor to be, with great respect,

Sir, your Excellency's most obedient servant,

WM. IRVINE.

[His Excellency, the President of the State of Pennsylvania.]

TREASURY DEPARTMENT,
REGISTER'S OFFICE, March 6, 1792.

These are to certify that James O'Hara, Esq., late Contractor for supplying the army with Provisions, and who occasionally acted as Quartermaster of the troops and agent for the supply of Indian goods, is not charged with any Moneys on the treasury books. That he has from time to time settled his accounts in a regular manner at the Treasury, and has given general satisfaction to the Treasury officers with whom he settled said accounts. (Signed)

JOSEPH NOURSE, *Register*.

WAR DEPARTMENT, April 19, 1792.

Sir:—The President of the United States, by and with the advice and consent of the Senate, has appointed you Quartermaster-General in the Army of the United States. You will please immediately to signify your acceptance or non-acceptance of this appointment. In order that you may judge of the pay, rations and emoluments for the commissioned and non-commissioned officers and privates in the service of the United States, I enclose you the Act of Congress relative to the military establishment.

I am, sir, your humble servant,

H. KNOX, *Secretary of War*.

[JAMES O'HARA, ESQ.]

PITTSBURGH, June 20, 1792.

Sir:—I have the pleasure to inform you that the Quartermaster-General's Department begins to bear such appearance in this country as strengthens my confidence in being able to perform the Duties in such manner as may be required. The Stores sent by Mr. Knox have arrived more expeditiously than I expected and in tolerable order; the brass cannon is at length received very safe. The conduct of Gist I represented to you in Philadelphia, he being there with his wagon. The Sheet Iron was delivered in due time, and the Camp Kettles are in a fair way of being ready. Every article furnished at this place will be of excellent quality. I expect some embarrassment in procuring Forage, chiefly owing to the very low state of the rivers, but with a little exertion I expect to raise the necessary supply. I have made such arrangements as was in my power for having the necessary magazines and Granaries erected at the Western Posts and for having dry Forage laid up, if possible; this will depend on the state of the Garrison. I cannot make any observations on the deficiencies of my department, having no returns of accoutrements, camp equipage and other articles, which I am informed are already procured, but shall certainly attend to it soon as may be in my power. Wishing to continue Major Craig as Quartermaster at this post, I have ventured to offer him Forty dollars per month, three Rations per day and Forage for one horse, which he does not consider a sufficient compensation and which I shall not exceed in any case without advice. Such Blacksmiths, Carpenters and Wheelwrights as ought to be employed as artificers, will not engage to serve for less than fifteen or twenty dollars per month and extra provision. Good Mechanics are indispensably necessary, and as I do not conceive myself justifiable in agreeing on such high terms, I wish to be instructed on both these cases. I have purchased but very few Horses, as having a great number on Hand would at present be attended with unnnecessary expense. I shall wait for particular orders on this Head, as a sufficient Number may be raised in a few days' notice. The Commander-in-Chief being here I shall not trouble you with any observations on the situation of our Frontiers, nor do I know that more can be said than that we seem to be in profound peace, surrounded by a cheerful people, possessing all the necessaries of life in the greatest abundance and on the most easy terms, although not altogether free from apprehension that this tranquillity may be again disturbed by skulking parties from Lake Erie, or by Muncy Vagabonds. I expect to be honored with your commands often as the service may require, and I now take the liberty of assuring you that no motive nor consideration can possibly interfere with the duties of my station, which I feel myself most religiously bound to execute agreeable to your instructions and my own judgment. A few loads of shot is received under Campbell's contract. They will not please, being too rough for brass pieces and not fair cast; of this they are informed.

I have the honor to be, sir,

Your most obedient humble servant,

JAMES O'HARA, Q. M. G.

[To the Honorable, the Secretary of War, June 20, 1792.]

WAR DEPARTMENT, June 29, 1792.

Sir:—I have received your favor of the 20th instant and I am happy to learn the confidence that you shall be able to perform the duties of your Department in a satisfactory manner.

I am really of opinion that Major Craig ought to have the pay and emoluments of a deputy quartermaster-general. His punctuality, fidelity and industry are such as to be of particular importance in the place where he is, as he has the charge of receiving and distributing all the public stores. I think you may engage good mechanics at fifteen dollars, besides extra provisions; but they ought to be engaged for two or three years, unless sooner discharged. I am glad you have not yet purchased many horses. The Commander-in-Chief being upon the spot, will instruct you upon that and all other parts of your duty.

The returns of the Tents and Camp equipage is presumed to be abundant; a particular return shall be transmitted to you, and if there should be any deficiency you will either provide them, or require them to be provided here.

I shall write to Major Craig about Campbell's shot.

I am, sir, your humble servant,

H. KNOX.

EXTRACT OF A LETTER FROM THE SECRETARY OF THE TREASURY TO THE SECRETARY OF WAR.

"TREASURY DEPARTMENT, August 6, 1792.

"All advances for supplies in the quartermaster's department will be made to the* quartermaster by warrants in his favor from the treasury, and he will have to account immediately to the treasury for the disbursement of the moneys committed to him.

"It will, of course, be necessary for the quartermaster to have an attorney or deputy at this place. No provision for compensation of a deputy having been made it is of necessity that he should depute some person who is otherwise in the employ of the government.

[Compared.]   "JN. STAGG."

HEADQUARTERS, PITTSBURGH, August 17, 1792.

Sir:—I have received the extract of a letter from the Secretary of the Treasury to the Secretary of War, relative to the appointment of an attorney or deputy at Philadelphia, and

* After the first of next month.

the Secretary at War's request that such appointment should
be immediately made. I cannot conceive that the allusion in
this Extract can be to you in particular, as the Secretary's
sentiments on this subject were the same several months
ago; nevertheless, your known Integrity merits my confidence.
Your industry and knowledge of the mode of doing Business
in the Publick Offices will no doubt entitle you to "such compensation as may be hereafter thought reasonable " for such
services as you shall tender in this line. Inclosed you have
a Letter of attorney that will enable you to receive the necessary supplies of money for my department. The purchases and
disbursements will be made occasionally, as may be legally
ordered.

I am, Sir, your most humble servant,

JAMES O'HARA, Q. M. G.

[SAML. HODGDON, Esq.]

HEADQUARTERS, PITTSBURGH, August, 17, 1792.

Sir:—I am honored with yours of the 7th instant, inclosing
an extract of a letter from the Secretary of the Treasury,
respecting the mode of advancing Supplies in the Quartermaster's department. In consequence of a letter received
from Mr. Hodgdon, and my knowledge of his integrity, I
have forwarded to him a power-of-attorney, that he may draw
money on my account, from the Treasury of the United
States, whenever it may be considered necessary, after the
first of next month. This is all I feel myself justifiable in
doing on this subject at present.

Mr. Belli's letter, dated Lexington, June the 8th, relative
to forage, was received and answered in due time. I am
under no apprehension on account of this article, although,
on a moderate estimate, the present Establishment will require one Hundred Thousand Bushels of Grain annually. He

17

applies to me for an additional sum of money, as the $25,000 he has received is the exact estimation for Purchase of the Cavalry Horses. The purchase of Oxen (in which he has been successful), the purchase of forage, his expenditures, the necessary assistance and other expenses, do require that he should be furnished with Ten Thousand Dollars, at least. I, therefore, request that this sum of ten thousand dollars be placed in the Hands of Colonel Hodgdon, who will transmit it to me by the first good opportunity.

I find that the Spades and Shovels required in my first Estimate have been entirely neglected. They are already in demand. I beg they may be forwarded, or part of them, as soon as possible. Should the present mode of Transporting public stores to this country be continued, every branch of the army must suffer not only great inconvenience, but their disgrace may be owing to the base speculations of a few ungrateful Wagoners, who seem to take pride in abusing that indulgence they have so often experienced. The high price given for carriage is the principal cause of its being so infamously executed. It is engrossed by the most insinuating and stowed away until they can trip it, or sell out, at two or three Guineas the load; then no responsible person will meddle with it, having been Witnesses to the tricks of those undertaken before; then have I seen Lading pass to the fourth hand before it reached this place. The only remedy for this growing evil is to reduce the price of Carriage twelve per cent.—viz., change the neat to Gross Weight, and cause every fellow who has trespassed to be dismissed. The best characters will then engage to deliver each load at this place in Twenty-five days, or pay four dollars for every day's detention after.

I am, Sir, your most humble servant,

JAMES O'HARA, *Q. M. Gen.*

[Honorable Secretary of War.]

LETTER TO HIS EXCELLENCY MAJOR-GENERAL WAYNE.

HEADQUARTERS, PITTSBURGH, August 30, 1792.

Sir:—I have the honor to inclose you a copy of a letter from Captain Haskell, dated at Marietta, the 21st instant, stating the disagreeable situation the Troops at that Post and Gallipolis are in "for want of clothing" and other necessaries.

Captain Haskell having made no regular returns of the Articles wanted, I beg leave to submit to your Excellency the necessity of furnishing him with temporary relief as soon as the communication will admit, as I apprehend that those Posts are not of such magnitude as will justify the appointment of subordinates in either the Quartermaster, Ordnance, or Clothing branch of the staff.

I am, sir, your most humble servant,

JAMES O'HARA, *Q. M. G.*

LETTER TO MR. ROBERT ELLIOT, CONTRACTOR.

HEADQUARTERS, MIAMI VILLAGES, October 5, 1792.

Dear Sir:—We arrived here safe on the 30th and in tolerable order, and with Extreme difficulty Barbees Brigade was prevailed on to go to Greenville for the last Escort, his people would not agree to bring any flour on their own Horses, the General has, however, wrote him by this Express, requesting him to prevail on them to load out.

It is very unfortunate that your new Horses will not be able to join this Escort, as it would complete this Post for a reasonable time, and I can assure you, that doing this after the army moves, will be very critical. I do not expect General Barbee can leave Greenville before the 9th, and were it possible for you to have him overtaken at Recovery by Express, I think he would leave a Detachment to bring you on, as you had some hopes of being at Greenville on the 10th, the whole Detachment could not wait as the army will be again on half allowance, notwithstanding all possible dispatch. I have ordered Butler to push until he meets you, and should this Effort have the desired effect it will be of very great importance to the army and to the contractors. The Fort goes on rapidly, and I have not the least doubt of the General taking up his line of march at all events on the 15th.

JAMES O'HARA.

LETTER TO THE HONORABLE THE SECRETARY OF WAR.

PITTSBURGH, October 19, 1792.

Sir:—In consequence of a requisition from the Commander-in-Chief for a supply of Forage and other articles, I take the liberty of representing to you the necessity of having the sum of Fifty thousand dollars, at least, advanced for the Quartermaster's department and transmitted to me, as soon as convenient. Annexed you have an estimate of the Expence that will Certainly attend the different Articles therein specified.

By letters of the 21st and 27th of September from Mr. Belli, I cannot depend on any considerable assistance with Forage from the country of Kentucky. I transmitted him ten thousand Dollars yesterday by Major Rudolph, being the first good opportunity.

The Articles of Boats, mentioned in this estimate, may appear to you extraordinary, having so great a number already on hand; they happen to be all at this place, and the Articles required are only to be found at a very considerable distance up the river Monongahela, and the flat and unwieldy Construction of the Boats preclude every idea of ascending the Stream with them. I shall, therefore, be oblig'd to procure others, more Convenient to the Cargoes. Colonel Hodgdon will wait on you, and should the present demand of Fifty thousand dollars meet your approbation, he will receive the Money as my Agent, and forward it soon as may be in his power.

I have the honour to be, sir,

Your most obedient humble servant,

JAMES O'HARA.

WAR DEPARTMENT, October 26, 1792.

Sir:—Your letter of the 19th instant has been received, containing a requisition for fifty thousand dollars for the objects specified. This request will be considered and transmitted to the treasury.

You will please to transmit to this office immediately a return of the pack-horses, oxen, carts and wagons in service, and the objects for and places at which they are employed. It will also be necessary that you transmit the objects for which the five hundred pack-horses mentioned in your estimate are destined. Mr. Belli, expecting his letter would come through the wilderness, transmitted a duplicate open of his letter to you of the 21st September, but as you have received the first I have retained the duplicate.

It is necessary that you should monthly transmit to me an abstract specifying generally the objects and amount of your payments. You will for the past exhibit a general abstract. It is not expected that this should be precise or accompanied with vouchers, but to serve as a general index of the expenditures.

I am, sir, your very humble servant,

H. KNOX.

LETTER TO THE HONORABLE THE SECRE-
TARY OF WAR.

PITTSBURGH, December 14, 1792.

Sir:—My being absent on several post days past, deprived me of the pleasure of acknowledging the receipt of the 9th ult. sooner. Please to accept of my sincere thanks for your particular attention to my last requisition for money. I am perfectly satisfied with the sum Advanced to my agent, as the ease and facility with which it may be transmitted appears now so obvious, that I shall certainly prefer drawing occasional supplies to having a large sum in my possession at one time, and therefore do dispense with any further application until necessity requires it.

The whole amount advanced for my department appears, by your statement to be One hundred and seven thousand Dollars. I am not informed how the Odd seven thousand were drawn, but presume they will be accounted for in the proper place. Twenty yoke of Oxen, mentioned in my return of the 2d of November, are all that have been in service. Mr. Belli's letter of the 21st of September informs that "some are used at the outposts and some engaged in carrying Forage from headquarters to Fort Hamilton," and answer very well. I ex-pected to have in my power to give you more satisfaction on this subject in the course of this Winter; having purchased ten yokes for the use of our new camp at Legionville. I never had any doubt of their performing well in Draft, but they come too high in this country, to purchase more than the number necessary for present use. A particular abstract of Major Craig's expenditures is now enclosed, by which you will be able to form an idea of the charges incidental to the department, exclusive of the necessary preparations.

Captain Pryor, with sixteen Indians, three squaws and three

interpreters, arrived here on the 7th, and proceeded on their way to Philadelphia on the 12th, all on horseback. I inclose a statement of their Expences from Marietta and at this place, which you will find to be very extravagant, owing principally to the dissipation of the Interpreters, who, I am well convinced, will afford you very little satisfaction, especially Mayo and Jaco are the greatest Ruffians I ever saw, and I am sorry to find that Captain Pryor conceives it his duty to indulge them in all their excesses at public expence. You have (inclosed) my instructions to Mr. Sallender, a French gentleman, well recommended, as a proper person to furnish the Indians on the road. He is to remain with them in Philadelphia or return immediately to this place, as you may think proper. The four hundred dollars advanced being considered insufficient by Captain Pryor, I gave him one hundred more, which he has promised to settle at the war office. You will also receive a copy of Mr. Belli's letter of the 28th of October, from Fort Washington, all his wants regretted in this letter were supplied by Major Rudolph, being the first good opportunity. Rudolph's pilot is returned, and brings letters late as the 14th ult., which you will probably see before this reaches you; however, I take the liberty of giving you an Extract, which states particularly the number of horses we lost on the 6th of November before Fort St. Clair. The Commander-in Chief has got his troops very comfortably encamped, and the prospect of forage and provisions is very favorable. I intend taking the advantage of the present open weather, to send off fourteen boats loaded with Forage, to Fort Washington; my principal motive for pushing on this quantity at this uncertain season is, the hopes of making our boats as useful as they should be in the Spring; could I preserve them, which I apprehend will be so very difficult and uncertain, that I am of opinion it will be very proper to have twenty new boats ready to launch for the reception of the Troops in March, as soon after as may be necessary.

I have the honour to be, your most obedient servant,

JAMES O'HARA, *Q. M. G.*

HEAD QUARTERS, LEGIONVILLE, February 12, 1793.

Sir:—I have been Favor'd with your letter of the 5th instant, enclosing a general statement of forage purchased, a statement of cash, with an Estimate of boats wanted for the ensuing campaign ; and have received a general return of Quartermaster's stores on hand the 20th of July, 1792, received since, issued and on hand up to the 1st February, 1793. If you have not already done it, I have to request that you will transmit a copy of it to the Secretary of War the soonest possible. I have examined your Estimate of boats, out of the twelve that you have calculated for the transportation of 2,000 men with their Arms, baggage and provisions sufficient ; we ought not to calculate upon a greater number of men than fifty to each boat, and I have seen it demonstrated that your large ferry-boat would not carry more than twenty horses and men across the Allegheny at one trip, with the men and horses all standing up and without forage. I should rather suppose it would require twelve boats to transport 160 horses and cattle, with the riders, drivers and necessary forage, so as not to crowd or injure the horses or cattle, and it will certainly require at least eight boats for the Artillery department. By the best calculation that I can make, it will require at least sixty boats, independent of those necessary for the Quartermaster's department—what number that may require, you are the best judge. The whole amount of the grain part of the forage ought most certainly to be procured, and the deficiency in hay to be made up by an additional quantity of grain, in the proportion of one thousand bushels of Corn for

every ton of Hay, which is upon the very lowest scale of
allowance per ration, i.e., 14 pounds of hay and 7 quarts of
corn. Enclosed is a return of articles immediately wanted,
and which must be forwarded, if possible, to-morrow. All
our smiths and armourers are idle for want of coal; the con-
sumption is, at least, equal to five bushels per diem; we have
made and used upwards of 150 bushels of charcoal besides the
stone coal; the whole is now exhausted. We shall want 150
bushels per month. What will be the best mode of forwarding the troops under Captain Slough? Their tents, if any,
may be stored at Pittsburgh; their other baggage may be
sent by water, and the Detachment to be ferried over the
Allegheny to-morrow and march the next morning early for
this place, where they will be immediately under cover. You
will, therefore, give the necessary orders, in addition to those
enclosed for Captain Slough.

I am, Sir, your most obedient, humble servant,

ANTY. WAYNE.

[To JAMES O'HARA, Q. M. G., Pittsburgh.]

LEGIONVILLE, March 26, 1793.

Sir:—I have the honor to enclose you an estimate of
money, absolutely necessary for carrying the orders of the
Commander-in-Chief into immediate effect; exclusive of
$18,000 lately drawn by Mr. Hodgdon, being very apprehen-
sive that Mr. Belli has involved the department at Fort
Washington, of which I can make no estimate at present.
On the 15th inst., I received orders to prepare for transporting the whole of the troops to Fort Washington. I had not
one boat fit for the purpose, at that time; however, they shall
be ready on the day appointed; and the forge will be complete, agreeable to the orders of September 10.

I hope Mr. Hodgdon will meet no difficulty in having at

least $60,000 forwarded to me as soon as possible, that I may
be enabled to furnish the necessary transportation and support on your first and best principle for ready money only.
My accounts for the present Quarter, with general returns,
will be presented at the Treasury by the next post, and in
future they shall be particularly attended to, agreeable to
your instructions.

I have reason to apprehend that the ground on which Fort
Fayette is erected has not been patented. When this work
was begun by Major Craig, the property was in the Penns,
and he informs me that he applied for a performance of their
moderate terms at the war office, and proceeded considering
the ground as public property. The lots are in George
Wood's Plan of the Town of Pittsburgh, numbers 55, 56, 57,
58, 91, 92, 93 and 94. Should any citizen take out Deeds for
those lots and persist in their right, perhaps five times the
purchase money must come out of the public treasury for the
property by the common law. I therefore request that those
deeds be immediately applied for in the name of the United
States.

Mr. Anthony Butler is the late Proprietor's present agent
and has full power to convey.

I have the honor to be your most obedient and very
humble servant, JAMES O'HARA, *Q. M. G.*

[The Honourable the Secretary of War.]

WAR DEPARTMENT, April 6, 1793.

Sir:—I have just received your letter of the 26th of
March last, with the list of articles enclosed, these shall be
duly considered and application made to the Secretary of the
Treasury for the necessary funds to be placed in your hands.
| The purchase of the lots on which Fort Fayette stands shall

be taken into consideration and such order taken thereon as shall appear to be authorized by the laws.

I am, sir, your humble servant,

H. Knox,

Secretary of War.

[James O'Hara, Q. M. G.]

War Department, April 12, 1793.

Sir:—I have received your letter of the 6th, inst. You will receive in a few days after this letter such proportion of the monies you have required to the 1st of July, as the Secretary of the Treasury and myself shall judge sufficient, with an assurance of a further supply from time to time as shall be judged necessary.

Your deputy, Mr. Belli, is here, and has presented his accounts to the treasury for settlement for whatever sum he shall produce, proper vouchers will be credited to your account. Before you descend the Ohio it will be indispensable that your accounts and vouchers to the close of the last year, shall be presented to the treasury for settlement.

Major Craig speaks of a balance due Turnbull and Marmie for the rent of this magazine, due before your administration. This account you will pay if reasonable, and charge the same in your account in consequence of this order.

I am, sir, with respect, your very humble servant.

Knox.

[James O'Hara, Esq., Quartermaster General].

Headquarters, S. W. Branch of Miami, Oct. 23, 1793.

Sir:—In obedience to the orders and instructions received from the Secretary at War on the 25th of May, 1792, directing me if there should be any defect in the transportation or supplies of provision (on the part of the Contractors) to make instant arrangements, at the public expense, to remedy the evil, in order to prevent any injury to the service. That defect having actually taken place as far as relates to the Contractor's means of transport, which is not more than one-half equal to the daily supplies and the necessary deposits ordered in advance at the respective posts and garrisons. You, as Quartermaster-General, will immediately purchase in behalf of the Public, and add 250 pack horses and 30 pair of oxen or 60 wagon horses to the Contractor's present means of transport, and for which this shall be your warrant and authority.

ANT. WAYNE.

[JAMES O'HARA, Esq., Q. M. G. of the Legion.]

LETTER TO HIS EXCELLENCY THE COM-
MANDER-IN-CHIEF.

PHILADELPHIA, April 3, 1794.

Sir:—I embrace this first opportunity to inform you of my progress in forwarding the necessary supplies for the Legion for the present year, and of expressing my regrets for the unavoidable delay attending it, being well aware of your solicitude for the regular support of the Army. I could not, with propriety, receive money nor permission to purchase until a few days ago, the Appropriation Bill having passed into a law, the business was immediately attended to by the Secretary of War and the Treasury. The stores and articles required to be taken from this place are now preparing, and those required from the Western country shall be forwarded agreeable to the enclosed schedules regular as possible. The sheet of bar iron, stationery and tents are under way.

Enclosed you will receive a general estimate of money required for use of the Quartermaster Department for the present year, to which no kind of objections has been made. Of this I have this day drawn $30,000. One half I send Mr. Belli by Mr. Carpenter ; the remainder I shall also send on in a few days. You have been informed of the fate of the Army Bill in Senate, it is again brought forward and certain means will be adopted to complete the Legion, at least the old and obstinate opposition becoming more and more confounded, and the spirit to stimulate daily increasing, the effects that those changes may produce will be indebted to the universal approbation of your proceedings in the Indian country.

The Secretary of War informed me yesterday that he had received returns of Hospital and Military stores required and that they should be immediately ordered. The clothing is in a very fair way, and five months' pay is preparing at bank. I will go on in the course of next week. My accounts being before the Comptroller free from all appearance of difficulty, I hope to get from this place in ten days, and as procuring and purchasing supplies on the Ohio will require some time to meet your Excellency's particular commands, either to attend to the execution of that duty or repair to the Army with such other orders as you may think necessary, would relieve me from great anxiety in case of active operations. I wish to be with you, otherwise I may be well employed elsewhere until your supplies are better secured. We daily wait the pleasure of hearing from you, in the meantime you may be assured that every thing in my power shall be done to support the department and accommodate the Legion.

I have the honor to be sir, your most obedient servant,

JAMES O'HARA, Q. M. G.

HEADQUARTERS, GREENVILLE, June 29, 1794.

Sir:—Since my letter of the 25th inst., I have received despatches and papers from the Secretary of War down to the 4th of this month; the intelligence therein mentioned will require some artillery and stores, which together with all such articles as may be necessary in your department must be forwarded the soonest possible. All the packhorses and cattle belonging to your department and that of the Contractor's, may be forwarded under the escort that is directed to be formed at Fort Washington in the course of three or four days, viz.: all the soldiers in that garrison fit for active service that can possibly be spared, the regular Dragoons under Captain Thomas Lewis and Cornet Blew, all the volunteers that Captain Kibby can bring forward agreeably to his instructions and ready to advance with the Convoy on or before the 5th of July; to these will probably be added twenty Choctaw Indians, who are now on their way to Head-Quarters, and who had arrived at Lexington on the 21st inst. You will probably have to purchase horses or good ox teams for the artillery and Tumbrils, which must be loaded with shot and shells agreeably to the invoice with which Captain Henley will be furnished; these last articles are to come forward under the immediate escort of Major General Scott; who you will please to furnish with four Harremen's tents and thirty common tents, and with forty packhorses, taking receipts for the same to be accounted for at the close of the campaign. All the horses belonging to both your own and the Contractor's departments are, and will be, fully employed in front.

Great caution must be observed in the next escort and convoy, as it would appear that the enemy are meditating a serious blow at some quarter. The opinion of our red allies is that they are now advancing to attack the Legion.

I had sent out three select parties, composed of Indians and spies, in order to take prisoners and make discoveries of the situation, force and design of the enemy, two of these parties are yet out. The other, consisting of forty-five Choctaws and ten of our best spies, were drove back to camp yesterday, by vastly superior numbers, according to the Choctaws' account, who lost one of their people at a place called Girtey's Town, on the St. Mary's, thirty miles advanced of this place, in a direct line towards Grand Glaize, and a few miles to the east of Fort Recovery, for which post Major McMahon marched this morning, at reveille, with a good detachment, having under his escort a large number of horses loaded with supplies. Perhaps the enemy may endeavor to prevent his progress, in that case his orders are to charge and cut his way through them to Recovery, regardless of number.

Then I shall endeavor to draw the attention of the enemy from our escort in the rear, and to create a jealousy for their own safety, as well as for that of their women and children. In the return you will give directions for improving every moment in forwarding corn to Fort Hamilton by every possible means. It would also be necessary to purchase a reserve of at least three hundred packhorses, to be ready in Kentucky at a moment's warning. Apropos, the war has assumed so new and so serious a complexion as not to admit of Mr. Belli's absence in furlough ; on the contrary, he ought to remain at Fort Washington, and you ought to be with the Legion, together with an able assistant ; you have nobody at this place but the most trifling thing, whose utmost stretch of abilities will not reach across the Counter.

You will please to inform the Contractor that his means of transport at this place is not half adequate to the purpose.

I also hope and trust that your own will be at least double

to what it now is at Greenville. Wishing you a speedy and safe arrival,

I am, Sir, your most obedient and humble servant,

ANTY. WAYNE.

[To JAMES O'HARA, Q. M. General.]

HEADQUARTERS, GREENVILLE, July 26th, 1794.

Sir:—Yesterday I received yours, dated the 11th June, which I presume was wrote on the 11th inst. Garner's dispatches have not yet come to hand. I have no objections to your progress in procuring Forage, and wish it all safe at Fort Washington; you are informed before this time of the ample state of our granaries, and in order to relieve you from the trouble of forwarding corn in the dry season, you will please to purchase no more for this country until further notice. I wrote you on the 14th and 21st, wherein I complain of want of bags, and of the delay of Sundry Articles of the department, which I expect will be remedied as soon as possible. My calculation respecting the volunteers was perfectly right, upwards of 1,500 are now actually coöperating with the Legion. General Scott arrived yesterday, and a forward move will be made in two days. Since my last several reconnoitering parties have returned from the Towns. Mr. Wells, one of our Spies, and his small party, brought in a Pocotawatomi, who was in the action of the 30th June; annexed you have the purport of his information; he was taken at Grand Glaize, July 21st, 1794, and being examined, says that by every account of the Delawares from Roche de Bout, the British have from fifteen to twenty pieces of Cannon at that place. That the British called upon all the Indian Nations to bring on all their warriors, and that they would bring more British soldiers than they could bring Warriors altogether. This was one moon before the action at Fort Recovery. The Indians having prepared for war told the British to raise their Strong Arm and come on ; their answer was to proceed and go on before, and they would wait with their Strong Arm to strike the Americans who were expected to come the other way, and strike them in the rear after the Indians would go to the war. That at the attack made on Fort Recovery on the 30th of June, there were of the Shawnese 160 warriors, Delawares 160, Wyandots 130, Six Nations 100, Pocotawatomies 40, Thawas 170, Chippewas 700, Miamis 78, Eel River 8–86–1,654, and in addition to them 650 had joined them after they were beat. Mathew Elliot and young McKee, a British officer, brought on four Matrosses and Ammunition, to batter the Fort, as soon as they could find the Cannon, that were hid by the Indians after General St. Clair's defeat, but were disappointed, as the cannon had been taken away. That the great man of Canada ordered them to go and take the first Fort and pass on and take all to the river, to overset General Wayne's army and roll them into the Ohio. The Indians thought their numbers equal to the Task, but were soon convinced of their mistake. He cannot tell the number of Indians killed before Fort Recovery ; the Indians carried off all their dead, except a few that lay too near the fort, in the course of the night after the Assault. He only saw of the killed nine Shawnese, six Pocotawatomies, ten Chippewas, two Wyandots and about sixteen Tawawas—the latter suffered most. There was a great number of Wounded carried off on horseback, and a number on biers, who are since dead. The Chippewas and Tawawas, and all the other Nations secrete their dead, nor do they like to talk of them, nor let one nation know how many another had lost. The Chippewas and Tawawas put their wounded in Boats at Grand Glaize, and went off immediately by water, disgusted and angry with the Shawnese, whom they suspected of having fired on their rear whilst attacking the Fort, they were jealous of the other Nations

18

and all the other Nations were jealous of them in consequence of mutual reproach for bad conduct during the engagement.

The Shawnese, Delawares and Miamis are very uneasy for their situation; the general opinion was they would be obliged to abandon their Country, as they cannot expect any further assistance from the Chippewas or Tawawas; their attention is totally absorbed in attending to the safety of their women and children, whom they were determined to move off (as soon as the army advanced) to Detroit, and up the Bear Creek branch of the Miami.

That the fort, built by the British at Roche de Bout, is a plain Stockade, comprehending all McKee's houses and stores.

Being present at the examination of this prisoner, I am of opinion that his answers to the General's queries were very candid. He was taken within sight of the house at Au Glaize; he was the seventh on hand. A variety of circumstances correspond to confirm a belief that the Indians must have sustained very considerable loss in Warriors. Before Fort Recovery three bodies have been found in the Woods, making the number thirteen, and the information of the Pocotawatami is corroborated in some measure from other quarters. My prospect of supporting the Quartermaster Department with general approbation are very flattering; the Legion and auxiliaries are in good spirits and well supplied, and you may be perfectly assured that we shall be in possession of Grand Glaize and Roche de Bout before the 15th of next month.

July 27th.—The General beats to-morrow morning instead of the Reveille—the whole army is ready to move in the most complete order at sunrise, and you may expect to be informed of an end being put to the business of war in this quarter and of Simcoe's* retrograde or defeat by my next letter.   I am, etc.,

JAMES O'HARA, *Q. M. G.*

---

* Governor of Canada.

It is a fact that upwards of twenty of our Chickasaws fell in with the rear of the enemy and killed a number undiscovered.

[To Isaac Craig, Esq., July 26, 1794.]

HEADQUARTERS, GRAND GLAIZE, Sept. 11, 1794.

Sir:—The enclosed letter to Elliot & Williams, with its enclosures will show you the present disagreeable and critical situation of the army, and the measures that I have been compelled to adopt, in order to hold possession of the country and prevent a famine.

After perusing those letters, which are necessary for your nformation, you will seal and deliver them to Mr. Elliot. I much fear that he has been deceived by his Agents as to Cattle, Horses, etc.; if upon a free communication with him you find this to be the case and that he cannot throw in the supplies demanded, in the course of four weeks from and after the 10th instant, you are then, in behalf of the United States, to make the necessary purchases of Cattle, Horses, etc., in order to supply the defect, of which you will keep a separate and fair account, to be settled at the treasury with the Contractors at a future day. In the interim you will forward as great a quantity of whiskey as practicable, as the public are greatly in arrears with the Legion, and volunteers with the Legion in particular, who have been on half allowance of flour for five weeks past and for these fifteen days on constant fatigue in rendering Fort Defiance impregnable to the force of Artillery and for which I have promised them, by way of a small compensation, one gill of whiskey per diem per man, when on this necessary fatigue and on short allowance.

I expect to march from this place on the 13th and to reach the Miami village on the 18th, in the evening, if not attacked by the combined force of the Enemy, whose long silence and great prospects of a powerful re-inforcement from the Lakes renders that event not improbable, add to this that our force will be much reduced by the absence of General Barbee's brigade and the garrison of Defiance; we shall, however, push hard for victory.

Interim, I am your most

Hum. serv't.,

Aɴty. Wɴyne.

[Col. James O'Hara, Q. M. G.]

Fort Washington, Oct. 16, 1794.

Sir:—I had the honor to write you from Greenville by Captain Gibson on the 18th, informing your Excellency of my great disappointment in finding the Horses on the way to Headquarters, to be under the one-fourth part of the number expected. General Barbee having but 38 instead of 300, and only 144 by Captain Gibson, instead of 400 as reported to you, on the 9th by Express and of the surprising deficiency of flour at Greenville, being 44,000 Rations instead of 120,000, by the same report. At Fort Hamilton the state of the Wagons was as suspected, not one to be found, nor the least information respecting them.

On my arrival here yesterday morning I met Mr. George Wilson, the Contractor's principal agent, setting out for Headquarters, and wasted the remainder of the day in prevailing on him to postpone this extraordinary journey, and in fruitless Altercations Notwithstanding the most liberal, pointed and repeated orders from Mr. Elliot, and the most solemn promises on his part, to have 500 Pack-horses at this place on the 1st instant, to continue purchasing until further orders, and to have 1200 Head of Cattle on the 15th. He has deceived his employers and involved the Army in a very serious scene indeed. He has not one Beef nor satisfactory information respecting any, and only one hundred Horses at this place ; and his apologies are if possible more criminal than his delinquencies. He asserts, that he had received neither instructions nor funds for any such purposes. That the contractor's bill had not credit. That Bank notes would not pass. That the price of Horses was too high, and on each of these ungenerous subterfuges being clearly confuted by my certain knowledge of the reverse, and after my offer of money and personal assistance to support the Contract agreeable to your requisitions, he concluded by declaring that the Horses could not be got in the state of Kentucky by any means whatever. The most favorable construction that can be put on this man's conduct is, that he has fallen into the fashionable error of thinking for others, and that the Army must return to Fort Hamilton and this Post, but his arrangements are deficient even in this case. On perceiving that I had determined to have five hundred Horses immediately brought forward for the Contractors, Mr. Wilson offered his service and actually promised to procure them in fourteen days, or, "in as short time as any man living could."

This inconsistency induced me to inform him that he could no longer be confided in, being alone culpable for all the consequences of his deception and neglect. An Express was dispatched on my arrival to forward a number of cattle, said to be at George Town. I shall receive two hundred horses on the 18th which shall be kept in motion ; the purchase of these Horses was deferred, that they might not interfere with the first purchase ordered by the Contractors. One hundred were this day collected and sent to load at Hamilton, to proceed to Headquarters ; this is all the visible means of assistance in my power at present, but I beg you to be perfectly assured that not one moment shall be omitted in removing your present Anxiety—of which I am very sensible—and of relieving myself from very uncommon perplexity. The wagons I have engaged to load and start from Hamilton on the 20th, having ensured them regular Escorts.

In order to keep the business of the contract as separate from my department as possible, I have furnished Mr. Wilson with money to assist my Agents in the purchase of five hundred Horses for the Contractors, and have instructed them in such a manner as cannot fail of success.

Mr. Samuel Culberson, one of the Contractor's agents, has charge of the horses now setting off. I expect he will be at Recovery on the 22d, and will give you all the candid information in his power, relating to the subject of this letter, having heard the disputes and equivocations to which it alludes. The state of provisions at the different Posts were October 12th, at Fort Adams, 600 lbs. flour, and 2 head of cattle. At Fort Recovery, as stated by Lieut. Drake, Oct. 13th, at Greenville, 720 lbs. flour and 20 cattle. At Fort St. Clair, 48 bbls. of flour, 30 lbs. of beef. 14th, at Fort Hamilton, 3,500 barrels and 1,300 kegs flour. The 15th, at Fort Washington, 1,000 barrels of flour and 40 barrels salt.

I am Sir, Obt. Hbl. Servt.

JAMES O'HARA, *Q. M. G.*

[HIS EXCELLENCY THE COMMANDER-IN-CHIEF.]

HEADQUARTERS, MIAMI VILLAGES, October 17, 1794.

Messrs. ELLIOT and WILLIAMS.

Gentlemen:—As contractors for supplying the Legion and the Western posts, you are to make immediate and effectual provision for 3,640 daily issues of complete rations until the first day of January, 1795, inclusively of 327,600 rations of good and wholesome provisions always in advance. The meat kind to be well and carefully salted and cured and the whole properly housed and stored in the following proportions, places and deposits, viz. :

	Daily Issues.	Rations
1st at Fort Washington	300	27,000
2d at Fort Steuben .	100	9,000
3d at Fort Massac	100	9,000
4th at Fort Knox .	100	9,000
5th at Fort Hamilton	100	9,000
6th at Fort St. Clair .	60	5,400
7th at Fort Jefferson	60	5,400
8th at Greenville .	1,500	135,000
9th at Fort Recovery	100	9,000
10th at Fort Adams .	60	5,400
11th at the Miami Villages . . .	—	54,000
12th at Fort Defiance (Grand Glaize)	—	2,700
13th at Pique Town, (Chilacothe)	100	900
14th at Lormies' Stores, N. Branch	60	5,400
15th at the old Tawa towns	100	—
Au Glaize	100	9,000

Total 3,640 daily issues, and in advance 327,600.

You will please to observe that none of the posts on the waters of the upper parts of the Ohio are mentioned, because the late commotions in the vicinity of Pittsburgh may eventually occasion material alterations, therefore, you will receive orders from the Secretary of War with respect to rations at those posts. The season for curing provisions being now arrived, you have not one moment to lose in making the necessary arrangements. The general interest of the United States, the security of the Frontier Inhabitants and the retention of the posts and country we have recently acquired, as well as your own interest and reputation, depend upon your punctual and faithful compliance with these orders and instructions. Hence I have thought it my duty to direct and order the Quartermaster-General, Colonel O'Hara, to supply any defect that may appear or happen upon your part and at your expense in behalf of the United States, to be settled at the Treasury at a future day ; and he is furnished with a copy of this letter accordingly. With a sincere hope, wish and desire that you may be able to comply with those orders in due season,

I am, gentlemen,

Your most obedient, humble servant,

ANTHONY WAYNE.

CAMP SITE OF THE MIAMI VILLAGES, October 18, 1794.

Sir:—I have a moment only in which to inclose a return of the provisions on hand this day and to tell you that Laselles' brother has been here and carried him off yesterday. I received him in the double Capacity of Spy and negotiator, being suffered to go at large. He witnessed the retreat of the volunteers and reconnoitered our Camp and fortifications. He gave us much good talk with apparent sincerity and is sanguine in his expectations of peace. The great exception which I make to him is on the score of his talks, which were all too good. The strongest circumstance picked out of him was that Simcoe, McKee and Brandt, with 100 Mohawks, landed at the post Miami on the 30th inst., direct from Niagara, and proceeded from thence with all the chiefs of this route to a grand Council now acting at the mouth of the Strait. Of what is this indicative ? Peace or War ? I say the latter, else why Brandt and his warriors. It appears to me that the pursuit of Peace by this route is not only enormously expensive but will eventuate in disappointment. Recollect that the transport of Army supplies by land has its limit, beyond which practicability ceases, and that the savages have behind them great space in which to retire before us. It would in two years produce a saving of one million of dollars and secure the object sought, did the government now determine to abandon this Route and put their whole force by Presqu' isle. You may have peace by the mediation of the British or by expelling them from the territory of the Miami. This last is the only mode in which to break the shackles in which the savages are now held. Here are some crude ideas for you and how do you like them? I will thank you very much if you will be so good as to order six tons of good Hay to be procured for me.

Dear sir, yours,   J. WILKINSON.

[COLONEL O'HARA.]

HEADQUARTERS, MIAMI VILLAGES, October 10, 1794.

Sir:—The unfortunate death of Mr. Robert Elliott, the acting contractor at this crisis, will render more defective and greatly derange that department, already but too defective and deranged; so much so as to hold up nothing but famine to the army and the western Posts. Under this alarming situation and circumstance and the pressure of famine hard upon us, it becomes my duty to remedy those defects without a single moment's loss of time in the best manner possible. You will therefore proceed to Fort Washington immediately, visiting the respective Posts on the way, taking an invoice of the stores belonging to the Contractors at each place and at Fort Washington, together with the means of transport, forwarding without a moment's delay as great a supply of flour, salt and cattle as every means of transport in your own department, as well as that of the contractors will enable you to do, for which purpose I have ordered a detachment of Dragoons and riflemen under the command of Captain Gibson as far as Greenville to escort the convoy to this place. You are not unacquainted with the small stock and state of provisions at this place—say, eight days' rations only, hence the indispensable necessity of dispatch. I will furnish you with a particular list of Posts and the quantum of supplies requisite for each by the first favorable opportunity; and for the present only mention in gross the rations necessary for the army from Fort Washington to the head of the line until the first of April next, viz., 555,000 complete rations, which will be three months in advance, exclusive of the daily issues; but should the Legion be completed, it will require at least 800,000 rations up to that day, by which time it is to be presumed proper arrangements will be made at the treasury for the regular supply of the Army. You will please to keep fair and particular accounts with the Contractors in behalf of the public of all expenditures made for the supply of this Army, and if upon obtaining all the returns or invoices of provisions and stores belonging to the contractors from this Post to Fort Washington, inclusive, you should find any deficiency, you are immediately to supply the defect by purchase of horses, cattle, flour, etc., as may be found deficient in the Contractor's department, which you will make in behalf of the public and for which this shall be your warrant. You will please to consult with the Contractor's principal agent upon this interesting subject and show him their instructions, offering him at the same time every assistance in your power to enable him to comply with the Contract of his principals, but you are not to relax in obtaining the supplies whenever you discover a deficiency; let me hear from you upon this interesting subject the soonest possible.

Wishing you every possible success, I am with sincere esteem,

Your most obedient humble servant,

ANTHONY WAYNE.

CINCINNATI, October 23, 1794.

Sir:—I had the Honor to write you on the 17th, by Pierce & Butler Express, informing your Excellency of the state I found the business of the Contractors on my arrival here, and my prospects of further supplies for the Army, which I hope you received. I shall have 200 very good Horses start this morning for Greenville with corn, 100 of the Contractors with flour, and upwards of 100 beeves, purchased by Mr. Wilson on his way to Kentucky, having yet heard of no part of his former purchases being on the way. Enclosed you have part of the correspondence that took place with the agent of the Contractors on his departure to Kentucky, by which you will perceive the difficulty that subsists in transacting this business, and of my arrangements for forcing forward the provisions. Mr. Day is the only agent present, he generally answers all my inquiries and requisitions by sublime strictures on men and measures, he writes to your Excellency by this opportunity. The clothing ordered on the 4th is safely arrived and stored at Fort Hamilton, in complete order, and the whole may be taken to Greenville by the wagons next trip, being in all thirty-three loads at 1,500 each. Should your Excellency approve of this most convenient and speedy method of transporting the clothing, the return of the wagons must be engaged by the Quartermaster, and such escort as you may please to order, made known to the owner ; this will not be interfering with the business of the contractors, being of the terms agreed on between Mr. Elliott and myself on their second trip from Hamilton. As the Beef ordered for the Miami village and for Fort Defiance, which will require 300 head, is not ready, nor a sufficient number of Horses, which ought to be 400, and as I presume your Excellency intends that the whole should go under one escort, I have directed the public horses to return to Fort Hamilton for another Cargo of Corn, the contractors may load with flour until the Cattle arrives. The Contractors have at this moment about 300 Horses on the line fit for service, should it appear to you that the number of 500 ordered in addition, is more than will be necessary I beg to be informed, as the purchase may yet be curtailed, and be assured that your further orders shall be most cheerfully executed.

I am with sincere esteem,

Your Excellency's obedient servant,

JAMES O'HARA, *Q. M. G.*

CINCINNATI, October 29, 1794.

Sir:—I received yours of the 18th with packet for the Secretary of War, and for the Contractor, late last evening, by a Sergeant of Dragoons, who cannot account for the uncommon delay of those dispatches, which I apprehend will in some measure interfere with your Excellency's orders respecting the convoy that ought to advance from Greenville by the route of Girty's Town; however, I am in hopes that Major Buell has received your instructions in due time to support that arrangement.

I had the honor to write you on the 17th by Butler & Pierce, and on the 23d by Campbell Express from this place, and having heard of neither since their departure, I enclose you a copy of my last, no material addition being since made, either in beef or means of transportation. You have enclosed a copy of a letter from Mr. George Wilson, the Contractor's agent, dated on the 20th, at Lexington. The cattle and horses promised by this letter are yet expected, one small drove of Cattle having only arrived on the 23d, which joined those mentioned in my letter of that date. He is mistaken in his statement of the number of horses on hand the 17th instant, fit for service, which Mr. Culberson, Superintendent of the Contractor's horses, can clearly explain.

The mysterious and obstinate conduct of the Contractor's agent, and of Mr. Day in particular, who has assumed the sole control of that department, renders my present situation extremely disagreeable and delicate. It appears very evident that he wishes no supplies to be furnished in front of Fort Hamilton ; he on the most ungenerous, ill-founded and avowed prejudices, not only refuses to give the least information respecting his arrangements and prospects, but also endeavors to move on such supplies as were in his power, without my knowledge, and consequently irregular ; protesting against all interference that has been or may be attempted, relative to the business of the contract, and instructs others to do so likewise. I take the liberty of annexing an extract of his orders to Mr. Carousay, Agent and Commissary at Fort Hamilton, per example :

"Remember well that if no Arrangement is made in writing by Mr. Elliott, signed for that purpose by his own hand, you are not to suffer a wagon to carry Whiskey for any man ; nor are you on any pretence whatever to make any arrangement with the Quartermaster-General or any one of that department ; each Department takes its chance." The teams here alluded to are the private property of the people who drive them, who had (as you have been already informed) quit carrying to Greenville, and were dispersed before my arrival here on the 15th, and were prevailed on by my interference to rejoin that business. In order to accommodate the contractors, and prevent disorder in engaging the teams (then upwards of sixty in number), I had made a former agreement with Mr. Elliott, that the whole should be employed in their name, reserving a right to load ten each trip from Fort Hamilton, and to have the one-half for one trip only if it should be necessary, an order in Mr. Elliott's handwriting, directing Mr. Carousay to have the number mentioned given, for use of the public, was last evening presented to Mr. Day, but was not sufficiently explicit to justify his permitting "the thing to be done." As Mr. Day must be convinced that all the wagons employed might be immediately engaged by the Quarter-master, it must also be his object, in order to add to his cata-logue another apology for the deficiencies at the outposts. As this is their principal mode of transporting flour at present, I shall give up my claim to any part of the teams, and en-deavor at the same time to prevent any ill consequences from attending the disappointment of the department. Your Excellency's letter of the 17th instant, containing your orders to the contractors, requiring supplies of provisions for the different posts, was handed to Mr. Day last evening, a copy of which I had received enclosed. I am not yet informed whether these orders are transmitted to Mr. Wilson or not, but this must be done. I have not received any further information respecting the invalid Dragoon Horses, but shall certainly attend to your orders on that point without delay. I have procured good pasture and forage at Columbia, in order to have them recruited, and shall dispose of them as may be judged most beneficial to the public and to the service. Your Excellency's orders respecting the escort are very agreeable, and will be properly applied. I now wait for the waters to rise to carry your very eligible plan of navigating the Miami to the Picquee Town into execution. Should this soon take place, the clothing being in handkerchiefs and large bales, may be transported in that way. Should it meet your appro-bation, and having directed the public teams to be filled up, they may be employed from Greenville to the landing to the best advantage.

I have the honor to be, etc.,

JAMES O'HARA, *Q. M. G.*

CINCINNATI, November 2, 1794.

Sir:—Enclosed you will receive further fair promises from Mr. Wilson. All communication with Mr. Day on public business being at an end, I cannot give the least information respecting the state of the provisions on the way, but I apprehend it remains, as I have endeavoured to represent to your Excellency by my letters of the 23d and 30th ultimo.

The Horses ordered to be purchased in Kentucky will certainly be on very soon, and if any faith or credit remain due to the positive language of Mr. Wilson's enclosed letter, a large drove of Cattle must be also on, and shall move forward without loss of time.

By letters from Pittsburgh I find that John Wilkins & Co. are the Contractors for next year, the provision to be delivered at Fort Pitt and Washington, of which I expect you are officially informed. This circumstance I hope will be a means of relieving me from a situation which has become intolerable, as the new contractors may operate with the old if necessary, especially after the first of January. The prospect of navigating the Miami has become very fair by the present cloudy appearance of the weather, and will be attempted as soon as an escort will be ready for that purpose.

I have the honor to be

Your Excellency's most obedient and humble servant,

JAMES O'HARA, *Q. M. G.*

[THE COMMANDER-IN-CHIEF.]

FORT WASHINGTON, November 8, 1794.

Sir:—I had the pleasure to write you on the 2d inst., covering a letter of Mr. George Wilson's from Lexington, containing a flattering prospect of an immediate supply of Beef, which has not yet arrived. I have a number of boats now under way for Still Water, loaded with Corn and Whiskey;

they are bound to take in the clothing at Fort Hamilton should your Excellency please to order it on that way. The whole will rendezvous at that Post in four or five days, and must there wait your pleasure respecting the clothing and such escort as you may please to order.

Should the difficulty of transporting the clothing from the mouth of Still Water to Greenville (which will require thirty wagons) induce you to defer ordering it by water, the private team may be engaged as proposed by my letter of the 23d. On their arrival at Headquarters, which will be about the 17th, the corn, being very portable, may go on; an extra escort will be wanted even then, which I hope will be at Fort Hamilton soon as possible or orders for the quarter-master to have the boats immediately discharged. I expect the honor of writing you with more satisfaction in a few days.

I am, Sir,

Your most obedient and humble servant,

JAMES O'HARA, *Q. M. G.*

[HIS EXCELLENCY THE COMMANDER-IN-CHIEF.]

CAMP, ROSTRAVE TOWNSHIP, November 8, 1794.

Sir:—Information has been received that Mr. Elliott, one of the Contractors, has been lately killed by the Savages; and Mr. Williams, his partner, has represented that this, without the aid of your department, may embarrass the measures for furnishing and forwarding the supplies required by the Commander-in-Chief. As it is all-important that these supplies should be duly furnished and conveyed to the respective posts, I must request and advise that you will co-operate in the article of transportation as far as may be necessary. For this purpose you will understand yourself with the Agents of the Contractors, ascertain what they can or cannot do, and endeavor to supply what may be deficient. In doing this

you will, of course, keep and furnish such a record and statement of the aid you give as will enable the United States to
make the proper charges against the Contractors, who are
bound by their contract to transport as well as to procure and
issue the provisions. It is understood that in the course
of the Campaign similar aids have been, from time to time,
given by your department. Of these, also, the Treasury
ought to have as accurate a view as is practicable; otherwise
the public will have to pay doubly for transportation—first in
the price of the rations to the contractors, and secondly, in
the expense of that which you furnish in aid of them.

With consideration, etc., I am, your obt. servant,

ALEXANDER HAMILTON.

[JAMES O'HARA, Esq., Quartermaster-General.]

FORT WASHINGTON, November 9, 1794.

Sir:—I am honored by yours of the 6th instant, and highly
flattered by that polite testimony of your Excellency's approbation of my conduct respecting the supplies for the Legion.

I wrote you on the 8th, by Express, and have now the pleasure to inform you that, on or before the 14th, six hundred
Horses of the two departments, one hundred and sixty Cattle,
and salt sufficient for the advanced Posts, will be at Greenville. I sent an Express into Kentucky yesterday, and, at his
return, two hundred fresh Horses shall set off from this place,
and good information, at least, relative to further supply of
Beef. Ten Boats will be at Hamilton, on the 12th, loaded
with corn, flour and whiskey for Still Water. The private
teams start to-morrow, entirely loaded with flour for Head
Quarters. The clothing may be transported, by either land
or water, by next return, as you will please to order. I hope
those arrangements will enable your Excellency, at length,
to have the advanced posts furnished with provisions agree-

able to your former orders; the flour for Head Quarters, Jefferson and St. Clair, will be complete in a short time.

I am, Sir, your most obedient, humble servant,

JAMES O'HARA.

[HIS EXCELLENCY THE COMMANDER-IN-CHIEF.]

FROM HIS EXCELLENCY ANTHONY WAYNE.

[TO COLONEL JAMES O'HARA.]

HEADQUARTERS, GREENVILLE, Nov. 14, 1794.

Sir:—I have to acknowledge the receipt of your several letters of the 3, 8, 9 inst., with enclosures; and am happy to find that your perseverance and decision have at last put the contractor's department into operation. Upon the receipt of your letter of the 8th inst., I ordered a detachment under Captain Bradley to proceed to Hamilton as an escort to the boats and sent Captain Shrimm to the confluence of the Stillwater with Greenville creek in order to determine the state of the water, which he found to be eighteen inches lower than it was last spring at the place where the boats unloaded, and that it was impracticable for them to get to that place until a rise of water—in fact I suspected that was the case, because when we crossed Stillwater on Hartzhorn's road on the 2d inst., it was lower than I had ever seen it, nor was this creek much raised although the St. Mary's had overflowed its banks and was swimming to the horses and detachment that escorted the cattle to the Miami villages at the usual crossing place between that Post and Fort Recovery on the 6th inst.; so that it is now reduced to a certainty that supplies may be transported by water from Girty's Town to Forts Wayne and Defiance in boats carrying fifty or sixty barrels, built in the form of the Adventurer, which was sent from the Miami villages to Grand Glaize. I therefore wish you to have at least one dozen built after that construction and sent up loaded to Fort Hamilton, from whence they may proceed at a proper season to Lormies' stores and be transported on waggons to the St. Mary's along a fine, dry, level road, not exceeding ten miles distant, when they may be reloaded and proceed on their voyage to the aforesaid Posts. It was on waggons that we transported our pontoons or boats for the purpose of crossing the Delaware and North River during the late war—one of those pontoons would have carried an hundred or more barrels. I have ordered the boats to be unloaded at Hamilton and sent back to Washington. I think it's more than probable by the time they return to Hamilton the creek will be in a proper state of navigation ; at least it was the case in the latter end of last November—which, from present appearances, will again be the case about the change of the moon, say on the 20th or 25th inst. The clothing will be ordered on by the by the next return of the wagons, and for which a proper escort will be furnished.

I received a letter from Mr. Charles Wilkins, dated Lexington, November 4, 1794, enclosing a copy of a contract made between Mr. Tench Coxe, Commissioner of the Revenue, and Alexander Scott and Matthew Ernest for supplying rations at Pittsburgh and Fort Washington. I really do not nor cannot understand it until I have official information of its being made and instructions upon the subject, neither of which have yet arrived. It will be necessary that Mr. Wilkins and Mr. George Wilson, as agents of the old and new Contractors, should attend immediately at Headquarters, perhaps it may be convenient for you to accompany them, in order that the present state and means of supplies, etc., may be properly understood.

I have ordered Mr. Newman to be sent to this place under a proper guard, which may serve as an escort to you. Captain Pierce will be directed to consult upon the occasion. Captain De Butts will trouble you with an invoice of certain articles of which we stand much in want. I pray you to procure them or let them be forwarded with Mr. Newman. I believe we have sufficient proof to establish the charge which will be exhibited against him.

Wishing you a safe arrival, I am with sincere esteem,
Your most obedient humble servant,
ANTHONY WAYNE.

HEADQUARTERS, GREENEVILLE, November 6, 1794.

Sir:—I have to acknowledge the receipt of your several letters of the 17th, 23d and 29th ultimo, with their respective enclosures; and sincerely thank you for the part you have taken and the pointed manner in which you have detailed the defects upon the part of the Contractors in point of supplies for and at the respective posts, as also their deficiency of means of transport. The enclosed report of provisions at this place will best demonstrate the indispensable necessity of your utmost exertions to supply, or to compel the Contractors' agents to supply, the rations mentioned in my letter of the 18th ult. At this moment we are on half allowance of beef, and even at that rate we have not six days' issues now on hand, you will therefore call upon the Contractors for beef cattle, and upon Captain Pierce, to furnish an escort to proceed with them to this place, without a moment's delay. All the cattle that came in were sent to the advanced Posts—say 250 head—except a small supply at each of the intermediate posts from Hamilton to Adams inclusive. All those Posts were destitute of beef at the time that supply was on the way, and until it arrived. One-fourth of those sent to the Miami villages were ordered to Fort Defiance, where I hope they have arrived, but there is not salt at either of those Posts to cure one thousand weight of beef, and should the Enemy determine to persevere in hostilities, those cattle must inevitably be lost; add to this that the pasture has totally failed, hence the immediate necessity of a full supply of salt, by the first convoy, and perhaps this will be the most favorable opportunity, as I have now at this place two *hostages*, one of them a chief of the Wyandots, until the return of a flag from *Sandusky*, which will be on or about the 20th inst. You will therefore, please to communicate the contents of this letter to the Contractors or their agents, and should you find any demur on their part in immediately furnishing the supplies called for, you are to supply the defect agreeably to the orders given you on the 10th and 18th ultimo.

I am, with esteem and respect,

Your most humble servant,

[COLONEL JAMES O'HARA.]   ANT. WAYNE.

FORT WASHINGTON, September 16, 1794.

Sir:—You will please to receive of Captain Peirce all the Quartermaster's stores and other public property delivered to him by Mr. Belli, and continue to perform the duty of Deputy Quartermaster-General until further orders. In order to prevent any deficiency in the Ordnance Department, I leave Mr. Hanagan and Mr. Oliver in the Quartermaster's stores, those gentlemen being well acquainted with the forms and method of doing the business, will enable you to attend to both departments till more permanent arrangements can be made, for which you will be allowed a reasonable compensation in addition to your pay as Commissary of Military Stores; being apprehensive that the clothing lately arrived is not in good order, you will have it immediately examined and repacked into casks and stored under cover at all events. Your knowledge of the different duties required of you and for which you will be accountable, render it unnecessary for me to be more particular in explaining them at present; therefore in perfect confidence that the interest of the public, the dignity of the department and your own honor, are safe in your hands, and wishing you health and pleasure in the execution of those duties,

I am your humble servant,

JAMES O'HARA,

Quartermaster-General.

[SAMUEL HENLEY, ESQ.]

GREENVILLE, November 14, 1794.

Dear Sir:—I had the pleasure to receive your favor of the 9th, the friendly and polite attention you have uniformly shown to me and to my interests has impressed me with very warm sentiments of gratitude and personal esteem towards you, and with a strong desire of being favored with an opportunity of evincing, by a reciprocity of good offices, that I am neither insensible nor unworthy of your regard. Although I shall feel much regret at your departure from the army, at any period whilst I shall remain in it ; yet my friendship would not permit me to wish your stay one moment to the injury of your domestic happiness and interest. I have been long of opinion that your private concerns called you loudly into private life ; but I had hopes that your appointment would be placed on a more liberal and respectable establishment ; such as might in some measure compensate for your relinquishment of other pursuits. I felicitate you most sincerely upon the happiness you will experience in carrying with you the releasing reflections of having discharged the important duties confided to you with ability and integrity, and to the entire satisfaction of all those whose approbation is desirable. I hope to have the pleasure of seeing you at the time mentioned in the General's letter—enclosed is the invoice of which he speaks. I hope you are aware that the drawing of the Federal lottery commences on the 22d of December; sooner, if the tickets should be sold. Your convoy arrived this morning; the cattle yesterday and before.

Believe me to be, dear sir,

Your sincere friend,

W. DE BUTTS.

[COLONEL JAMES O'HARA.]

GENERAL WILKINSON.

Nemat Calistai:—Kahela noolabindam ailey m'bindamin K'langandawokan? N'winga Kahama Kinémin, Kee, ock Kinashawshin (Sheeky aughqué) ock abschy Meetchy Ki mitcheewouckan, ock miney K'wine, Shuck, thamsy alindy matta Gusky ninélay, unéy Kisquee Paghaquike, qui Kwique indagh.

Neeshee okunachoky uney,

IMBAHANY.

Brother Calistai: Yes I rejoice because we hear you make peace? I am willing, if we know, you go, and shall take care (assuredly) and always. Already your provisions I have gathered here, and fit for you to eat. But sometime some if not to-day certainly, a guide about Noon goes to visit towards you; he will travel the road alone.

IMBAHANY.

[Original in the writing of James O'Hara, Quartermaster-General. Translated by Mary O'H. Darlington.]

HEADQUARTERS, GREENVILLE, 3 February, 1795.

Sir:—Agreeably to the verbal orders I gave you at this place, you will previously to your departure from Fort Washington make the necessary and effectual arrangements for the transport of every species of supplies for the use of the Legion and for the respective posts and garrisons in every direction, as by the new Contract with Messrs. Scott & Ernest the public are to be the carriers of all the rations in future, from the general deposits at Pittsburgh and Fort Washington, add to this the defect on the part of the old Contractors of 120,000 Rations from this place to the head of the Line, inclusive; nor is there the least prospect of this deficiency being made up, as Mr. Wilson has not as yet sent forward but 15,800 rations of flour towards it, notwithstanding his promise to complete the whole by the 8th Instant. We have but twenty days issues of flour now at this place and but fifteen at Recovery; nor have we at this moment more than eight weeks' issues at any of our Posts. Hence you will have to commence the transport of provision under the New Contract earlier than what was expected—say, on the 1st of March, *i. e.*, in the course of three weeks, and of which you will please to give M. Wilkins (their agent) immediate Notice so as to have the flour part ready to deliver at Fort Washington on or before that day, agreeably to the orders given him on the 13th ultimo, to the end that advantage may be taken of the first rise of the waters upon the breaking up of the ice, & which from present appearances will soon be the case. I therefore wish you to have the boats in readiness at Hamilton, etc., for the transport to this place and Lormies' Stores, & hold the wagons and pack-horses in readiness for the portages at the shortest notice, with proper persons to superintend and direct the water & land carriage, so that there may be no time lost upon any occasion whatever, and send forward Mr. Sharp upon sight to build the boats for the St. Mary's.

The prospect of a General Treaty of Peace, with all the Hostile tribes of Indians North West of the Ohio on or about the 13th of June, renders it expedient that you repair to Philadelphia *via* Pittsburgh as soon as you have made the arrangements before mentioned, in order to procure and forward the articles wanted in your department for the present year, as also the Indian goods and articles wanted for the pending treaty, agreeably to the invoice, provided it meets the approbation of government upon being presented to the Secretary of War.

In the interim it will be indispensably necessary that you forward (from your own private Stores at Pittsburgh), a temporary supply of clothing, Wampum, etc., for the use of such deputies as will naturally be coming in with overtures from the different tribes of Indians, between this time and the day appointed for holding the General Treaty. Had I the means I would prefer separate treaties, in order to avoid the idea of a General Confederacy, but the disposition of those people must be consulted. You will also please to forward all such Public Stores as may be at Pittsburgh for the use of the Legion and designed for this Quarter, belonging to your own and to the ordnance and Hospital departments, immediately upon your arrival there, in order to take advantage of the water transport to this place and to the head of the line, which you know we can't count upon after the Middle of April at furthest, either on the Miami or the Ohio, or the St. Mary's or Au Glaize; this is an object of very considerable consequence and will save an immense expense, trouble and fatigue if timely attended to.

I begin to feel very uneasy with respect to flour. The New Contractors have none at Washington, and the ice will prevent any from descending the Ohio for some time yet; perhaps not before the middle of March; they therefore must purchase from the old Contractors at all events, and which might have been done with advantage to the Public and them· selves some time since; perhaps it will not be the case now; yet the thing must be done and the sooner the better. From this statement of facts you will see the absolute necessity of putting everything in a proper train before you leave Washington. Among other Matters, provisional means ought to be directed for mounting the Dragoons in case it should be found expedient, and materials furnished for repairing the old furniture, to serve until new comes forward. Wishing you a safe and speedy arrival at Pittsburgh and Philadelphia (after you have put everything in a proper way) and a speedy return to this place,

I am, with Sincere Esteem,

Your most obt., humble servant,

ANTHONY WAYNE.

[COL. JAMES O'HARA, Q. M. G.]

FORT WASHINGTON, Feb. 8, 1795.

Sir:—I am honored with your letter of the 3d instant and find your apprehensions, respecting the immediate transportation of flour to headquarters but too well founded, none of that article having yet come to hand. The Ohio and Miami rivers being in very good order I was tempted to load and dispatch twelve Boats with corn for Still Water, and if they meet with no unforseen demurage, they may be returned to Hamilton and the mouth of the Miamis before the provisions will arrive for a second Cargo. The necessary and effectual arrangements shall be made for the transporting and furnishing the necessary provisions and every species of supplies for the Legion and for the respective Posts and Garrisons on

the line before my departure from this Post, and preparation
shall be made for carrying your Excellency's orders, respecting Massac, Fort Knox and Steuben, into immediate effect
as soon as you will please to direct. By the enclosed papers
you will see all the communication that I have had with the
Agents of the new Contractors. My arrangements for forming further means of transportation and the rates of freight
for Still Water established with the owners of Craft on that
Service.

Your Excellency will perceive the necessity of a covering
Party at the landing of the cargoes ; as much depends on the
Boats being instantly discharged, in order to meet the flour at
the mouth of the Miami in due time.

Mr. Mathews is ordered to attend to the receiving of the
cargoes and forwarding the property to Headquarters. Mr.
Donwoddie, with a few additional teams, will attend to the
transportation and Mr. George Adams has charge of the
public Boats now under way.

The extravagant speculations held in View by the owners
of the private teams that have been employed by the Contractors having rendered it absolutely necessary to erect a
number of public teams for the road, I beg leave to submit
the propriety of having the road from Hamilton to Recovery
repaired soon as possible, being at present impassable for
wagons. If the old road from Hamilton was cleared out and
a few swamps Bridged or causway'd it would, in wet weather,
be preferable to the new, at all events, it will be a good alter-
nation.

I have conversed with the old Contractors' agent here and
have some reason to expect that they will yet furnish the
stipulated quantity of provisions. They have sent on seventy-
five fresh Horses, lately purchased, which will increase their
whole number perhaps to one hundred and fifty and may be
a means of supplying the outposts without delay.

A number of Horses start to-morrow with a supply of iron, stationery and other stores for headquarters.

The time of my going from this place being very uncertain, I may be yet honored with your further commands, which, with those enjoined by your last letters, shall be religiously complied with.

I have the honor to be with the most sincere attachment
Your Excellency's most Ob't, Hum. Serv't,

JAMES O'HARA.

[HIS EXCELLENCY, THE COMMANDER-IN-CHIEF.]

TO COLONEL JAMES O'HARA, Q. M. G.

WAR OFFICE, March 14, 1795.

Sir:—On looking over the return of Indian goods on hand at Greenville, I am inclined to think that a small additional supply will suffice for the occasional demands of the Indians, until the treaty should be held for making peace. The following articles are all that I would have forwarded until the terms of purchase shall be settled here between you and the treasury department. About 400 calico shirts No. 8; the smallest trunk of linen shirts containing 189. Case No. 13 containing blue, green, brown and white, half thicks and two diaper rugs. The bale No. 15, containing twelve pieces of blue stroud, one piece of Scarlet stroud of 17 yards and one of blue containing 15 yards.

Seventeen hundred of black Wampum and the 5½ pounds of vermillion. The whole should be examined, and particularly the woolens before they are forwarded; there is much danger that woolens are moth eaten, as they have lain so long on hand. Nothing should be sent that is not in good order. Colonel Meigs will be employed to take charge of the goods in the Indian department, and perhaps of the clothing of the

Army ; I expect if not now, that he will shortly be at Pittsburgh. Should he not arrive in time, Major Craig may receipt for them. I am your humble servant,

TIMOTHY PICKERING.

WAR OFFICE, April 23, 1795.

Sir:—The articles requisite to be purchased here in the quartermaster's department were selected, and the list thereof with the supposed prices yesterday presented to the treasury.

I shall be obliged by your making out a list of Indian goods to the amount of twenty-five or thirty thousand dollars, assorted according to your opinion of the wants and conveniences of the Western Indians. I am Sir, your obedient servant,

TIMOTHY PICKERING.

[COLONEL O'HARA.]

GREENVILLE, Sept. 21, 1795.

Dear Sir:—I don't know whether my impatience to have the papers (now sent) dispatched from hence, equalled yours, but I am correct in assuring you it was very great. I could have wished the trunk to have gone sooner—and it had been ready waiting in the Quartermaster's possession for several days—but it was not thought expedient to send it before yesterday, as the dispatches for you could not follow it before to-day. I send the key by Captain Taylor, which I pray you to return after forcing open the trunk deposited in your stores at Washington in 1793, and transferring its material contents into the one now sent.

The General has received your letter of the 15th and I yours of the 18th instants ; they afforded the same satisfaction which your letters have uniformly imparted.

A knowledge of Mr. Harragan's unadorned worth, renders his appointment in your department very pleasing to the

General, and no attention in my power shall be wanting to give him support and confidence in his office. Mr. Clark's equipment, in your hands, was expected to be as respectable as the occasion required. His barge and crew—should they make a speedy voyage—may return time enough for a certain expedition; this is to be wished, as the crew are chosen men and will in all probability be well trained.

Mr. Caldwell has not yet applied; your wishes respecting him shall be complied with.

I think you will have not a disagreeable passage at this time to Pittsburgh; the season is favorable and the equinox may perhaps afford you water sufficient. I congratulate you sincerely on your return to your family after your long and eminent services, and I wish you from my soul, every success which your most sanguine wishes may lead you to hope for, in the execution of the designs which shall for the future employ your attention.

It appears rather problematical at this moment whether I shall ever be so fortunate as to derive advantage from your knowledge and experience by a partial union of our respective interests, and as I cannot at present advance anything new or decisive on this subject, I am constrained to be silent until I shall have the pleasure of again seeing you. I transmit enclosed with many thanks for the loan, three hundred and fifty-six dollars, the amount of my note in your hands.

I hope you will have the goodness to write me a few lines before you leave Fort Washington, and be ever persuaded that the best and warmest wishes will attend you, of

Dear Sir, yours with real esteem and friendship,

DE BUTTS.

[COLONEL JAMES O'HARA.]

GREENVILLE, September 22, 1795.

Dear Sir:—The business of yesterday, in despatching Captain Taylor with the General's packets for you, occupied my time so completely that I could scarce find enough to scratch the few lines I sent you by him, and induced me to keep one of his dragoons until this morning in order to have the pleasure of talking a little more to you. I received unfeigned pleasure in reading and transmitting the General's letter of yesterday to you. So just and so full a testimony of your abilities and conduct, of his approbation and friendship, I am sure you will consider as the dearest reward that an officer can receive for his public labors. A copy of it, and of yours of the 25th ultimo to the General, are contained in the dispatches you carry forward, accompanied by a long paragraph, in one of his public letters, expressive of the regret he feels at your retiring from the service, of the entire confidence he has always so justly placed in your worth and conduct, of the high sense he entertains of your ability and resource, and of his fears lest the office should not be filled by a successor of equal merit. These are tributes, my dear sir, that will ever attend worth and virtue, and administer the sweetest satisfaction, not only to the object to whom they are offered, but to all those who are interested in our fame and happiness. What would you think of the General's partial regard for and opinion of me when, almost in the same sentence in which he pronounces your eulogium, he should propose me as your successor? However strange and unexpected the thing may appear, the fact is so ; and he has fortified his recommendation with so many flattering expressions, and so much further strengthened them by his voluntary responsibility for my conduct at the head of the department, that I shall not be much surprised should I really be appointed. He deems it advisable that I should acquaint you, in confidence, with this circumstance, as he imagines your regard for me would interest you in the issue, and you may be persuaded my reliance on your friendship and judgment anticipated the advice. I shall say nothing further to you but to request that if my name should occur during your intercourse with the Secretary of War on the subject of your vacancy, that you would be good enough to advise me with your observations on the occasion. This matter is intended, for the present, to rest silent in the General's, in yours, and in the breast of

Your sincere friend,

DE BUTTS.

[COLONEL O'HARA.]

PHILADELPHIA, February 24, 1797.

Sir:—A Regiment of Troops is ordered to rendezvous at the mouth of the Big Miamis on or before the 20th of April next, from whence, after a few days' halt, they will be marched by the most direct route to Knoxville in the State of Tennessee. I give you this reasonable information of the movement for your accommodation and have to require that you may take the necessary arrangements for provisioning the troops, at mouth of the Miami and on the march, at such times and places as Lieutenant-Colonel Butler may regulate with you.

With respect, I am, Sir,

Your most obedient servant,

JA. WILKINSON, *B. General.*

[COLONEL JAMES O'HARA.]

TREASURY DEPARTMENT,

COMPTROLLER'S OFFICE, December 28, 1798.

Sir:—Your accompt as Deputy Quartermaster-General at Fort Washington for services performed and supplies purchased to the 30th of June, 1796, has been adjusted at the Treasury, and the amount disbursed found to be ninety-nine thousand seven hundred and twenty-seven dollars and ninety-nine cents, which will be passed to the credit of James O'Hara, Esq., late Quartermaster-General in the books of the Treasury.

The amount of the Abstracts, on which this settlement is predicated, is one hundred thousand three hundred and seventy-seven dollars and eight cents; is six hundred and forty-nine dollars and nine cents more than the amount above stated, and arises from the following deductions, viz :

This sum being the amount of sundry errors, $25.23 ; this sum being the amount for public horses sold, $508.86 ; this sum being an advance to Captain Shaumburg, pursuant to General Wilkinson's Warrant, which is referred to the War Department for settlement, $100 ; this sum being a payment for services performed in September, 1796, which will hereafter constitute a credit to the present Quartermaster-General, as per receipt in his favor, $18. Difference above stated, $649.09.

I am, Sir, very respectfully,

Your obedient servant,

JAMES STEELE, *Comptroller.*

[DANIEL HARAGAN, Esq., Deputy Quartermaster-General, Fort Washington, Northwestern Territory.]

TREASURY DEPARTMENT,

COMPTROLLER'S OFFICE, Oct. 11, 1797.

Sir:—Your account as late Quartermaster-General, for disbursements made at Philadelphia, by your Agent, Samuel Hodgdon, from the 1st of January to the 30th of June, 1796, has been adjusted at the Treasury, in consequence of which, the amount so disbursed, being $10.816.70, will be passed to your credit in the books of the treasury. Your account in the capacity aforesaid, for disbursements made at Pittsburgh by your deputy, Isaac Craig, from the 1st of February to the 14th of October, 1796, has also been adjusted at the Treasury, and the amount so disbursed found to be $30,064.12, which will likewise be passed to your credit in the books aforesaid.

I am, Sir, very respectfully

Your obedient servant,

James Steele, Compt.

[James O'Hara, Esq.]

New York, May 12, 1799.

Sir:—If you have not previously been apprised of it, it is proper you should be informed that an Act of Congress of March last entitled " An Act for the better organizing the troops of the United States and for other purposes," contains the following provisions :

Section 19. That a ration of provisions shall henceforth consist of eighteen ounces of bread or flour, or when neither can be obtained, of one quart of rice or one and a half pounds of sifted or riddled Indian meal, one pound and a quarter of fresh beef, or one pound of salted beef, or three-quarters of a pound of salted pork, and when fresh meat is issued, salt at the rate of two quarts for every hundred rations ; soap at the rate of four pounds, and candles at the rate of a pound and a half for every hundred rations : *Provided always*, that there shall be no diminution of the ration to which any of the troops now in service may be entitled by the terms of their enlistment.

Section 22. That it shall be lawful for the Commander-in-Chief of the Army, or the commanding officer of any separate detachment or garrison thereof, at his discretion to cause to be issued from time to time to the troops under his command, out of such supplies as shall have been provided for the purpose, in quantities not exceeding half a gill of rum, whiskey or other ardent spirits, to each man per day, excepting in cases of fatigue service or other extraordinary occasions, and that whensoever supplies thereof shall be on hand, there shall be issued to the troops vinegar at the rate of two quarts for every hundred rations.

These provisions are, of course, to govern your future issues. But as the promise with regard to troops who may have enlisted on the stipulation of a different ration may require circumspection on the application of the new rule, the commanding officer must concert with you this application.

With consideration, I am, Sir,

Your obedient servant,

ALEXANDER HAMILTON.

[JAMES O'HARA, Esq., Contractor, Pittsburgh.]

LETTER FROM GENERAL HAMILTON TO JAMES O'HARA, ESQ.

NEW YORK, November 7, 1799.

Sir:—The recruiting rendezvous in Virginia are: 1. New London; 2. Powhatan Courthouse; 3. Petersburgh; 4. Suffolk and Kemperville, either or both for one; 5. City of Richmond; 6. Williamsburgh; 7. Acomac Courthouse; 8. Northumberland Courthouse; 9. Bowling Green; 10. Culpepper Courthouse; 11. Fauquier Courthouse; 12. Leesburgh; 13. Fredericksburgh; 14. Charlotteville; 15. Winchester; 16. Staunton; 17. Fincastle; 18. Abingdon; 19. Moorefield; 20. Morgantown.

The rendezvouses in Maryland are: Georgetown, Hagerstown, Porto Bacco, Annapolis, Fredericktown, Easton, City of Baltimore, Centreville, Elkton, Close.

In Delaware the rendezvouses are: Wilmington, Dover, and New Castle.

In Pennsylvania they are: Wyoming, Reading, North-umberland, Philadelphia, Lancaster, Bristol, Yorktown, Carlisle, Lewistown, Bedford, Greensburgh, Washington, Pittsburgh.

Some changes may have taken place, which you will learn from the particular officers. There are two companies at Fort Mifflin, one company on the Schuylkill, two at Norfolk, and one at Baltimore. It is intended to station three regiments at Harper's Ferry on the Potomac, and a battalion of artillery too. But the difficulty of obtaining winter quarters at this place may cause two of the regiments to be stationed at Fredericktown, in Maryland, or Carlisle, in Pennsylvania, one or both of these places. The Seventh Regiment, under the command of Colonel Bentley, will pass the winter in the vicinity of Richmond. For more particular information concerning Virginia it will be proper to consult General Pinckney.

With great consideration, I am Sir,

Your obedient servant,

[JAMES O'HARA, ESQ.] A. HAMILTON.

P. S.—By letter received this day, it appears that there will be no troops quartered at Fredericktown, but pretty certain that one, Colonel Moore's, the 10th, will be stationed at Carlisle.

--

NOTE.—Fort Lafayette contains two barracks, three hexagonal towers in wood, containing artillery and powder magazine. The inclosure is composed of large pointed stakes, closed together, fifteen or sixteen feet high, the fort is square, of weak defence.

ARY

FORT PITT
in
1795.

FRANKLIN ROAD

ALLEGHENY RIVER

OHIO RIVER.

Siteof
FORT
DU QUESNE

FORT
PITT

HAY
MARBURY
ST.
ST.
ST.
PITT

MONONGAHE

SAND

Beech island ground

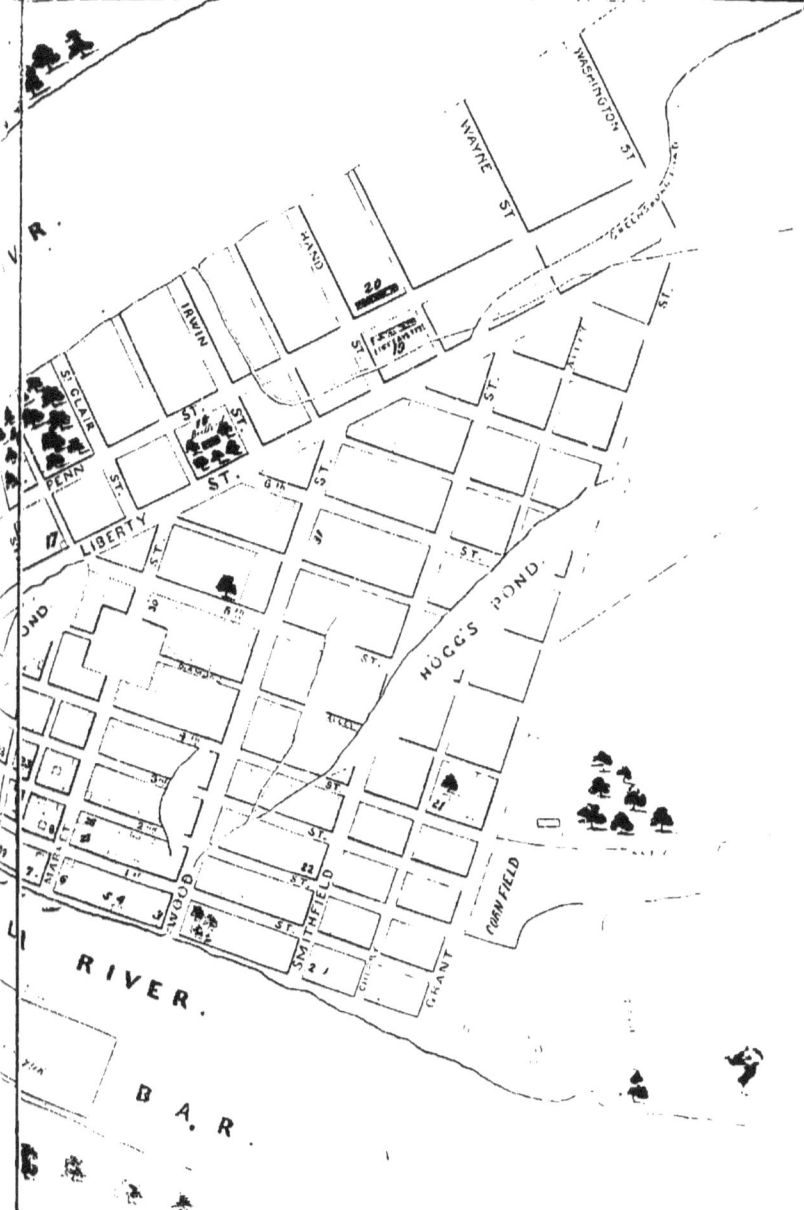

ERECTION AND ORGANIZATION OF ALLE-
GHENY COUNTY—1785 TO 1788.

By William M. Darlington.

1785. The earliest movement towards forming the county of Allegheny appears to have been in the year 1785, when, on Monday, the 7th day of March, in the General Assembly of Pennsylvania, at Philadelphia, "A petition from a number of the inhabitants of the town of Pittsburgh and county adjoining, within the counties of Westmoreland and Washington, was read, praying that part of the counties of Westmoreland and Washington may be erected into a new county, and that the seat of justice may be fixed at the town of Pittsburgh, or upon the tract reserved by the State, on the west side of the Allegheny." The petition was laid on the table, nor does it appear that it was taken up for consideration during that session.

The representatives from Westmoreland, William Findley, Thomas Morton and William Todd, probably were opposed to it. On September 2, 1786, a like petition was presented to the Assembly, read and laid on the table. The term of the Assembly ended at the close of the same month.

In October following, at the general election, Hugh H. Brackenridge, of Pittsburgh, William Findley and James Barr were chosen members from Westmoreland County for the ensuing year.

The first session of the next House of Representatives opened at Philadelphia, October 23, 1786.

(301)

The returns from Westmoreland County were not received until November 2d. Mr. Brackenridge took his seat in the House on the 13th of November. On the 16th of the same month " Petitions from a considerable number of the inhabitants of the counties of Westmoreland and Washington, read in the late and former House of Assembly, March 7, 1785, and September 2d last ; praying a part of the said counties may be created into a new county" were presented to the chair, read and ordered to lie on the table. On the 21st they were taken up, read the second time and referred to Messrs. Ross, of Lancaster ; Piper, of Bedford County; Finley, of Westmoreland ; Brackenridge, of Pittsburgh, in Westmoreland County ; Flenniken, of Washington County ; Gilchrist, of Fayette County, and Carson, of Dauphin.

On the 29th of November the report of the Committee was read the first time, and on the next day, the 30th, a second time, and adopted as follows, viz. : The Committee on the Petition praying that a new county be laid off, comprising the town of Pittsburgh, are of opinion that it may be expedient, and offer the following resolution :

Resolved, That a new county be laid off by the following boundaries, viz. : Beginning on the Ohio River, at the mouth of Flaharty's Run, and thence with a direct line to a point on Chartier's River, two miles below the mouth of Miller's Run, and thence with a direct line to the Monongehela River, at the mouth of Youghiogheny River, and with that river to the mouth of Turtle Creek, and with that creek to the mouth of the most northerly branch, and with that branch to the head, and from the head of said branch to the head of Plumb Run, and with that run to the Allegheny River, and ascending that river to the boundary of Northumberland County, at the mouth of Conewago River, and with that river to the northern boundary of the State, if the said river shall extend so far, or if it shall not extend so far, then with a north line to the said northern boundary, and with the said boundary to the western boundary of this State, and with that line to the Ohio River, and with that river to the place of beginning.

Your committee also taking into view the value it will give to the tract of land reserved by this State on the west of the Ohio and opposite the town of Pittsburgh, to have the seat of justice located on that tract, and also that but small segments have been taken from the counties of Westmoreland and Washington on this side the Ohio to the new county, offer a further resolution :

Resolved, That the seat of justice be located on the said reserved tract, and that in the meantime, until a courthouse and gaol can be built on the said tract, the courts shall be held in the town of Pittsburgh, and the commissioners of the county shall be empowered to rent convenient buildings for a courthouse and gaol, at the expense of the county ; that the sum to be expended in building a courthouse and gaol shall not exceed £——.

Ordered, That Mr. Ross, Mr. Piper, Mr. Findley, Mr. Brackenridge, M. Flennikin, M. Gilchrist, and M. Carson be a committee to bring in a bill agreeably to the foregoing resolution.

On December 6th the committee reported a bill, which was read the first time and ordered to lie on the table.

December 8th, the bill was read a second time and debated by paragraphs. It was then ordered to be transcribed, and in due time printed for public consideration. Nothing further was done with the Act that session of the Assembly, which adjourned on December 30th, until February 20, 1787, sat until the 29th of March, and then adjourned to the 4th day of September next.

On the 7th of September, 1787, it was, on motion of Mr.

Brackenridge, seconded by Mr. D. Clymer, ordered that the bill be called for reading on Friday next (14th inst.). On Saturday, September 8th, Mr. Brackenridge presented petitions from 1,363 inhabitants of Washington County, praying that the lines of the new county proposed might be extended so that they might be annexed. On September 13, 1787, petitions from 753 inhabitants of the counties of Westmoreland, Washington and Fayette were read, praying parts of the said counties may be erected into a new county. Ordered to lie on the table. On the 14th, the bill being the order of the day, was read the third time, and on the question "Will the House take up the same for debating by paragraphs?" And upon reading it over a long debate occurred. Mr. Whitehill opposed it; he thought something should be done to show the propriety or necessity of passing it before going further with it; he thought the expense would be too great for the population. He said it was too late to run the boundaries, the people could not be informed before the next election. Mr. Brackenridge, in reply, urged the disadvantages of the distance of the courthouses of Washington and Westmoreland from the centre of population. At the erection of Washington County, Pittsburgh expected to be made the seat of justice, but it was not obtained, though they deserved it. Mr. Wright opposed it on account of the small population and the expense. He remarked, "Will five hundred people be able to support the expense, especially if we consider the law laying out a town on the Allegheny River and the Ohio? The people will all have to cross the river to attend the courts, the county town and gaol being on the west side, and there is not a soul to commit unless it is the bears, for there is not a soul living on that side of the river Ohio." Mr. D. Clymer referred to a petition sent in to fix the new county seat at Milmont, near the habitation of Mr. De Vore. The question was now put on taking the bill up by paragraphs, when the yeas were 25, nays 33.

On October 22, 1787, the Assembly convened at Philadelphia. At the late election Mr. Brackenridge was not a candidate, Messrs. Findley and Barr, old members, with John Irwin, new, were the representatives from Westmoreland. From Washington the old members were chosen. On November 20th, a petition of a committee chosen by the inhabitants of Pittsburgh and the neighboring county was read, referring to the petition to former members of Assembly, and praying that the parts of the counties of Westmoreland and Washington may be erected into a new county, and by special order the same was read a second time. Ordered that it be referred to Mr. Clymer, Mr. Lewis, Mr. Lowrey, Mr. G. Heister, Mr. Findley, Mr. Irvine, Mr. McDowell, Mr. Philips and Mr. Schott to report thereon.

On the 21st of November, the petitions read in the last House of Assembly, on the 13th of September, were presented to the chair and read and referred to the above committee.

On the 27th of November the report read on the 21st was read the second time, and the further consideration of it postponed. The committee again reported on the 29th. Ordered to lie on the table. Nothing further on the subject was brought up during the remainder of the session. The Assembly adjourned on the 29th of November to the 19th of February, 1788.

February 23, 1788. A petition from 90 inhabitants of the county of Washington was read, remonstrating against the petitions presented to this and former Houses of Assembly, for erecting parts of the counties of Westmoreland, Washington and Fayette into a separate county and establishing the seat of justice for the same at the town of Pittsburgh, and suggesting the propriety, in case it should be deemed expedient to erect a new county, that the courts of justice may be established at the mouth of Beaver Creek, or at Old Logstown.

Ordered to lie on the table.

March 22, 1788. The House resumed the consideration of the report postponed November 27th last on the petitions of a number of the inhabitants of the counties of Westmoreland and Washington and appointed a committee to decide on the boundaries of a new county.

The committee reported March 26th.

Ordered to lie on the table.

House adjourned March 29, 1788.

House met September 2, 1788.

September 9th. Petitions presented from 700 inhabitants of the county of Westmoreland were read, praying that the bill entitled " An Act for erecting parts of the counties of Westmoreland and Washington into a separate county," may be so amended as not to extend further up the Youghiogheny than Crawford's sleeping place and from thence by a straight line to the mouth of Plum Creek on the Allegheny River. Ordered to lie on the table.

September 11th. Ordered that Tuesday next be assigned for the third reading of the bill entitled " An Act for erecting parts of the counties of Westmoreland and Washington into a separate county," and that it be the order of the day.

September 16th. The bill was read the third time and the further consideration postponed until Saturday.

September 19th. Petitions from 1,573 inhabitants of the counties of Westmoreland and Washington were read, praying that the bill may be passed into a law. Ordered to lie on the table.

September 22d. A petition from a number of the inhabitants of the county of Washington was read. Ordered to lie on the table.

September 24th. The bill entitled "An Act for erecting certain parts of the counties of Westmoreland and Washington into a separate county," having been brought in engrossed, was compared at the table, enacted into a law and the Speaker directed to sign the same.

INDEX.